MEDIA MONSTER

OMJ RYAN

www.omjryan.com

"Whether you think you can or whether you think you can't, you're right."

-Henry Ford

O J
___

Enjoy the 'Monsters'

Dedicated to Michael Ryan.

A more honest man, you would struggle to meet.

I'm so grateful you read it and loved it pops!

xxx

PROLOGUE

Monday 11th May 2015.
Studio 1 – Talk105, Media City Manchester.

As the time approached 8.20am, breakfast show host Marty Michaels gently pulled down his microphone fader, taking a gulp of black coffee, savouring the rich Colombian blend. Laminated signs adorning the walls proclaimed hot drinks were banned from the newly refurbished studios. *Whatever,* he thought.

Across the desk sat the newly elected British prime minister, Nicholas Fay. His advisors had made it clear: all questions relating to his involvement in the advisory committee on Operation Yewtree were totally off-limits. The senior management team at Talk105 had greedily accepted the terms to secure the first interview since the election. Marty Michaels, however, had not. *Following the rules – where was the fun in that?*

The eleventh-hour decision by Nicholas Fay's party to promote him to leader was a gamble that worked spectacularly, winning by a landslide just three days ago. Partly, considered Marty, because he was a dead ringer for Hugh Grant's prime minister in the movie *Love Actually*, and partly because Fay had replaced a man of incredible ineptitude. The outgoing prime minister, a multi-millionaire Old Etonian, had shown himself to be truly detached from the reality of modern-day life. Switching to Fay brought unprecedented media support and one of the most one-sided election wins for a single party since Tony Blair's New Labour in 1997.

As Marty sipped his coffee, Fay continued to deliver a well-rehearsed answer to a question on immigration, but Marty had stopped paying attention. His listeners tuned in for political blood each morning, and it was time for him to deliver.

So far in his first one-to-one radio interview, the new PM had done a decent job of sounding as if he knew what he was doing; he'd been earnest and refreshingly open about his own party's shortcomings over the last ten years. If truth be told, Marty quite liked him – it was hard not to. He certainly looked the part in a simple, well-fitting charcoal suit matched with a white shirt and a red-and-blue-striped tie. His strong jawline and bright blue eyes were framed by a shock of dark brown hair, greying slightly at the temples. His easy smile exposed large dimples on either side of his mouth, making him appear genuine and warm, and one could easily believe Nicholas Fay was that rare breed of politician: in government because he wanted to make a difference. None of which mattered to Marty.

Broadcasting daily across England, Scotland, Wales and Northern Ireland for the last fifteen years, *The Morning Show with Marty Michaels* had become an institution. Marty ranked alongside Jeremy Paxman and John Humphreys as one of the toughest talkers in the business. Famously loquacious politicians were rendered speechless on many occasions.

This morning's interview was Fay's first beyond the scope of mass-media press conferences, and marked his debut with Marty. So far, he had taken it easy and the new PM seemed relaxed. His guard had lowered somewhat, just where he wanted him. Placing his coffee cup on the right side of the desk, he pushed his own microphone fader to the top level, illuminating the red 'mic-live' button on the panel in front of him. As Fay finished talking, Marty allowed the silence to linger a moment longer than would be comfortable in any normal conversation. The PM stared at him, quizzically.

'Prime Minister, it's my duty to speak on behalf of the British public.'

Fay opened his mouth to speak but Marty closed his microphone, silencing any protestation. With the PM now helpless, he ploughed on.

'As leader of the advisory committee investigating the "Savile" scandal of 2012, you promised to expose anyone abusing children or teenagers within the public sector, including the House of Commons.'

Nicholas Fay looked uncomfortable now, 'Yes I did.'

'So how many arrests have been made?'

Fay flinched. His press team, watching through the glass from the adjacent studio, stood rooted to the spot, awaiting his response. He stumbled slightly.

'Erm, well...'

Marty smiled coldly as he activated Fay's microphone. 'Were you not expecting that question, Prime Minister?'

The PM shifted in his seat. 'Well, I guess not, considering we were just discussing immigration,' he said, trying to sound light-hearted.

'Would you prefer *not* to answer the question, Prime Minister?'

Fay raised his hand. 'No, no. I'll answer it,' he said, clearing his throat before continuing. 'Obviously in government we have a duty to ensure children are protected and nurtured...'

Marty cut Fay off mid-flow. '*How many arrests*, Prime Minister?'

'It's really not that simple,' offered Fay flatly.

Marty snorted his disapproval. 'It really *is* that simple. If someone in government had done something about the likes of Savile, Glitter, Harris or Smith, we could have protected thousands of kids from those vile abusers. Abusers with lifestyles financed by the public purse. Abusers protected, and in many cases, *lauded* by successive governments, given knighthoods for God's sake!'

The colour had drained from Fay's face and he stared blankly at Marty for a moment, as if hoping to find the answer he sought.

'I'm afraid I cannot speak about events that happened over thirty years ago, under a different government...'

Marty cut across him again. 'Really, Prime Minister? Many people believe those associated with the abuse are still active today in local and national government. Yet no further investigations or charges have been brought against anyone since Harris was jailed in 2014 and Glitter in 2015.'

Marty sensed Fay was doing his best to appear calm, but his face gave him away; he had him on the ropes.

'It is my understanding that the investigations are *still* ongoing, which means it would be inappropriate to discuss them, even if I wanted to. At such time as we have information we can share with the public, we will do so.'

'Prime Minister, forgive me but the British public don't need empty promises, we need action and we need it *now*. How many more children are to be abused before you do something about it?'

'Let me assure you and the country as a whole that these are not empty promises. I'm simply saying the appropriate protocols are in place and anyone identified as an abuser will be brought to justice, regardless of their line of work, position or relationship to government.'

Marty paused for a moment to scan the Twitter feed on the monitor in front of him. Comments supporting his stance appeared rapidly one after another.

'So, for the purposes of clarity,' he said, 'if I were to present you with a list of people accused of abuse, working within your *own* government today, would you bring those people to justice?'

Fay shot a glance at his press team next door.

'Your press team don't have the answer, Prime Minister. You need only look at me.'

Fay appeared embarrassed by Marty's remark and his cheeks flushed.

'I will investigate all allegations, yes,' he said nodding his head at Marty.

'No matter who they are?'

Fay stared at Marty intently now, moving his mouth closer to the microphone before responding in a low voice.

'Yes, we will investigate all allegations of abuse, *whoever* they may be linked to. You have my word on that.'

Marty allowed the prime minister's answer to land, savouring the silence. He stared at Fay, who was holding his gaze, looking more than a little angry after the unexpected ambush.

Marty smiled broadly. 'Well, we have you on tape now, Prime Minister, the people of the UK can expect to see those responsible for abusing the young people of Britain swiftly brought to justice, *no matter who they are.*'

Fay nodded sagely before agreeing.

'Thank you, Prime Minister,' Marty said, as he began delivering one of his trademark Churchillian speeches. 'I, myself, am appalled by the behaviour of these so-called trusted men and women hiding in plain sight; and many in my own profession who have sullied the world of media and entertainment. I promise I will not rest until every single one of these evil perverts who prey on the weak and vulnerable are brought to justice. They must be rooted out and punished for destroying the lives of so many innocents!'

Nicholas Fay appeared lost for words and wisely stayed silent. The signals coming from the next studio made it clear the interview was over.

Marty was satisfied. His comments and interrogation would be headline news, replayed across the country and even worldwide, further enhancing his reputation as a hard-hitting interviewer.

He flashed a smile as he closed Fay's microphone and delivered some 'housekeeping' content.

'With the time coming up to eight-thirty, let's cross to the Talk-one-oh-five newsroom for the latest update where you live.'

CHAPTER 1

Marty touched the soft white sheets covering his body and slowly opened his eyes, fighting against the sticky pus that had almost sealed his eyelids shut. His head throbbed at the temples, his view of the darkened room impaired by something pressing against his face. Carefully he touched the fingers of his right hand to his cheek and recoiled as he felt the hard, smooth material. He sank his fingertips through a large hole around his right eye, touching the skin, before drawing an imaginary line down to his mouth where his fingers met the coarse edge of metal that framed his lips. He followed the material round, under the back of his head where he met another metal strip. *What on earth?* Pulling back the sheets, he was aware of his naked form; instinctively he sat upright, using his hands to steady himself, before swinging his legs off the side of the bed causing a wave of nausea to crash over him.

He touched his face again. *What is this thing?*

He needed a mirror.

The room was cloaked in darkness with only a tiny sliver of light framing what appeared to be a floor to ceiling window. He was sure he wasn't at home.

Taking a deep breath, he moved to his feet, swaying unsteadily as blood rushed to his head, black speckles against brilliant white dancing across his vision. He resisted the temptation to collapse back down and moved across to the window, pulling the curtain back quickly, regretting it immediately as blinding light flooded the room. Squinting and hiding his bare flesh with the curtain, he took in the view in front of him. Missing his contact lenses, he could just about make out the blurred cityscape, registering the heavy steel framework that formed the roof of the Great Northern building directly in front of him. To the right, he recognised the distinctive curved form of the G-MEX Centre with the clock tower of Manchester Town Hall just behind. To his immediate left was Deansgate, the mile-long avenue running a river of cars through the centre of Manchester. He had experienced this view many times on boozy nights in the Sky Lounge, the Metropolitan Hotel's über-trendy cocktail bar, positioned high up on the twenty-third floor of the iconic Sky Tower.

He must be in one of the hotel's rooms, he thought – but how did he get here?

Another wave of nausea crashed over him and he grabbed at the curtain, resting his head against the cold glass of the window, fighting an overwhelming desire to vomit.

As his palate began to water, he turned quickly to face the room, now illuminated, before launching himself in the direction of the bathroom. Slamming through the half-open door, he dropped to his hands and knees in front of the toilet basin, just as vomit erupted through the metal hole framing his mouth. Over and over, he spewed foul, hot liquid, until his throat burned with acid and his body ached for respite. Eventually, when he had nothing left to bring up, he crashed sideways onto the cold tiled floor and closed his eyes, exhausted.

He lay there motionless for a long time trying to orientate himself. The smell of the wet, disgusting liquid filled his nostrils; he needed to clean himself up. Opening his eyes and using the basin for support, he lifted himself from the floor, clumsily rubbing his right hand against the wall before finding the light switch and flicking it on.

The shock of his reflection in the mirror caused him to cry out, and despite his blurred vision, he could clearly see he was wearing a 'gimp' sex mask, made infamous by the hit movie, *Pulp Fiction*. He touched his face again and could see it was made of PVC. The metal zip was covered in congealing vomit. Wildly, he grabbed and pulled at the zip running up the back of his head but it appeared locked. Turning to the left, he attempted in vain to get a visual on it and caught a glimpse of something metal swinging from the back of his head, like a tiny circular ponytail.

Craning his neck, he was suddenly aware of something reflected in the mirror that made his blood run cold and his heart jumped in his chest. Slowly turning towards the shower cubicle behind him, he came face to face with the naked body of a teenage boy slumped on the other side of the glass, his skin pressed flat against the shower door. His black, dead eyes stared ahead, a red ball gag made of plastic, metal and leather fixed to his face and mouth, a thick strap locked around his neck. His hands and feet were tied with plastic cable ties so tightly that they had broken the skin, leaving congealed blood and dark purple bruising. Marty had no clue who the boy was or what he was doing in this bathroom. Stepping closer, he gently pulled open the creaking glass door, recoiling as the boy's body slumped heavily on to the floor. He knelt down next to him and checked his pulse at the neck but felt nothing. *Shit! Shit! Shit!*

Whoever and however this boy had ended up in this bathroom, Marty knew for certain – he had to get out of the mask and out of the hotel *fast*. If even a hint of this got to the press, he was ruined.

Instantly focused, he leapt to his feet and moved back into the bedroom in search of his phone. At times like this, there was only one man to call: his agent, Rob Woodcock. They had been together for almost twenty years and he was an expert at getting Marty out of trouble. Finding his phone on the bedside table, he selected Rob's number from his favourites and dialled. After what felt like forever it connected.

'Rob?' he said, struggling against the mask.

'Marty, is that you, mate? You sound different. What's up with your voice?' Rob's thick Essex accent belied the razor-sharp business brain that had made both he and Marty very wealthy men.

'I don't have time to explain, but I really need you to come to the Metropolitan Hotel right away.'

'The bar or the hotel?'

'The hotel, Rob, *quickly!*'

'Is everything OK?' Rob asked, clearly concerned.

'Look Rob, I don't have time for this. Just get down here now, will you?'

'OK mate, keep your hair on. I'll come right over. What room you in, then?'

Marty paused for a moment. He had no clue.

'I dunno. Just get here and call me. I'll have figured it out by then.' he said impatiently.

'Jesus, must have been some night, fella!'

'You have no idea.'

Rob was laughing now. 'You dirty bastard!'

Ignoring the comment, Marty asked, 'And can you bring some pliers?'

'Pliers? What *have* you been up to?'

'Don't ask!' Marty said flatly before ending the call.

He checked the time on his phone – 11.08am.

Noticing the deathly silence in the room for the first time, he slowly perched down on the end of the thick mattress and placed his head in his hands. What happened? How had a bound-and-gagged teenage boy ended up dead in his bathroom? More pressingly, how was he ever going to make this *go away*?

Suddenly there was loud knock and Marty's head shot up, staring in silence at the door. He thought he had imagined it, but there it was again. Slowly and silently, he crept forward and placed his eye to the peephole. On the other side, three men stood staring back at him, their bodies curved in the fisheye lens. All three were wearing suits, their expressions grave.

CHAPTER 2

'Who the bloody hell are you?' Marty whispered to himself as he peered out onto the dimly lit hallway. The three men stood intently, as if staring straight at Marty through the peephole. The smaller man at the front stepped forward and knocked on the door once more, this time noticeably louder. 'Mr. Michaels, can we come in please?' he said, just short of shouting.

Marty swallowed hard. His heart pounded so loudly in his head, he was convinced they could hear it through the thick door. How did they know he was here? He touched the PVC mask before looking down at his naked body through the eyelets. It didn't take a genius to realise just how much shit he was in. Headlines played out in front of him like a bad movie: MARTY MICHAELS – MASKED RADIO STAR FOUND NAKED WITH DEAD BOY. Marty Michaels, pervert and sex fiend – forevermore talked about in the same breath as Savile, Glitter and Harris – but even worse, a murderer. Permanently shamed and excluded from the celebrity world he had ruled over for almost two decades. *He had to hide.*

He ran across to the window and yanked open the curtains, his hare-brained hope of finding an escape route instantly dashed. The hotel had no balconies or windows that opened.

The banging resumed, this time even more aggressively, as the same man shouted at the top of his voice. 'Mr. Michaels, I know you're in there. Can you please open the door? If you do not let me in, I have the authority to enter the room using my own key.'

Shit.

Marty dropped down on all fours and lifted the sheet from the side of the bed hoping to hide under it, but it was no use; there was an inch at best between the bed base and the carpet. *Bollocks.* Jumping to his feet, he ran into the bathroom, but the sight of the body slumped on the floor sent him fleeing like a cartoon character in the opposite direction.

He was running out of time to hide. In desperation, he flung himself under the desk opposite the bed, pulling the office chair in around his hunched body, just as the door tentatively opened.

The first man to speak had a posh Mancunian accent, but in a way that sounded affected, like a common-man hiding his roots. 'Mr. Michaels? My name is Thomas Holmes, I'm the hotel duty manager. I'm here with the police, who would like to speak with you. Mr. Michaels?' he said moving through the room, stopping just inches from Marty's head. The next voice he heard had a very different accent – London he guessed – spoken by a man who would probably pronounce it 'Laaarnden'. He talked loudly and with confidence as if he had done this a million times before.

'Mr. Michaels, this is Detective Sergeant Jones. I'm here with my colleague, Detective Constable Bovalino, and we're from the Greater Manchester Police. We know you're in this room and we'd prefer it if you could show yourself and save everyone a whole lot of embarrassment. Mr. Michaels?'

The room fell completely silent for a moment and Marty's body started to shake as his back and shoulder muscles convulsed, trying to force open his mouth to let in some oxygen.

'Bov, check the bathroom, I'll have a good look round this room,' Jones said, casually stepping past Marty's position.

A moment later Marty heard the third man shout from the bathroom.

'Jonesy, in here!' he said in a thick Mancunian accent.

Marty watched as Jones obediently moved towards the bathroom and the location of the boy's body – *it was now or never.*

Finally allowing himself to breathe he gulped in air and thrust the office chair out into the room, exploding like a sprinter from under the desk. He ran headlong towards the door and the man he guessed was the hotel manager, who opened his mouth to speak. Marty lunged past him, slamming through the open door and into the wall in front of him, instinctively turning right, hoping it would take him to the elevators.

Behind he could hear voices shouting. The two officers alerted to his escape gave chase.

He ran as fast as his overweight body would allow, and up ahead could see a break in the corridor. Praying for an elevator with an open door, the voices of the men following drew closer with every passing second.

He reached the elevator and noted he was on the sixteenth floor as he hammered his fingers on the call button like a pinball machine. To his left, he could see the two police officers rushing towards him as he urged the doors to open.

'Come on! Come on!' he repeated under his breath before deciding to keep moving, setting off down the corridor like a man possessed, trying to stay out of range of the officers. Not easy considering he was totally out of shape. With every ounce of strength he could muster, he pumped his arms and knees trying to keep moving, but soon realised he was running out of corridor. A split second later, he felt the full weight of one of the men crash down onto his shoulders, stumbling painfully to the floor. In an instant, his captor expertly forced his knee into the small of Marty's back, yanking his arms together into handcuffs.

'You're nicked, mate,' said the man, his voice thick Mancunian. Bovalino, Marty guessed.

The other officer, who Marty assumed was Jones, arrived a split second later, just as he was dragged to his feet and presented like a prize by his captor.

Marty arched his head away from the man who stepped in close towards his face, peering through the mask's eyelets.

Jones was thin with gaunt, angular features covered by grey skin. His bloodshot eyes were framed with dark shadows and as he opened his mouth in a half-smile, he exposed crooked, tobacco-stained teeth.

'Well, well, well, what do we have here?' he said, his breath sharp and pungent.

Marty remained silent.

'Bov, If I'm not mistaken, inside this mask,' he said tapping his fingers loudly on the PVC material, 'we'll find the one and only, Marty Michaels.'

Bovalino laughed loudly.

'Let's get back to the room, We can unwrap *this* and see if I'm right.'

'Yes, guv,' Bovalino replied, tightening his grip on the cuffs, digging them into Marty's wrists. 'You got it.'

CHAPTER 3

Time passed slowly for Marty, sat on the edge of the bed, still naked, the room rapidly filling with more and more police personnel, called into action by Jones as soon as Marty was in handcuffs.

'Now then – let's see if you are who we think you are,' Jones said smugly, peering into the eyelets of the mask. Marty had still not spoken, somehow hoping he could get out of this mess without them seeing his face, or hearing his distinctive voice.

'Bov, grab those pliers, mate,' Jones said pointing to the pair being held by one of the uniformed police officers stood to Bovalino's right. 'And get this guy something to cover himself,' he added.

Bovalino was a big man all over. With his huge barrel chest, he looked as wide as he was tall, about six foot, Marty guessed, with close-cropped black hair and a five o'clock shadow across his swarthy face. He had the thick forehead of a man who enjoyed contact sport, and looking at his fleshy cheekbones and flat nose, one could assume he had spent a fair bit of time in the boxing ring.

Walking behind Marty, Jones grabbed at the zipper on the back of the mask and jammed the pliers painfully against his head, forcing him to cry out.

'It's alive!' Jones laughed and continued his attempts to release the locked zipper. After a few more minutes he succeeded, the zipper releasing noisily, before he grabbed the mask and pulled it away from Marty's face.

'Oh dear, son – it's just not your day, is it?' Bovalino said laughing.

'The press are gonna have a field day with this!' Jones said enthusiastically. 'The great Marty Michaels found naked in a sex mask with a dead body in his shower!'

Marty spoke for the first time now. 'I haven't done anything. I've never seen him before. I swear it's true!' he protested.

Jones faced Marty and leaned in close, his voice almost a whisper, his tobacco breath rancid.

'So how did he end up dead in your shower?'

Marty held his gaze.

'I'm telling you, I've never even seen him until just a moment ago. I woke up with this thing on my face, and not the first idea how I got here. I know it sounds far-fetched but it's the truth!'

'So why did you run when we came in? Why not just tell us this back then?' Bovalino asked.

Marty paused as the question sank in; now he looked twice as guilty.

'I ran because, as you've just demonstrated, I'm Marty Michaels and anyone with *half a brain,* let alone you two, can see this looks bad.'

Jones ignored the dig and stood up straight, turning to face the bathroom door as two men in white forensic suits entered the room carrying various boxes of equipment. He looked at Bovalino, smiled and turned back to Marty.

'I think you'd better get dressed, Marty. We're going to need to ask you a few more questions down at the station,' he said still smiling.

'I'm not going anywhere with you!' Marty protested loudly.

Jones leaned in again, this time his face just centimetres from Marty, the smile gone.

'Oh yes you fucking are,' he growled as Marty pulled his face away.

'I know my rights. Am I under arrest? You can't make me go anywhere if I'm not under arrest and you have nothing to tie me to that body in there, so nothing to arrest me for. I'm going nowhere and you can take these bloody cuffs off as well!' he said shaking his hands behind his back for effect.

'Bov, place Mr. Michaels under arrest,' he said.

'On what charge?' Marty yelled.

'Possession with intent to supply!' Jones said as he produced a large plastic zip-lock bag filled with white powder, holding it opposite Marty's face.

'That's not mine!' He protested.

Jones continued unabated, 'Oh? This stash of drugs just happened to be under your pillow. Did the coke fairies come in the night?'

'I'm telling you, that's not mine!'

Jones smiled broadly and his crooked, stained teeth made Marty remember his nausea.

'Caution him, Bov, and let's get him down the nick while the forensic team goes through this place,' Jones said as Bovalino moved in closer.

'I want to speak to my lawyer!' Marty shouted.

Jones threw Marty's jeans at him. 'I'm sure you do, mate. I'll tell you what, you can use the phone down at the station,' he said laughing as he walked away, leaving his oversized partner to help Marty get dressed.

'Find my contact lenses, you big lump,' Marty growled under his breath. 'I can't see a damned thing.'

CHAPTER 4

The three men entered the elevator with Bovalino ushering Marty inside. Holding his cuffed wrists securely against his backside, the big man manoeuvered Marty around to face the doors alongside Jones who stood to their left. 'Hit "Lobby", Bov,' he said smugly.

'Lobby?' Marty looked shocked. 'Shouldn't we be heading to the basement and the service entrance?'

Jones's crooked smile was back. 'Now, why would we do that, Marty?'

'To get me out of here unnoticed, of course...'

Jones and Bovalino said nothing, smiling at one another.

Marty's gaze darted between them, '... to protect my reputation, my career and my livelihood. How about that for starters?'

'Again, why would we do that?' Jones said almost laughing now.

Marty stared in silence, his eyes wild, chest heaving as he struggled to maintain his composure.

'Guys, surely I'm innocent until proven guilty? Give me a chance. Shit like this sticks and could ruin my career!'

'Dead bodies, gimp masks and drug possession? Yep, I'd say shit like that *could* ruin your career, eh Bov?' Jones said with a broad grin.

Marty was incredulous.

He had never liked the police, in particular, the Greater Manchester force, and had been publicly critical of them over the years. He had experienced corruption first-hand, plus he had never forgiven them for allowing drug and gang crime to ruin the streets of his beloved Manchester, especially Whalley Range, where he had grown up. Throughout the eighties and nineties he had watched it turn from a salubrious lower-middle-class suburb of family homes into a toxic, dangerous rabbit warren of dark roads and lanes, filled with crack dens, brothels and street-walkers. His own parents had been burgled so many times they had reluctantly agreed to leave their treasured four bedroom family home, moving to a smaller house in the much safer suburb of Gatley.

Marty's eyes scanned the digital display above the door as the elevator descended.

'Please, guys? They'll make me out to be a pervert – I'll lose everything.'

'Yeah, just like Freddie Tate did,' Bov said flatly.

'Freddie Tate?' asked Marty.

Jones sneered now. 'See that, Bov? Doesn't even remember his name. Ruined Freddie's and his family's lives, but doesn't care. What a total bastard you are, Michaels!'

'I don't understand. I don't know a Freddie Tate,' pleaded Marty.

Bovalino growled in his ear from behind his head. 'Just like you don't know that dead boy in your bathroom? You're going down for this one, mate!'

Marty pulled away and craned his neck trying to catch sight of Bovalino's face.

'Seriously, *what are* you talking about? Who is Freddie Tate and how did *I* ruin his life?'

Jones turned to face Marty now, his eyes narrow. 'Freddie Tate was one of the best coppers ever to wear the uniform. Thanks to *you,* he killed himself; left a wife and two young kids without a dad. Ring any bells now?'

Marty's mouth was open but no words would come out. Totally confused, his eyes darted away from Jones's face back up towards the digital floor display. They were only seconds away from the lobby.

'Come on! Say something, you perverted prick!' Jones screamed into his face as Bov twisted the cuffs up his back, causing shooting pains in his wrists.

Marty cried out in agony and doubled over as Bovalino continued to push his arms upwards, growling through gritted teeth as blood rushed to his head. 'I honestly have no idea who Freddie Tate is or why he killed himself. I swear on my mother's life!'

'With your track record that's a very dangerous thing to do, Mr. Michaels,' Jones said sarcastically.

A split second later, the elevator came to a complete stop and a loud chime signalled they had arrived at the lobby level.

'Straighten up our special guest, Bov,' Jones said flatly. 'It's showtime!'

CHAPTER 5

The silver doors appeared to slide apart in slow motion. The elevator flooded with noise from the horde of paparazzi waiting in the hotel lobby on the other side, magnified by the polished marble floors and wood panelled walls. Bovalino's grip increased in intensity and the big man pushed Marty forward as Jones lead the way through flashing camera bulbs and shouting, moving backwards with the procession. Jones appeared to be in no hurry, walking steadily and deliberately through the mass of bodies and rapid questions from all sides.

'*Marty, is it true a young boy was found dead in your room this morning?*'

'*DS Jones, is this arrest part of Operation Yewtree?*'

'*Marty – how long have you been a fetish freak?*'

'*Is your career over, Marty?*'

'*Marty! This way, Marty, this way!*'

Stony-faced, Marty remained silent as Bovalino pushed him through the lobby towards the all-glass main entrance. He could see the unmarked police car waiting in the street, in full view of the surrounding crowd of paps and a number of camera crews with broadcast trucks, set up waiting to deliver live pictures to eager newsrooms across the country. Marty's head sank to his chest as he realised his career was finished. Being innocent meant nothing in these cases; when it came to sex crimes and the media, it was always 'guilty until proven guilty'.

He lifted his head to see his agent Rob Woodcock rushing through the main doors and his heart lifted. He was a big man, an ex-footballer from West London who had made it to the Premier League and the African Cup of Nations thanks to his grandfather's Nigerian heritage. Pushing his way towards his client his expression was grave.

'Marty, *what the fuck* is going on?' Rob said walking sideways as Jones continued to direct the procession towards the exit.

'I swear I don't know, Rob. I've been set up; it's all bullshit!' he shouted above the throng of reporters.

Rob turned to Jones now. 'What are you doing arresting my client? He's an innocent man!'

Jones glanced sideways and smiled.

'Your client is under arrest and the nature of our investigation is confidential,' Jones said.

'Confidential? So how did this lot get here?' Rob protested.

'Mr. Michaels is a celebrity. Maybe they were just following him around?'

'Don't make me laugh; this is a stitch-up and you know it!'

Jones did not respond. Instead, he carried on walking through the melee of reporters and paps, jostling for the best picture of Marty.

Rob gripped Marty's shoulder as he walked alongside.

'Don't worry, Marty, I'll call Andrew. We'll have you out of this in no time.'

Marty nodded. If anyone could clear up this kind of mess, his lawyer Andrew Johnson could.

'Where are you taking him?' Rob asked.

'Ashton House,' Jones replied without missing a beat as Bovalino pushed Marty into the huge revolving glass door, deliberately walking him slowly towards the awaiting media outside.

As the door finally opened onto the forecourt, a second wave of noise from the TV camera crews enveloped Marty, their bright lights forcing him to turn his head away as more questions fired in his direction.

'Marty – why have you been arrested?'

'Is it true a male prostitute was found dead in your room?'

Marty stopped in his tracks; a male prostitute? Bovalino pushed him on.

'Are you now expecting a government enquiry into this sex crime, Marty?'

Bovalino's big frame cut through the sea of people like a hot knife through butter. Rob, suddenly caught up in the throng of bodies, shouted to Marty not to worry, that Andrew would get him out. Bovalino opened the rear passenger door to the police car, his thick hand clamping down hard on the top of Marty's head as he pushed him into the back seat before the door slammed shut. A moment later, Jones and Bovalino jumped in the front seats, closing their doors in unison, silencing the world outside.

Jones tapped his hand on the dashboard. 'Away we go, Bov,' he said cheerfully as the car slowly moved through the crowd.

Marty glanced out of the window to his left as he tried to place Rob, his attention suddenly drawn to the familiar yet unexpected face of Simon Williams. Williams was a freelance broadsheet journalist who wrote regularly for the *Independent* and the *Guardian*, considered one of the country's sharpest minds on current and corporate affairs. His presence struck Marty as very odd: *what was he doing at a feeding frenzy like this?*

CHAPTER 6

Ashton House, situated in Failsworth on the outskirts of Manchester, was headquarters to the Greater Manchester Police. After being processed, Marty sat quietly on a red plastic chair in Interview Room Three, handcuffs removed, staring at his reflection in the mirrored wall. He had never believed this kind of set-up existed outside of US TV shows, but clearly it did. Surrounded by windowless breeze block, he noted the grubby fingermarks and boot scuffs that covered the whitewashed walls. The floor was polished concrete. The Formica table opposite was framed by two more red plastic chairs pointing towards him. Above his head, strip lighting buzzed as it cast an unpleasant synthetic glow across the small space.

Marty suspected he had been left to 'sweat'. It was working, as the events of the last couple of hours played over in his mind; waking naked in a hotel room, seeing his reflection wearing a gimp mask, nausea like he'd never known, the dead boy in the bathroom, the police turning up, and the paparazzi on hand to capture every sordid detail. Once again, he asked himself what had happened. None of it made the slightest bit of sense. In fact, right now *nothing at all* made sense. All he knew was his career was heading down the toilet rapidly.

The door opened to his left and he turned to see a tall blonde woman stepping inside the room. Her hair tied back in a short ponytail, she wore thin, metal framed glasses, a white blouse and a charcoal-grey trouser suit. She smiled without feeling and held out her hand to Marty.

'Thanks for waiting so patiently, Mr. Michaels. I know this can't have been easy for you. I'm Detective Chief Inspector Phillips. I just have a few questions and hopefully we can get all this straightened out.'

Marty said nothing, staring directly at Phillips as she took a deep breath and paused a moment, smiling broadly before leaning closer to him, 'And can I just say, I'm a huge, *huge* fan of the show.'

Marty allowed himself a smile; he had fans *everywhere.*

Detective Chief Inspector Jane Phillips. Known within Greater Manchester Police as one of the brightest detectives on the force, she was a law graduate who spoke fluent Cantonese after growing up in Hong Kong, where her father had been a high-ranking police officer.

As a child, she had loved the excitement of her father's career, and from a very early age had decided that following in his footsteps was all she wanted to do when she grew up. She was a young teenager when the province returned to Chinese rule and her father had retired, moving the family back to her mother's home town of Manchester, where Jane finished school a year early and then graduated from Manchester University with a first in law.

Totally focused on her desire to become a police officer, she had enlisted straight out of college, much to her mother's considerable displeasure; she wanted more for her daughter than the grubby world of British police work.

Excelling in firearms training she was offered a fast-track path to SCO19, the elite armed response unit of the Met Police, but she wanted to be a detective. Since leaving the academy, she had risen quickly through the ranks. Many of her male colleagues had suggested the lack of senior female officers had helped her trajectory. She attributed their comments to jealousy and sexism, still rife in the modern-day police force, despite the efforts of the top brass to persuade the public to the contrary.

She was unmarried and devoted to the job. With one of the highest conviction rates in the country, she offered the right image for a police force rebuilding its reputation, tarnished after decades of alleged corruption, racism and brutality. She was, in the eyes of Assistant Police Commissioner Blake, the perfect face for a high-profile case involving a prominent celebrity.

Sat opposite that same celebrity, she produced a manila folder, placing it on the desk in front of Marty. She pressed 'Record' on the digital recorder to her right and a small red light illuminated. By way of explanation, she smiled and said, 'For the record. I'm sure you're quite used to having your voice on "tape", Mr. Michaels?'

'Not in these circumstances, no. Shouldn't I have my lawyer present?'

Phillips smiled and her face struck Marty as very attractive.

'You can if you wish, of course, but naturally it will slow down the process. I'll have to place you in a cell while we locate them. I have a feeling this is all one big misunderstanding. We can have you out of here much quicker if you answer my questions now.' Phillips's voice was calm and reassuring.

Marty thought for a moment, trying to decide if he was heading for a fall without his lawyer. His gut told him to wait but the thought of not knowing what the world was saying about his arrest, without being able to answer his critics was unbearable. He was desperate to get out and he knew he had nothing to do with the dead boy; besides, he was *Marty Michaels* and if he could take on world leaders in heated exchanges, he could easily handle a young detective. He nodded his agreement.

'It's OK, let's get this over with.'

'You're sure now, Mr. Michaels?' Phillips said, smiling once again.

'Quite sure,' he said, his tone condescending, 'and you can call me Marty.'

'Very well, *Marty*. So, how well do you know Paul White?' she asked casually.

'Paul White? Who is Paul White?'

Phillips smiled coyly. 'I'm sorry, the young man we found dead in your bathroom.' She passed him a photo of the boy Marty had seen in the hotel shower, clearly taken at the scene. 'His name was Paul White.' Phillips's tone was measured and focused now.

'Never heard of him.'

'You're saying you've never met Paul White?'

'That's exactly what I'm saying.'

'So you've never shared a drink with him or met him at a social event?'

'If I've never met him, I wouldn't have shared a drink with him, would I?'

Phillips stared at Marty for a long moment. Her tone was suddenly ice-cold, 'And you never hired him for sex?'

'What? This is outrageous!'

Phillips continued, pressing Marty hard now. 'Paul White was a male prostitute, Marty. He had sex for money. I'd like to know if you ever paid him for sex?'

'Don't be ridiculous! I'm not gay – *quite the bloody opposite!*'

'What do you mean by that, Marty?'

'I mean that, as a fan of my show, you'll know I'm a red-blooded heterosexual. I'm also a Catholic, for crying out loud.'

Phillips allowed his words to sink in and once more stared at Marty as if trying to solve a puzzle. She smiled quickly and without feeling before opening the manila file fully.

'Such passionate feelings, Marty,' she said flatly.

Marty leaned back in the chair, his hands flat on the table in front of him. 'I'm a passionate man,' he said breaking out into a big smile, 'as many of my ex-girlfriends would testify to.'

'Probably not necessary, Marty,' Phillips shot back dispassionately.

Marty's smile dropped along with his arms, which he folded across his stomach, 'Oh I see, touched a nerve, have I, Detective?'

'I'm not sure I know what you mean, Marty?'

'Woman in a man's world? Usually means they're more man than woman, doesn't it?'

'Are you suggesting I'm gay?'

'If the flat shoe fits, love,' he giggled to himself.

Phillips held his gaze a moment then dropped her head towards the manila file, before looking up at Marty once more.

'You see, Marty, the one thing that's puzzling me is that you claim to be passionately heterosexual and that you've never met Paul White, yet here you are having a drink with him, a male prostitute, in the Sky Lounge at the Metropolitan Hotel, *last night*.' Phillips placed a black-and-white A4 photo in front of Marty.

He looked at the photo. It was a grainy image, obviously enlarged from the original. It definitely looked like him, but it couldn't be.

'It's a still shot taken from the CCTV camera that sits just behind the bar. The quality's not fantastic, but I can assure you the video is picture-perfect. That is you in the photograph, isn't it Marty?'

'Well... erm, I guess, it kind of *looks* like me...'

'I'd say it's a dead ringer and the man sitting next to you...' Phillips tapped her index finger on the photo '... is Paul White.' She passed across another photograph. 'This is a clearer picture of him, a mugshot from a previous arrest for soliciting two years ago, aged just sixteen. The deceased found in your bathroom, the man you were drinking with until just before midnight. Can you explain that, Marty?'

Marty looked up at Phillips, his face like that of a little boy lost, all the swagger and cockiness vanished. Now he was scared. Phillips pushed on.

'Marty, are you still saying you've never met Paul White?'

'I... I...' For once in his life, Marty was lost for words. 'It looks like me but I don't remember.'

'You don't remember drinking with him or you don't remember tying him up and strangling him in your bathroom?'

Marty suddenly felt very nauseous again. 'I don't remember anything about last night,' he said weakly.

'Why don't you just tell me the truth, Marty?' Phillips's voice was soft now. 'Things got out of hand last night, sex game gone wrong, and you ended up killing your lover, Paul White?'

'I've never met him,' he pleaded.

'But this picture says otherwise, Marty,' Phillips said tapping the photo of them sitting together at the bar.

'That picture has been fabricated. Someone is out to get me. I have enemies. This whole thing has to be a set-up,' Marty said.

Phillips stared at Marty without blinking for a moment before passing him another black and white CCTV still. 'I'd like you to take a look at this photo as well, Marty, from the camera outside the room you were arrested in this morning. As you can see, it shows you and White entering your room just after midnight last night. It would seem you were very close at that moment. That is your arm around his shoulders, isn't it?'

Marty stared at the photo. His mind was racing. He had no memory of any of it but he knew it was his face smiling in the pictures. How could he not remember? What was he doing with a male prostitute – *in his room*? His stomach sank. He had a sudden urge to empty his bowels and panic rushed through every fibre in his body as his nerves ran hot, then cold.

'Marty, that is *you* in the pictures, laughing with Paul White, isn't it?' Phillips asked.

Marty looked up, his face a mixture of confusion and fear.

'I want to speak to my lawyer – *now*.'

CHAPTER 7

By the time Marty called his lawyer, Andrew Johnson was already on his way to Ashton House; one of his junior clerks had alerted him to Marty's predicament after witnessing his arrest on Twitter. Johnson had been on the fifteenth hole of Worsley Park Country Club when the call came through, enjoying a rare day off with his father-in-law, himself a lawyer who practised on the corporate side of the business.

Johnson cut an impressive figure. After reading English and French at Cambridge, he had studied law at The London School of Economics. He had all the attributes of public school life, the air of arrogance that comes from 'money'. He had successfully defended Marty many times against multi-million-pound libel cases and was now a constant presence in his life.

As soon as he was off the golf course, Johnson had launched into damage control, ordering his partners and clerks into action as they raced to file injunctions that could keep Marty's arrest out of the press and off TV. Despite their best efforts, it was too little, too late, and by midday, Marty's arrest was headline news UK-wide. When it came to the British media, Marty had made enemies through the years and, sensing blood, the vultures were circling.

When Marty had finally spoken to Johnson on the phone, his lawyer's directive had been crystal clear, 'Not a word, Marty; not a single fucking word!' He was happy to do as told, for once.

He sat alone in a holding cell now. Detective Chief Inspector Phillips had made her excuses and left shortly after Marty's request for his lawyer. His mind was racing, trying to make sense of what he had seen in the photographs, but he could not remember anything. He kept asking himself: *What happened?* But the answers continued to evade him.

The silence was deafening and Marty hated silence. It unnerved him; he struggled to think when it was quiet. His mother often remarked he was destined to be a radio host because as soon as he was able, all he ever wanted to do was talk. She joked she could not remember a time when he wasn't talking about something or somebody.

Marty allowed himself a smile at the thought of his mother and tried desperately to remember the sound of her comforting voice. She was very sick now, bedridden in Wythenshawe Hospital, suffering the effects of a severe stroke that had left her unable to talk. The irony was not lost on Marty and he felt sick to his stomach thinking about her, so frail and frightened.

He was the only child of his parents' loving marriage. After his father passed five years earlier in a car crash along with his best friend and producer, David, Marty had vowed to spend more time with his mother. However, overwhelmed by grief, his job had filled the huge void left behind, and over time his visits home had reduced from once every couple of days, to once a week, to finally every month or so. Sitting in the holding cell thinking of her with no living relatives but him, he felt shame. She was the one decent thing left in his life and he had treated her visits as some kind of moral obligation. He wished he could talk to her now. She would know what to do.

The cell door opened interrupting Marty's thoughts, and he was escorted back to interview room three, where Andrew

Johnson was waiting for him. The big lawyer strode confidently towards him, his right arm outstretched, his left hand holding a briefcase by his side. Marty instinctively took his hand. Johnson's handshake was unnecessarily firm. 'Marty, good to see you. I wish it were in better circumstances!'

Johnson was in his early forties, a tall man at six foot three, with broad shoulders. He had been a rower during his time at Cambridge, a 'blue', but these days preferred early morning 10K runs. The prematurely greying hair looked almost white against his tanned face but rather than making him seem old, gave him the George Clooney look that many found very attractive. His pinstriped suit was immaculate, bespoke-tailored and at considerable cost, from Savile Row in London. He could easily afford it and the others hanging in his Prestbury home, just three streets from Marty's own house. He was one of the elite lawyers in North West England earning serious money with an attitude to match. Marty had liked him from the moment they met.

'Bearing up, old boy?' he said with a hint of a smile as Detective Chief Inspector Phillips entered the room.

'Has *she* told you why I'm here?' Marty snapped.

'She has indeed, Marty. Terrible business, this White fellow getting himself killed; awfully sad for his poor family – assuming of course he has one – but as I just explained to DCI Phillips, quite what it has to do with you is beyond me. You are here on circumstantial evidence and there is little to hold you. The best they have is a potential possession charge on the cocaine; at worst, a simple summary offence – *providing they can prove it was yours, of course*; there were two of you in that room, after all. So, as it stands, I'm taking you home.' He smiled widely, his perfect white teeth almost glowing under the fluorescent light.

Marty's relief was palpable, exhaling loudly as his body softened. He was free to go; Andrew as ever had sorted it. In an instant, his relief turned to anger as the last few hours caught up with him. He turned to Phillips, pointing his index finger directly at her face. 'Don't think you've heard the last of this!' he raged.

DCI Phillips was unmoved. 'Oh, I'm quite sure we'll talk again, Marty. As *I've* just explained *at length* to Mr. Johnson here, the results of Paul White's post-mortem will be back in the next couple of days. Call it a hunch, but I have a feeling you and I will talk again.' Marty shot a glance from Phillips to Johnson and back to Phillips as she continued. 'You know, I'm not a gambling woman – but if I *were*, I'd bet my last fiver you'll be back here very soon,' she said, half smiling.

Phillips's confidence made Marty uneasy but he pushed it to the back of his mind. He was free to go. He snorted dramatically, heading for the door and was almost out of the room when Phillips stopped him in his tracks. 'Oh, Marty, one more thing. I have explained this to Mr. Johnson, but there's no harm in you hearing it too. If, for some reason, you suddenly have a desire to leave the country and head for your villa in Spain, you need to understand that wouldn't look good for your case. Am I making myself clear?' she said, her voice almost threatening.

Marty stared at Phillips, his rage like a living thing inside him, desperate to be let loose. Johnson placed a comforting arm around his shoulder and ushered him out before he could respond.

Perplexed, Marty looked up at his lawyer hoping for some reassurance. 'My *case*? Andrew, what does she mean? I'm off the hook, aren't I?'

Johnson never broke stride and continued to walk Marty along the corridors towards the exit, calmness personified. 'Of course you are, old boy,' he said. 'It's just standard practice, police talk. Look, she's trying to scare you, that's all. Let's get you home while I see what we can do to limit the coverage of this unfortunate situation.'

Marty nodded weakly. He wanted to believe it would be that easy, but he knew it would not. After his very public arrest, he was certain that even Andrew with his silver tongue, sharp suits and bank of highly paid partners could not stop him becoming the lead story of every radio show, TV programme and newspaper in the UK. The beginning of a feeding frenzy by a British press that resented Marty's power and influence. He knew what was coming; after all, in his fifteen years at the top, he had gone after hundreds of fallen celebrities himself, building his own career on the demise of others.

At that moment, as he moved closer to the uncertainty of the outside world, he felt like a lamb to the slaughter. He had a foreboding sense it was about to get very messy indeed. As his ex-wife had warned him many times, *'Karma's a bitch!'*

CHAPTER 8

Andrew Johnson dropped Marty off at his Prestbury house, but decided against going in. He had a busy night ahead with a fresh set of injunctions to force through, to limit the damage the press could do to Marty's career. His client's outspoken views had led to at least one libel case a year for Andrew over the last seven years, a rich stream of income that needed protecting.

It was almost ten o'clock when Marty stepped inside the darkened house, a purpose-built box made from steel, oak and glass. A classic example of the popular architecture that had sprung up across the UK in the last ten years.

In true Marty Michaels style, his was the biggest house on the block. A sweeping pebbled drive accessed by electric gates, provided the only way through the fifteen-foot-high white concrete walls, surrounding all sides of the house. It boasted a heated twenty-five-metre indoor pool with a separate hot tub, games room, private cinema and six bedrooms, all nestling in three acres of land rolling down to farmland behind the property. He switched on the reception hall light that also lit the stairs, and hurried up to his bedroom.

Throwing off his clothes, he walked into his wet room, turning on the huge overhead shower. The powerful spray crashed over his body and he lifted his head to face the water. He held it there for several seconds before turning away, gulping in air, repeating the ritual over and over, trying desperately to wash away the last thirty-six hours, to clear his head, to make sense of the strangest day of his life so far.

After twenty minutes, he gave up. His mind still searched for answers that would not come.

Marty wrapped his soaked body in a long white towelling dressing gown, tying it purposefully at the waist before heading downstairs to the kitchen, flicking on the lights. With the rest of the house still in darkness, Marty felt an overwhelming sense of unease. This had been his home for the last ten years. His sanctuary against a sometimes unforgiving outside world, he had almost lost it in a messy divorce from his first and only wife, Rebecca. It was an expensive separation that forced him to remortgage in a desperate attempt to keep the house. Despite his £1.3 million annual income, Marty's debts were sizeable.

Since the divorce from Rebecca, he had remained resolutely single. Proudly known in the media world as a red-blooded straight man, he was not averse to sharing his opinions on Manchester's prominent gay community.

A big part of Marty's 'act' relied on his right-wing views of sexuality, abortion, drug abuse and immigration. The very idea he was connected to a male prostitute was ludicrous.

The more he reflected on events, the more he believed he had been set up. Plenty of people had the motive. Jeremy Day sprang to mind. He was the drive-time presenter and Marty's main rival at the UK's number-one-rated commercial radio station, Talk105.

Day was much younger than Marty. He was part of a new generation of radio presenters, good-looking, super-fit, tanned and blonde, a stark contrast to Marty's post-forty ageing-rocker appearance. Day was the blue-eyed boy of COMCO – The Communications Consortium – parent company of Talk105, which owned and operated a portfolio of fifty radio stations across the UK. As with Marty's breakfast show, Day's drive show was syndicated across all fifty COMCO stations. Despite being on the network for only eighteen months, he was quickly becoming a household name to rival Marty. Many, including COMCO's current CEO Colin Burns, saw Day as next in line for Marty's coveted breakfast show, recognised by those in the industry as *the* gig in UK commercial radio. During his fifteen-year tenure on the show, Marty had seen off many pretenders to his crown, but times and tastes were changing. Day, more than just well-known, was well liked and a serious threat.

Marty shook his head vigorously hoping it would clear, but he remained dumbfounded by the events of the last thirty-six hours. He moved into the kitchen and with his overwhelming sense of unease growing, flicked on the house master-switch, turning on every light on the ground floor including the pool. He fixed himself a Scotch and ice in the lounge room, and pulling back the French doors, stepped out onto the decked terrace that led out onto the garden. Looking up, the sky was crystal-clear. The stars sparkled brightly without a breath of wind. It had been an unusually warm summer so far this year and he could feel the evening heat enveloping his body. 'What the fuck is going on, Marty?' he whispered to himself.

He took a moment to allow his thoughts to quieten, and closed his eyes, the only sound the distant hum of a flight taking off from Manchester Airport, just five miles away. Finally, a light calmness started to fill his body. *Everything would be OK,* he thought. Clutching the glass, Marty rolled the mixture around, absent-mindedly listening to the ice as it clinked back and forth. Lifting the glass to his lips, he took a big gulp of the liquid. It tasted good, warming his insides, and he greedily drained the glass, immediately beginning to relax.

The serenity was broken when the house phone rang. He did not intend speaking to anyone tonight, and so he let it go to voicemail, moving closer to the open door so he could hear who was calling as the message tone beeped.

'Hi Marty. I tried your mobile but it's switched off.' Marty recognised the voice immediately; it was his agent, Rob. 'Call me, we need to talk, mate.'

Rob had been Marty's agent for almost ten years and since David's death, he was the closest thing he had to a best friend. A cruciate ligament injury had cut short his promising career with Manchester City. Retired from the game at twenty-six, he jumped straight into life as a sports agent, moving quickly into entertainment in the years that followed. He was a likeable rogue and had established himself as one of the 'good guy' agents in the UK. They had been through a lot together and Marty relied on Rob to keep him out of trouble.

Darting inside, he picked up the handset.

'It's me.'

'Marty? How are you?' Rob said, relief evident in his voice.

'How am I? Let's see. Well, I woke up in a hotel room with a dead body in the shower and a bag of coke under my pillow. I've been arrested, manhandled, "papped" and humiliated, not to mention locked up for almost eight hours. *How do you think I am, Rob?*'

'I know, Marty, it's shit the way you've been treated. Look, do you want me to come over?'

'No, I want to be alone.'

'OK, mate. Let's meet tomorrow for breakfast and talk.' Rob called everybody mate, whether he knew them or not.

'Fine, I'll come to your office after the show.'

Rob paused for a moment.

'Marty, there's no easy way to say this… there is no show tomorrow.'

'What are you talking about, Rob? Of course there's a show tomorrow, it's Monday!'

There was another pause on the line, and Marty could sense Rob was trying to pick his words carefully.

'Look, mate, when all this broke I called Colin Burns. He was very clear; until this is cleared up, the board want you off the show. I'm sorry.'

'What do you mean "until this thing is cleared up"? I'm innocent. The police let me go. There's nothing to clear up. White's dead but I didn't kill him. Andrew said it was all a scare tactic, circumstantial bollocks.'

'*We* know you didn't do it but the investigation is still pending and until the police officially clear you, Burns and his cronies want you to keep a low profile. Advertisers are already pulling ads from the station; this kind of publicity is bad for business.'

'Sod Burns! I'm doing my show tomorrow no matter what he wants!'

'Marty, I get you're angry, but this won't help. Lay low for a few days; try to relax a little. It'll blow over and you'll be back on air in no time, mate.'

'But if I don't go on air tomorrow people will think I'm guilty!'

'Honestly, they won't. This is the right thing to do. Trust me.'

'Who's covering?' Marty asked, fearing the answer.

There was another long pause on the other end of the phone.

'Jeremy Day,' Rob said finally.

'For God's sake! I might as well just hand him my job on a platter!'

Marty's frustration was palpable. He was desperate to set the record straight and tell the world of his innocence. Now according to Rob that wasn't going to happen. Worse still, Jeremy Day was about to get a shot at his show.

'I have to do the show, Rob! I can't let Day get his hands on it. You're my agent – you're supposed to be looking out for me!'

'I am, Marty. When have I ever let you down or got it wrong? Come on, mate, you know it makes sense.'

Marty said nothing, instead he breathed heavily through his nose into the phone to ensure Rob could hear his frustrations.

'Marty, you know I'm right. It's just a few days.'

'It better had be, Rob, or I'll be looking for another agent!' Marty yelled into the phone without waiting for an answer. Ending the call, he launched the handset across the room where it landed with a loud bang against the wall.

'Bollocks!' he murmured as he stomped into the lounge room. 'I need a line!'

CHAPTER 9

Marty kept a small silver box of his favoured pick-me-up, pure Bolivian cocaine, in his lounge room for those days when he struggled to be 'Celebrity Marty Michaels'.

He paid over market value for the pure white powder because he was assured of quality and discretion; his dealer was very discerning, choosing to offer quality high-grade coke to a select few in the media world, and every line was a winner.

Marty perched on the edge of one of two oversized cream leather sofas and poured out a small pile of the cocaine onto the original Rennie Mackintosh glass coffee table, in the middle of the large room. Hunching forward he carefully and expertly chopped out three fat lines of powder, each about the length and width of a cigarette. He rolled up a twenty-pound note, dropped to his knees and leaned down to the glass, hoovering up the three lines one after the other, before quickly arching his body and leaning his head back so as not to lose any of the precious powder to gravity. Pushing his left nostril closed he sniffed hard to draw back any remnants of coke into his right, and let out a deep growl, signalling the process was complete.

Within a minute, he felt better, more in control, and soon after, he felt *good*, supremely confident. Marty reasoned Andrew would sort out the issue with White, and he would then relish taking Phillips, Jones and Bovalino to the cleaners. They would regret messing with Marty Michaels as their careers went down the toilet. Once he was finished with those bottom feeders, he would wage war on the leader of Greater Manchester Police, Assistant Police Commissioner Blake – a man he knew well and had once considered a golfing buddy but had been noticeable by his absence since Marty's arrest. He would ruin them all. He would teach them not to cross Marty Michaels; many had tried over the years, and he had used his immense power and influence to destroy every one of them. In the last fifteen years as host of the UK's number-one commercial radio show, he had earned the network in excess of a hundred million pounds in advertising revenues, not to mention the tens of millions' worth of free PR he had generated for the station and the network. He was revered in the industry, a money-making machine. With money came power, lots of power. Marty had chosen to use his to ruin countless political careers, influence public opinion and helped build and break businesses as he saw fit. He feared no one. In fact, five years ago he had even stepped into the murky underworld of Manchester, using undercover reporters to expose prostitution, human trafficking and drug-dealing on an international scale. The result being two organised crime leaders were now serving long sentences in Hawk Green prison. Both had vowed to get even with Marty. Every day since then, he had been looking over his shoulder, although it didn't bother him; it came with the territory. An essential sacrifice to stay on top.

It wasn't just criminals Marty fought – he took on the police too. Some years ago, as a young up-and-coming radio presenter, he had suffered personally at the heavy hands of Manchester police, arrested on a jumped-up soliciting charge, roughed up and humiliated by the officers involved when he protested his arrest. Two of the officers had later visited him in his cell and offered to make the case go away in exchange for five thousand pounds each. Marty had point-blank refused, instead insisting on seeing a lawyer. This had led to his first experience with Andrew, who quickly and expertly destroyed the case. The damage, however, was done.

In the late seventies and eighties, everybody suspected there was a large element of the police playing fast and loose. After a very public clean-up in the nineties, the outside world believed things had changed for the better. They started to look away. Marty did not.

Since his initial arrest, he was on a mission to expose the corruption he believed was still endemic in the British police, in particular the Manchester force. So savage was his contempt for them, and so strong his influence over public opinion, that when APC Stuart Blake entered office five years earlier, rather than reduce crime or increase arrests, his primary goal had been to befriend Marty Michaels and shut him up once and for all. The force simply could not move forward with Marty constantly and very publicly undermining them.

Blake had gone about his task with a level of ferocity that could only bring success. No sacrifice was too great, even enlisting Marty as the toastmaster for his eldest daughter's wedding. His daughter and wife had never forgiven Blake. Forcing Marty into their big day had been a complete disaster as he got tremendously drunk and called the bridesmaids 'a bunch of whores', before grappling with the best man and groomsmen as they tried to eject him.

In spite of his wife and daughter's anger, Blake had continued with his charm offensive towards Marty and they had become regular golfing buddies. Every second Saturday morning, usually sporting an enormous hangover, Marty would join Blake and two other unfortunate members of Worsley Park Country Club for a four-ball match of painful proportions. Each time Marty delivered his usual rendition of 'Army Golf', hacking his way from rough to trees and trees to bunker before electing to score himself impossibly low at the end of the round. If his scores had ever been near the truth, he would have easily been club champion – but the reality was, Marty was a cheat, a dreadful golfer and a terrible sport. To say he had pulled Marty onside would have been overstating it, but Blake's charm offensive and personal sacrifice had certainly tempered Marty's disdain for the force. That was all about to change. It was time for payback. Left to fend for himself by his so-called good friend APC Blake, it was clear that the gloves were off. Such was Marty's rage – growing ever stronger as the pure white powder coursed through his veins – he fully expected Blake would relinquish his position and step down in a matter of days.

As soon as he was back on air, the war on Greater Manchester Police would resume. Marty would not stop until every wrong was righted, every smart remark retracted and every minute of his confinement compensated in job losses.

Marty growled loudly like a pro wrestler psyching himself up; he was ready for the fight.

He needed another line.

Marty chopped out an extra-fat line this time and swept his Platinum American Express card across the glass in a figure of eight motion, carefully collecting any lose remnants of the precious white powder, neatly adding them to the long, chunky mound. He stared at it admiring its form, his mouth open and his tongue flicking furiously across his teeth; the coke had control now. Rolling the twenty-pound note into a tube he snorted the cocaine in one noisy movement, sniffing hard, forcing any remaining powder deep into his nostrils, as a thick, bitter residue slid down the back of his throat and his tonsils began to numb.

'You're gonna crucify them, Marty!' he shouted in triumph and leapt upright, ready to fight an imaginary foe.

Pacing the lounge rapidly, he muttered words of encouragement, psyching himself up for the battle that lay ahead. He felt strong, confident. He was ready to face them right now but that would have to wait. He certainly would never forget what Blake, Phillips and all the other bastards had done to him.

However, he trusted Rob and at times like this when everything seemed so completely messed up, he realised his agent was probably right. *They* may have won the first battle, but *he* would win the war.

Slumping down into the armchair, he stared at the silver box of cocaine for a long moment as it glistened on the coffee table in front of him, still half full. Thanks to Paul White and this whole, stupid mess, he had nothing to do for the next couple of days. Tipping a large pile of the contents onto the glass, he leaned forward. 'Fuck it!' he said loudly to himself. 'Don't mind if I do!'

CHAPTER 10

Marty woke with a start. As he opened his eyes, he blinked hard, trying to focus on the room around him. For a moment, he thought he was back in the Metropolitan but quickly realised he was in his own lounge room, lying prostrate on one of his oversized sofas. He prayed the last forty-eight hours had been a very bad dream and his spirits rose for a split second at the thought of returning to his normal life. Then he caught sight of the silver box of cocaine, which lay open on the glass coffee table along with his credit card and a twenty-pound note. Memories of his arrest, Andrew's intervention, his suspension from work and his subsequent drug binge came flooding back, filling him with dread.

He sat upright slowly and peered on to the glass table. He had shown some modicum of restraint in not finishing off all five grams of coke, but realised with some apprehension that he had devoured at least half of the pure white powder; quite a night for a man alone in his own home. His body was suddenly aware of the poison coursing through it and he immediately felt nauseous and weak, his head throbbing. He hated the blackness descended with a comedown and, staring at the remaining coke, contemplated getting high again to take the edge off the depression that now gripped him like a vice. He pulled the table closer to him and stared down at the contents, his body willing him to chop out a line, his heart begging him to leave it alone.

His mobile phone rang. A welcome distraction from his inner demons. He spied it vibrating on the sofa opposite. He stood awkwardly, doubled over, shuffling like an old man across the room to pick it up.

It was Rob.

'Hello?' he said weakly as he answered.

'Marty, thank God. Where've you been, mate? I've been calling all morning!'

Marty felt totally disorientated. He had no idea how long he had been out of action. 'What time is it?'

'Almost ten, mate.'

'Ten am?'

'Yes, it's ten am – ten am Monday! Are you all right, Marty?'

'I was exhausted last night, that's all. It was a big day, thought I deserved a lie-in this morning,' he lied.

'Well get up cos I'm only five minutes away from your place and I need you to let me through the gates when I arrive.'

Rob was a regular visitor to the house but never called ahead to warn Marty. It seemed odd that he would make a point of doing so today.

'Just press the buzzer as normal,' Marty instructed.

'Mate! Have you looked outside this morning?'

'No, I just woke up. Why?'

'There's an army of press camped outside, that's why! Turn on the news; you'll see your house!'

'What?'

'Your arrest at the Metropolitan was all over social media yesterday and across the news on all major channels by six o'clock last night. Some bastard in the police must have leaked your connection to Paul White's death – it's all over the papers, TV and radio this morning; unofficially, of course, and all just rumours, but you're everywhere!' Rob added, for a split second almost sounding proud.

'Jesus,' Marty managed to say, his voice barely audible.

Neither man spoke for a moment as they processed the conversation. Finally, Rob broke the silence.

'Look, Marty, don't panic. I'm sure we can turn this thing to our advantage. Just let me through in two minutes. When you see my car pull up on the security screen, open the gate, all right?'

'OK.'

'Good on yer, mate,' Rob said far too cheerfully for Marty's liking and ended the call.

CHAPTER 11

As soon as Rob's grey Range Rover had cleared the automatic gates, Marty fired them shut. He flicked on the master switch to the security blinds he had had fitted after the Moss Side gangland arrests and plunged the entire house into darkness, before turning on the lights in the kitchen. He wanted to keep Rob out of the lounge room after last night's exploits.

A couple of minutes later he opened the front door, careful to stand behind the thick oak panels to avoid being captured by any telephoto lenses.

Rob stepped inside the hallway and seeing the house drenched in darkness, awaited instructions from his client. As usual, he was smartly dressed in a grey suit with a crisp white shirt open at the neck with no tie. In his right hand, he carried a soft tan leather bag that matched his Italian shoes, the keys to his Range Rover and apartment jangling noisily in his left. He was a man who looked after himself, and still trained hard four times a week. In an attempt to intimidate opposition defenders during his playing days, he had chosen to shave his head to the skin, wearing it like that ever since above well-trimmed designer stubble, only one week away from a full beard. He smiled at Marty and his perfectly straight teeth set in his thick jaw gave him the look of an Armani model. Marty gestured for Rob to follow him through to the large open-plan kitchen and he obediently followed.

So voracious was Marty's appetite for information, he'd had flat-screen TVs installed in every room of the house, the fifty-inch screen on the wall of the kitchen was switched on with the sound down. Twenty-four-hour rolling news was showing, the main story being Marty's arrest. An old publicity picture of him looking younger and much healthier filled the screen with the caption 'MICHAELS ARRESTED' underneath.

Rob glanced up at the TV as he walked in and appeared slightly uncomfortable standing opposite Marty now, who handed him a mug of coffee before sipping slowly from his own cup.

'Thanks,' said Rob half smiling, unusually unsure of himself. He somehow had the appearance of a naughty teenager, waiting to see if his parents knew he had been up to no good. Marty stared at him for a moment without saying a word.

'You look like shit, mate,' Rob blurted out awkwardly.

'You don't look so hot yourself!' Marty shot back, which wasn't true.

Rob put his mug down on the kitchen bench and shrugged.

'Sorry Marty – I didn't mean to make you feel bad.'

'You got a funny way of showing it.'

Rob raised his hands in surrender. 'I was messing with you. I'm sorry.'

'The last thing I need right now is you telling me I look like shit when my life is falling apart!' Marty growled in a low voice.

'Come on, mate, it's really not that bad. We'll get through it.'

'Easy for you to say, it's not your career. If this goes south you lose fifteen per cent; I lose everything Rob, *everything!*'

'That's not fair, Marty, we're in this together and you know it. I'm not here to protect my investment or to keep a client on the payroll; I'm here as your friend, to support you. When have I ever let you down?'

There was a long pause as both men digested Rob's words, eyeing each other cautiously.

Marty had never apologised or backed down in his life, and he sure as hell wasn't about to start now, so instead he changed the subject, staring at the TV screen behind Rob's head, using his coffee mug to make his point.

'But how can they link me to a crime I've not been charged with? It's libellous, for God's sake!'

'I know, mate, and I put a call into Andrew about that very same thing on the way over. He's looking into it and he'll call me back as soon as he has anything.'

'We could sue, right?'

'Absolutely!' Rob said, his confidence returning now. 'With the amount of media companies and coverage involved, you'll be set for life. You know, this could actually be a blessing in disguise, Marty. Imagine it, millions in damages, you'll never have to work again.'

Marty stared at Rob for a long moment. 'But that's not the point. I'm Marty Michaels, I'm supposed to work, I want to work, the British people *need* my show. They depend on me to look out for them, to protect them. I can't just walk away!'

'Mate, you've been getting out of bed at 4am for fifteen years, aren't you ready for a change? Don't you want to start taking it easy? Maybe now you can finally move on. It's been *long enough*, Marty,' Rob said, his words tailing off.

'What the hell does that mean?'

Rob had just entered dangerous territory.

'Marty, you've done nothing but work since you and Rebecca split, that's five years next month. You're drinking more than ever and I know you enjoy more than just the occasional line of coke. You got high last night; I can tell you've hardly slept.'

'I wasn't high – I just couldn't sleep with all this going on in my head,' he lied again.

'Come on, Marty, you forget I know you too well. I bet if I walk into your lounge, that expensive glass coffee table of yours will have tiny fragments of Bolivian marching powder on it. Am I right?'

Marty said nothing, taking a large gulp of coffee as he tried his best to avoid eye contact.

'I thought so. It's not healthy, mate; in fact, there's only one way to go if you carry on like this. You're my best mate as well as my client and I'm not planning your funeral. You can sue the bastards – *all of them* – for a million quid each and start a new life away from this bullshit business.'

Marty dropped his head and stared into his coffee cup, Rob's words cut deep and he said nothing for almost a full minute. When he spoke, he didn't look up and his voice was low, brimming with emotion. 'I'm not ready to walk away, Rob,' he said quietly. 'The show is the only thing I have left.'

Rob stared at Marty before stepping forward and placing a reassuring hand on his shoulder.

'Hey, mate, it was just an idea. I know the break-up with Becks really messed you up. I want to try to help you move on, that's all. Look, don't you worry, they're not going to take your show, Andrew and I will see to that! We've got you out of some pretty bad scrapes before, right? We can do it again, OK?'

Marty looked up and smiled weakly. 'Thanks, mate,' he said, nodding.

He hoped with all his heart Rob was right, that this would all go away and things would be back to normal, just as they had on previous occasions; but this situation was like nothing they had faced before. His intuition told him everything had changed in the last forty-eight hours and life would never be the same again.

CHAPTER 12

Marty showered while Rob prepared breakfast of bacon and eggs. By the time he returned to the kitchen, barefoot, dressed in blue jeans and an old grey AC/DC T-shirt, the breakfast bar was set with orange juice and a fresh pot of coffee. The TV was on, the volume turned up high, and Rob had opened one of the window blinds; the kitchen was now bathed in morning sunlight making the cutlery glisten like precious metal.

Marty wasn't hungry – nothing kills an appetite quite like two grams of coke and being linked to a man's death – but he knew he needed to eat, and Rob insisted. He obediently slipped on to the breakfast stool and ate slowly, forcing down every mouthful. Opposite, Rob remained standing, his jacket off and shirt sleeves rolled up exposing his heavily tattooed wrists, the black ink visible but not stark against his black skin. By contrast to Marty, the former athlete virtually inhaled his plateful whilst keeping a close eye on his client.

When they had both finally finished, Rob slipped onto the breakfast stool and pushed his plate away, replacing it with his leather-bound notepad and cherished Montblanc fountain pen: a gift from Marty when he brokered their first million-pound deal together. Marty looked at it and allowed himself a slight smile; they were happy times.

Rob muted the TV on the wall and set the remote to the side of his notepad.

'OK, so I spoke to Andrew while you were in the shower and it looks like we have a couple of options here,' Rob said.

'What do you mean?' replied Marty casting his plate sideways as he buried his nose in a large mug of black coffee.

'Well, he believes the evidence against you – that we know of so far – the photos at the bar and outside your room, well, they're purely circumstantial. On those alone they could probably charge you but they'll struggle to get a conviction – although *nothing* is impossible with the law.'

Marty was listening intently, his eyes locked on Rob as if interrogating a guest on his show.

'You said "that we know of so far"; what does that mean?'

'Right, yeah,' Rob said, shifting uncomfortably on his stool. 'Andrew reckons we'll pretty much know the extent of the case against you once the post-mortem on White is complete, and the forensic sweep of the hotel room is done. We should hear more in the next couple of days.'

'Well, they won't find anything – so once that's done, I'll be in the clear, right?' Marty asked hopefully.

'Right,' Rob said without conviction.

Marty eyed him suspiciously; he knew Rob had more to say.

'What else did he say, Rob?'

Rob took a gulp of coffee and fiddled with his cup, as if trying to find the right words. 'OK,' he said, 'so the thing is, mate, Andrew says that although they haven't charged you as yet, he seriously thinks they will.'

'But I thought the evidence was purely circumstantial?'

'It is. It is. But Andrew thinks there is probably enough to go to trial and with you in the public eye, the CPS will feel compelled to do that.'

'Why does that make a difference?'

'They can't be seen to be letting celebs walk away from dead teenagers in S&M gear, Marty, especially when one of your mates is head of the Manchester force!'

What? You mean that prick, Blake… if we're such good mates, why haven't I heard a word from him since the arrest? Why was I locked up and humiliated? That's just bollocks!'

'Look, mate, I know that, but the press is out for blood and the police would prefer to spill yours than theirs. We're gonna have to play smart here.'

'So what do we do now?'

'Well, there may be a quick way to get the police off your back for good and the press on our side again.'

'And that is?'

Rob paused for a moment. 'Andrew reckons you'd be better off giving them a DNA sample.'

Marty could not believe what he was hearing.

'A DNA sample – what for?'

'To prove you didn't shag him or kill him,' Rob said very matter-of-factly. His words seemed to suck the life out of the room; the silence was deafening.

'You what?' Marty finally managed to mumble in disbelief. 'I have to prove *I didn't* have sex with a male prostitute and then murder him?'

Rob continued, unperturbed. 'I'm sorry to say this, Marty, but if you want this to go away quickly *and for good*, then *yes*.'

'Let me get this straight. Not only do I have to prove I didn't sleep with a man full stop – I also have to prove I didn't sleep with a man who has sex for money. Not only that, but I didn't then kill him too. Are you mental? No, I'm sorry, Rob, you can tell Andrew he's dreaming! Absolutely no way.'

Rob raised his palms in defence.

'I know mate, it's bullshit, but you've got to think about it logically. It's a confidential test and it's conclusive. You know you didn't sleep with White—'

'Or any man for that matter!'

'Well, if we can demonstrate conclusively that you never touched him, we can prove you didn't sleep with him and you didn't kill him. You know the game, Marty. The bad press is crucifying you right now – guilty until proven guilty in sex cases, especially on radio and TV after Yewtree. This could rumble on for months, *years even*.'

'But that's so unfair! I didn't do anything!'

'*We know that*, Marty, but the media doesn't. Andrew reckons if you volunteer a sample, you'll be clear within forty-eight hours. That means I can have you back on the radio by the end of the week. One swab of your mouth and all this will go away; ancient history. Plus, with no case against you, we're in a strong position to start libel proceedings. Once it's thrown out, trust me, everyone will settle. You'll be a very rich man again, Marty. Imagine that, a grovelling apology from the papers and TV – and a shitload of money to boot. Like I said, this could turn out to be a blessing, mate.'

Marty said nothing and instead stared out of the window as he gathered his thoughts. After an awkward length of silence, he turned to look straight at Rob again, his face sullen.

'You said there were *two* options here – what's the other?'

'Well, yeah, I'm not sure you'll like that either. The second option is we hold tight as we are and wait for the post-mortem and forensics to land with the police. If they have nothing to tie you to White – *which of course they won't* – then they'll need to work a lot harder to persuade the CPS to charge you.'

'That's good, right?'

'Yes, of course it is, but it's a much slower process and the stigma will stay with you. Everyone will always wonder; did Marty Michaels kill that male prostitute? Not great for your career, that's for sure.'

Marty paused again, trying to take it all in. 'And how long will that take? How long before I can get back to the show?'

'That's the unknown. If we're lucky, it goes away straight after the post-mortem, but as I said, Andrew thinks they will try and charge you. The prosecution has a high-profile celeb in their grasp, a very vocal celeb who has been a thorn in the side of the police and judicial system for the last decade. They see a chance for some serious payback, Marty – they won't give you up without a fight.'

Marty allowed the words to sink in. His mind was awash with questions. He still couldn't believe his situation.

Rob closed his notepad laying the fountain pen on top. When he spoke, his voice was soft, almost paternal. 'Look, I know it's a lot to take in, mate. But right now, if we're going to get you out of this, you've got to try and stay focused on the end game – keeping you out of jail and getting your career back on track.'

Marty shook his head in disbelief.

'I can't believe it's come to this – me having to prove I didn't shag and kill a male prostitute. What will my mother think? This could kill her.'

'Mate, if we're smart she doesn't need to know. If you do the DNA swab quickly, by the time she's well enough to read the papers or watch TV you could be back on-air. Think about it, Marty; it looks like the right way to go all round.'

Marty was still not convinced, leaning back on his stool, pressing his hands against the breakfast bar.

'It just feels risky to me. I mean what if someone really has set me up for White. What's to stop them doing it again?'

'We'll get a duplicate done by your own doctor – a fail-safe to ensure the police results match ours.'

Marty said nothing, his gaze returning to the garden and indoor pool building beyond. He realised he had not swum in it since the August bank holiday; that was almost a year ago.

Working the hours he did, it had become easy for him to take his home for granted; now he was in danger of losing it. Without his considerable salary, he could not afford the mortgage and after his divorce and the impact of the global financial crisis on house prices, he was now in negative equity meaning he could not afford to sell it either. He needed to prove his innocence quickly and get back on the payroll; a few million in damages was beginning to look more appealing too.

'Just one thing, Marty; with your memory loss, there's no chance your blackouts could have come back, is there?'

Marty shook his head as he turned to face Rob. 'My epilepsy? No, no way. I'm super strict with the meds; haven't had one for nearly two years now,' he said. 'I'll admit it did cross my mind but I only used to blackout for a few minutes back then. This was different; I lost the whole of Saturday.'

'OK, mate, I had to check.'

Marty took a swig of coffee, his attention drawn to a face he recognised on the TV above Rob's head.

'I don't believe it!' he shouted angrily, slamming his fist down on the kitchen bench.

Rob turned to face the screen, as shocked as Marty by what he saw.

'Oh God, no...' Rob managed to mumble as he grabbed the remote and turned up the volume.

'What the hell is he doing?' Marty growled.

The rolling news was still on, and the headline across the bottom of the screen flashed the words 'BREAKING NEWS – COMCO DROP MICHAELS'. In the centre of the screen was Marty's boss, Colin Burns. He was standing in front of COMCO's World Tower HQ in central London. Burns was a North Walian from Conwy who had moved to Manchester in the mid-nineties. In less than ten years he had worked his way up from sales director at Talk105 to CEO of the ever-expanding parent company, COMCO. He was a tall, well-built man with a full head of red hair on top of an equally red face, filled with a permanently austere expression. Marty had never liked him and the feeling was mutual. Burns was facing a collection of different microphones, each emblazoned with individual station names, jostling for precious position on the TV. Camera bulbs flashed and clicked continuously.

Burns pulled out a single sheet of paper and began reading from it, glancing into the camera lens as he did.

'It is with regret that COMCO announce the suspension of Marty Michaels from our Manchester-based national station Talk105 until further notice.'

His nasal North-Wales accent was still audible, but polished now.

'Mr. Michaels is, at this moment in time, involved with an ongoing investigation and we feel it is in the best interests of the business – and Mr. Michaels himself – that he be allowed time to focus his full attention on helping the Greater Manchester Police with their enquiries. Jeremy Day will take over the breakfast show indefinitely. COMCO will be making no further comment at this time.'

Despite his final words, a throng of questions erupted from the crowd. Burns remained resolute and ignored them all, turning away and walking quickly back towards the World Tower building.

Marty stared at the screen open-mouthed.

'He can't do that!' Rob said angrily. 'I'm your agent. We agreed he'd talk to me before he talked to the press!'

'You knew about this?'

'No, I didn't! Well, only what I told you. The board wanted you off air for a couple of days to let things calm down. We never once discussed doing anything official. Or statements or going public. And *indefinitely* was never mentioned, that's for sure!'

Marty eyed him suspiciously.

Rob raised his hands in defence again. 'I swear on my mother's life, Marty – I didn't know he was going public!'

'Those wankers!' Marty said shouting at the screen. 'After everything I've done for them! All the money I've made them over the years and this is how they treat me? They abandon me!'

'I won't let them get away with this, Marty – believe me,' Rob said trying his best to sound assured.

Marty continued staring at the screen as the news anchor repeated the breaking news.

'This morning's headline news once again – Talk105 radio host Marty Michaels has been suspended indefinitely following his arrest on Sunday, thought to be in connection with the death of a man found in his hotel room in the early hours of Sunday morning…'

Almost like a volcano erupting, the rage that had been building inside Marty exploded out of him. With all the force and focus of an American Football quarterback, he launched the remote control at the massive TV. 'Bastards!' he yelled, as the screen shattered on impact, sparks flying and smoke rising up to the ceiling.

He turned to Rob who was staring back at him with a pained expression.

Marty took a deep breath and as he exhaled, growled loudly, 'Get me a DNA test now!'

Rob nodded without saying a word.

'Nobody messes with Marty Michaels!' he raged, yanking open the patio doors. '*Nobody!*' he yelled again louder as he stormed out into the garden.

CHAPTER 13

Twenty-four hours later, Marty's house looked very different. The security blinds were open, every window now exposed to the outside world as the mid-morning sunlight drenched almost every room. Rob had insisted on hiring in his own firm of cleaners to remove any evidence of Marty's bad habits and every surface now glistened in the light. He had also hired in a private security firm consisting of ex-military types who now controlled the front gate and patrolled the grounds to keep the ever-more-creative press and paparazzi at bay. Since news of Marty's arrest had first broken, the 'vultures of the press' as Marty called them had continually attempted to breach the perimeter walls; the unfortunate price of celebrity.

After an early morning haircut, his thick locks remained shoulder-length but tidy, and a cut-throat shave had taken years off him. He stood now on the back deck wearing blue linen shorts, brown leather boating shoes over bare feet and a fresh white cotton shirt. He sipped the herbal tea Rob had insisted he drink. It tasted foul but with the promise of a rebalanced system and 'good energy', he had given it a go. Who would have thought an ex-footy player could be such a hippie?

Behind his back, he heard footsteps and quickly turned to see Rob stepping out on to the deck, followed by Andrew. Both men were dressed in their usual attire, Rob in a crisp blue suit, white shirt and no tie, Andrew in a Savile Row pinstripe navy suit over a plain blue shirt with a white collar and pink silk tie; both the picture of success and wealth standing together. Both at well over six foot tall, they had the look of a formidable forward line for any sporting team.

Rob did his best to sound supportive. 'They're here, Marty. I've put them in the lounge. Are you ready, mate?'

'Not really,' Marty said flatly.

'It'll all be over in a matter of minutes, old boy,' added Andrew.

'Are you both sure this is the best way to go – a DNA test, I mean? It seems extreme. Shouldn't we just wait it out?'

Rob stepped forward now and patted Marty on his right shoulder, a habit from his playing career that Marty had never really noticed before but which had become very evident in the last couple of days; a footballer's way of showing support. 'Mate, it'll take ten minutes tops to do the test and with our own doctor doing duplicates there's nothing to worry about, it'll all be kosher. In a matter of days, the results will be conclusive and you'll be fully vindicated, heading for a serious windfall in libel settlements. Come on, you know it's for the best.'

Andrew stepped forward now, unbuttoning his suit jacket the way lawyer do in court when they approach a witness, his left hand casually placed in his trouser pocket. 'Marty, rest assured I wouldn't be allowing any of this to go ahead if I didn't think it would produce the best results. As it stands, the police have yet to charge you, but I have it on good authority they *are* building a case against you. DNA samples from the hotel will be the next natural step. Rather than wait to be a passenger, I'd much prefer to be in the driving seat. We can prove you and White were not lovers, and you didn't kill him.'

'But what if they don't ask for DNA? Aren't we jumping the gun here?' Marty asked nervously.

Andrew's voice was calm yet strong and direct; he was in no doubt of the best outcome. 'It's only a matter of time, standard procedure. This way we're able to use our own doctor to take the swab and ensure we do a duplicate test. Trust me, leaving something this important in the hands of the police and expecting them to be honest and fair is not something I want to risk Marty, and nor should you.'

'I guess you're right,' Marty said, still not totally convinced.

'He is, mate,' added Rob, his hand back on Marty's shoulder.

Marty stared at them both and said nothing for a moment. Clapping his hands together, he took a deep breath before he spoke. 'Right then, let's get on with it, shall we?' he said, opening his arms out wide as he ushered the two men back inside the house.

CHAPTER 14

Greater Manchester Police had sent what appeared to be a platoon of people to Marty's house. Detective Chief Inspector Phillips greeted him as he entered the bright, sunny lounge room. She looked good, Marty thought, her crisp black suit accentuating her tall, athletic frame. He had not noticed quite how striking she was during his detention. For good reason, he thought. She reached out a hand for Marty to shake, which he took in spite of himself, before introducing the group in front of him. He instantly recognised the rat-like appearance of Detective Sergeant Jones next to Bovalino. Marty made no move to acknowledge either man, his total disdain evident for all to see. Adjacent to the two detectives were police surgeon Dr. Fitzpatrick and his own doctor, Clive Chorlton, a short, rounded man in his fifties with thinning fair hair that seemed to cling to his forehead, above thick, black-rimmed glasses. The entire group remained politely standing in a way that appeared awkward and impatient. Marty decided the best option was to treat the process like an interview and take control from the outset.

'Right, so how are we going to do this?' he said in his best attempt to appear relaxed.

DCI Phillips responded first. 'OK, Marty,' she said confidently. 'It's really very simple. You invited us here to perform this test, which naturally entitles your own doctor to collect a duplicate sample for individual analysis. If you'd like to take a seat, Dr. Fitzpatrick will take a sample swab from your mouth followed immediately by Dr. Chorlton.'

Andrew stepped forward now and produced a small HD video camera no bigger than a mobile phone. 'I'm sure you won't mind if I video the whole process to ensure we capture everything as it happens,' he said, an ironic smile crossing his face.

'Not at all,' replied Phillips with a smile to match.

Marty purposefully chose a seat as far away from the police surgeon as possible; he made no fuss as he sat down on the end of the big leather couch.

The whole process took no more than ten minutes and Marty's eyes never once left the swabs that collected the samples. His paranoia had left with him zero trust of the police and in his current predicament, his own doctor was not beyond reproach. With all the samples collected and packed away in security-sealed containers Marty stood, signalling it was time to leave.

Rob stepped forward taking Marty's lead. 'OK, folks, it looks like we're about done here, so if I could ask you all to follow me out to the main entrance,' he said brightly as he pointed to the door, attempting to warm the icy atmosphere.

Bovalino and Jones needed no encouragement and Dr. Fitzpatrick tucked in behind as they headed out of the house. DCI Phillips hesitated and turned to Marty. 'The preliminary results of White's post-mortem will be back tomorrow,' she said flatly. 'I just thought you'd like to know.' Her eyes seemed to reach into Marty's soul, as if she could sense his heart sinking and his fears rising.

Marty tried his best to appear calm and unmoved. 'Good!' he said with a little too much enthusiasm. 'I look forward to it. At least this bloody nightmare will be over!'

Phillips continued to stare at him. 'Quite,' she said coldly.

There was an awkward moment where no one in the room said anything before Andrew stepped in, extending his left arm towards the door. 'Well, Detective Chief Inspector, I look forward to hearing from you sometime tomorrow,' he said with the same ironic smile he had produced earlier.

Phillips eyed him cautiously in return. 'Of course,' she said without feeling, before turning to follow Jones and Bovalino to their waiting car.

CHAPTER 15

Marty was tempted to stay and hide under the hot flowing shower, but he knew the clock was ticking. Rob would be arriving soon to take him to Ashton House for 'further questions' from the dreaded Detective Chief Inspector Phillips. Less than an hour ago, Andrew's phone call had woken him from a fitful sleep to break the news they were needed at the station by 9am for the results of White's post-mortem.

Reluctantly he turned off the shower, wrapped a towel around his plump waist and hurried into his walk-in wardrobe.

Looking at his gold Rolex watch resting on the red leather chair in the corner of the room, he could see that he had just ten minutes before Rob arrived at 8.15am. His black leather Paul Smith loafers sat waiting for him to slip on, next to his empty belt rack; the over-zealous housekeeper must have tidied everything away again. No matter how many times he told her he liked everything in his walk-in closet left just as she found it, she believed she knew better, much to his annoyance.

He turned to face his wardrobe and suit choices for the meeting and caught a glimpse of himself in the mirrored door. He looked tired, his grey lifeless eyes hung in the dark recesses of his face. His skin looked almost transparent. He had aged about ten years in the last five days.

He tried to focus on the task in hand – his face-to-face with DCI Phillips.

He had to look good. If the press captured any images of him leaving the house or entering the police station, he needed to look respectable and therefore innocent. He had seen too many celebrities presented as monsters because of bad wardrobe choices and cunning paparazzi photographers catching them unawares. Marty was too smart to fall into that trap.

Anything black would appear too severe – obviously guilty. Blue was too light-hearted, very dangerous for someone connected to a man's death. He opted for his favourite charcoal-grey Hugo Boss suit – conservative yet respectful. He laid it on the chair before slipping on the tailored pants and felt uncomfortable as they pinched at the waist a little more than he remembered. It had been a while since he had last worn them, but they still looked good. Next, he pulled on a crisp white Gucci shirt with French cuffs and diamond-encrusted cufflinks, a wedding gift from the late British fashion icon Alexander McQueen – the only remaining memento of his marriage to Rebecca. Finally, he slipped on the loafers and ran a comb through his wild, wet hair. To his surprise, he looked almost human again.

Despite his tight-fitting suit pants, Marty wanted his matching Hugo Boss black belt to finish the outfit properly. After wearing it for a host of post-marriage one-night stands, it had acquired 'lucky' status and as a supremely superstitious man, he now wore it every time he went out to party or had an important meeting to attend; it gave him good luck.

With the clock ticking to Rob's arrival, he began his search for the belt, trying to guess where the housekeeper would have hidden it. He hoped it would be coiled up in the top drawer of his integrated wardrobe; it wasn't. He tried the next drawer down, and the one below that, and again below that, but had no luck.

He was angry and agitated now, slamming the sliding doors open and closed, muttering loud complaints directed at her as he searched obsessively for his lucky belt.

Finally, he found a hanger in an empty section of wardrobe filled with an array of belts in varying colours, each hanging by the buckle from the metal neck of the hanger; but still his Hugo Boss belt was nowhere in sight.

A crippling feeling of foreboding rushed into his gut as his mind flashed to White's dead eyes, the thick strap pulled tight against his neck, followed by images of Phil Spector and OJ Simpson in austere US courtrooms, on trial for their lives. Was that what lay ahead for Marty Michaels? It was the unthinkable possibility he had been avoiding since his arrest; this might be one situation even Andrew couldn't get him out of. In reality, he could not remember anything beyond Saturday afternoon, but if the post-mortem results warranted an urgent face-to-face with DCI Phillips – did that mean he was *somehow* involved?

When they last met, Phillips had produced a host of images that showed Marty drinking alongside White in the Sky Lounge on Saturday night. They appeared clearly in front of him now and the panic engulfed him; his chest tightened and he felt a sudden urge to lie down, dropping quickly to all fours, rolling onto his back as he closed his eyes, attempting to steady his rapidly rising heartbeat. He lay motionless for about a minute, his heart rate dropping as his body relaxed back into a regular breathing pattern. His mind drifted quickly back to his situation and no matter which way he looked at it, it did not make sense. He had no memory of ever meeting Paul White and the photos of them together in Sky Lounge Bar were stills from a CCTV camera – he reasoned the poor image quality could have been doctored or faked; God knows he'd made a lot of enemies in the last fifteen years who would have a vested interest in seeing him fall. Was someone framing him? He had no memory of events, but he had to be innocent, *had to be*; anything else was unthinkable.

Marty opened his eyes, suddenly very aware of his position on the floor of his walk-in wardrobe. He immediately sat bolt-upright, leaning back on his hands. He chastised himself for winding himself up. He had to remain positive. Speculating over what awaited him was no use. He had to finish getting dressed, look smart and play the part of 'Marty Michaels, innocent man, wrongly accused'.

Dismissing his elusive belt and vowing he would finally get a new housekeeper, he finished dressing quickly. In the absence of the Hugo Boss version, he grabbed a plain black belt from the clustered hanger and threaded it through his trousers, before pulling on his suit jacket and clipping on his Rolex. He checked his reflection in the mirror – he looked crisp, smart and in his opinion, anything but guilty. He allowed himself a faint smile and grabbed his wallet and phone. He was heading downstairs when his mobile exploded into life. It was Rob letting him know he was on his way up the drive. Marty didn't hesitate. He focused on the task in hand – it was show time.

Grabbing his keys and Ray-Ban sunglasses from the hall dresser, he swept through the huge double-height main lobby and out into the warmth of the morning sunshine. He was just in time to see Rob's glistening gunmetal-grey Range Rover pull up in front of the oversized oak front door, the tyres grabbing noisily at the gravel drive as he braked to a halt. Marty flashed up his right hand to acknowledge Rob's arrival before jumping in the passenger seat, slamming the door shut behind him.

The car was ice-cold, the air conditioning on full blast.

'Hey, mate,' Rob said his voice positive. 'Beautiful morning!'

'Is it?' Marty shot back.

'Yeah, well, sorry. I didn't mean—'

Marty had no interest in his response and cut him off abruptly.

'So what's the crowd like at the gate?'

Rob seemed pleased to change the subject. 'To be honest, mate, it's busier than it has been, almost twice as many as yesterday. I reckon they could have been tipped off.'

'Of course they have! Someone is really doing a number on me. Who knew about this police visit?'

Rob thought for a moment. 'Well, you, me, Andrew and the coppers. That's it.'

'And you haven't said anything to Vanessa?'

Vanessa was Rob's long-term assistant.

'No way, mate!' Said Rob, his tone confident. 'She knows I'm seeing you because it's in my diary but nothing about the reason for the meeting.'

'What about Andrew? Could he be the link?'

'Marty, I know you're struggling with this, but Andrew? That's ridiculous; he's as straight as they come. He's been on the payroll for years and, more than that, he's a friend.'

'He's a bloody shark and you know it! That's why we use him – "whatever it takes" is his motto – he's a ruthless bastard!'

'Yes, he *is* a ruthless bastard, but he's *our* ruthless bastard. I guarantee it's nothing to do with Andrew. I'd put my life on it, Marty.'

Marty removed his Ray-Bans and looked Rob dead in the eye now. 'Yeah, well it's not your life that's at stake here, "mate" – it's mine!' There was an awkward moment of silence between the two men that said so much. The outcome of the next couple of days would determine whether their partnership would survive.

Rob broke first. 'So are you ready for the drive-through when we get out of the gate?'

Marty was well versed in the various protocols practised by 'hunted celebs'.

'Ready as I'll ever be. Do we cover our faces or are we going for the "open and nothing to hide" approach?'

'It's gotta be about having nothing to hide, mate. We keep a straight face all the way through. I won't stop the car but depending on the amount of people around us, I'm going to have to take it slowly. The last thing we need right now is a journo or pap crying to the press about being hit as we speed past. No mate, it's gotta be "slow and steady, innocent, nothing to hide".'

'OK, Rob, I'm inclined to agree. Still, I can't say I'm looking forward to sitting there whilst they swarm around with their cameras.'

'Me neither, mate. I've only had the Rover a couple of weeks.'

Marty was incensed. 'I'll tell you what, Rob; you can take the damage out of my next deal! My entire future is on the line here and you're worried about your bloody paint job! Now I *really* know who the shark is!' he raged.

'That's not fair, Marty and not what I meant. Look, I'm sorry. I'm not thinking straight.'

'Well, start – *and quickly*. I need your A-game right now. I can't do this on my own, OK?'

'Of course, Marty, you're right. I'll get us through the crowd in no time and before you know it we'll be sat by your pool sipping cold ones and laughing about how much money you're going to make from suing everyone.'

Marty was staring straight ahead and nodded slightly; he wanted desperately to believe that could happen but his heart was not buying it.

'Right, there's no point putting it off any longer. Let's do this!' Marty said loudly with a forced confidence as he slipped his Ray-Bans back on. Rob nodded and the big SUV slowly pulled away from the house, back towards the main gate and the unavoidable reunion with the waiting press and paparazzi, baying for Marty's blood.

CHAPTER 16

Marty's heart rate seemed to double as the big Range Rover approached the solid oak gates; beating like a drum in his head, he could almost hear the hot blood coursing through his veins. With one last nod to reassure Rob he was ready to face what awaited him on the other side, Rob triggered the automatic gates and they began to open.

As a gap appeared Marty could clearly see two large men in black combat uniform including what looked like snipers' caps standing in the way of a sea of journalists and photographers; two of an eight-man private security team hired by Rob to keep the house secure. Even from inside the cool, air-conditioned SUV, Marty could hear the volume of the mob's chants increase excitedly as the gates opened. Feeling overwhelmingly vulnerable, Marty gripped the soft leather seats on either side of his legs and readied himself to drive through the crowd. 'It's OK mate, we can do this,' Rob assured him softly. 'Walk in the park,' he added without conviction.

The two security men suddenly became four as the gates opened wider still, forming a human chain-cum-barrier to the reporters and paps who began to surge forwards towards the car.

'Remember, mate, head up, look calm and show no emotion. We want to minimise the chance of dodgy photos or videos, right?'

'I can't do this…' Marty mumbled as his overwhelming fear took hold. He felt completely helpless.

'Marty, stay with me, mate. This will all be over in a matter of minutes. No matter how scared you feel, remember, show no emotion, no emotion at all.'

Marty remained silent, staring straight ahead into the heart of the crowd.

'Marty, no emotion – are we clear?' Rob asked, his own voice brimming with tension.

Marty nodded and the car moved forward.

The two security men in the centre of the human chain separated and created a space for the car to move through, instantly filled by reporters and paps, desperate for a glimpse of Marty Michaels, the accused. Rob stopped the car suddenly as a small film crew jumped in front of the bonnet. The big SUV sat motionless as the crowd quickly surrounded it on all sides. Camera bulbs flashed like machine-gun fire and a cacophony of voices shouted Marty's name as he blinked frantically in the frenzy of noise and light.

The questions came thick and fast through the glass; muffled but still audible.

'Did you kill Paul White, Marty?'

'Are you gay, Marty?'

'Is it true you've done a deal and you're on your way to be arrested for murder?'

Their words felt like gunshots to his fragile mind.

'Get us out of here, Rob!' he said trying hard not to move his lips.

'I can't move, mate; they're everywhere.'

'Please get me out of here, Rob, I can't handle it,' Marty pleaded through gritted teeth. His nerves were jangling and panic was building inside him. The nervous energy of fear filling his system made him want to smile and laugh out loud but that would be disastrous – the press would present him as the remorseless killer. Surrounded by the baying mob he was unable to defend himself or show the slightest hint of reaction or emotion to his terrifying situation.

'Rob, please do something,' he said under his breath.

Before Rob could reply, the security detail in front of the car doubled in size as four more reinforcements arrived, quickly placing themselves between the SUV and the mob, pushing the crowd back to create more space for Rob to exploit.

'Stay with me, mate; we'll be out of here in a second, I promise,' assured Rob.

Marty's jaw was locked in a nervous clench as he desperately tried to hold it together. Teetering on the edge of losing control, he had to stay focused on getting through; it would all be over soon. At least he hoped it would.

The cameras continued to flash like a disco strobe, the bright white lights making everything seem like it was happening in slow motion. The shouts and questions continued but Marty pushed them into the background; just noise now.

As the security team worked overtime to force the mob back, the car moved ever forward, inch by inch. Marty could see clear road and freedom ahead.

Careful to avoid any bodies, which appeared to be bouncing off the sides of the big Range Rover, Rob began to gather speed. As they cleared the deep sidewalk and the front wheels dropped onto the asphalt, Marty allowed himself to breathe out and relax for a second, just as his eye caught a familiar face to the left of the car – the journalist, Simon Williams. The same person who had been notable by his presence at Marty's arrest. Anything but a celebrity hack, what was he doing here on a Thursday morning? The two men locked eyes for a moment and Marty's blood ran cold. Williams's emotionless face seemed to bore directly into him. Suddenly all four wheels connected with the road and Rob gunned the engine, speeding away down the wide avenue towards the city, the noise of the crowd fading away.

'We're clear, mate! We're out of here!' Rob shouted in celebration, punching the steering wheel in triumph as he let out a huge sigh of relief. 'Well done, mate, you did brilliantly,' he added and slapped Marty on his right shoulder.

CHAPTER 17

Returning to Ashton House police headquarters filled Marty with a sense of overwhelming dread but he took solace from the fact he was not alone. Having entered through a back service entrance to avoid the press camped out front, he and Rob nervously waited in the large open-plan reception room just inside the ground-floor parking garage. Both men had signed in with the attractive young receptionist and were now standing away from the main entrance doors in the middle of the sterile room, sporting visitor tags attached to the breast pockets of their matching charcoal-grey suits.

Andrew joined them, impeccably dressed as ever, his black pinstripe suit, crisp white shirt and bright blue tie accentuated by his richly tanned skin. Almost a perfect match for the soft leather briefcase he carried in his left hand. He flashed his dazzling white teeth as he approached.

'Gentlemen, how are we?' he said warmly, offering his outstretched right hand, first to Marty and then to Rob.

Marty twitched uneasily. 'I've been better.'

'Quite,' replied Andrew sombrely.

'I keep telling him it'll all be over soon,' added Rob nervously.

Andrew smiled again and glanced at the receptionist before stepping closer to Marty and Rob. He spoke in hushed tones.

'Now Marty, despite Rob's confidence that this will all go away quickly, I'm afraid I can't promise DCI Phillips won't try and push this all the way to a very public court case. You are a high-profile fish on a rather large hook; for an already under-pressure Greater Manchester Police to dismiss the charges against you just days after your arrest looks unlikely. However, that said, whatever happens in this meeting will at least reveal a little more of their hand and allow my team to get this ridiculous situation resolved as quickly as possible. I just need you to stay calm and no matter what games Phillips tries to play – and she will try to unsettle you, be sure of that – *whatever* she throws at you, you must let *me* do the talking and only speak when I give you the signal to do so. This is very important. *Do you understand, Marty?*'

Although Marty nodded, he was absent from the conversation. His mind was elsewhere, racing at lightning speed towards the darkest possibilities of his bleak future – a life inside Hawk Green, Greater Manchester's maximum-security prison. Terrified of the images running through his head, he forced his attention back to Andrew.

'What did she say on the phone?' he asked.

'Simply that she had the results of the DNA test and would like to see you and me in person.'

'That could be good, right?' Marty's tone appeared desperate, almost childlike.

Andrew's voice dropped an octave, rich and reassuring. 'It's certainly possible, but honestly Marty, I tend to find it's best not to speculate in these situations. There could be a hundred and one reasons for her calling us down here and, in my experience, a man could go insane trying to second-guess the Greater Manchester Police.'

It was Rob's turn to be supportive now, stepping closer still to Marty, his left arm reaching around his shoulders.

'He's right, mate. Let's just wait and see what she has to say. We can deal with it together,' he said, trying to reassure his friend, 'we'll both be in there with you.'

Andrew flinched slightly and turned to face Rob square on. 'I think it's best Marty and I do the meeting *alone*, Rob – far less complicated, I'm sure you'll agree.'

Rob's body visibly tightened at the rejection. 'As Marty's *foremost* advisor I really think that *I* should be in this meeting!' he protested far louder than necessary in the quiet room, drawing a fleeting glance from the receptionist. All three stood silently for a moment, aware of her gaze before she turned her attention back to her computer screen and the conversation resumed.

Johnson's face had changed now, gone was the calm, casual smile, replaced instead with a sharp and ferocious glare. 'And as his *legal counsel* I'm telling you that's a bad idea, *Rob!*'

Marty quickly broke up the fight, his tone unapologetic. 'No! We do this together. Rob's been with me since day one. I trust him with my life and I want him with me every step of the way. This is no time for divide and conquer.'

Johnson softened once more; Marty's determination was clear for everyone to see. 'OK, Marty, as you wish – but I must point out it's highly irregular.'

CHAPTER 18

DCI Phillips's timing was perfect as she entered the room from behind the reception desk a moment later. Stepping away from the desk, she walked quickly and confidently towards the three men carrying a brown manila folder under her right arm against her chest. She looked fresh-faced and refined in a white blouse and a grey skirt cut just above her shapely knees. Her long legs ran smoothly into surprisingly expensive-looking black shoes with a slight heel. Her hair pinned back and up, she wore tortoiseshell-rimmed glasses, which made her look intelligent but could not hide the natural beauty of her face.

'Gentlemen, thank you for coming,' she said casually as she strode straight past them across the reception room to a door marked 'Private'. She opened it, switched on the light inside and gestured for the three men to enter. 'This way please,' she said, a half-smile on her face.

All three obediently followed. Once inside, they sat together on one side of a large grey veneered desk on red plastic chairs opposite Phillips, also now seated, the beige folder laid closed in front of her. Marty sat on the middle chair, flanked protectively on the left by Rob with Andrew to his right. The room itself was quite large, another windowless box. The breeze-block walls were covered in white emulsion, the floor was polished concrete, as appeared standard throughout the entire building, and the air was filled with the now-familiar smell of industrial-strength disinfectant. Marty noted there was no mirrored wall in this room but instead a small wall-mounted closed-circuit video camera directly above and behind Phillips's head.

The door opened abruptly behind the three men and Phillips smiled widely as she was joined by a face Marty knew well. Phillips continued smiling as she introduced her colleague. 'I'm sure you all remember Detective Sergeant Jones, the arresting officer in this investigation.'

'Detective Sergeant,' offered Andrew with a slight nod of acknowledgement.

Marty and Rob chose to say nothing, instead staring straight at the newcomer, their hostility apparent to even the blindest of eyes.

Jones pulled up a chair and sat quickly. As he did, he laid a large yellow Jiffy bag on the table in front of him before leaning back in his chair and folding his arms, staring straight at Marty, a lopsided grin fixed to his face. Marty's contempt for him was evident and not for the first time he felt a deep fear of the man who had instigated his nightmare. Glancing quickly at the yellow Jiffy bag, Marty wondered what it contained.

The atmosphere in the room was palpable. Detective Chief Inspector Phillips broke the tension first.

'Thank you all for coming in this morning. Before we begin, I must first inform you that, as is customary in these situations, I'll be recording our conversation for the purpose of any future prosecutions. In this instance, everything we say will be taped on this digital recorder, and filmed on the camera just behind me,' she said as she gestured behind her head.

In spite of himself Marty shot a glance directly at the camera as Phillips continued, 'I just want everyone to be crystal clear on that.'

Johnson was keen to get Phillips on the back foot. 'Really, Detective Chief Inspector, is all this completely necessary? My client is here of his own free will after all.'

Phillips returned the volley in a flash. 'Standard procedure, Mr. Johnson, and with your client's publicly stated concerns around Manchester Police procedures, we wouldn't want to be accused of not following the letter of the law, now would we?'

Marty was boiling inside now, his mouth opening to speak, desperate to respond. Andrew placed a calming hand across his right wrist on the table before responding to Phillips's jibe.

'Careful now, Chief Inspector. I'm sure the force wouldn't want to be accused of prejudicing my client based on previous actions or comments.'

Phillips flashed her smile again. 'Not at all, Mr. Johnson,' she said, her eyes cold as they fixed on Marty. 'This one will be done by the book. On that you and your client have my cast-iron *guarantee*.'

Marty felt a chill run down his back as Phillips's lingering look seemed to bore into him.

It was Andrew's turn to break the ice now. 'Very well, Chief Inspector, as you wish. Now would you be kind enough to explain what was so important that it warranted my client making a personal visit so early this morning?'

Phillips moved her gaze back to Andrew. 'Of course, Mr. Johnson, of course,' she said as she pulled the manila folder closer to her. She opened it fully on the table between her hands, which she laid flat on the table for a moment, before taking out a series of A4-sized black-and-white pictures and placing them in front of Marty. 'As you'll see from these pictures taken on Saturday night directly from the video feed at the Sky Lounge in the Metropolitan Hotel, this is your client drinking alongside the victim, Paul White. The time stamp says 11.15pm.'

Andrew did his best to sound exasperated for dramatic effect. 'Yes, yes. We've seen the photos, Chief Inspector. Frankly, if that's all you've got, they prove nothing more than my client likes to drink in the Sky Lounge, but then who doesn't? The cocktails are to die for,' he said with a confident smile and a flash of his perfect teeth.

Marty flinched at Andrew's choice of words.

DCI Phillips laid out another series of A4 black-and-white shots directly in front of Marty and Andrew. 'And these pictures clearly show your client and Paul White entering room number 1609 shortly after midnight.'

Johnson's tone was deliberately one of condescension now. 'Chief Inspector, *once again for the record*, we've seen these photos, we acknowledge my client and Mr. White may have spent a short time together in the corridor, but without cameras inside the actual room it proves nothing of how White died or more importantly, how my client is any way connected,' he said continuing to act bored of the game the detective was playing. '*Really*, DCI Phillips, if you dragged us all the way down here to show us these then I'm afraid it's a further waste of our time and the taxpayers' money. It's quite ridiculous.'

Phillips eyed Johnson cautiously but chose not to react, instead reaching into the folder for the next set of documents.

'This document shows the DNA results we took with your client's permission two days ago, on Tuesday 14th July,' said Phillips.

Andrew straightened fractionally and Marty felt a rush of adrenalin punch the air from his lungs, making him cough.

Phillips turned the sheet to face Marty, Andrew and Rob. Her gaze fixed on Marty as he stared blankly at it.

Phillips continued, 'We found traces of semen in White's mouth post-mortem.'

'He was a prostitute, hardly surprising,' said Johnson, quick as a flash.

'The samples taken from White's mouth are a direct match for your client's DNA, Mr. Johnson. So with a sixteen-million-to-one chance someone else has the same DNA, it's safe to assume the semen found in White's mouth belongs to your client, *Marty Michaels*,' she said, staring directly at Marty as she said his name.

The world seemed to slow down for Marty as he stared at the page of results in front of him. He could not read or understand the charts but Phillips's words rang loudly in his ears. How could that even be possible? He had never had a gay relationship in his life. Not even as an experiment, not once. How could he now be facing the possibility that White had performed oral sex, *on him?*

Despite the evidence on show, Andrew responded quickly to protect his client as best he could.

'Chief Inspector, you may well have a positive match for my client's DNA in semen found in White's mouth but it does not make him a killer. You know that and so do I. So, unless you have something that ties my client to White's death, this conversation is over,' he said curtly as he pushed his chair back and began to stand. Marty and Rob instinctively followed his lead, standing too.

Phillips lifted her arms in surrender and smiled wryly. 'Please don't rush off, gentlemen; Detective Sergeant Jones has something he wants to show you,' she said gesturing for them to sit. 'Take a seat, you may need it.'

Jones leaned forward and opened the Jiffy bag. Reaching inside, he fumbled for a moment, as if milking the tension like a game show host, before finally laying a clear plastic bag on the table in front of the three men, a black object inside.

Marty's world crumbled in that instant. He recognised the black leather belt in front of him. It was his favourite and, up until that very moment, his missing Hugo Boss belt.

Phillips allowed the moment to sink in before explaining what they were looking at.

'This is a black leather belt found in Mr. Michaels's hotel room, we believe used to strangle White to death. Traces of skin found on the belt are a match for the victim and other samples match the DNA taken from your client,' said Phillips, confidence oozing from every pore. Sensing her opponent's obvious shock and bewilderment, Phillips pressed on. 'There are also clear fingerprints all over this belt, and I'm guessing when we take your client's prints, Mr. Johnson, we'll find they're a perfect match.'

Andrew Johnson was, for once in his life, at a loss for words.

Marty desperately wanted him to take control, to bat her accusation into the long grass and tell him everything would be OK. Instead, there was silence, Johnson clearly as shocked as Marty. Rob coughed again nervously.

Finally, Johnson spoke. 'I need a moment with my client.'

Phillips's smile was gone now, replaced with a steely, determined glare. 'I'm afraid that's not possible, Mr. Johnson. You can speak to him in your allocated time before court tomorrow morning,' she said as she gestured for Jones to follow the next steps of official protocol. Pushing back his chair, he stood pulling out his handcuffs.

'Marty Michaels, I'm arresting you for the murder of Paul White. You do not have to say anything. But, it may harm your defence if you do not mention when questioned something which you later rely on in court. Anything you do say may be given in evidence.'

As Jones moved around the table, Rob stepped into his path, speaking for the first time since entering the room. 'There's no need for this!' he said as he laid his large hand on Jones's chest.

Jones said nothing, looking down at Rob's hand and then up into his eyes. The ex-footy player seemed to dwarf the skinny officer.

'Take your hands off me, sir, or you'll be joining your friend in the custody suite tonight,' Jones said coldly.

Rob reluctantly stepped aside and Jones moved forward. He turned Marty round to face Johnson as he dragged his hands behind his back and snapped some cuffs tightly on his wrists with a loud click.

Marty's world was falling apart around him and he was powerless to stop it. He physically began to shake.

'Do something!' he pleaded to Johnson. 'For God's sake, man – stop this madness!'

Johnson grabbed Marty by both shoulders and stared him squarely in the eye. 'It's a temporary setback, Marty. We will get you out of this, I promise.'

Marty nodded.

Phillips appeared to sneer now, her voice laced with sarcasm and self-satisfaction. 'He is right, Marty. If you're lucky you'll be out of Hawk Green in no time – *give or take twenty-five years.*'

CHAPTER 19

Held overnight in a police cell, Marty appeared before a magistrate the next day where he was officially charged, and the case was promoted to crown court. Remanded once more, he awaited his fate.

Spending two consecutive days in a holding cell facing murder charges was not something Marty had ever expected to experience in his lifetime. Being locked in a ten-foot-by-twelve-foot concrete box with no belt or shoes was degrading enough; trying to sleep on the blue urine-stained plastic mattress whilst doors slammed and drunks argued with the detention officers was another level of degradation entirely. He felt lower than dog shit on someone's shoe as he was 'woken' at 7am on day two to the loud click of his cell door opening. He was allowed to shower and shave and handed fresh clothes, delivered by Andrew the previous evening. Dressed in a navy blue suit and white shirt, he was handcuffed and frogmarched to the waiting security van, for transportation to court. How had he become a murder suspect?

Placed in a caged section of the van, the journey to Manchester Crown Court took around thirty minutes. As he slid left and right on the plastic seats in the back of the reinforced steel truck, he realised he had never been more terrified, or felt more alone in his life.

The van rolled noisily up to the court building before stopping as the gates to the car park slowly opened. With news of his arrest leaked to the media, he could hear a frenzy of shouts from outside as paps jostled for position. Camera flashes illuminated the dark interior as they thrust their lenses against the tinted two-inch-thick glass above his head, hoping for a shot of the 'prisoner'. Fear gripped him like a thick arm around his throat, stealing the air from his lungs.

A moment later, the van moved forward and descended into the underground car park of the court building as the shouts and camera flashes faded into the distance. The vehicle stopped and the engine died. Seconds later, the back door opened into an eerie silence, the car park dimly lit and empty. His cage was unlocked and he was escorted into the building.

The next twenty minutes were a blur as Marty was once again frogmarched into the secure custody suite under the court, used exclusively by prisoners and police. He passed through a maze of gates. Thick doors opened and closed to a chorus of barked orders on his way upstairs towards court number four, before being forced down into a plastic chair in the visitors' area, to the left of the courtroom.

Seated at a large table in the middle of the room, he waited in silence for fifteen minutes for Andrew to arrive. Staring at his hands cuffed together he began to laugh, overwhelmed by the absurdity of his situation. The laughter soon gave way to tears and his body began to heave as he broke down and surrendered to the emotions flooding his battered mind.

A moment later, the door opened. As Johnson entered the room, Marty pulled himself together in an instant; it was not the time to show any weakness.

Impeccably dressed as ever in his trademark pinstriped navy suit, this time matched with a pink fitted Gucci shirt and silver tie, Johnson took a seat opposite Marty and began talking quickly.

'Right, Marty, we have five minutes before your hearing, so listen to me very carefully.'

'Five minutes?'

'Look, they're simply playing games to unsettle us by giving us the minimum amount of time required by law, so we really don't have time to waste discussing the merits of their tactics. We literally have five minutes before going in front of the judge. So Marty, with all the love and respect in the world, shut the fuck up and listen to me very carefully, OK?'

Marty nodded silently, like a chastised schoolboy.

'Good,' Johnson said. 'So the evidence against you is potentially damning, my friend. We can use reasonable doubt to weaken the photos from the hotel. However, with the prosecution claiming traces of your semen was present in White's mouth, and your fingerprints on the murder weapon, if they get a conviction, they could send you to prison for a very long time. Marty, if I'm going to defend you I need to know – and trust me it's all confidential – *did you kill White?*'

It was as if Johnson had hit him with a hammer. His own lawyer, and someone he considered a close friend, doubted his innocence. 'No, I damn well didn't!' he yelled loudly, his eyes wild as he stared at him. 'I'm innocent. I'm being set up!' he said, shaking his cuffs.

'OK. I'm sorry. I had to ask, Marty. I need to know what I'm dealing with. Some clients do lie to me. I can't help my people if they lie to me.'

'I'm not lying. I've never met White, or at least I don't remember meeting White, and I've never had sex, be it full or oral, with a man – *ever!* Are we clear on that, Andrew? Or do I need to pay a thousand pounds a day to another lawyer, one who believes me?'

Johnson ignored the question and moved straight onto the briefing, giving Marty the rundown of his appearance in court.

'Right, in a couple of minutes I'll head into court through the main door and you'll be taken in through that one there,' he said pointing behind Marty's head.

'You'll sit next to me at the defence table and when asked by the judge to stand we'll stand together. He will ask for your plea and you say simply "Not guilty".'

'And what about bail?'

'Not possible for me to argue, we'll need a barrister to secure that in Crown Court. I'll get Ruben Cole on the case as soon as I get back to the office.'

'How long will that take?'

Johnson paused longer than was comfortable for Marty.

'Andrew, how long will that take?'

'Look Marty, it's not that simple I'm afraid.'

'Yes it fucking is! If OJ can get bail then so can I!'

'That's US law, Marty. UK law is very different and far more complex. It's very rare that anyone charged with murder is granted bail unless the circumstances clearly warrant it.'

'Such as?'

'Most of the precedents involve children. I'm struggling to think of any adults who made it out before trial.'

'So what happens to me until then?'

'I'm afraid you'll be remanded into custody and sent to the nearest prison.'

'Which is Hawk Green, right?'

'Correct.'

Marty tried to digest the information. 'Fuck!' he managed to whisper. 'That's category A – maximum security, murderers, armed robbers and paedophiles?'

'Yes it is, but if anyone can find a way to secure bail given enough time, it's Ruben.'

Marty wanted to believe Johnson but the reality was terrifying. 'That's just it, Andrew. I don't have time. If I go to Hawk Green I'm a dead man. I won't last five minutes. Keats and McCloud are in there because of me.'

'We'll apply for protective custody.'

'By the time you get that, I'll be dead.'

Before Johnson could reply, the door from the main corridor opened and a female court bailiff stepped inside, dressed in a security uniform.

'You're first up today, gentlemen; time to go, court is in session.'

Johnson stood and Marty's gaze followed him like a lost puppy. Grabbing his briefcase, he stared straight at Marty, his face stern and serious. 'Trust me, Marty, you'll be fine. We'll get you home soon enough,' he said and left the room without looking back.

CHAPTER 20

The courtroom scene played out exactly as Johnson had said it would. Marty took his seat behind the table on the left next to his lawyer facing the judge. The prosecution's team of two sat behind the table on the right.

Marty was in his seat for all of sixty seconds before standing to face Judge John Mellor, a 'ready-to-retire' right-wing homophobe. As Marty pleaded 'Not guilty', there was an audible sneer from Mellor. He appeared to have reached his verdict on the case already, casting his own judgment with a loud exhale of air, before impatiently asking the prosecution if they had anything to add.

The chief prosecutor was Josh Lei, a young lawyer with an impressive record for securing convictions. He was the poster boy for law and order in Greater Manchester, the son of a Chinese immigrant father and Polish mother who owned a small restaurant in the city's Chinatown. Lei had paid his own way through university and risen through the ranks of public office after graduating top of his class with a double first from Manchester University. He was good-looking with strong chiselled features, and at over six foot in height, he carried the genes of his Northern Chinese ancestry. He was dressed sharply in a tailored suit that fitted his slim frame perfectly, and he appeared effortlessly calm, charming and confident around the courtroom. Marty hated him immediately.

Lei stood slowly to answer the judge, fastening his suit jacket as he did.

'Nothing at this stage, Your Honour.'

'In that case, the defendant will be remanded into custody until trial,' Mellor said coolly.

Marty looked up at Johnson, 'Does that mean I'm going to Hawk Green?'

'For the moment, yes,' Andrew said matter-of-factly. 'But I'm confident we'll get you into protective custody'.

'Andrew, I don't want to hear confident – I need to hear certainty! I'll die in general population. You know who's in Hawk Green – Clarence Keats, Vic McCloud – *and the rest*. I'm a dead man!'

Johnson put a reassuring hand on Marty's arm as the bailiff approached.

'Try not to worry, Marty, I'm sure you'll be OK,' he said unconvincingly.

CHAPTER 21

Built in 2010 to replace its decaying Victorian predecessor, Hawk Green Prison was home to maximum security Category A and B males, located twenty miles south of Manchester city centre, in the middle of the Cheshire countryside. Following the well-worn design of modern British prisons, its five cell blocks housed seven wings each following the standard 'H' layout, safely locked down behind two thirty-foot walls, forty minutes on foot to civilisation in all directions.

Its was almost 5pm on Friday when the prison transport carrying the remanded defendants from Manchester's Crown Court pulled into the entrance to Hawk Green Prison. Some of the UK's most dangerous criminals called it home and for the foreseeable future, so would the self-proclaimed 'King of Radio', Marty Michaels. Ironic, considering his own Prestbury mansion was just a short drive away. With Johnson's application for protective custody denied due to overcrowding, his client now sat handcuffed and very afraid in the back of the transport, alongside four other inmates.

The intake gates opened, the truck moved inside the compound and the gates closed behind them as they moved forward for another minute, before coming to a shuddering stop. Next, the doors to the transport truck opened, correctional officers barked orders and the prisoners got out. It appeared to be a well-rehearsed routine and everyone complied.

When it was his turn, Marty stepped out into the summer evening sunshine. The bright sunlight burned his eyes forcing him to raise his cuffed hands to his face, turning his head away from the entrance gates to face the foreboding form of Hawk Green Prison.

In stark contrast to normal life for Marty, there was no 'celebrity entrance', no VIP wing and no special treatment, all made abundantly clear by the prison transport officers earlier when he had been loaded into the truck. Along with the other inmates, he was quickly marched inside the intake block, told to strip naked and stand inside an observation booth to be checked by two officers for any hidden contraband. The next stage of the process involved the transferral of all his personal possessions and clothes into a sealed box, taken away until his release. He was handed prison-issue underpants, an oversized grey tracksuit and white slip-on sneakers, ready for deployment to general population; a folded blanket and a pillow were lain across his outstretched arms. He was a mirror image of his four companions, who had formed a line facing the long corridor to A-Wing.

Marty had never felt more terrified as they left the safety of the intake block, walking slowly in a single-file procession. As they moved through the building, gates opened loudly and each time they moved through to the next secure area, the gates closed behind them with a deafening thud, plunging them deeper and deeper into the belly of the prison. Every step took Marty closer to hell. His heart pounded erratically until he struggled to force any breath into his heaving lungs. He wanted to cry out, overcome by an overwhelming urge to shout for his mother. He knew it was ridiculous for a grown man to break down and cry like an infant, but prison does strange things to people, and right now Marty wanted his mum to sweep in and make it all better; just like she did when he was a kid.

A moment later, the entrance gate to the main detention block of A-Wing rolled open noisily and the procession of men obediently moved forward into general population, with Marty the last man in the line. His fear was overwhelming as they moved into plain sight of the rest of the inmates.

The noise was the first thing that struck him, like a wave crashing over every sense in his body, disorientating and terrifying. News of the celebrity guest arrival had spread fast and the parallel landing floors above filled with inquisitive faces. A mixture of sneers, laughter and total indifference. Inmates chanted, whistled and shouted, while absolute terror surged through every fibre of Marty's body. He had arrived at the gates of hell and he was now at the mercy of some of the most evil men on the face of God's earth; and even God could not help him now.

Above, the cacophony of chants and screams was almost impossible to decipher as the line moved slowly forward, but two loud voices became instantly clear.

As part of his daily radio show, Marty played a jingle package and audio piece that said confidently, *'Demand the King at Breakfast – DEMAND MARTY MICHAELS!'* Now, here in the middle of A-Wing, he could hear that jingle sung in unison. He looked up to the first-floor landing in the direction of the singing. To his horror, he saw the broad smiling faces of Vic McCloud and Clarence Keats. Marty stopped in his tracks before the prison officer bringing up the rear of the procession ushered him forward.

He kept his eyes fixed on McCloud, who pointed his index finger back at him before running his outstretched thumb across his own throat, and both men laughed loudly as he stared back in terror. A second later, Keats and McCloud stepped away from the rail as a group of prison guards ushered the inmates back into their cells, trying to calm the baying masses. Marty's arrival was a break from the boredom of daily life in prison. It had caused an over-excited reaction from the inmates, which without proper management could easily turn volatile. Within minutes, a temporary lockdown was in effect and the landings and cell-block floors were empty; each of the prisoners was locked behind six inches of steel and glass – their maniacal chants and screams, though muffled, still audible as they echoed around the large prison wing.

Marty finally reached his cell. Locked inside his twelve-foot-by-ten-foot room, alone for his own safety, he would remain that way until morning.

He was now officially remand prisoner number 865439 of HMP Hawk Green.

Today was without doubt the worst day of his life. He had *no doubt* if McCloud and Keats caught up with him tomorrow, it could well be his last.

CHAPTER 22

Marty did not see his attackers coming.

It was Saturday morning. Having made it through the shower he was forced to take by prison staff, followed by the loneliest breakfast he'd ever eaten – isolated on the end of a long bench in the mess hall – Marty had returned to his cell trying his best to avoid Saturday recreation and bumping into McCloud or Keats in the yard. He was perched on the end of his bed with his head in his hands when the three men arrived.

They moved quickly through his cell door and as Marty reacted, he felt a heavy blow on the left side of his head that knocked him sideways onto the mattress. Before he could respond, they struck him again, this time on the back of his head. Pain surged through his body; dizzy and disorientated, he tried to cry out for help. A thick hand covered his mouth as they dragged him to the floor, his face pushed down hard onto the cold concrete, still unable to see his attackers.

As he attempted to kick and scream his way to freedom, two of the men held him down whilst the third man pulled thick duct tape over his mouth, before binding his hands and ankles with cable ties. He leaned in close to Marty's right ear and whispered in a heavily accented voice, 'Don't struggle. Just enjoy a cell-warming present from your friends, Mr. McCloud and Mr.

Keats.' He laughed a cold, hoarse belly laugh. His friends joined in.

Marty, filled with a terror he had never known, tried desperately to breathe through his nostrils, as he wriggled, writhed and screamed under the tape. His attempts to fend them off inspired even more laughter as one of them closed the cell door. Marty still could not see any of the men from where he lay, but he sensed one of them had left the cell. As he lay on the ground, gripped with fear and begging for mercy, he made nothing but muffled noises.

Laughing like giddy children with a new toy, one of them, yet to speak, forced his knees onto Marty's shoulders, pressing his head to the floor, trapping him under his heavy, hot, sweating crotch. The second man pulled Marty's tracksuit bottoms down around his knees, before yanking down his underwear to expose his backside, running his rough fingers delicately over the exposed skin. Marty squirmed, attempting to kick the men off, but it was no use; they were heavy and he was totally incapacitated.

He could hear the man who had spoken to him laughing as he stood up above him for a moment, before pulling down his own tracksuit bottoms, allowing them to fall to the floor. A moment later, he dropped back to his knees and leaned in close to Marty's right ear again. 'This may sting a little,' he whispered as Marty kicked and wriggled frantically underneath him, 'but you'll soon start to enjoy it.'

A second later, the big man began forcing his erect penis roughly inside Marty's backside, grunting heavily as he did. The pain was unimaginable and tore through Marty's insides. He began to cry and scream uncontrollably underneath the tape. Tears poured down his face as the man began to thrust back and forth, over and over for what felt like an eternity. Suddenly the third man returned, warning the prison guards were on the landing below, heading towards their *own* cells.

'Shit, that's all we need!' said the man on top of Marty as he leapt off him and quickly dressed. His accomplices roughly pulled up Marty's tracksuit bottoms up and dragged him back onto his bed, his hands and legs still tied. Frozen with shock, Marty stared at his attackers for the first time, blinking wildly as they stood above him – three dark-skinned men, heavyset, potentially Greek or Lebanese. One of the men leaned in close, a small razor melted into a toothbrush in his hand, and smiled wickedly. As he spoke, Marty recognised him as the man on top. 'Welcome to Hawk Green,' he whispered before laughing hard and turning to share the joke with his mates. He turned back to Marty, the smile gone now.

'I'm going to cut your hands and feet free and take off the tape. *You* are not going to mention any of this to anyone or we'll come back again tomorrow, *and finish this off.* Do you understand?'

Marty nodded quickly, his eyes wide and wild.

'That's a good boy,' said the man, tapping the blade on Marty's cheek. 'And if I were you, I'd stay in my cell and get some rest. It's been a big first day, superstar!' he said and laughed loudly as he cut the cable ties from Marty's wrists and ankles before painfully pulling off the tape.

There was a sudden flurry of movement, and something heavy smashed into Marty's skull and his world went black.

CHAPTER 23

Lying on the cool grass of Alexandra Park opposite his family home in Whalley Range had always been a favourite pastime for Marty as a child. Most summer days after school, he would head across the road and into the park, watching excitedly as the bigger boys played football or cricket each evening. He so wanted to be like them, but as his father had told him many times over, *he was not the athletic type.*

Despite his obvious shortcomings in sport, he was never happier than when he could feel grass under his feet; halcyon days, ending each time with the shouts of his mother, calling him into their warm, welcoming home for dinner. He remembered it like it was yesterday. 'Marty! Marty! It's dinnertime!' she would shout in a thick County Mayo accent from her position on the front step. Reluctant to leave the park, more often than not, he would fail to answer her call. Then the shouts would turn more formal, using his 'Sunday' name, 'Marty, Marty Michaels!'

He could hear his mother now as he lay on the grass, revelling in the feeling of the cool cushion under his body as he stared ahead at the bright blue sky above him.

'Marty… Marty… Marty Michaels!' came the shouts.

He smiled, lifting and turning his head towards his family home, but he could not see his mother, despite hearing his name repeated over, and over.

'Marty... Marty... Marty Michaels!'

Sat upright, his mother was nowhere in sight and he blinked slowly as the world around him changed, the bright blue sunlit sky turning grey, then white and suddenly morphing into fluorescent tube lights and what looked like ashen white roof tiles ahead of him.

A woman's face appeared. 'Hello, Marty,' she said, her voice was soft and reassuring.

He turned his head slightly to look at a dark-haired woman and the smiling elfin face that greeted him was warm and filled with kindness. He smiled weakly as he looked into the big brown eyes staring down at him. She touched his wrist reassuringly, her voice loud and certain. 'Marty, you've had an accident. You've been unconscious for almost two days. You're in the hospital now. I'm Nurse Cavanagh,' she said, her accent reminiscent of his mother's.

Marty's mind raced and replayed the events of the previous week; the blackouts, the arrest, Paul White, prison; it had all been a comatose dream. A horrible, terrifyingly realistic dream – *thank God.*

'Wait there a moment, Marty, I'll be back in a minute,' said Nurse Cavanagh as she walked away.

Marty's relief was palpable and despite the overwhelming pain in his head, his body began to relax into the soft white sheets and his pillow seemed to wrap around his head, neck and shoulders, like a childhood hug from his mother. He closed his eyes and for the first time in twenty years said a short silent prayer of thanks, a smile touching the corners of his mouth as fatigue enveloped him. He lay there motionless for a few minutes until a loud male voice interrupted his thoughts.

'Mr. Michaels?'

Marty opened his eyes with a start and followed the guttural drawl to his left, coming face to face with the saggy features of a man in his late fifties. He wore wire-framed glasses and his breath carried the stale, sour smell of a heavy smoker.

'Mr. Michaels, I don't think we've actually met. I'm Jim Morrell, Governor of Her Majesty's Prison Greater Manchester. I am of course familiar with your work, as you are with mine after your week-long exposé last year on the staffing crisis within Hawk Green. It really was *fascinating!*' he said sarcastically.

Every fibre of Marty's body stood on end and he wanted to scream; the nightmare of the last few days had been all too real. Sinking into the pillow, the pain from his injuries suddenly came into sharp focus.

As if sensing his discomfort, the dark-haired woman gripped his wrist gently as she spoke. 'Marty, I'm the prison nurse. You've suffered severe injuries to your head and posterior and been unconscious for over thirty-six hours,' she said and smiled gently. 'We thought you'd fractured your skull but the X-rays have so far come up clear. There doesn't appear to be any internal bleeding but you'll need a full MRI and CT scan to be sure.'

Marty stared at her blankly for a long moment as he attempted to process this information before he spoke, very quietly, his voice brimming with fear and confusion. 'No scans, no press,' he said, shaking his head.

'Marty, I really must insist we get you thoroughly looked over at a proper hospital,' Cavanagh said.

Marty ignored her plea. 'What day is it?'

'It's Monday,' she said and checked her chest-watch, 'just after 8am.'

'Monday, Monday morning?'

'Yes, Marty.'

Marty stared ahead silently before he turned to face Cavanagh.

'How long can I stay here in the infirmary?' he asked desperately.

Nurse Cavanagh began to speak but Morrell cut across her bluntly, his hand falling heavily on the bed frame.

'*Two to three days at most I'd say,* Mr. Michaels, but it really all depends on how quickly your wounds heal. Ideally, you'll back on the wing by tomorrow night!' he said, sneering.

'I can't go back there! They'll kill me!'

'Nonsense, and besides, based on this unfortunate incident, your legal team has successfully petitioned to place you in isolation until the trial. I am, of course, only too happy to oblige. I just hope we have enough staff to ensure your safety,' he said, his tone still thick with sarcasm. A second later, he appeared to stand to attention, his voice suddenly light and jovial. 'Right, well I can't stand here all day chatting when I have a prison full of nasty bastards out there. Good day, Mr. Michaels,' he said turning towards the open door, before adding 'and good luck' as he marched off.

CHAPTER 24

After discharge from the prison infirmary late on Wednesday evening, under rule 45, Marty moved to the segregation unit or 'Seg' for his own protection. Despite the overcrowding in Hawk Green, the transfer of a less-high-profile inmate to Liverpool had created space for him in the ultra-secure unit, isolated from the rest of the prison in a single cell, under the constant watch of two officers. Sitting in the small space with the door locked he felt a mixture of relief, shut away from Keats and McCloud, and a creeping sense of anxiety that this soulless existence was to become a way of life for him.

Having spent just a few days in prison he had yet to earn any privileges and the room was devoid of any creature comforts. The mattress was standard prison-issue blue, and there was no TV or radio to help pass the time. The cell smelled of stale smoke and bleach, and the nicotine-stained walls bore the marks of previous inmates' posters, since removed.

After making his bed as best he could, he lay down and stared at the ceiling as the light began to fade through the window above his head, casting shadows across the plain white walls. Closing his eyes, he tried to calm his racing mind as he replayed the rape over and over again. In spite of the locked door and thick glass, he could hear the muffled chants of his neighbours echoing around the unit, calling him a 'nonce' and telling him what they intended to do to him should the opportunity arise. Finally, he broke and curling into the foetal position, began to sob, as quietly as he could at first, before the events of the last four days in Hawk Green overwhelmed him, his muffled sobs turning to the wailing scream of a tortured soul, much to the amusement of his fellow inmates.

*

Next morning, two prison guards escorted Marty to the shower block. Under their constant supervision he quickly washed and shaved alone, before dressing in a fresh tracksuit and being escorted back to his cell, where he was locked inside for his own safety. As the thick door slammed into the metal frame, he stared at it for a long moment before turning and moving to the small window overlooking the main block of the prison. Red brick, concrete and razor wire surrounded him in all directions and he felt an overwhelming sense of claustrophobia; would he ever get out of this place?

Some time later, the loud grinding of keys in the door echoed behind him and he turned to see the officers from earlier that morning entering his cell. Mr. Mayhew was a young, fresh-faced officer of average height and build with olive skin covered in a thick, well-groomed black beard and appeared new to the role, constantly deferring to his partner next to him, Mr. Clarke. Clarke was an older, taller man whose shirt strained against his muscular physique and his close-cropped hair and stiff gait gave away his previous career as a Royal Marine.

'Michaels, you've a visitor waiting,' Clarke said in the booming tones of a sergeant major.

'Visitor? Who is it?' Marty asked suspiciously.

'Do I look like your fucking secretary?' Clarke replied.

'Come on, Michaels, we'll take you up to see them,' Mayhew added with a warmth that caught Marty off guard.

Cautiously, Marty stepped out into the segregation block and was relieved to see he was the only inmate outside of his cell, and walking between Clarke and Mayhew, made his way to the visitors' block.

After a security pat-down by Mayhew as Clarke watched on, Marty slipped on a red bib to identify him as a prisoner and moved inside the big room. He estimated the floor space was about the size of a tennis court, with neat rows of tables and chairs laid out directly in front of him, currently empty. As a segregated prisoner he was kept away from general population prisoners at all times, joined only by his fellow 'seg' inmates. To his left in the far corner of the room a series of eight booths lined the wall, allowing a little more privacy for visits, usually used by inmates and their legal teams. All but one was currently occupied. Right on cue, Andrew Johnson stepped through from the civilian entrance and a huge wave of relief crashed over Marty; he could not recall ever being so happy to see his lawyer. Mayhew walked in front and Clarke fell in behind Marty as they made their way across the room.

Johnson's outstretched hand was waiting for Marty as the two men came together.

'How are you holding up?'

Before he could respond, Clarke barked instructions. 'You have thirty minutes, so make the most of your time,' he said as he and Mayhew stepped away to observe at a distance.

Johnson gestured for Marty to take the seat opposite him and both men sat down in unison.

'You've got to get me out of here, Andrew!' Marty said desperately.

'We will, Marty, in time we will.'

'Time is the one thing I don't have in here! Keats and McCloud are trying to kill me!' he said in an agitated whisper.

'I know, it's easier said than done, but try not to worry. Because of the attack, you'll remain in segregation until the trial. Two officers will be watching you at all times. Keats and McCloud cannot get to you in there.'

'That's bollocks, Andrew, and you know it! I'm not safe as long as I'm in Hawk Green. You have to get me out!'

'Ruben is working on it but the precedents for bailing murder suspects are rare and generally only happen in the most extreme circumstances.'

'Such as?'

'Such as a vulnerable child being charged with killing an abusive parent. There's nothing on wealthy celebrities on remand for killing a male prostitute.'

Marty was shocked by Johnson's blunt response and it showed on his face.

'I'm sorry, Marty, I don't mean to be cruel, but you're charged with a very serious crime and even though we're looking at every possible angle to get you bailed, you would be well advised to focus on coming to terms with being in here until your trial.'

'But how long will that be?'

Johnson paused for a moment, before answering. 'There's no way to sugar-coat this Marty. Ruben estimates anywhere up to six months depending on the prosecution's case.'

Marty stared back wide-eyed, his mouth open but unable to form any words. Johnson continued.

'I know that's not what you want to hear, but I can only present the facts as I find them,' he said flatly.

Marty finally found his voice, 'Six months in this shithole? Are you fucking kidding me? If Keats and McCloud don't get me, then insanity will. I won't survive in here for six months, Andrew!'

Johnson's voice softened now, 'Look, as I said, Ruben is looking at every angle. He's one of the UK's top barristers and if there's a loophole in the law, he'll find it. In the meantime, try to take it one day at a time. Thinking long-term will send you mad.'

Marty said nothing as he tried to take in Johnson's words, before rubbing his palms down his face and changing the subject. 'So where's Rob? How come he's not with you?'

'This visit is in my capacity as your lawyer. Rob will need to come during general visiting. I'm in the process of getting him added to your visitor list. He'll be here as soon as he's approved.'

Marty nodded, 'And what is the outside world saying about me?'

Johnson again took his time to answer, 'I won't lie, Marty, people are not being kind, but I really don't recommend you expend any energy on what the media think of this. They all have agendas and your celebrity creates news, drives page impressions etc.'

'What are they saying, Andrew?' Marty asked firmly.

Johnson sighed. 'Very well. Thankfully, because you've now been charged, no one can make any comment on the case or they'll face contempt of court. So a lot of the media are looking through your past, dragging up old stories as they try to paint you as a man capable of murder, without actually accusing you of anything specific. Your ambush of the prime minister after the election is getting a lot of airtime by social commentators.'

Marty snorted his contempt, 'So it's trial by media?'

'I'm afraid so.'

'Ironic really, considering how many times I've done it to others myself,' Marty added.

Johnson nodded, 'Ironic certainly covers it, old boy.'

Despite his initial protestations, Johnson spent the next twenty minutes walking Marty through various high-traffic media outlets and their view on his arrest and remand, punctuated by a constant stream of profanity from his client. By the time he had finished, Marty felt like a coiled spring, ready to explode. Johnson clearly sensed his unease.

'I did try and warn you, Marty. It's not pretty.'

'It's a fucking witch-hunt, is what it is!' Marty growled.

'Look, Marty, you know this game better than anyone. If someone else were in your shoes, you'd be doing exactly the same. Try not to take it personally.'

Marty slammed his hand down on the table in frustration, drawing disapproving looks from Mayhew and Clarke. Marty raised his hand by way of apology before lowering his voice to almost a whisper, 'I do take it personally, Andrew. This is my life going down the toilet. I've worked too damn hard to get to the top to just sit back and let them destroy me. You have to get me out now so I can defend myself!'

Johnson placed a reassuring hand on Marty's across the table, 'Ruben is doing everything he can to make that happen. In the meantime, keep your head down and watch your back.'

Marty nodded as Mayhew and Clarke arrived.

'Time's up, Michaels,' Clarke said curtly and both men stepped back to allow Marty to stand. He shook Johnson's hand and turned, stepping out into the main visitors' room. There was a flurry of movement from the booth to his right as someone lunged towards him screaming, 'Die, you fucking nonce!' In an instant, he felt agonising pain in his neck below his right ear and instinctively raised his arms in defence as his attacker kept coming, forcing Marty to the floor, before Mayhew and Clarke managed to pull Marty free and two other offices restrained his attacker.

He could feel the hot blood running down his neck and onto his torso. He raised his right hand to stem the bleeding, and realised his wrist was also pumping out thick, almost black, blood onto the floor. 'Fuck,' he managed to mutter before passing out.

*

According to the consultant in charge of Wythenshaw A&E, Marty had been incredibly lucky, even joking he should buy a lottery ticket, before remembering his patient was an inmate of Hawk Green, and making his apologies. The double-bladed weapon used in the attack had severed veins in his neck and wrists but somehow missed the main arteries in both. Thirty-four stitches later, he sat on the edge of the hospital bed in the treatment cubicle, bandaged and awaiting transport back to the prison infirmary. Mayhew and Clarke watched on in silence.

News of his attack had already made it into the public domain and a nurse just starting her shift updated Marty on the large crowd of paps and journalists congregating outside. She had a kind face and her green eyes sparkled under her thick auburn fringe.

'Love the show, Marty,' she said in a soft Scottish accent, 'Looks like a stitch-up to me – no pun intended,' she added, winking, before heading off in search of her next patient.

Marty allowed himself a smile. Maybe not everyone in the world thought he was guilty.

Clarke's phone beeped, 'Right, the van's here,' he said louder than necessary in the confined space before cuffing himself to Marty and gesturing for Mayhew to lead them out.

Moving through the maze of corridors they passed a number of patients in dressing gowns and slippers, wandering the corridors at a snail's pace in stark contrast to a host of visitors in such a rush to get to their final destination, they barely flinched at the cuffed celebrity in their midst. If only the waiting media pack would have the same ambivalence.

As they approached the exit, Marty spotted a couple of uniformed police officers waiting to escort the party to their transport, and he braced himself for a repeat of the scrum he had experienced at the Metropolitan Hotel. He would not be disappointed. Stepping out into the summer sun, he raised his left hand to shade his eyes as the noise erupted. Unlike Bovalino and Jones, neither Clarke and Mayhew nor the police officers had any desire to be the centre of attention, barging their way through the mass of bodies grappling for a shot of the prisoner. An assault on the senses ensued. Even in the bright sunshine, Marty was dazzled by the rapid-fire camera-flashguns thrust in his face, as shouts and taunts overwhelmed his ears. Silently coaching himself to stay calm, he did his best to block out the noise, staring straight ahead as they moved ever closer to the safety of the prison van, waiting to take him back to Hawk Green.

With just a few steps left to the van, a sudden surge of bodies knocked Clarke off balance causing him to fall onto the concrete path, dragging Marty onto his knees alongside him. Blind panic ensued and Marty cried out as people began to trample over his legs and feet, but Clarke was not a man to lie down for long. Using his muscular frame to great effect, he dragged himself and Marty back to their feet as the two police officers and Mayhew stepped in to push back the crowd.

A moment later Clarke virtually lifted Marty into the van, jumping in behind him and slamming the door shut on the mini riot outside. He was safe, for the time being at least.

CHAPTER 25

Marty's bail was confirmed at 4pm on Monday 1st June, too late to process his release the same day. Johnson had visited Hawk Green that morning under tight security to share the good news; Ruben had agreed a deal with the CPS to allow Marty out on bail. Johnson believed the uber-ambitious Josh Lei wanted to make an example of Marty in court to supercharge his career trajectory. After two serious assaults since his remand, if Marty died in prison, Lei's opportunity would die with him. The terms of the deal were simple and required him to remain at home under permanent curfew, which was just fine by Marty; there was nowhere else he would rather be.

After spending another lonely, sleepless night in segregation, a sneering Governor Morell informed Marty of his release schedule at 7am Tuesday and an hour later, he was handed over to his court-appointed guardian, Andrew Johnson.

Marty was dressed in the blue suit and white shirt he had worn to court four days earlier. His shoulder-length hair was wet and combed back against his head, his neck and arms tightly bandaged.

A large steel door opened and stepping painfully into the public reception area, Andrew greeted him.

'Marty, how are you?'

He ignored the question and moved past Johnson as if looking for something, his mind elsewhere, before turning to face his statuesque lawyer.

'Where's Rob?' Marty asked abruptly.

'He thought it best I come alone; less chance of the media linking us to you.'

Marty nodded silently as if satisfied by the answer but his face betrayed his true feelings.

'So, it's not the case he's distancing himself from a damaged client?'

'Marty, it's not like that at all, I can assure you,' Andrew said smoothly.

'Really, you don't think it's odd that as soon as I'm suspended from my million-pound job and publicly humiliated, my agent and so-called best friend suddenly goes AWOL, leaving me to rot in this hellhole? He then decides it's in *my best* interests for *him* not to turn up when I'm released. Hardly the actions of a committed agent and friend, wouldn't you agree?'

'Marty, it's nothing like that, honestly. You are front-page news right now and everybody knows Rob is your agent. We *both* figured you'd have more chance of getting out of here without a full press pack if I came alone. Your release will become public record at 9am, so if we move quickly we can get you home before the mass media get hold of the story. Rob will meet us at your house later.'

Marty nodded unconvincingly as Johnson raised his left arm, gesturing towards the exit. 'Come on; let's get you out of here.'

CHAPTER 26

Just before 9am, with the help of the temporary security firm standing guard at the main gates, Andrew effortlessly swept past the now-depleted press pack outside Marty's Prestbury home. The blacked-out rear windows of his S-Class Mercedes made it impossible to catch a glimpse of his passenger, huddled in the back of the car.

With the big gates firmly locked behind him, Marty retreated to the security of his beloved house and a red-hot shower, as he attempted to wash away the events of the last few days in Hawk Green Prison. Standing with his face directly under the hot stream of water, he finally dared to curse the three men who had so brutally violated him. Anger rose up inside him like a volcanic eruption; picturing their sneering faces, he wanted to execute each of them without mercy.

Placing his hands flat to the marble walls of the wet room, he pressed his forehead against the cold surface and stared at the water swirling around his feet, his jaw locked in a painful clench as he struggled to deal with the torrent of emotions flooding his mind. He closed his eyes, took a couple of deep breaths and let out a long, guttural scream as he repeatedly slammed the side of his fist against the wall, over and over again. He screamed louder and louder until he could scream no more and, eventually, exhausted and broken, he slumped slowly and painfully to the floor and cried like a petrified child as the hot water bounced off his battered, heaving body and blood from his weeping wrists swirled around his feet.

Half an hour passed and when it seemed his tears had finally run dry, he painfully lifted himself off the wet room floor, turned off the shower and dressed in his white towelling robe. He dried his hair roughly and pulled it back against his head, tucking his wet locks behind his ears, before limping slowly down the big sweeping staircase to the ground floor of the house, gripping the bannister tightly with each step.

Marty could hear two men talking. He assumed Rob had arrived and readied himself to share his feelings on the current 'distancing' strategy. Following the voices, he eventually found Andrew in the lounge room, but there was no Rob. Instead, Andrew was talking to Marty's personal physician, Dr. Clive Chorlton.

'I invited Dr. Chorlton over here to change your dressings and give you the once-over,' Johnson said calmly, as if it was perfectly normal for him to invite whomever he liked into Marty's home.

'I'm fine, I don't need it. Where's Rob?'

Dr. Chorlton remained silent but watched Johnson as if ready to take his lead.

'Rob will be here later. Look Marty, I could hear you shouting upstairs. I'll never understand what you went through in there, but your injuries could be far more serious than we've been led to believe. I'd feel much more comfortable if Dr. Chorlton looked you over.'

Marty turned to face the doctor. 'Look, no offence, doc,' he said. 'You've looked after me and my mum for a very long time and I appreciate that, but I really don't need an exam. I just need some time on my own. I just want to put the last few days behind me rather than dwell on it.'

Johnson's toned changed now, his voice stern, the public-school accent sharp as a blade.

'Marty, do me favour and have the exam. If not for your own health, then do it for the sake of your case. I need a full evaluation of your injuries, so that when we get you off these ridiculous charges, we can sue the arse off the prison system. It was completely unacceptable for you to be attacked twice in almost as many days, and in the case of the second instance, directly under the noses of the officers assigned to protect you in segregation. If we can demonstrate the extent of your injuries and prove there was negligence, it's potentially worth an awful lot of money to you. So please, Marty – for me, and for your desire to hang onto this ridiculously expensive house, take the sodding exam, will you?'

Marty stared at Johnson in silence for a moment and then slowly nodded his approval as he shuffled towards the couch. On cue, the doctor stepped forward and sat down on the sofa, placing his bag on the seat beside him. 'Right then, Marty, let's get you stripped to the waist, shall we?' Chorlton said warmly.

CHAPTER 27

'You've had a rough few days,' Dr. Chorlton said with no hint of irony as he finished replacing Marty's dressings.

Johnson was in the kitchen 'making calls'.

Marty shook his head. 'I just don't know what's happening,' he said. 'One minute I'm finishing my radio show on Friday morning and heading home for the weekend, the next thing I know I'm waking up in the Metropolitan and being accused of murder. How could this have happened?'

Dr. Chorlton placed a stethoscope on Marty's chest, instructed him to take a few deep breaths, before nodding and pulling the stethoscope out of his ears and clipping it round his neck.

'Well, your breathing is fine, no damage to your heart or lungs. Is that *really* all you can remember – *Friday morning?*'

'*Yes!* I remember being in the studio and recording the weekend promo because we were due to have the Health Secretary on the show on Monday morning. I argued with Jon my producer because he wanted two different versions to run on rotation across the weekend, and I didn't agree. For me it was a simple promo – *Join me Marty Michaels on Monday morning as I grill the newly appointed Health Secretary.* It was her first official one-to-one with any media so it was a big deal, but Jon wanted a version that also promoted some client-funded thing we were running as well.'

Dr. Chorlton shone a light in his left eye, his face so close that Marty could smell the coffee on his breath as he spoke in a hushed, slightly distracted tone. 'And *you* didn't want to run two?'

'No chance! Clients pay to be associated with *my* show and *my name*. Without me, there would be no audience and no clients – so I have final say on the show and that includes the promos. Sales are always trying to get me to read stuff for their clients but if I don't endorse the company, they don't get in the show. It's simple, either *I* get my cut or it doesn't happen.'

Chorlton moved to the right eye.

'And your bosses are OK with that?'

'They have no choice, it's part of my contract. The fact is *I am* the show. I pull in a weekly audience of seven million listeners – and *The Morning Show with Marty Michaels* brings in annual revenues in excess of ten million pounds. The advertisers want to be part of *my show* – which puts *me* in control.'

Chorlton checked Marty's ears next, the head of his otoscope catching the left side of Marty's head; he cried out in pain.

'Sorry, Marty, your skull is very tender on this side.'

Marty gently touched it. 'I'm not surprised; whatever they hit me with was bloody heavy.'

The doctor checked both ears fully before pressing his fingers lightly up and down both sides of Marty's face, each impact on the left side drawing a painful grimace from his patient.

'Now I don't want to panic you, but I think we need to do a full CT scan – just to be on the safe side,' Chorlton said.

'No scans, doc, no hospitals. I don't want to go outside again.'

'Look, it's probably nothing, but you have some sensitivity on the left side of your head which is beyond the norm, and it feels a little unusual to the touch. It *is* very swollen, which doesn't help, as there is a lot of damaged tissue which could potentially be masking all kinds of problems underneath. Looking in your ears there's no obvious signs of fluid, which is good, but I can't rule out the possibility of a skull fracture.'

'But I'm fine, honestly.'

'Patients can often function perfectly well with a fractured skull for days, even weeks at a time, without it being detected. Then one day, something as simple as turning their head in bed can release tiny particles of bone into the bloodstream, which can lead to a stroke, cardiac arrest or even serious brain damage. Trust me, Marty; let's get you booked in for a CT scan. We'll do it at the private hospital and make sure security is ultra-vigilant to protect you from the press.'

Marty thought about the doctor's words for a moment and finally nodded his agreement.

The doctor smiled and began to pack away his medical bag, both men silent for a moment before Marty spoke.

'Doc, is it really possible for someone to suffer from amnesia – you know, to lose two days' memory like I did?'

'It is possible, yes; very rare, but it does happen.'

'What causes it?'

'Most often it's trauma of some kind, physical or mental, or sometimes both. It's as if the brain shuts down to protect itself.'

'But before the attack in Hawk Green, I was perfectly fine, no injuries whatsoever.'

The doctor nodded. 'Yes, it does seem highly unlikely.' He paused for a moment. 'There is of course another possibility,' he ventured.

Chorlton stopped packing his bag and sat perfectly still, staring straight at Marty.

'Memory loss such as yours is often seen when the victim is drugged. In the last decade, we've seen the use of Rohypnol increase exponentially.'

'The date-rape drug?'

'It is sometimes referred to as that, yes.'

Marty shifted on the sofa, clearly agitated.

'I wasn't raped, if that's what you're thinking.'

The doctor raised his hands, palms facing Marty. 'I'm not saying anything of the sort, not at all,' he said. 'I was merely commenting that Rohypnol, along with a host of other tranquillisers, can be used to induce a loss of consciousness and leave the victim with no memory, sometimes for days at a time depending on the particular drug and strength of dose. If administered in drink, particularly alcohol, they are virtually tasteless and if the intended party is already intoxicated, I'm guessing it's relatively easy to spike their glass without being noticed.'

'Jesus, I was drugged.' Marty's words seemed to tail off.

'Well, it could be a plausible explanation for your memory loss.'

Marty was nodding feverishly now. 'It had to be drugs, how else would I lose two days? The pictures the police showed me had me sitting at the bar at the Metropolitan drinking whisky. I have a weak bladder at the best of times, but especially on the spirits. I'm always going to the bathroom, anyone could have spiked it.'

Dr. Chorlton nodded his agreement, 'Well, there is one way to be certain; a urine test. But I'd suggest we do it now as all drugs flush out of your system at different speeds. That said, depending on the drug and when it was administered, there's a slim chance it could *still* be detectable.'

Marty nodded as Dr. Chorlton handed him a sample cup. He stood awkwardly as he took it.

'One more thing, doc…'

'What's that?'

'I'm gonna need an HIV test too.'

CHAPTER 28

The doorbell rang loudly through the ground floor of Marty's house, followed by Andrew's brisk footsteps as he moved quickly from the kitchen to answer it.

The doctor was packing his case and saying goodbye as Andrew entered the lounge and silently introduced Rob to the room. As he stepped from behind Andrew, Rob's face betrayed the fact he was clearly uneasy, and Marty spotted it instantly.

'Hi, Marty,' Rob said quietly.

Marty said nothing, instead eyeing his agent and 'best mate' cautiously as he stood like a naughty child in front of him, his grey suit pants and crisp fitted white shirt adding to the image.

'So you decided to grace us with your presence then?' shot Marty, his voice laced with venom.

'Oh, come on, mate, don't be like that,' Rob hit back.

Dr. Chorlton made his excuses and promised to organise the CT scan as he left the room, quickly followed by Andrew who reminded everyone how busy he was as his phone rang.

Alone now, the two men stared at each other; Marty sat on the large white leather sofa, Rob standing directly in front of him.

'I know you're angry, but I was trying to protect you,' Rob said.

'By leaving me alone in Hawk Green?'

'Look, Marty, the press knows I'm your agent. They would've had a field day if I'd gone to pick you up. They're watching my house too, you know! I wanted you to be able to leave the prison quietly, and it worked, didn't it?'

'That's not the point, Rob; you and I have been mates for over fifteen years and not a word the whole time I was in there.'

Rob looked to the floor, his face filled with shame.

'I tried, Marty, I really did.'

'Bullshit, Rob, you left me there to rot. Over a week I was in that place and the only person I saw was my bloody lawyer – and he gets *paid* to kiss my arse!' Marty yelled, pointing towards Andrew who was now in the kitchen. 'Technically as my agent, so do *you*, but above all else, I thought we were mates, Rob!'

'We are mates!'

Marty jumped up from the chair, his eyes wild with rage, his face filled with pain from his injuries.

'Do mates leave each other to be brutalised by a bunch of fucking savages?' he yelled grabbing Rob by the shirt, just inches from his face, his eyes filling with tears.

Rob gently prised open his grip and stared open-mouthed into his face, 'My God, what did they do to you in there?'

Marty turned his face away from Rob. 'Nothing anyone needs to know about, Rob. *Not even you*,' he said.

'Please, mate, talk to me.'

Marty shuffled back to the sofa and dropped down gently onto the leather.

'Over a week, Rob, over a week, and not one word from you.'

Rob crossed the room and sat down next to Marty, his voice soft as he spoke. 'They wouldn't let me see you. I tried but you went in on Friday night and by Saturday evening, you were in the infirmary. There was no way of getting to you.'

Marty stared silently at Rob, studying every curve and bump on his face for signs he was lying but there were none; he seemed genuine enough.

'I honestly tried,' Rob repeated.

Suddenly Marty felt very tired.

'OK,' he said standing slowly as he walked towards the door. 'Look, I'm tired. I need to sleep. Can you tell Andrew I'm going to bed and let yourself out?'

Rob's eyes followed him, 'Sure thing, Marty. But if you need anything, just call me, right?'

'I will,' he said absent-mindedly as he continued walking, before suddenly stopping in his tracks. 'In fact, the doc wants me at St. Xavier Hospital tomorrow afternoon for a CT scan. Can you speak to Andrew about getting approval from Lei's team? If they say it's OK I'll need you to drive me over there.'

'Of course, mate. You got it!' Rob said just a little too enthusiastically.

CHAPTER 29

Saint Xavier Hospital is less than a mile south of Manchester city centre nestled between the two suburbs of Whalley Range and Hulme.

True to his word, Dr. Chorlton had insisted on a security upgrade for Marty's visit, with only a select few staff members made aware of his treatment. Lei's team had approved the visit but only under the supervision of Jones and Bovalino who had followed Rob's Range Rover from Prestbury through to the private hospital, where they escorted Marty to the X-ray and scanning department. Thirty minutes later, on the second floor of the building, Marty lay prostrate on the bed of the CT scanner, naked all but for a pale green hospital gown tied loosely at the back. His eyes searched the ceiling above for some form of comfort; he hated hospitals at the best of times but after his nightmare experience at Hawk Green, the fear now ran much deeper.

Sasha, the tall, dark-haired radiologist managing Marty's scan, explained the process that was about to happen, in a thick Central European accent, before retreating to the small office opposite the big machine. A moment later, the bed rose gently and Marty was manoeuvred slowly into the tight metal ring and the scan began.

The noise from the spinning scanner was deafening and terrifying as claustrophobia enveloped him. Forced to stay completely still, he gritted his teeth painfully and closed his eyes, trying hard to steady his breathing as his pulse raced.

He could feel his head throbbing as the scan continued, round and round and round, appearing to close in on him. *Stay calm Marty, you have control, you're safe*, he repeated over and over in his mind until eventually the noise stopped and he was released from the grip of the machine.

Sasha returned and touched Marty's arm gently, a smile forming on her face. 'It's all over now, Mr. Michaels,' she said reassuringly. 'You can get dressed and head back to the waiting room. One of the consultants will be with you shortly to talk you through the results.'

Marty turned his head to face her and managed a weak smile.

'Thank you.'

He dressed quickly and returned to the empty waiting room, anxious for the results.

Grabbing an iced water from the fully stocked fridge in the corner of the room, he purposely avoided the muted television showing rolling news of the day. Instead, he walked to the window and stared out through the half-open vertical blinds to the street below. It was a beautiful summer's day in Manchester and the world outside continued about its business, oblivious to Marty Michaels watching over them. His mind wandered and before long, he found himself once again questioning the events of the last week. How had his world changed so quickly? Once a cash-rich millionaire with the world at his feet, movie stars and politicians to call on as friends; now after an expensive divorce and no work coming in, he was going broke. With a murder charge hanging over his head, it didn't look like things would get better any time soon either.

A little while later, the door opened behind him causing Marty to jump; Hawk Green had made him impossibly edgy. A slim Middle Eastern-looking man in an expensive black shirt but no tie, dark suit pants and brown shoes stood holding a clipboard and smiled at Marty.

'Mr. Michaels, I'm Dr. Ashard, the consultant neurologist here at Saint Xavier's. I have your scan results,' he said and gestured for Marty to sit down on one of the two light green fabric armchairs opposite him.

'I'm fine standing,' Marty replied curtly as he stepped forward to inspect the ID hanging round the man's neck. 'Just checking,' Marty added abruptly. He wasn't about to let his guard down, even if this was a private hospital.

Satisfied he was indeed Dr. Ashard, Marty nodded for him to speak.

Ashard took a step closer. 'The good news is there is no skull fracture, and brain activity looks normal. You have, however, sustained a fractured cheekbone on the left side and your jaw directly below the fracture is also very swollen.'

Marty nodded distantly. 'So does that mean I can go home now?' he asked.

'Yes, of course. However, I would like to refer you to a colleague of mine who can fix your cheekbone.'

'Dr. Chorlton will sort all that for me. I'd just like to get out of here quickly please. Hospitals make me nervous.'

'As you wish, Dr. Chorlton is waiting for you outside. I'll make the necessary arrangements and let him know you can go home now.'

Without acknowledging Ashard, Marty turned away and gazed again at the street below as the door opened behind him. He recognised the voice of Dr. Chorlton who exchanged pleasantries with Ashard before both men stepped outside. A few minutes later Dr. Chorlton returned and Marty turned to face him.

'Good news, Marty, no skull fractures,' he said cheerfully.

Marty was in no mood for pleasantries and got straight to the point. 'Do you have my blood test results?'

The doctor's expression changed, instantly serious. He gestured towards the two armchairs in the middle of the room. 'I think you may want to sit down,' he said.

Marty gulped, the words almost catching in his throat as he sat, 'What is it? What did you find?'

'Look Marty, you won't like what I'm about to tell you, but there may well be some kind of explanation that's not immediately apparent.'

'Cut the crap, doc. Just tell me, do I have AIDS?'

Dr. Chorlton snorted heavily, 'God no; not at all, in fact you don't have *any* STIs.'

Marty's body visibly softened and he exhaled loudly as relief washed over him.

'Oh, thank God.'

'Did you seriously think you might be HIV-positive?'

Marty deliberately ignored the doctor's question. 'So what *did* you find?' he asked instead.

'Well, it appears you were indeed drugged. We found traces of cocaine, plus Methaqualone in your system, although you may be more familiar with the street vernacular, Quaaludes.'

'The tranquilliser?'

'You are familiar with it. It's a very powerful drug and may have accounted for your memory loss.'

Marty hammered his fists on the arms of the chair as he shot to his feet, regretting it as pain shot through his torso.

'I knew it! I knew someone had drugged me! The bastards!' he shouted as he paced the room. 'I bet it was Jeremy Day or Burns who set me up, all so they could get rid of me. They've been undermining me for years. Rather than face me head-on, they resort to this underhand shit!'

Chorlton remained seated but raised his hands to try to calm his patient.

'Look Marty, I know you're angry but we have no idea who put the drugs in your system. Are you sure you didn't take anything at the weekend yourself? Whilst Methaqualone can be detected for up to fifteen days, cocaine flushes out after three.'

Marty shot the doc an angry stare. 'Yes, I'm sure! I don't do coke anymore,' he lied.

After a long moment of silence, Marty turned to face Chorlton, bending forward and leaning with both hands on the arms of the doctor's chair, staring him straight in the eye.

'Doc, considering the amount of Quaaludes in my system, do you think it's possible I could have killed a man on Saturday?'

Staring back at Marty, Chorlton took a moment to answer.

'I honestly don't think so; if for example you had taken cocaine then I'd say it certainly would have been possible, but the levels of Methaqualone in your blood indicate it would have been very difficult for you to function normally. Quaaludes are very powerful tranquillisers, capable of incapacitating for quite some time. Take too many and your lungs can even shut down. In my opinion, you were not capable of *any* physical movement with the drugs you had in your system.'

'Just so I'm clear, you're saying in my condition, it would have been impossible for me to fight with, let alone overpower and strangle, a fit and healthy young man?'

'In medicine there are no real definitive answers, but looking at the facts and the sheer volume of 'ludes in your system, in my opinion it would have been virtually impossible.'

'And you're *sure*?'

'Based on the facts at hand, I'm as sure as anyone can be.'

'So I couldn't have killed White!' Marty said giddily. 'I didn't bloody kill him, I'm innocent. I'm innocent!' He grabbed Chorlton on both sides of his face before kissing the top of his head. 'You little beauty, doc! I'm innocent!'

Dr. Chorlton stared at Marty, a look of bemusement on his face as his patient stood up straight and clapped his hands together. 'Right, I need to call Rob; it's time to get my bloody job back!'

CHAPTER 30

The journey home from the hospital had passed without incident, Jones and Bovalino following Rob's large SUV to ensure he made it back to Prestbury unscathed. The conversation between Marty and his agent during that time had been distinctly more challenging. With Dr. Chorlton suggesting drugs with extreme sedative effects were the most likely cause of his memory loss, Marty had petitioned Rob to call Colin Burns and discuss a return to work. Rob, ever the pragmatist, had cautioned against the idea, insisting Marty needed to keep a low profile, not to mention the fact he was still under permanent curfew. All very true, but not what his client wanted to hear and when Rob pulled up outside the house, Marty had got out of the car without saying a word.

A moment later, he entered the house without looking back and as he slammed the heavy oak front door, the walls appeared to shake across the entire ground floor. He was angry and frustrated beyond belief, his body arching forward with his arms out wide, as if preparing to wrestle an invisible opponent.

'Everyone's against me, *even though* I'm clearly innocent!' he screamed to the silent hallway.

Pacing furiously, he moved into the kitchen and using all his body weight and grunting like a tennis pro, threw his house keys at the polished white cabinet directly in front of him, producing a loud crack that sounded like gunfire and left a small, dark hole from the impact.

'Arseholes!' he raged as he moved back and forth across the polished concrete kitchen floor.

During the journey home, Rob had reiterated COMCO's stance which was crystal-clear: they could not publicly support Marty unless cleared by a jury or the charges were dropped, which seemed ever more unlikely.

A trial of such profile and complexity could take six months to prepare, and would be played out in the spotlight when it did finally get to court. Marty's celebrity status and finances could not handle that amount of time without work or pay.

He walked quickly into the lounge room, his fingers interlocked behind his head, elbows flush against his temples.

With no one there to listen, he talked aloud to himself, 'Who do they think they're messing with? Seriously? I'm Marty Michaels! I *made* COMCO! Before me they were an "also-ran" with a market share of four per cent and losing ten million pounds a year! I dragged them kicking and screaming up to a double-digit share. *I* gave them the means to pull in forty million profit every year! If they're trying to destroy me, I won't go down alone – I'll take them all with me!' he raged as he slumped onto the sofa.

He stared out of the large floor-to-ceiling windows that ran the length of the room. A pair of magpies called to each other in the back garden and he watched as the branches of the large willow tree outside swayed in the breeze, the daylight beginning to fade across the farmland in the distance.

Fuck.

After a long moment, he had decided what to do.

Stepping up, he walked to the secure white cabinet in the corner, unlocked and opened the heavy double doors. He pulled out the solid silver coke box and returned to the sofa, placing it on the glass coffee table in front of him. Opening the lid, his irritation immediately intensified when he realised his supply of high-grade cocaine was exhausted. *Dammit!*

Returning to the cabinet, he pulled out a cheap plastic pre-paid mobile phone and pressed redial. It rang five times.

The deep baritone voice on the other end was cautious, the accent Eastern European, the English almost perfect.

'Hello?'

'G, it's me.'

'Account code?' came the muted reply.

'Eighteen-eleven-seventy-one.' Marty used the code agreed with his elusive contact, G – real name Gerard Wizkowsky, or 'G-Wiz' as he was known in the trade – a Polish national now residing in Manchester. G was a used book trader according to Greater Manchester Council's records – but to those who knew different, he was a purveyor of high-grade amphetamines to the great and good of Cheshire.

'What do you need?'

Overly paranoid, Marty was careful to follow the well-rehearsed script.

'Five classics.'

G interpreted this as five grams of the drug dealer's classic – cocaine.

'That's a lot more than usual, you sure?'

'Yes, business is booming and I've run out of stock.'

'It must be; I only dispatched six to you on Saturday. You moved them on already?'

'You what? What are you talking about, what six from the weekend?' Marty replied, taken aback.

'I packaged up and processed six classics for you on Saturday afternoon.'

'This Saturday, just gone?'

'Yeah. A car came to pick them up around 6pm. Tall blonde collected the books, said she was new to the payroll.'

'Are you sure it was for me?'

'Damn right, gave me the correct code – paid cash. Good-looking girl, too.'

This was all news to Marty.

For good reason, he had always insisted on never meeting G or handling cocaine outside of the safety of his own home. He had seen too many high-profile careers go down to the toilet thanks to 'drug busts' and tabloid exposés; he himself had led the way on many a celeb hunt.

Instead, he would send private couriers and radio station runners to pick up the drug orders. His 'mules' were told that Marty was buying rare books from a private dealer in the leafy suburb of Didsbury, five miles south of Manchester city centre, and they always paid cash for the large sealed Jiffy bags handed to them on arrival. Unbeknownst to them, they actually contained hollowed-out hardbacks, filled with two large tablets of the purest cocaine available in the Northern Hemisphere. Marty was careful to ensure there was no physical trace back to him at any level.

In the event of any arrests, he would deny all knowledge of the deals. His word against the mule's – *no contest.*

To buy the drugs from G, all the mules needed was the cash and the code.

'Eighteen-eleven-seventy-four' referred to the initials of Marty's ex-wife, Rebecca Kate, the eighteenth and eleventh letters of the alphabet, and her year of birth, '74; fairly rudimental but memorable, and very difficult to connect anything to Marty.

Marty's mind raced in all directions, his heart pounding, the rancid taste of adrenalin seeping from his palate. He struggled to speak and his voice cracked as the words came out.

'Mate… I didn't order anything on Saturday and I don't have anyone new on the payroll.'

G took a drink of something before responding, 'It did seem odd you hadn't ordered directly, especially as it was triple the normal amount, but she said she worked for you, and gave me your account code. I just figured you were busy and forgot to tell me.'

Marty was silent for a moment whilst he processed the information.

'Describe the girl again.'

'Er… well. She was Asian, blonde and tall. Very tall actually, around six foot. She had very long legs, that's what really stood out to me, and she was wearing a black coat, like a mac… oh and leather boots that went up past her knees. They were nice – but it seemed a strange outfit for six o'clock in the middle of summer.'

Marty racked his brain for anything he recognised.

'Anything else, eye colour, distinguishing marks?'

'She had sunglasses on the whole time but when she handed me the money I did notice she had a black dragon tattooed on her wrist. It was small but very detailed and looked like a good one.'

'How did she get in contact with you?'

'Like I said, I got a call, she gave me the code and she made the order.'

'And she specifically ordered on *my* behalf?'

'For sure, yes. She asked for your usual "titles" along with a couple of special imported extras but nothing you haven't had before so it all seemed OK.'

'And how did she get to the house?'

'Cab waited while she paid and took delivery.'

'What was the name of the taxi company?'

G thought for a moment, Marty could hear him rubbing his stubble next to the mouthpiece.

'I think… it was a Blu.'

Marty knew them well; one of the fastest-growing taxi fleets in the city with well over a hundred cars roaming Manchester at any given time.

'Did you get the registration plate?' he asked desperately.

'What am I, Columbo? All I know is, it was red with a buckled back bumper.'

'And you're absolutely sure of the time, 6pm?'

'Yes, the football was on, I was watching the first half with a few beers when she arrived.'

'That's good to know.'

It was clear G was tiring of the questions now, keen to get back to his life of idle TV watching.

'So do you want any new books or not?' he said sharply.

Marty could hear the words but his mind was miles away.

'Sorry? What did you say?'

'I said do you want the five books you rang to order?'

'Er... no,' Marty was already planning his next move. 'That... that won't be necessary.'

'Suit yourself,' G said and the phone went dead.

Marty stood totally still for a long moment staring out of the window and slowly closed the plastic phone. He ran the facts through in his mind: a tall, tattooed Asian blonde, wearing sunglasses and a long coat, bought drugs on his behalf, using his top-secret code, from a dealer no one knew he used. She picked them up personally at an exclusive address very few people knew existed.

He was clueless as to what was going on but he was sure of one thing; whatever it was, someone was going to an awful lot of trouble to get close to the underbelly of his life; a terrifying thought made even worse by the fact he had absolutely no idea what they would do next.

CHAPTER 31

'You called your dealer while under curfew?' Andrew's usual calm and collected demeanour had completely dissolved. 'Are you insane?'

'Look, you're missing the point – we have a lead on a girl who could be connected to White's murder somehow; surely that's a good thing?' Marty shot back.

Andrew continued to pace around Marty's lounge room, shaking his head, unable to process the conversation he was having with his client. Rob stood between the two men, silently refereeing the fight.

'Let me see if I'm hearing this right – you're telling us that you rang your fucking coke dealer, from your home phone, *and ordered takeout?*' Andrew continued.

Marty protested, 'No! I was careful; I called him on an untraceable mobile. I still have it – look…' he said grabbing the plastic phone from the cabinet and passing it to Andrew, who held it for a brief moment before discarding it on the couch.

'OK, that's *one* thing in our favour, but seriously Marty, I'm good at looking out for you, but I'm not a bloody miracle worker. If you are caught in possession of a class A drug, on bail, *and* under house arrest, they'll lock you up and the game is over.

No more career, no more money – no more anything – just plenty of time to wish you'd made better choices, stuck in Hawk Green with your pals Keats and McCloud.'

Rob stepped forward and tried his best to look in control. 'I thought you told me you had quit that shit?' he said.

'Oh, come on, Rob, not you as well! I was having a rough time of it. You had just told me Burns and COMCO rejected Dr. Chorlton's view on the Rohypnol in my system, and there was no way I was getting back on-air until after the trial. That could take a year. I was pissed-off and had a momentary lapse of concentration – you can't blame me for that. The show is my life; it's all I have left, for God's sake. And anyway, I didn't order any coke in the end, so this is all irrelevant.'

Rob tried his best to calm the situation.

'You said this dealer of yours, G, mentioned a girl had picked the drugs up on your behalf. Why don't we all just sit down and you can tell us more about that.'

Each man nodded his agreement and took a spot on one of the three large white leather sofas while Marty relayed every detail of his conversation with G.

'See, that's got to be a lead, right?' he concluded with forced optimism.

Andrew said nothing, lost in thought for the moment. Rob chipped in.

'I don't know, Marty, seems like a long walk to me, an Asian woman wearing knee-high boots in a cab on a Saturday night in Manchester – tricky one, mate.'

'Yeah, but let's not forget a *tall* Asian woman, almost six foot according to G, blonde with an intricate dragon tattoo on her right wrist. Not your everyday sight, even in Manchester. It's gotta be something? And it's a damn sight more than we had this morning – *which was zero!*'

'I guess so,' Rob said, sounding unconvinced.

Marty was not giving up and he directed his thoughts to Andrew now.

'For me, it does two things. Firstly, it proves someone else is involved in this whole thing besides White and me; and secondly, it gives us a potential witness to the murder – someone who's NOT dead and could potentially clear my name. Surely, that has to be a good thing, a bloody great thing, in fact. It gives us hope at least!'

'Yeah, of course,' Rob replied without conviction.

It was Andrew's turn to speak now, cutting across Marty whose mouth was already forming his reply.

'I know a guy who can find her,' Andrew said very matter-of-factly.

Marty smiled widely.

'I knew you would!'

Andrew Johnson was notorious for finding unorthodox solutions to his cases and with an almost ninety per cent win rate, his methods clearly worked.

Andrew ignored Marty and continued, his face focused and cold.

'He's ex-close-protection police; freelance now. Used to work for Blair and Brown, went all over the world with them; stopped some nasty people doing a Manchester version of the 7/7 bombings. Hard as nails and very effective. He left when Cameron got in, total lefty, couldn't work for a Tory government.'

'Sounds ideal,' Rob added sarcastically.

Andrew pressed on. 'He's expensive, but worth it. *When* he's available I use him to find "information" the police can't, if you know what I mean. He's incredibly well connected and has access to police and government data even the regular police don't have.' There was an air of excitement in Andrew's voice now.

'Well, let's call him now and get to work!' Marty said.

Andrew's tone was uncompromising.

'No, that's not the way he works. Only I speak to him. I'll brief him and get back to you. It's better that way; what he does isn't strictly legal – and the less *you* have to do with him the better.'

'OK,' Marty replied cautiously, 'as long as you're sure you got all the details? You didn't take any notes.'

Andrew stood and buttoned his suit jacket, tapping his right temple, 'I have it all in here, and I'm sure we can find your mystery woman. Leave it to me,' he said picking up his case and walking towards the door. Marty and Rob stood in unison and followed him out.

Just before he reached the front door, Andrew turned to face both men.

'Oh, and Marty…'

'Yes?

'If you do actually want to keep out of Hawk Green – make sure you stay off the nosebag, OK?'

CHAPTER 32

Twenty-four hours later, Marty was experiencing serious déjà vu, and Andrew was obviously feeling the same.

'Anyone else got the sense we've been here before?' he said with a smile as he opened his briefcase.

'Tell me about it,' Marty said. 'I'm going stir-crazy in here. There is absolutely nothing to do. I can't even listen to the radio or watch TV because everything is about *me* and the case.'

A slight exaggeration, but it was fair to say Marty's case was still high on the daily news agenda. However, with no new developments to report, the papers, radio and TV stations had resorted to simply regurgitating the facts to date as well as speculating, where they dared take the risk. As long as they steered clear of prejudicing the case against Marty, they were OK.

'You've got a home cinema, mate,' Rob reminded him, relaxing back on the chair and crossing his leg over his knee revealing expensive brown Italian loafers and sockless ankles under grey suit pants. 'You should take advantage of it, download a stack of porn and get some beers in!' he said laughing, but stopped quickly when he saw Marty's expression.

Marty stared at him silently for a moment, irritation etched on his face, before turning to face Andrew sitting down opposite him.

'You said you had something, Andrew?'

'Indeed I do,' Andrew replied, pulling a file out of his briefcase. He placed it on the glass coffee table between the men.

'Wow, that was quick!' Marty said.

'I told you he was good, plus he rushed it through for me as he's going overseas later in the week. That's why he's expensive. He wants five thousand for this little lot.'

Rob sat forward. 'Five grand? Jesus, forget expensive – he's extortionate!'

Marty was growing impatient. 'Never mind all that,' he snapped. 'It costs what it costs; we can worry about that later. What did your man dig up?'

Andrew opened the file and pulled out a black-and-white CCTV still shot of an Asian woman in what appeared to be a taxi, with blonde hair and sunglasses. He placed it in front of Marty who greedily picked it up and stared at it wide-eyed like a small boy on Christmas morning.

'Gentlemen, meet Rochelle,' Andrew said, with an air of theatrics.

'Jesus! Where did he get this?' Marty asked, his voice high with excitement.

'Like I said, he's very well connected. Actually, in this case it was quite easy by all accounts. Through his contacts, he was able to hack into the cab firm's database and cross-reference all cars to Didsbury on Saturday night. He simply matched roadside CCTV footage with the fender bender description we got from your "friend" G – and, voila! He came up with this little lady.'

'And where did this headshot come from?' Rob asked.

'Inside the cab; the taxi company keeps CCTV records for seven days and Rochelle happened to be sitting right in front of the camera; they're so small now she probably didn't even know it was there.'

Marty was very excited. 'So we've got her?' he asked, a broad smile spreading across his face. 'She can tell us what really happened?'

'Not quite,' Andrew said flatly. 'There are one or two complications around that, I'm afraid.'

He passed another photo over to Marty, this time of an Asian male's passport identity page.

'Who's this guy?' Marty asked, confused.

'That is Ashraf Tan.'

'And what has he got to do with Rochelle – or *me* for that matter?'

'Well, here's the thing,' Andrew said cautiously. 'Ashraf Tan *is* Rochelle.'

Marty took a moment to catch on.

'What, you mean… she's a *he?*'

'Not necessarily. Gender reassignment may well have taken place. We won't know for sure until we speak to Rochelle. What we do know as of now, is that Ashraf Tan came into the country five years ago on a student visa from Malaysia studying business and media at Manchester Met, but he dropped out of college a couple of years later and disappeared off the radar. We're not sure how it happened, but Ashraf is now believed to be working as a transgender prostitute. My guy thinks she's employed at The Purple Door on Demesne Road in Whalley Range – but as yet that's unconfirmed.'

'And does he have a home address for her?'

Andrew shook his head. 'I'm afraid not,' he replied. 'As you can imagine, the brothel doesn't keep employment records, so he's drawn a blank on the address for now.'

'But he's going to find her right?' Marty asked, his tone desperate.

Andrew flashed his 'work smile'; Marty had seen it before, usually when he was attempting to play his cards close to his chest.

'He'll find Rochelle, he's absolutely sure of that, but he can't guarantee timescales. He reckons the best option is to stake out The Purple Door and follow her home. Then he'll send the address to me.'

'OK, but can he give us *some kind* of idea of how long this could take?'

'If Rochelle was involved in the murder of White and was part of setting you up for it, it's likely she's not working alone. If that is the case, she may have been told to lay low for a while. We'll just have to wait and see. Hopefully she'll show up before my guy goes overseas.'

'Hopefully?' Marty didn't need that; he wanted certainty right now.

Rob tried to lift the mood, clapping his hands together and exhaling loudly, 'Right! Well, it's certainly looking more positive than twenty-four hours ago. If we find this girl... we're somewhere closer to proving your innocence, mate!' he said.

'*If* we can find her, Rob, *if*. That's an awfully small word to hang my entire life on right now.'

CHAPTER 33

The empty six-bedroom house felt bigger than ever as Marty meandered through the ground floor trying to find something, *anything*, to occupy his mind. Andrew and Rob had left two hours ago, both promising to keep Marty in the loop on any developments in the hunt for Rochelle. He was already struggling waiting for news. Could he trust Andrew's mystery man was working with the same urgency as he would himself? He wished he knew who he was; then perhaps, in some way, he could help him find Rochelle.

He wandered into the dining room with its floor-to-ceiling windows overlooking the deck and garden beyond. In the centre of the room sat a large chrome-framed, rectangular frosted glass dining table surrounded by a raft of chairs, leading the eye to the glorious view over the Cheshire countryside. This room had been Rebecca's favourite and in happier times they had entertained regularly into the wee small hours. Marty smiled as he allowed himself to remember his beautiful ex-wife.

Rebecca Fox had been the love of his life. A journalist at COMCO, they had met when Marty was a young enthusiastic presenter, covering any holiday and weekend shifts he could get his hands on. Blonde and bubbly with a great figure, he had fallen for her instantly. She hadn't quite seen him in the same way though, and it took many months of trying to finally persuade Rebecca. Their first date was at his favourite tapas restaurant in the city, El Torero. That night he was on sparkling form and had made her laugh so hard her mascara had run. They had giggled at how much she looked like a panda as they jumped in the cab back to her apartment and, fuelled by two bottles of red wine, had made passionate love into the early hours. From that moment, they had been inseparable.

They married quickly and lived a happy life together for almost eight years as both their careers advanced, him to breakfast radio stardom, her to television and anchor of the Network News national evening program. They fast became a powerful couple within the UK media and as they moved into their dream home in Prestbury, life, it seemed, could not get much better.

Then one tragic evening whilst attending the National Television Awards, their world had crumbled. Marty had been booked to host one of the evening's key awards, and with Rebecca herself nominated for the People's Choice gong for her work at Network News, Marty had decided to make an event of the evening at the National Hotel ballroom in Manchester city centre. He invited his father as well as best friend and producer David to attend the dinner; his mother, suffering from flu, had stayed home, much to Marty's disappointment.

The evening had started well enough but Marty had seemed uncharacteristically nervous. Over the course of the event, he drank far too much to drive home as originally planned and David, a recovering alcoholic, sober for seven years at that point, had offered to drive Marty's brand new Bentley, as well as his father, Peter, home.

Drunkenly hugging both men as the valet parking attendant delivered the car to the front of the hotel, Marty could never have imagined it would be the last time he would see either of them alive. Fifteen minutes later, both men died instantly when the powerful car came off the road and collided with a tree on the way to Marty's family home in Gatley. Dental records helped identify the charred remains of his father and best friend and worse still, the post-mortem claimed David was twice the legal limit at the time of the crash. No matter where it was written, or who was saying it, Marty could never believe his best friend since childhood and the man he treated as a brother had been back on the booze, or that he would ever have knowingly put his father's life at risk.

It was a dark night that changed him forever, as a little bit of Marty died too. The trauma of the event and the pain that followed also caused Rebecca to miscarry their unborn child at ten weeks.

Consumed by guilt, believing *he* should have been behind the wheel instead of David, he retreated into himself and began drinking heavily, using harder and harder drugs, eventually driving Rebecca into the arms of another man. She had tried to help him find his smile again, but as time moved on it was clear to everyone, apart from Marty himself, that work, alcohol and drugs were his only solace. It was as if he thought punishing himself every day would somehow make the pain go away.

Sadly, after eighteen months of trying, Rebecca Michaels finally left the family home and filed for divorce, plunging Marty into an even deeper depression.

Standing here now, Marty felt the huge loss of the woman who had helped him understand what true happiness meant. She had taught him to laugh at the world and himself, and to appreciate life. Since their divorce, he had grown used to the hollow feeling of emptiness that clung to him daily. He wished more than anything he could pick up the phone and call her, to tell her how much he still loved her and ask her to come home, but they had rarely spoken since the divorce and her life had changed dramatically. Still a successful TV news anchor working with the BBC News Channel in Manchester's Media City studios, Rebecca had moved on, marrying a banker and giving birth to twin boys, fulfilling her lifelong dream to be a mum.

As the pain gnawed at his insides, Marty turned away and left the room. He had to get out of the house and needed a drink. Grabbing a bottle of Scotch and a glass tumbler from the lounge room he pulled open the French doors and walked out into the warm early evening air.

The sun was going down and it felt 'close', as if a storm was brewing in the distance. Across the garden, he spied his red-and-black Ducati Scrambler motorcycle parked at the side of the garage – a plaything he had bought a year ago and hardly used. Still carrying the bottle of Scotch in one hand and a full tumbler of the liquor in the other, he wandered over to it before straddling the big machine as he gulped down the hot liquid in one movement. He refilled his glass and repeated the exercise before placing the bottle on the ground, the effect of the alcohol already hitting him as he sat back upright, a deep sense of agitation bubbling inside him. He was still angry with Rob for leaving him in Hawk Green and pissed-off at Andrew because he was still not clear of the charges. He was mad at his mum for being vulnerable; mums were supposed to be strong, always there for you. Then, as his thoughts turned to the mystery man supposedly out there trying to find Rochelle, his rage almost boiled over. This woman was his only chance of avoiding a long prison sentence and a life in hell. So why hadn't he found her already? Surely it couldn't be that hard to find a tattooed, six-foot Asian woman in a Whalley Range brothel for God's sake?

Marty gulped down another tumbler of Scotch. Attempting to calm his racing mind he gazed across the three acres of garden in front of him, leading to the tree-lined lane running the length of his property into the farmland beyond. Way in the distance, he could just about make out the top of the Sky Tower, home to the Metropolitan Hotel in Manchester city centre and scene of his arrest. Staring at it, he was suddenly possessed by a moment of clarity and knew exactly what he needed to do, and without hesitation, jumped off the bike and ran headlong into the house.

CHAPTER 34

It had been surprisingly easy to find Rochelle at The Purple Door massage parlour in Whalley Range. Calling on the untraceable mobile he used for contacting his dealer, Marty had quickly ascertained Rochelle was indeed working that evening, and would be available for a 'consultation' at midnight. He was in luck according to the very forthcoming receptionist, who explained tonight would be Rochelle's last for a while. Giving a false name, Marty had booked Rochelle for an hour-long 'massage' and spa; code for what he suspected could be anything his sexual appetites desired. As he imagined confronting her, a surge of excitement rushed through him.

He immediately called Andrew to pass on the details to his man on the ground, so *he* could take the midnight appointment and ensure Rochelle came clean. Annoyingly, Andrew's phone had gone straight to voicemail. After leaving instructions to call back urgently, he called Rob, but again got no answer. The one time he truly needed them, and they both decided to go missing.

Marty tried both men repeatedly for the next hour, his frustration mounting with every missed ring; after tonight, Rochelle would disappear. He paced the floor willing his phone to ring, swearing repeatedly under his breath. He checked his watch, 10.49pm; the appointment was just over an hour away. Trying to calm his nerves, he walked onto the back deck and

159

stared out into the night, racking his brain for a solution that would not come. After a few minutes, he called Rob and Andrew one last time, each without success. *Dammit!*

He checked his watch again: 10.57pm.

Staring across at his Ducati, Marty made a decision.

Gathering his phone, he took a deep breath as he attempted to sound sober and dialled Rob's number. This time when it landed on voicemail his message was calm and steady; he knew what he needed to do.

'Rob, it's me. Look, I've found Rochelle and I'm going to talk to her. I know I'm not supposed to leave the house and what that could mean if I'm caught, but it's vital I speak to her *tonight*. I'll explain more when you finally call me back.' He paused for a moment, as if testing his resolve to do what he was about to. 'Look, just call me back ASAP. I've gotta go!'

He ended the call, and exhaled loudly, before heading back into the house to get his keys and crash helmet.

CHAPTER 35

Despite the whisky running through his veins, Marty felt confident he could handle the Ducati Scrambler at night. Zipping up his protective jacket and slipping on his gloves, he made his way out to the big machine, his right arm looped through his crash helmet.

Fully aware there were still some die-hard paps and journalists at the front of the house, he rolled the bike silently across the grass towards the back lane and farmland. The private security team hired by Rob had fortified the lane the day of their arrival and a couple of men, permanently positioned at either end, had ensured his path into the fields behind his house was unobstructed. Having ridden trial bikes as a kid, he was confident he could handle the terrain ahead, although riding through fields in darkness was certainly new.

He unlocked the large metal gate at the bottom of the garden and slipped quietly through, walking the Scrambler down the lane towards the heavy wooden gate that secured the entrance to the farmer's field. The last thing he wanted was the GPS built into his phone pinpointing his location to those looking to find him, so he switched off data roaming, the wifi connection and Bluetooth. A moment later, the bike roared into life and his journey into the city was underway.

Marty chose to ride without lights across the first couple of fields as he attempted to make his way, undetected, to the A34 that would lead him back towards the city. After a couple of near misses with tree stumps and rabbits, he reached the main road within ten minutes. Checking both ways to make sure there were no cars coming, he joined the carriageway and turned on the headlights before accelerating away towards Manchester's CBD, the deep growl of the engine filling the night air.

*

The Purple Door looked like any other Victorian townhouse in Manchester. Tucked down a residential road just off the main drag of Princess Parkway, you would think the residents were out of town. With few lights visible there were absolutely no clues alluding to the activity happening behind the ornate shutters covering the windows at the front of the house.

Marty approached the front door with caution.

Many times during his career he had attempted to expose this very brothel to Manchester police, but had drawn a blank at every turn; it was widely rumoured some of those within the higher echelons of the force were regular patrons of the illicit den. Marty had often attempted to draw the public into the debate around prostitution, but The Purple Door had somehow escaped any real criticism or condemnation from the people of Manchester. Under the radar for twenty years, Mancunians had accepted it.

Standing outside the dark foreboding building, his best chance of staying out of jail waiting for him inside, he was glad those attempts had failed.

Arriving at exactly midnight, he pressed the intercom at the front door and hid his face from the CCTV cameras above his head as he waited for a response. A few moments passed before the silver box attached to the red-brick wall in front of him sparked into life and a deep male voice barked at him.

'State your business?'

Marty continued to cover his face.

'I'm here to see Rochelle, I have an appointment at midnight,' he said nervously.

'Name?'

Marty hesitated. 'Er… Jack Steel,' he said giving the false name he'd made up as a young boy, and used regularly in his teens to get him out of trouble.

'Remove the hat, please,' the gruff voice ordered through the tiny speaker in front of him.

Marty's heart rate elevated and his breathing shortened, a shot of cold adrenalin rushing through his chest and neck. He decided to bluff it out and said nothing.

A moment passed before the voice barked again, 'Take off the bloody hat!'

This time Marty did as told and removed the hat slowly, attempting to keep his face away from the camera, perched above his head.

The voice growled again, 'Face the camera.'

Again, Marty did nothing.

The voice returned, angry and impatient.

'Look, mate, I really don't care who you are but I need to see your face before I can let you in. It's policy, so look into the camera above the door or your appointment is cancelled, OK?'

Marty stood motionless trying to figure out his next move.

The intercom barked again, 'And I haven't got all night!'

He finally faced the camera, looking straight at the little black lens, which appeared to stare back at him. His heart pounded like a maniacal drummer. A million thoughts flooded his brain: *who was on the other end of that lens, had they recognised him, was he in danger, were they calling the police?*

Finally, the small speaker crackled back into life.

'Ok… push the door.' A loud buzz signalled the door had unlocked.

Marty steadied himself on the wall and allowed his breathing to slow and his heart rate followed. He felt sick, his legs suddenly heavy and any kind of movement awkward. Wiping sweat from his face and replacing his cap, he stepped inside, greeted by a long, narrow corridor covered in purple velvet wallpaper running down both walls, above a thick white shagpile carpet underfoot.

He moved forward carefully towards the soft music and soon found himself in a reception area. It reminded him of a small boutique hotel he and Rebecca had stayed in during a trip to Barcelona. At the centre stood a tall, old-school curved reception desk, in front of an arch leading to an unknown and obscured room. Behind it sat a professional-looking receptionist. Only her torso was exposed but Marty noted her black silk blouse open at the neck with a small but attractive line of cleavage exposed. She had a pretty but relatively ordinary face, and dark black hair, cut into a severe bob with a razor-straight fringe that sat millimetres from her eyes. To her left stood a man-mountain and, for a split second, Marty mistook him for Bovalino; his size, shape, skin-colouring and hair were almost identical. After an involuntary double-take Marty realised – to his considerable relief – it was not.

The big man straightened, his eyes fixed on Marty.

The receptionist smiled as she spoke and her tone was warm. 'Can I help you?'

'I'm here to see Rochelle,' Marty replied quietly.

'Mr. Steel?'

'That's correct'

'Have you been to The Purple Door before?'

Marty shot a glance back at the big man who maintained his gaze.

'Er, no… first time.'

She passed over two white towels and a matching robe with a large locker key balanced on top of the pile. 'Please change into this robe and wait in the lounge. Rochelle won't be long,' she said warmly, pointing to a door just beyond the man-mountain. 'Drake here will show you through.'

Marty nervously took them, the process feeling eerily reminiscent of his first day in Hawk Green – *without the key of course!* As 'Drake' turned and opened the door behind him, Marty followed and they moved through a dimly lit corridor of red walls. A moment later, they stopped at a door marked 'Lockers'. The big man held it open in silence as he signalled for Marty to enter.

Suddenly he had a very bad feeling about the plan and turned to walk away, but Drake's vice-like grip locked on his left shoulder, propelling him back towards the room.

'Get changed here and then follow the signs for the lounge,' Drake said flatly.

'What?'

Drake pointed his right arm to the other end of the dark room. 'I said, get changed here and then follow the signs for the lounge. And make sure you either take anything valuable with you or put them in your locker; shit gets nicked here all the time.'

Marty nodded to the big man who closed the door without a word.

Still holding his towel and robes, Marty surveyed the space and realised he was in a changing room about the size of a large family bathroom; the walls were filled with lockers, some locked, others wide open, with small wooden benches in front.

He quickly undressed, placing his clothes in the locker provided as he prepared to move to the critical stage of his plan; in a few moments, he would finally come face to face with Rochelle.

CHAPTER 36

Sitting in a crisp white robe over black boxer shorts, Marty tapped the arms of the cream leather chair waiting for Rochelle to appear.

The room itself was the size of a double bedroom, which Marty imagined it had probably once been. The ceilings were high with ornate period detail around the central light fitting still intact and surprisingly well maintained. Large wooden shutters covered the three tall windows to his right, keeping the world on the other side out. It was obvious that somebody cared about this place, and the details *mattered*. The walls were warmly lit and painted red, the carpet beneath his feet similar to the entrance hall: cream, deep and luxurious. Fixed rigidly between two identical unmarked doors on the wall opposite him, a flat-screen TV played music videos silently. To his left a small glass-fronted fridge, containing bottles of water and soda, hummed a gentle rhythm.

There was still no sign of Rochelle. *What was taking so long?*

Marty scanned the room looking for anything untoward, not that he knew what *untoward* would like in a place like *this*. His mind began to race ahead of him. *Was this delay a ruse? Had they recognised him outside and let him in on purpose; was an ambush about to happen?*

The alcohol had almost completely worn off now and his nerves were getting the better of him.

He drummed his fingers loudly on the arms of the chair as he tried to distract himself, but could not avoid the stark reality of his situation. For all intents and purposes, he was a sitting duck. He had voluntarily walked deep into the heart of a notorious brothel, one frequented by high-ranking police officers as well as known and hardened criminals with potential connections to McCloud and Keats. His mobile phone, and only connection to the outside world, was in his locker. Plus, the woman he was here to meet had, on Saturday night, tracked down his ultra-secretive drug dealer, utilised his top-secret and very protracted buying routine, as well as handing over a large amount of cash for an order on *his* behalf. All without Marty knowing a thing.

The absurdity of it all hit him like hammer to the head.

He jumped to his feet, almost rolling his ankle in the ill-fitting slippers as he did. He had made a *huge* mistake; he had to get out *right now*. He moved back towards the door he had entered through and grabbed the handle roughly. A small black swipe-card entry system sat neatly next to the door; a tiny red light illuminated, indicating it was locked. Crossing the room, he tried the two doors on either side of the TV but the same security system was in place. *Shit!* He tried the heavy window shutters next with no luck. His eyes darted around the room searching every nook and space for a way out, but he was trapped.

How could he have been so stupid?

Circling the room, the walls appeared to move towards him. Initially it had felt spacious and open, offering him a potential way out of his nightmare if he could talk to Rochelle. Now, locked in, it felt small, oppressive and appeared to be shrinking.

His mind suddenly replayed the horror of the rape in Hawk Green and a childlike helplessness clawed at his throat, his heart pumping wildly. He wanted to cry out, run away and hide. His breathing began to shorten as adrenalin surged through his body. He wanted to vomit and began to feel faint; he had to sit down quickly before he collapsed. Slumping into the chair, he stared mindlessly at the TV screen in front of him as the music videos played out silently, before placing his head in his hands, his long hair falling through his fingers and covering his face.

At that moment, the door clicked open and Marty looked up, his face hidden under his hair. A tall, elegant Asian woman stood before him smiling. She had soft features and long dark glossy hair. Her impressive legs ran into black stilettos, her torso wrapped in a black corset with white trim. She was a strikingly beautiful creature and for a moment, Marty lost all fear as she stepped forward, the door clicking shut behind her. She spoke softly but with a heavy accent; Malaysian, Marty assumed.

'Mr. Steel, I am Rochelle, welcome to The Purple Door; whatever you want shall be my pleasure.' Despite the accent, her tone was silky smooth, deeper than most women, but undeniably sexy.

'May I sit?' she asked pointing to the chair opposite Marty.

She had not recognised him. He nodded his agreement whilst keeping his head tilted upwards, hair still covering his face.

Rochelle sat in one elegant movement, crossing her legs seductively as she made herself comfortable, before leaning closer and speaking again through her wide, perfect smile.

'So what would you like me to do, Mr. Steel, or can I call you Jack?'

Marty peeled his hair back with both hands to reveal his face.

'How about you call me Marty – and you can start by telling me why you set me up!'

The shock was evident on Rochelle's face, her body recoiling instinctively as she tried to evade Marty's hand which shot out and locked on her right wrist in a flurry of movement.

'I don't know what you're talking about,' she pleaded, struggling to maintain the softness of her female form. She tried to stand but Marty's grip tightened as he leaned in close to her face.

'You'd better start telling me the truth and quickly, Ashraf Tan!' he said twisting her arm over to reveal an intricate dragon tattoo, just as his dealer G had described it.

Her mouth fell open for a moment, before quickly regaining her composure.

'That's right, I know all about you, Ashraf. So will immigration if you don't tell me what I want to know. It will be bye-bye UK and back to Malaysia. So stop fucking me about and start talking!'

Rochelle dropped her head towards the floor. She held it there for a moment before lifting it again and facing Marty. Her eyes were moist and she looked ready to burst into tears at any moment.

'OK, OK. Please let go of my arm. I'll answer your questions. I cannot go back to Malaysia.'

Marty released his grip slowly. 'No funny business – OK?'

Rochelle nodded and sat back in the chair, brushing her hair away from her face and trying her best to look composed. She took a deep breath and smiled awkwardly.

'What do you want to know?' she asked calmly.

'Did you kill Paul White?' Marty asked flatly.

Rochelle shook her head vigorously, 'No! I loved Paul, he was my soulmate; I could never hurt him.'

'Then *who* did and *why?*'

'Please don't ask me that, not here.' Rochelle's eyes darted towards the double doors.

'Look, Ashraf…'

'I am Rochelle! I will not answer to Ashraf; Ashraf is dead.'

'OK, just tell me who killed White – because I know for sure it wasn't me. There were so many different drugs in my system I couldn't have walked to the bathroom unaided, never mind strangle a fit and healthy young man.'

Rochelle's body flinched as Marty described White's violent death. He sensed from her reaction they had obviously been close.

'Why did you buy the drugs on my behalf?'

Again, Rochelle looked towards the double doors.

'What's on the other side of the doors, Rochelle? Are we being watched?'

Rochelle leaned in closer to Marty and whispered, 'I don't know, there are cameras and people watch sometimes yes, but the sound is not so good. They could be listening, I don't know.'

'Who's they?'

'Security.'

'Do they know I'm here?'

Rochelle shook her head. 'Drake, the man who let you in, he's not a smart man. He pays no attention.'

'What about the receptionist?'

'Debra? She's different. The owner's daughter, very smart; she knows everything that happens in here.'

'I doubt we have much time in that case. Please, tell me – who killed White?'

'I don't know. It wasn't supposed to happen. They offered Paul money to take you to your room and have sex with you. I was there to take pictures.'

'You were there?'

Rochelle nodded.

'Jesus! So why the hell were you taking pictures?'

'I don't know. It was a simple deal, pictures of you and Paul having sex and taking drugs together.'

'So why use my dealer? Why go to all that trouble and expose yourself?'

'I didn't know who he was, I just followed the instructions to pick up the drugs and take them to the hotel.'

'So, what happened in the room, Rochelle?'

She looked to the floor once more, her hair falling forward and covering her face again.

'Did Paul have sex with me?'

Rochelle nodded and lifted her hand to her face as she began to sob silently.

'But I passed out?'

'Paul slipped a Viagra in your drink along with something to make you sleep. Then when I arrived he gave you oral sex for a while and I took pictures and filmed it.'

'That's rape, damn it!' Marty said angrily.

Tears rolled down Rochelle's cheeks now as she spoke. 'I told him not to do it,' she sobbed. 'I kept saying it was wrong but he just told me to think of the money.'

'Where are the photos and video now?'

'I don't know. When Paul was finished you were still unconscious, and I went home. He was supposed to leave soon after to take everything to the man who hired us. But he never came home and when I saw the news – a man had been found dead in your hotel room – I knew it was Paul.'

'Who hired you?'

'I don't know his name, Paul did it all.'

'Why did you do it? *Why me?*'

'I didn't know who you were. It was just a job. I needed the money to pay for my surgery. Paul wanted me to be happy; I was finally going to fully transition. It was just supposed to be photos and video; no one was supposed to die.'

Marty sat back in his chair trying to come to terms with the information. *Why set him up with the photos? Why go to the trouble of using his dealer? Why kill White?* None of it made any sense.

He leaned in close, 'How much did they pay you?'

'Nothing!'

'What? I don't understand.'

Rochelle sobbed heavily as she spoke now.

'Paul was due to exchange the photos for twenty thousand that night.'

'Twenty grand? Is that all it costs to ruin my life?'

Rochelle nodded.

'He never came home. We got nothing.'

Marty studied her in silence.

'Right, that's it. You have to come with me to the police and tell them the truth.'

'No! I'm leaving the UK tomorrow for good. I'm going to Europe to start again.'

'You can't leave; you're the only person who can prove I didn't kill White!'

'His name was Paul, and I loved him,' she sobbed.

Marty realised he needed to change tack. He spoke softly and warmly; a technique he used many times in the studio to get what he needed from a reluctant interviewee.

'I'm so sorry, Rochelle. Look, I need your help to prove I didn't kill Paul so his real killer can be brought to justice. We can do that, together,' he said as he placed both hands around her wrists. 'Please, for Paul.'

Rochelle stared straight at Marty before shaking her head.

'No, I can't, I'm sorry. Please leave.'

Marty was suddenly angry, his hands gripping tight around Rochelle's wrists. She cried out, 'You're hurting me!'

He was not about to give up.

'You have to help me! I can't go back to prison. Please! I need you to talk to the police.'

'I can't. I'm leaving tomorrow and I never want to see this city or anyone in it ever again. I'm sorry, but I have to go,' she said as she stood up quickly and headed for the twin doors.

Marty leapt to his feet, '*I'll* give you the twenty grand!' he blurted.

Rochelle stopped and turned to face Marty.

'I'll give you the twenty grand and you can disappear, become who you really want – *who Paul wanted you to be.*'

Rochelle stood watching him, and Marty's face softened as he tried desperately to persuade her.

'Just record your version of events, I'll get you the money and you can leave the country before I share it with anyone, I promise.'

Rochelle stepped back closer to him now.

'I want it in cash.'

'Of course, whatever you want.'

Rochelle nodded her agreement. 'Meet me near the airport tomorrow night,' she said handing him her business card. 'Text me your number tomorrow and I'll send you the location when it's safe. Bring the cash. Just you, anyone else comes near me, and the deal is off. I'll disappear.'

'OK, sure. I can do that,' Marty said realising he had to find twenty grand in just over thirteen hours.

'For twenty thousand, I can give you something more than the confession. I have videos of others like you,' Rochelle said.

'What?' Marty asked.

'Paul and I had done this before, many times. He knew we were dealing with bad people and felt we needed some insurance – so he always made copies of the videos he was involved in before he handed them over.'

'How many do you have? And who's on them?'

'Over fifty I'd guess; I don't know the people in the videos, but Paul did and he said they were powerful people who would not want them to be seen. He guessed they were for blackmail and extortion. So he made copies for us to use if we got into trouble. He was also very smart with computers. He managed to hack into the business records of the man who hired him. I have those too. He put them on a stick and told me to keep them safe.'

'Jesus,' Marty whispered.

'You bring the cash tomorrow, I'll give you everything.'

Marty nodded without speaking.

'I have to go now,' Rochelle said and headed towards the door. 'I'll tell reception you changed your mind. The doors will unlock automatically. You'll only pay the booking fee.'

Marty opened his mouth to speak but Rochelle was already gone.

CHAPTER 37

Bounding through the reception area, Marty rushed past Drake without speaking. He nodded quickly to the girl behind the desk who was talking on the phone, as he dropped two twenty pound notes on the counter. 'I changed my mind,' he mumbled and continued walking at pace as Drake let out an audible grunt of disgust. Marty could have sworn he heard the word 'homo' muttered behind him.

Outside on the darkened main street he grabbed at his iPhone; *finally*, a signal. He punched in the access code and hit the flashing voicemail button as it pinged twice, indicating two new messages. The first was from Rob urging caution on whatever he was planning, that he wanted to meet – to talk, *before* Marty did something he may regret. The second was from Andrew, his sharp public-school tones cutting and acidic.

'Marty, what the *hell* are you doing at The Purple Door? Seriously, I'm trying very hard to keep you out of prison but you are not helping me. If you value your freedom, call me the moment you get this! *The moment!*'

How had he known he was at The Purple Door? He picked out Andrew's number from his favourites and it seemed to take an age for him to answer. When he finally did, his tone left Marty in no doubt he wasn't a happy man.

'*Finally!* I've been calling you for over an hour. Where are you?'

'Look, I know what you're going to say, Andrew, but I had to see Rochelle tonight.'

Andrew cut across him; his tone was urgent and anxious.

'Look Marty, if you're anywhere near The Purple Door get away right now. Run as fast as you can, and as far away as possible, the police will be there in a matter of minutes! They're on their way to arrest you *right now.*'

'The police, but how could they possibly know I was here?'

As if on cue, the sound of sirens in the distance wafted on the evening breeze, getting louder as they approached from the city centre.

'That's not important, Marty. If you want to stay out of Hawk Green, you need to get away now.'

'OK, I'm on the Ducati; I can be miles away in minutes.'

'No Marty, you can't use the bike; the police are already looking for it and it's hardly quiet. You'll have to go on foot.'

'But where?'

'I don't know Marty; use your imagination. Just bloody run, *now!* I'll call again soon.'

He did not wait for Andrew to finish, instead killing the call and running up Manley Road towards the intersection with Spring Bridge Street. Once he reached it, he shot a glance left and right as the sirens howled ever louder behind him; he guessed they were just a couple of streets away now. Running like a child with his head down, he darted left towards Alexandra Park. Zigzagging his way through the parked cars on the darkened street as he tried to stay out of sight of the police cars, which had come to a stop, somewhere behind him. He was totally out of shape and his prison injuries had still not healed, making progress much slower than needed.

As he reached the park and entered through the gate by the pond, he was sure he heard footsteps from the shadows, but when he stopped to focus on where they were coming from, saw nothing. Had he imagined it? He took a few seconds to catch his breath; his heart was beating so quickly it felt like it could burst. Still, he had to keep moving. He checked once more for a tail, but saw nothing, so moved on quickly through the shadows of the trees as fast as his heavy legs and burning lungs would allow. Finally, when he was sure he was far enough away from the sirens, he stopped in the darkness, slumping against a wide tree trunk, gasping for air.

Still struggling to regulate his breathing and slow his heart rate, he squatted forwards steadying himself on his fingertips, before falling fully onto his hands and knees. He coughed as his body retched; the lactic acid surging through him making him nauseous and light-headed.

His phone rang loudly causing him to panic, fearing it would give away his location. Grabbing wildly at it in his pocket, he wiped his drooling mouth before swiping the answer icon to the unknown Manchester number, but said nothing.

Andrew's tone was tense.

'Marty? Is that you? Are you OK? Did you get away?'

'Yes…' he said weakly between short breaths. 'How… did you… know about The Purple Door and the police?' he asked as he rolled heavily onto his backside and leaned back against the tree, his eyes scanning the area back towards Spring Bridge Street.

'The guy I had looking for Rochelle spotted you going in and called me,' Andrew said.

Marty's breathing was slowly returning somewhere near to normal. 'You had him *follow* me?' he rasped.

'No, he was stationed outside.'

'But I didn't see him,' Marty protested.

'Of course you didn't, and that's why I pay him three hundred pounds an hour, you weren't supposed to see him and neither was Rochelle. His plan was to follow her home tonight and, shall we say, *persuade* her to talk to us.'

'That still doesn't explain how the police knew I was there.'

'I must admit that bit is puzzling. But then this is the GMP – they have eyes and spies everywhere.'

'But how did you know they were coming for me?' he asked.

'My guy is well-connected; he also has a police scanner and your name came up just after you walked out of The Purple Door. He contacted me immediately. I was on the phone to him when you called, actually; thank God for "call waiting" or you'd be heading back to Hawk Green.'

'I'm never going back there, Andrew. I'm a dead man if I do.'

'I understand, Marty, but I'm afraid to say it's looking more likely now.'

'But I didn't do anything!' Marty protested.

'The simple fact is you broke the terms of your bail and it's unlikely the prosecution or judge will let you stay on the street. Your best bet is to meet me at my office and we'll work out a plan to talk to Josh Lei. Ask for forgiveness; say it was a moment of madness from a desperate man. See if I can get you into a low security detention centre until the trial, in isolation *for your own protection*. It's the best we can hope for now.'

'Best we can hope for? No chance, *no way*, Andrew. I'm not spending another night in prison, ever again – I'd rather die. I'm meeting Rochelle tomorrow. She says she'll admit on camera that I couldn't have killed White because of what they did to me in that room. She also has copies of videos she thinks could help me. White gave them to her as security.'

Andrew snorted. 'And you believe her? A call girl?'

'Seriously, what choice do I have? Right now, my life is over. I have to believe there's a way out of this, and I need your help!'

Andrew paused for a moment on the other end of the phone.

'Look, Marty, I know you're scared and want out of this situation, but we have to box clever. Let me come and get you and we can work this out together. I can talk to the prosecution; keep you safe. Why not let me talk to Rochelle on your behalf, that way *I* can protect you.'

Marty was in no mood to surrender or put his life in the hands of anyone else. 'No Andrew,' he insisted. 'I'm doing it *my way*. I'm meeting Rochelle tomorrow. I need to make sure she comes through as promised.'

'Are you saying you don't *trust* me?' Andrew said, clearly agitated.

'Look, mate, I don't trust *anyone* right now. My life is on the line and I'll do whatever it takes to protect myself.'

There was a long pause before Andrew finally responded. 'OK, Marty, we can do it your way, but please, let me help you. You need to listen to my instructions carefully if you're going to stay out of custody.'

'OK,' Marty said, getting to his feet. 'But be quick, I need to keep moving.'

'Well you can't go home; my guy says they've already sent a couple of cars to your place in case you show up.'

'Shit! Well I guess I'll have to get to my mum's place.'

'Not a good idea, I'm afraid. They'll be all over that within the hour.'

'You're really not helping, Andrew!' Marty barked.

'Don't shoot the messenger, Marty. This is your reality right now. Your best option is a faceless hotel. Somewhere with an automated check-in like a Premier Inn. I can send you my business credit card details to use.'

Marty considered what Andrew was saying before responding, 'OK, there's one by the Mancunian Way I can try. It's out of the way and hopefully full of tourists.'

'Great. And please make sure you don't call anyone you know, not even Rob, as the police can trace it.'

'But what about this call now?' Marty asked.

'Payphone,' Andrew said very matter-of-factly. 'I've been in the game a long time, Marty; I know how to play it. That said, they'll be tracing your mobile soon enough so I need as much info as quickly as possible, and then you need to switch off your phone.'

Marty could not comprehend the conversation he was having with his own lawyer. It was like something from a spy movie, on the run, staying under the radar and off the grid, totally surreal.

Andrew continued with his instructions. 'Now remember, you pay cash and avoid ATMs like the plague, your credit cards are no good to you now. Aside from walking into Ashton House, using a credit card is the quickest way to get yourself caught. I'll call you again in an hour.'

'Right! Got it,' Marty said before a hefty pregnant pause.

'What is it, Marty?' Andrew asked eventually.

'Look, mate, I'm gonna need some cash.'

'OK, that makes sense, how much do you need?'

Marty hesitated for a moment, 'Twenty grand.'

'Twenty grand? Jesus, Marty! What for?'

'It's a long story…'

'It always bloody is with you!' Andrew said, half laughing. 'We clearly don't have time for that, so best you give me the super-quick version!'

CHAPTER 38

Alexandra Park fell quiet around Marty as he switched off his iPhone, pushing it into his jeans pocket, the cars running along the Princess Parkway dual-carriageway a hundred feet away, the only sound breaking through.

Andrew had assured him he would do his utmost to raise the £20,000 in time for his meet with Rochelle, but was unable to guarantee the money in cash, which would almost certainly be a problem. He racked his brain for a way to access the cash himself, drawing a frustrating blank at every turn. He would have to hope Andrew would come through.

Content he had not been spotted, he scanned the grassland and trees around him, and began to relax for a moment. The sound of cracking wood caused him to tense, his eyes darting back and forth across the trees and shadows, but he saw nothing. Cautiously, he very slowly lifted himself up onto his feet as he continued to search the darkness around him. There was another loud crack, closer this time.

A burst of adrenalin shot through Marty's body and his heart began pounding so loudly he could no longer hear anything else. His head whipped left and right; but he found nothing in the darkness. He was rooted to the spot, as if glued to the ground. His heart pounded louder, each beat gaining pace with every second that passed. His mouth bone-dry, he desperately needed to swallow but feared the loud crack of his throat would give him away. Regaining control of his limbs he began to edge sideways to an illuminated area of the park, close to the road which was about fifty feet from his current position. Step by step, he moved closer to the light. Another loud crack, in front of him this time, stopped him in his tracks. Holding his breath, he attempted to remain unheard.

As the silhouette came into view, an icy chill ran the length of his body. The athletically built man was well over six foot tall, standing motionless in the darkness staring straight at him, a hooded top casting his face into darkness. Like a Mexican standoff, both men said nothing.

Suddenly Marty's feet were moving without instruction, stepping slowly backwards at first, quickly gaining momentum as he turned to the right of the silhouette and began sprinting towards the road. The man immediately followed. Marty's legs and lungs burned as he drove them into action. At forty-two and weighing over sixteen-stone, he felt like he was running through treacle, as the loud and rapid footsteps behind him drew ever closer. He could hear Andrew's words now – *Run, Marty, run!*

Lifting his knees high and pumping his arms, he began to pick up speed but the man directly behind him matched him step for step. Still he pushed every fibre of his body but he could feel the man gaining ground to within touching distance – *Run, Marty, run!* It was no use. A split second later, the full weight of his pursuer enveloped him, forcing him to the ground.

Winded and lying with his face in the grass, he tried to shout for help but there was no air in his lungs as the man lay heavily upon him. Marty's mind flashed back to Hawk Green and he began to kick out, jabbing his elbows backwards, but whoever was above him was too strong and he quickly found himself flipped over onto his back. The man used his knees to subdue Marty's flailing arms before placing his thick, heavy hands over Marty's nose and mouth. He moved his face closer, the hooded top still hiding his features.

'Hold still and be quiet… I'm here to help you, Marty.'

Despite the man's reassurances, Marty felt a desperate need to get away and he began to wriggle like a rugby league player breaking loose from a tackle. He tried again to shout through the hands covering his mouth.

'Shut the fuck up or we're both dead!' the man added, his face suddenly within inches of Marty's and visible in the glare of the street lights casting their glow from the Parkway. Marty stopped struggling and stared up at a face he now recognised – Simon Williams, the Guardian reporter.

'I'm taking my hands away now, Marty, so I'm trusting you to be quiet,' Williams whispered, nodding as he released his grip and lifted himself off Marty's chest, before kneeling silently on the grass as he waited for him to respond.

Marty pulled himself up onto his hands, staring at Williams. After a long moment of silence, he finally spoke.

'What are you doing?'

'I'm trying to save your life, you idiot.'

Marty was even more confused. 'Save my life? From what?'

'More like from *whom*,' Williams said.

'What do you mean? The police?'

Williams looked around them before speaking.

'Look Marty, it's complicated, but the long and the short of it is, I'm one of the few people in the world who *doesn't* think you killed White. In fact, I have good reason to believe you were set up to take the fall for his murder.'

Marty shifted awkwardly on his hands for a moment before joining Williams on his knees.

'I knew it! Who set me up? Who was it? Tell me!' Marty said a bit too loudly for Williams.

'Ssh! Not here, it's not safe. You need to come with me now.'

Marty lifted himself up onto his feet.

'*No fucking way.* I'm not going anywhere with you or anyone for that matter. Not now, not ever,' he said.

'I know this is tough for you to believe, but I can promise you I'm not trying to set you up. I really do want to help you.'

'Why? What's in it for you?'

'The story, of course; the exclusive,' replied Williams.

'What exclusive?'

'Mate, come with me and I'll explain. Trust me; you need to hear what I have to say.'

Marty shook his head and began to walk away in the direction of the Parkway.

'No thanks, I need to get away from here and out of sight. I'm not going back to Hawk Green.'

Williams ran to catch him up and blocked his path, pressing his hands against Marty's chest.

'Look, Marty, I swear to God this isn't a set-up. I've been following this story for the last *two years*, long before you became part of it, and I'm getting close to cracking it wide open, but I can't do it without you.'

Marty said nothing as he processed this new information.

'I'll give you *anything* you need,' Williams said desperately.

Marty thought for a moment.

'*Anything?*' he said.

'Well, within reason. I can't promise a million pounds or a Ferrari, but I'll do what I can.'

'How about twenty grand?' Marty asked flatly.

Williams appeared stunned by the directness of the request. He laughed before responding, 'You're serious?'

'Damn right I am!'

Williams shrugged his shoulders. 'OK, sure. I guess that's doable.'

'Cash!' Marty shot back. 'It has to be cash and I need it when the banks open in the morning.'

Williams again took a moment to respond.

'Yeah, OK. Whatever.'

'No *whatever*. I need certainty. Can you get me twenty grand cash by midday tomorrow?' Marty asked impatiently.

'Yes! Yes, I can, *definitely*,' Williams replied confidently.

Marty stared at Williams to see if he could spot any signs he was lying but it was too dark. In truth, he had few options to raise the cash before Rochelle disappeared, and he was willing to take the risk. He extended his hand out to Williams.

'Ok, for twenty grand cash, you've got yourself a deal.'

'Just one thing,' replied Williams. 'What's it for?'

CHAPTER 39

'Keep your head down,' Simon Williams had ordered before the ten-minute car journey from Whalley Range to his apartment in Manchester's uber-trendy Northern Quarter. To avoid any CCTV en route, Williams had suggested Marty lie across the back seat of his 3-Series BMW with a picnic blanket over his head. To say he felt vulnerable was an understatement. As the car rolled onwards, he prayed Williams was telling him the truth and he was safe; the alternative was too frightening to contemplate.

Throughout the journey, he had tried to orientate himself, listening intently to the sounds around him, following the movement of the car left and right. To his considerable relief, when the car finally stopped, he recognised the buildings surrounding him as belonging to the Northern Quarter. Williams was true to his word, *so far so good.* They waited for a moment as the metal gates to the apartment block rolled back, before Williams guided them below ground to his private space beneath the building. He killed the engine and they sat in silence for a moment before Williams spoke. 'Right,' he said, 'we need to get you upstairs unseen, which will be easier said than done in this place; there are more security cameras than MI6.'

Marty glanced across the silent car park. 'How far do we have to go?'

'Top floor,' Williams replied. 'Penthouse,' he added.

'Nice and easy then,' Marty said sarcastically.

Williams handed Marty a baseball cap and dark sunglasses.

'I know it's a bit clichéd but it's all we've got right now, and it's better than putting a blanket over your head!' he laughed.

Marty nodded and Williams opened the driver's door. 'Come on, let's get you inside and out of sight,' he said as he stepped out, opening Marty's door gently to let him out.

They moved cautiously across the brightly lit car park, Marty taking special care to keep his head down and out of clear view of the CCTV cameras positioned across the garage. Reaching the elevator, they waited for the doors to open, Marty pulling the peak of his cap down over his face. When it finally arrived, it was mercifully empty.

Williams punched '10' on the panel and as they began to ascend, Marty breathed an audible sigh of relief.

'Almost there, mate,' Williams said reassuringly and Marty nodded, still keeping his head turned towards the floor to avoid the camera in the corner of the elevator. A moment later, the digital display signalled they had reached the top floor and the doors opened into total darkness. Marty's guard was up as Williams stepped out and the lights immediately flickered into life. He motioned for Marty to follow him, which he obediently did.

As they walked quickly along the narrow corridor, Marty was struck by the 'new home' smell that lingered in the air, and noticed the communal areas were spotless and appeared brand new.

'That's mine at the end,' Williams said pointing; Marty nodded silently.

Williams opened the door and as Marty stepped inside the apartment he had mixed emotions; relief coupled with fear - he still did not completely trust Williams.

Almost immediately, a pungent aroma filled his nostrils, which Williams attempted to explain.

'Sorry about the smell, there's something wrong with the carpet,' he said smiling. 'Apparently, the glue they used reacts to the heat of the apartment below. My landlord reckons he can't smell *anything* so won't replace it. Seems to get worse when it's really hot or the carpet gets wet.'

Marty nodded cautiously as Williams continued.

'I spilled a beer on it a few days ago and it flared up again,' he said casually.

Is that really what it is? Marty asked himself, vowing to stay vigilant.

'Hang on here, I'll get the air freshener and open a couple of windows,' Williams said as he headed down a narrow hallway to what Marty could see was the bathroom. He returned a moment later, spraying the air wildly, filling the room with the smell of something perfumed. Marty followed him into the lounge area, and through double glass doors into what estate agents called a 'winter garden' – a small sealed balcony filled with a glass-top dining table and four stainless steel chairs. As Williams pulled at a long cord to the right of the space, the floor-to-ceiling blinds quickly retracted revealing stunning views of the Manchester skyline.

'Wow, that's some view,' Marty said stepping into the winter garden to get a better look.

Williams turned and smiled. 'Makes putting up with the smell worthwhile,' he said. 'My landlord is a very laid-back Greek guy who wants little or nothing to do with the place, and for this location it's pretty cheap. Heaven forbid he ever took an interest and checked market rates, it'd be way out of my price range, that's for sure!'

Marty nodded and turned to look at the lounge. It was cleaner than he would expect of a hard-nosed hack, and furnished in white throughout. A few black-and-white pictures of cities from around the world adorned the walls. A modest flat-screen TV was fixed to the main wall, opposite a cream IKEA-style sofa and armchair and smoked-glass coffee table; it was minimal to say the least. The only concession to the clinical and overtly tidy finish was a tall bookshelf, again some kind of flat-pack creation, rammed full of books in what resembled organised chaos. Williams followed Marty's gaze to the bookshelf, 'I like order in my life, but when it comes to books I have little control,' he offered by way of explanation, before gesturing for Marty to take a seat on the sofa.

'Do you fancy a beer, or maybe something stronger?' Williams asked.

'Whisky, if you have it?' Marty replied sitting down.

Williams smiled broadly. 'I have just the thing,' he said heading out of the room.

Marty checked his watch; it was 02:08, and he suddenly felt very tired.

A moment later, Williams returned with two glass tumblers in one hand and the distinctive dark green bottle of Glenfiddich Scotch in the other. He sat heavily in the armchair to Marty's right, and resting the tumblers on the glass coffee table between them, poured two generous measures of the whisky. Clinking his glass against Marty's he drained the contents in one loud motion. Marty watched as he poured himself another large drink, before sitting back in his chair and rubbing his eyes and nose nosily with his thick fingers, his face reddening.

Marty took a gulp of his drink. As the warm liquid coated his insides, he reluctantly began to relax a little, sinking slowly into the sofa.

'So, you wanna know who's setting you up, right?' Williams said almost cheerfully.

Marty nodded, 'Of course!'

Williams stared at Marty without speaking for a long uncomfortable moment. Marty, in response, shifted in his seat and downed his remaining whisky, his glass quickly refilled by Williams who seemed to be enjoying himself now.

'OK. Do you remember about four years ago, an Asian corporation tried to buy the Fontaine Radio Group?' Williams asked.

'TW Holdings?'

'That's the one, based out of Singapore.'

'Of course I do! I lobbied John Stone as PM at the time to block the move. I felt it would lead to consolidation and job cuts for the radio industry.'

'I remember that, you giving him serious grief on your show, calling him a traitor!'

'He bloody well was, trying to persuade me that rolling over and letting TW buy Fontaine was the natural next step for UK radio. They wanted to deregulate the industry, which would have left smaller local stations totally unprotected from big business and profit-making. He actually had the nerve to claim that because my show was national, I was in no position to judge the deal.'

'Yes, I remember thinking he did have a point on that one,' said Williams.

'Rubbish!' snorted Marty. 'Just because my show is nationally networked doesn't mean I can't have a view on those stations that deliver content locally. In fact, as the loudest voice in UK radio, I have a duty to speak up for the smaller stations and the people who rely on them in our towns and cities. Deregulation and consolidation by an overseas owner means less control from the UK, which in turn means less freedom for broadcasters. They could force us to toe the corporate line, like they do in the States and end up ditching the truth in favour of big business, backhanders and pseudo-sponsorships. *I* wasn't going to let that happen!'

'And that's when you set up the official petition, right?' Williams interjected.

'Yep, and it worked too! Over a million of my listeners signed up ensuring it was debated in parliament. And as we know, it caused a massive stink publicly and the government eventually did a U-turn and vetoed the takeover.'

'But it didn't really work, did it, Marty?' Williams said.

'What do you mean? Of course it did!'

'What I *mean* is, it's only a matter of time before overseas ownership becomes the norm in UK radio, in fact in all media. But that's not really the issue *right now*, is it?'

'So what is? And for that matter what does any of this have to do with me or White's murder?'

Williams shifted forward in his seat, moving closer to Marty. 'Do you know COMCO is up for sale?'

'That's not true, surely?'

'I'm afraid it is, my friend. The company is on the market for a cool four hundred million sterling.'

Marty took a large swig of whisky, grimacing as the heat of the liquid hit his stomach. 'I just can't believe that,' he said. 'COMCO's a cash cow, why would they sell it?'

Williams finished his second whisky and poured himself another, picking up the glass and cradling it between the fingers of both hands.

'Doesn't make sense, right? I thought the same, so I started digging into the finances of COMCO and oddly, there was incredibly little on file. I asked a very reliable source of mine in the government for some insight. I gotta tell you – what came back was shocking.'

'Go on,' Marty said eagerly.

'Well, it appears they've been diversifying the business since the global downturn. When advertising revenues dropped off a cliff in 2008, Colin Burns, who had previously worked in oil and gas in Scotland and the Middle East, came up with the idea to branch out into other industries including tin mining in China – which, to be fair, looked like a no-brainer: low cost and high profits. At the time, they raised over a hundred and fifty million pounds through private equity investment in the form of loans, channelling those funds into what became known as the 'China Project' operating under the trading name of EXPO C. They were hoping for substantial returns to see them through the uncertainty of the financial crisis. The idea was they would mine the seams extensively over a five-year period, exporting the tin directly to the UK in a cosy partnership with the British government – notably via a deal brokered directly with the then Chief Secretary to the Treasury, *Nicholas Fay*. I'm sure it won't surprise you to know that the government received a substantial contribution to their party funds not long after Fay ensured the deal was agreed with China.'

'Jesus,' Marty muttered under his breath as Williams continued.

'Looks like the plan was for COMCO to sit back and enjoy the profits before eventually selling the mine when the tin became harder to extract, and further investment would be needed.'

'I can't believe it. I've worked for COMCO for twenty years. I was in the building every day. And I never knew any of this!' Marty exclaimed.

'Nobody did, that's the benefit of getting into bed with the government. If they really want something hidden, it will stay hidden. Plus – to all intents and purposes – EXPO C wasn't in any way connected to COMCO. Neither was it a public or limited company in the UK so they had no duty to reveal any of their affairs to anyone.'

'But surely they had to have declared the dividends from EXPO C? COMCO is a public company after all. Any profits would show up on their books, wouldn't they?'

Williams nodded. 'Of course, but if you look really hard you'll find that COMCO is in fact registered in Jersey and as such is not liable to the same scrutiny as UK mainland businesses. Instead, they can claim non-dom status on the majority of their overseas interests, particularly EXPO C who, according to all records, made zero profit since launch. Instead, the backdoor COMCO investors simply received loan repayments against the money they put in. It's a perfectly legal way of avoiding tax.'

Marty exhaled loudly. 'Bloody hell,' he mumbled before draining his glass, which Williams duly refilled with another generous measure of whisky.

'It was a brilliant deal. With the taxman effectively looking the other way and large profits for the investors, everyone involved made a killing – including the majority shareholders of COMCO, helping it become one of the most powerful media companies in Europe if not worldwide; totally untouchable.' A smile of satisfaction crossed Williams's face.

Marty digested the information for a moment.

'But I don't get it; I openly rallied against the government and no one ever tried to stop me.'

'You had become too powerful, Marty. They couldn't risk you finding out what they were up to and whipping up a media frenzy or another petition to Parliament. It appears that they left you to it and instead, pulled people like Jeremy Day into the mix. If you recall, sometime in 2010, he suddenly started disagreeing with you and your opinions on everything, including the government. *He* was the one toeing the company line.'

'And I always thought he was just disagreeing for the sake of it, you know, to get some attention!' Marty growled, sitting forward now.

'He was. Having met him, it's clear he's not the smartest of men. I very much doubt he understood the bigger picture, or knew who the puppet master was; instead, I'm led to believe he was quietly told to disagree with you and undermine you at every opportunity with the promise he'd eventually get your breakfast show, arguably the most coveted gig in UK commercial radio,' Williams said.

'How do you know all this anyway?' Marty said.

'Like I say, I have friends who are *extremely* well connected.'

'*Covert* more like!'

Williams smiled and pressed on. 'Anyway it seemed life could only get better for the COMCO boys. With the mining seams delivering healthy repayments on the loans, when the TW takeover deal for Fontaine eventually fell through, COMCO seized on the opportunity. Buoyed by the success of EXPO C they tried the same trick to raise more private equity funding and picked up Fontaine for two hundred million – which, with sizeable stations in major cities like Glasgow, Manchester, Birmingham and London, was a bloody brilliant piece of business.'

Marty nodded.

'Anyway, the good times couldn't last, and in 2012 it all started to come down around their ears when *the accident* happened.'

Marty leaned in closer still. 'What *accident?*'

Williams moved closer in reply, his words coming out in a conspiratorial whisper, as he looked left and right searching for an invisible foe.

'In their haste to make money, EXPO C cut a few corners. Shall we say, safety wasn't what you would call *paramount.* With more people working the seams under less structural support than was strictly legal, the mines suddenly caved, killing *hundreds* of locals.'

'I never heard about that!' Marty protested.

'And why would you – the deaths of three hundred people in Northern China, a country of over 1.3 billion? The story never made it out of the province, never mind the country; shut down immediately by the government-controlled media. The Chinese were not at all happy, foreign-owned mines killing *their* citizens – not a great look for the party. They closed the mines down immediately pending a "state investigation", and three years on, the seams remain dormant. That's a lot of money invested not making any kind of return.'

Marty whistled quietly. 'Jesus, you're not kidding,' he said.

'With the mines suddenly mothballed indefinitely, COMCO's quarter-of-a-billion-pound investment was suddenly buried deep in Chinese bureaucracy. Add in the two hundred million they borrowed for Fontaine, and they're faced with debts of almost half a billion, and crippling interest, which is driving them deeper and deeper into the red.'

'COMCO going bankrupt? Jesus,' muttered Marty, taking in the enormity of the statement. 'If this is all true…'

'It's true, mate, it's true.'

'OK, so if it *is* true, I still don't understand what that has to do with me, or the failed TW deal – *and White's murder, for that matter?*'

Williams sat back now and took a long slug of whisky.

'Look, I can't prove it yet – but I'm *certain* they are linked.'

'But how?'

'OK, here's what we know. Five years ago, an unknown and very secretive Asian corporation tried to buy the Fontaine Group and *you* got in their way by causing a very public stink at government level, meaning the buyout never happened. *You*, my friend, stopped a lot of people getting very rich and you embarrassed a lot of powerful faces in government, including the current prime minister.'

'Sure I did, but that was *years* ago. I don't understand how any of this is related to me and White *today*.'

'I don't know yet, but I'm sure it's all connected to COMCO and new overseas ownership. My source tells me Burns has been over in Asia a lot recently, specifically Laos, flirting with business consortiums in the hope of drumming up a sale.'

'But they can't do that, that's what they tried five years ago with Fontaine; the government and Ofcom vetoed the sale,' Marty said.

'Exactly, you said it, *five years ago*. But Fay just got into office and things can change quickly when the PM is a "friend". Plus, deregulation is just a couple of years away by all accounts.'

Marty rubbed his hands down his face, slowly dragging his fingers over his mouth, holding them there as he spoke. 'Why would he do that now? That's a public shit-storm waiting to happen. He can't possibly risk that as his first action as PM.'

'*True*, but that shit-storm would be a lot smaller without you banging your incredibly loud drum, wouldn't it? I mean, look at what you did to Fay after he was elected. He was totally humiliated; you made him look like an amateur over his involvement with Yewtree. Listen, I can't prove anything at this stage, but Fay has powerful supporters, many from overseas. Last week's election was the closest since the coalition in 2011, and he got in by the skin of his teeth. Seriously Marty, do you *really* believe Fay got himself elected after just three months as party leader based solely on his personality and sharp suits?'

'What are you saying? The election was rigged?' Marty asked.

Williams took another loud gulp of whisky. '*Maybe*,' he said. 'Nicholas Fay also spent a lot of time in Asia this year courting investment and foreign trade, some of it coinciding with Burns's visits. It was a big part of his election manifesto, becoming a big hitter in the Asian economy, trading outside of Europe with the Asian superpowers to make the UK a dominant worldwide force once again.'

Marty took a moment before speaking, shaking his head as he did. 'It makes sense when you say it, Simon; but at the same time, it's a long walk – a radio company involved in a government conspiracy?'

'I know it's a lot to take in, but I bet if we start digging further we'll find more to connect the fire sale of COMCO to the current government. I'm sure of it.'

'Even so, do you really think COMCO and the government would set me up for a murder just to get me off air?'

Williams nodded and looked into his glass. 'Yes, Marty. Yes I do, and I'm afraid you're not going to like my reasoning for thinking that.'

'Go on.'

'I can't be certain, Marty, and I'm just putting the pieces together at the moment, but...' Williams paused, as if trying to find the words, '... look, this may be hard for you to hear...'

'Spit it out, man!' Marty barked.

'Look, I have reason to believe that the death of your father and your producer David were also connected to the failed Fontaine takeover.'

Marty stared at Williams, his face ashen, almost grey.

'What did you say?'

Williams sat forward once more, his voice softer now. 'Marty,' he said. 'I did all of this for the right reasons, but I had a friend in the Met Police look into the GMP files around their deaths. They were killed driving *your* car.'

'I'm fully aware of how they died, Simon; I think about it every single day,' Marty said coldly.

'I'm sure you do. But knowing what you know now, think about it from the outside looking in; at the time they died, your campaign to stop the Asian takeover was in full flight with a huge amount of public support. PM John Stone and Nicholas Fay were under enormous pressure to back Ofcom and veto the deal, but initially they were adamant the deal should go through.'

'I remember that, of course I do, but...'

Williams cut across Marty. 'And the Finance Minister, Catherine Smith, even appeared on your show to cement their stance, stating the sale was in the best interests of the economy and had the government's full support.'

'Yeah, I destroyed her argument that day as I recall.'

'And then, just two days later, on the very public night of the NTV Awards, the accident happened.'

Marty's eyes dropped to the floor now, the grief was still a living thing inside him.

Williams continued, more gently now. 'A tragic accident where your producer and best friend – as well as your father – were both killed when your *brand new* Bentley, a car *you* should have been driving home that night, left the road and hit a tree.'

Marty nodded silently without looking up.

'Death caused by drink driving, according to the coroner's report.'

'I know all this Simon,' Marty said in a low murmur. 'What's your point?'

Williams's voice was warm, almost tender now. 'Marty, do you really believe that Dave was back on the sauce?'

Marty looked pained as he remembered that fateful night, 'I honestly don't know, Simon. As far as I was aware until that night he'd been sober for five years, but the coroner's report said he was three times over the legal limit.'

'And did you see him drinking that night?'

Marty closed his eyes and shook his head.

'I'm sorry, Marty but *I* believe that the car wreck was no accident and Dave was somehow set up. It's just a theory right now, but I think that it was *you* and your campaign against the government that were supposed to be killed that night.'

The realisation of what Williams was saying hit Marty like a hammer blow.

'I *was* supposed to be driving... that was the plan all along. I'd just got the car and made a big deal of it on the show in the week leading up to the awards. As usual though, I got pissed and Dave ended up bailing me out and driving Dad home.'

Williams nodded. 'Whoever did it hadn't planned for that, Marty.'

'*They* killed my dad and best mate instead of me?' Marty slammed his drink down on the table and leapt to his feet pacing back and forth. 'Fuck, *I* as good as killed them both!'

Simon stood and followed Marty, putting an arm out to steady him as he stumbled around the lounge room.

'Look mate, I know it's hard to hear and I can't prove *any* of it yet, but my gut tells me COMCO and the government are somehow involved in your current situation and White's death. With what I've uncovered so far, it's just too much of a coincidence for me.'

Marty felt punch-drunk and drained, his legs close to jelly as he turned to face Simon. 'I don't get it. Why kill White? If they want me out of the way so badly, why not just kill *me*?'

Simon clapped his hand on Marty's back and let out a half-chuckle. 'I have absolutely no idea, but we *really* need to find out. Maybe your Malaysian girl will have some answers for us, hey? That's the first place we can start.'

Marty, feeling suddenly broken, slumped back down onto the sofa. Dropping his face into his hands, he began to weep, overcome by a mixture of fear, grief and anger.

CHAPTER 40

Marty woke with a start as Williams nudged his shoulder and handed him a cup of black coffee to match his own. He had clearly fallen asleep on the couch, a black blanket laid across his body. He rubbed his face with his hand as he sat upright before taking a gulp of the filtered coffee; a good blend, South American he guessed. Williams took a seat in the same chair as the previous night and stared at Marty without speaking for a moment.

'What time is it?' Marty asked.

'Just after eight: you had about five hours. Fell fast asleep after the third whisky.'

'Yeah, it can do that to me,' Marty said lightly.

Williams stayed silent for a moment before asking his question; his voice measured when he finally spoke.

'You still wanna do this, Marty?' he asked taking a gulp of coffee.

'Too bloody right I do. What other choice have I got?'

Williams nodded. 'I get that but I need to be one hundred per cent sure you're gonna come through for me on this. Twenty grand is a lot of money. It's going to take some doing pulling it together for your mystery woman – if she even turns up, that is.'

'She'll turn up,' Marty said confidently.

'OK, say she does, we need to be really clear here, Marty. If I'm right, the people we're looking to expose in all this don't fuck about. This could get very messy and bloody serious, very quickly. It's OK for me, I'm a free man, but if they get *you* back in Hawk Green, anything could happen.'

Marty closed his eyes for a second as he fought to block the images of the rape, but it appeared in full colour in his head. He opened his eyes quickly and nodded as he stared straight at Williams.

'Simon, I have never been more determined to expose anyone or anything in my life. If you're right and this *is* all connected to Dave and my dad's deaths, then I won't rest until these bastards are held to account by the highest level of the law!'

Williams let out a loud guffaw and shook his head.

'I wish I shared your optimism, mate. Lately it appears the law is laughable. The reality, it seems, is if you have enough money, you're pretty much given carte blanche to do whatever the hell you like!' he said before dropping his coffee cup on the glass table and standing. 'OK, Marty, we're in this together now. The banks open at nine and I have a meeting with my editor at ten. I hope we'll have the money we need to make this work by midday and I'll be back as quick as I can. In the meantime, don't use your mobile, someone could trace it; instead you can use my landline. Oh, and I'd avoid telling *anyone* where you are, especially your lawyer. I never trust lawyers. You'll be safer that way.'

Marty nodded and a moment later, Williams closed the apartment door as he headed to the office.

Left alone, Marty took a shower and put on the spare white cotton shirt Williams had left out for him. They were about the same size, although Williams was taller so Marty had to fold the sleeves back, exposing his freshly bandaged wrists. All in all, though, it was a decent fit tucked into his blue jeans and made him feel a little more human, *a little less 'man on the run'*.

After admiring the daylight version of the city skyline view from the sunroom over another filter coffee, Marty returned to the lounge, switched on the TV and flicked to the Network News channel. As he suspected, reports of his disappearance and bail violation were top of the agenda. Newscasters and so-called experts relayed the police manhunt now underway, all the time speculating on his whereabouts, state of mind, plus his motives for going on the run. Marty had built his career on this kind of ill-informed information delivery, derived from minimal facts. Until this moment he had never appreciated the damage his ruthless 'hunting' had inflicted on so many innocent people caught in difficult situations. He had lived by the mantra, *'throw enough mud and eventually some sticks.'* It had never been truer than right now, ironically. The realisation of who and what, he had become over the years left him feeling sick to his stomach.

Hoping to receive the location of this evening's meet with Rochelle, he switched on his iPhone. A moment later, the voicemail icon appeared on the home screen. Disappointedly, Marty listened to a panicked Rob, who according to the message had been trying to get hold of him all night.

Marty contemplated calling him back but after Williams's revelations the previous night, Marty's fear of conspiracies and dark operations was at an all-time high. The last thing he wanted was someone tracking his phone. He considered switching it off again but he couldn't do that until he had heard from Rochelle. Instead, he placed it on the coffee table in front him and turned his attention back to the TV.

Colin Burns's public statement made after suspending Marty, was replaying on the news. His very public suspension and current AWOL status made him look guilty as charged in the eyes of the unforgiving and cynical British public. As the footage came to its conclusion, Marty prepared to switch channels, just as another face he recognised appeared on screen, that of Assistant Police Commissioner Blake, his one-time golf buddy.

Standing outside Ashton House Police HQ, Blake had adopted his 'serious face'. Marty had seen him switch it on and off many times over the years at press conferences and fund-raising police junkets. Ironically, right now as he attempted to project to the world his sincere concentration and focus on the matter in hand, Marty was sure of one thing: APC Blake did not care about anyone but himself; his lack of support for Marty after his arrest had been clear evidence of that. Marty turned up the volume as Blake spoke to well-known Sky News reporter, Sally Scott.

'I want to assure the people of the North West that the Manchester Police force is doing everything we can to find Marty Michaels and ensure he faces trial for the murder of Paul White. I would ask anyone who might be helping Marty, or even hiding him somewhere in the city, to consider the ramifications of such an act. Murder is a very serious charge and we will enforce the law to the full extent of our powers.'

Sally Scott – managing the interview from behind the camera – fired a question it appeared Blake was not expecting.

'Assistant Police Commissioner Blake – what do you say to those people who are demanding your resignation? Considering your evidently close relationship with Marty Michaels, some would say your judgment and objectivity is in question and there is no place for you in this investigation. Are they right in their assumption, APC Blake?'

A tiny movement flashed across Blake's face betraying his true feelings of disdain, before managing to smile as he threw the first punch of his defence.

'*Mr. Michaels and I were members of the same golf club. That was the extent of our relationship...*'

The reporter cut across him.

'*And as I understand it he was also the toastmaster at your only daughter's wedding. Is that correct?*'

Blake paused for a moment before expertly returning the conversation to the matter he was there to discuss.

'*Let me say again, finding Marty Michaels is the number one priority for every Manchester Police officer. We will leave no stone unturned until we bring him back into custody, where he will face the charges brought against him in relation to the murder of Paul White. Now if you'll excuse me, I have a briefing on this very matter I need to attend urgently. Thank you,*' he said with a firm nod before walking back towards the main door of Ashton House.

As much as it pained him, Marty had to admire APC Blake. Caught in the headlights he had ensured the last thing he left the public with was a clear picture of Marty's supposed guilt, effectively masking much of the negativity around himself.

Marty felt a rage building inside him as he watched Blake disappear into headquarters.

'I'm gonna get you for this, Blake, you bastard!' he said loudly at the TV. 'Corrupt and stupid, the lot of you. How do you think the public would feel if they knew your number one suspect was sitting just a few miles away from your fucking press conference?' Marty said and started to laugh.

His attention suddenly drawn to his iPhone, it pinged to let him know he had a text message. He prayed it was from

Rochelle with the meet details and was again disappointed to see it was from Johnson.

WE NEED TO TALK. HOW CAN I REACH YOU?

Marty sent the landline number back via text and a moment later the house phone rang. He picked it up without speaking.

'Marty, it's Andrew, are you there?' said the voice on the other end. It was strangely reassuring to hear the sharp angular tones of his posh lawyer.

'It's me, mate.'

'Thank God. Are you OK? Where are you?'

'I'm fine and I'm safe; staying with a friend.'

Johnson had bad news.

'Look, Marty, I couldn't get you the cash you needed. I'm sorry.'

'I thought as much.'

'Look, to be honest, I think the best option is for you to give yourself up. Tell me where you are and I can come and get you. We can work this out together and surrender on *our* terms.'

Surrendering was not an option for Marty. Seeing the TV reports, it was evident any jury would convict him.

'Sorry, Andrew, I can't tell you where I am, and I have no intention of handing myself into the police. APC Blake as good as said I'm guilty on TV just now. My best chance of getting out of this is for *me* to prove *myself* that I didn't do it! The only way that will happen will be getting what I need from Rochelle. Hopefully tonight.'

'Marty, as your lawyer, I simply cannot advocate this course of action,' Johnson said sternly. 'And neither can I help you in your endeavours; the police hunt is growing more intense by the day and soon it'll be impossible for me to help without implicating myself. If you insist on going down this route, then this will be our last communication until you're ready to face the authorities. At that point, I'll of course give you my full support.'

Marty knew what Johnson was saying and what it meant for him. In a world of lies and deceit, it was refreshing to hear some straight talking.

'Andrew, you've been a valuable attorney and a good friend to me over the years and please believe me, I understand what you're saying. I know you think this is the wrong way to go, but mate it's the *only way* from where I'm standing right now. I have to meet with Rochelle.'

'OK, I get that, but is it safe for you to do so?'

'I honestly can't say, but I have to give it a go. It's all I have.'

'So where will she meet you?'

'I'm not sure yet; still waiting for a text from her.'

Right on cue Marty's iPhone alerted him to a new message on the home screen. He picked it up and to his considerable relief it was from Rochelle.

EXCHANGE AIRPORT HOTEL 8PM TONIGHT.

Johnson pushed Marty. 'What is it, is everything OK?'

'Yeah, Rochelle has just messaged me with the details for tonight.'

'Where does she want to meet?'

'I don't think I should say. It's probably better that way,' Marty replied.

'I'm your lawyer. Someone has set you up for murder. The people working against you are clearly dangerous. For your own sake, someone needs to know where you're going.'

Marty considered his words for a moment; should he tell him? It probably did make sense if this all went belly up, but he still had a nagging doubt as to whether he could truly trust him. He decided to take the risk. 'OK, Andrew,' he said, 'but you seriously can't tell anyone, not even Rob, understood?'

'One hundred per cent. You can trust me, Marty, I'm on your side.'

Marty paused for a moment while he considered the option one final time, 'OK, but I'm seriously going out on a limb here. I'm meeting her at the Exchange Airport Hotel at 8pm tonight. She claims she has evidence that proves I didn't kill White. I can have it in exchange for twenty grand cash.'

'You have the money?'

'Not yet; but it's coming'.

'Jesus, Marty. Where did you get it?'

'A friend.'

'That's some friend.'

'Let's just say it's more of a transaction – quid pro quo, so to speak.'

'I'm not sure I want to know, Marty,' Johnson said.

'I'm not sure you do.'

After an awkward silence, Marty decided there was nothing to gain from continuing the conversation.

'Look, Andrew, I'd better go. I'll be in touch as soon as I have what I need.'

'OK, good luck, old boy.'

'Thanks, I'll see you soon,' Marty replied quickly as he hung up, hoping he was making the right choice.

CHAPTER 41

Marty and Simon sat in the BMW and prepped the route to the airport hotel one last time; after all, they were about to head to one of the world's busiest airports swarming with CCTV. Marty was wearing a baseball cap and sunglasses to hide his notorious face. A rucksack containing twenty grand cash sat in the footwell between his legs. When both men were happy with the plan, Williams started the car and headed out of the parking garage into the Northern Quarter. They were soon on the inner ring road towards Manchester Airport. As they drove, Williams questioned Marty on the details of his phone call to Andrew Johnson.

'Did you tell him where you were staying?'

'No, of course not.'

'And what about tonight? Did you tell him about the meet?'

Marty paused for a moment and looked left out of the window as they approached a set of red traffic lights.

Williams pressed Marty now, his voice agitated. 'Does Andrew know where we're going tonight?'

Marty turned to face him, his expression pained. He nodded. 'Yes, he does.'

'Oh, for God's sake, Marty, we agreed you wouldn't talk to him!'

'I know, I know, but he's my lawyer and he's been a friend for a long time,' Marty protested.

'Trust me, there's no such thing as a friendly lawyer. It's like saying you're mates with a crocodile and you fancy a swim; it's in its nature to eat you. Lawyers are no different. They cannot help but get involved and, in my experience, screw things up. He could have told the police for all you know.'

Marty exhaled loudly. 'Look, I know Andrew and he wouldn't do that. The truth is I'm pretty bloody scared right now and it actually felt good to have someone else rooting for me. I'm sorry if you think it was a mistake, but Andrew's one of the few people who's been there for me from the beginning of this mess, OK? I mean, he could say the same about you. Do you think he'd advise his celebrity client to meet a prostitute with a reporter in tow?'

Williams said nothing for a moment before conceding Marty had a point. 'Look, I'm sorry. I know this is difficult for you. I get it, honestly I do, and I'm sure I'd probably have done the same in your position.'

Marty nodded but said nothing as the car moved forward and eventually joined the Mancunian Way, a dual carriageway cutting through the heart of Manchester. After a few minutes, Williams probed again.

'Does anyone else know where we're going? Rob, maybe?'

Marty shook his head. 'Absolutely not; no way,' he replied.

Williams stared at Marty for a moment. 'Are you sure, fella?'

'Absolutely; one thing I know about Rob is the man *cannot* keep secrets. He's like an old woman at times and he'd have to tell someone or he'd burst.'

'OK, well that helps.'

'It's just you, me and Andrew,' Marty said.

Williams paused for a moment, 'Well... not *quite* just the three of us,' he said sheepishly.

'What? So *you've* told someone, after just this minute lecturing *me?*'

Williams raised his left hand in defence. 'Woah! Hang on here! I'm handing over twenty grand cash to a murder suspect, ten grand of which is from my editor's safe. That's a month's worth of source payments for the paper, not to mention ten grand from my own savings account, which I'm going to have to filter through expenses over the next six months if I ever want to get it back. Plus in case you missed the news today, I'm officially aiding and abetting a wanted man. That's serious shit, Marty. I wasn't going to walk alone into the unknown with my cock in my hand and my cash in *your* pocket!'

Marty was angry but deep down understood Williams's reasoning.

'So, *who* did you tell?'

'My editor, Chris. He's been in the game long enough to know to protect a source. He understands your situation and the danger you're in; and the danger I'm in for that matter. He wants the exclusive when we blow this open so he'll keep quiet. I can guarantee you that.'

Marty didn't respond and instead stared out the window in silence as Williams took the off-ramp leading to the Princess Parkway and a direct road to the airport. A moment later, they passed under the Hulme Arch. His guts turned as he considered the meeting ahead and his mind filled with questions. Would Rochelle show? Would she actually bring anything he could use? Once he had anything that proved his innocence, would he be able to stay out of jail long enough to use it? More to the point, considering the people he was up against, could he *stay alive* long enough to use it? He tried to assure himself everything would be fine, but he didn't believe it.

The rest of the journey passed in silence and took around fifteen minutes through stop-start traffic, with Marty covering the left side of his face with his hand to avoid detection.

As they rolled past the intersection of Chorlton and West Didsbury, Marty's thoughts drifted to APC Blake and his public rebukes. It maddened him to think he had once considered him a genuine friend. Sure, he knew they would never share their deepest fears with each other, but after two years of golf and Marty serving as the toastmaster at his daughter's wedding – albeit with a few questionable comments – he really had thought there was a bond between them. To see Blake so publicly distance himself, and more or less accuse Marty of the crime, was tough to take. Not only did he feel rejected, he felt hurt by someone he thought he could trust; something he had never found easy to do. Yet, here he was, driving to a clandestine meeting with a prostitute, twenty grand in cash between his feet and a hard-nosed hack as his driver. As he considered what he was actually doing, he almost laughed; it was ludicrous. Yet it was all he had. The prospect of going back to Hawk Green made Marty's blood run cold and his stomach churn. After the brutality of the rape, he knew jail meant there was little chance he would see his next birthday.

He closed his eyes and slumped down into the passenger seat as he tried to prepare himself mentally for the task in hand; Rochelle was his only hope now.

Sometime later, the car began to slow and as Marty opened his eyes, he came face to face with the Exchange Airport Hotel as Williams pulled the car into the car park.

Marty's mobile was locked tightly in his fist as he awaited instruction from Rochelle and bang on cue, it signalled he had another message: ROOM 317, 3RD FLOOR.

He stared at the words for a moment before exhaling loudly like an athlete at the starting line; game on.

CHAPTER 42

The hotel lobby was mercifully quiet. The bored-looking receptionist stared lazily down at her computer monitor. Marty – wearing a black baseball cap and sunglasses – moved quickly across the polished marble floor towards the elevators adjacent to the concierge desk. His body tightened as he prepared for the grey-haired man in a charcoal uniform to look up and make eye contact. Much to his relief his head remained down, his eyes fixed on the sports pages of the *Manchester Evening News*.

Pressing on, he hit the central call button, lighting up the two elevators in front of him. His eyes darted between the digital screens above each pair of metal doors. 'Come on! Come on!' he muttered under his breath as he hopped from foot to foot. Finally, he heard the welcome sound of an elevator arriving at the ground floor. The doors opened and a couple pulling suitcases stepped out, unaware of the celebrity-cum-fugitive in their midst. As the pair moved towards reception, Marty took their place in the elevator, pushed '3' on the gold panel inside the double doors, and jabbed at the 'door close' button, sealing himself inside. After a minute the doors opened on to a generically decorated beige lobby which thankfully was empty; so far so good.

Glancing quickly at the room numbers and arrows on the wall ahead, Marty decided to go right. Moving along the surprisingly long corridor, he kept one eye on the ascending room numbers on either side, and one on the fire doors placed at equal intervals along the way – his exit strategy.

Up ahead, a door opened and the noise of a TV filled the corridor causing Marty to jump. A man in a hotel robe stepped out and placed a room service tray on the floor. He stared at Marty for a moment before appearing satisfied, stepping back inside. The door closed and the silence returned.

Marty experienced a sudden wave of paranoia. Had the man recognised him? Was he watching through the spyhole to get a better look? Was he just surprised to see a man wearing a cap and sunglasses inside? Either way, he had to keep moving and ploughed on with his face turned away as he passed at pace.

Room 317 was the last door on the left-hand side of the corridor and as Marty approached, his mouth suddenly dried and butterflies filled his stomach. He took a long, deep breath, to steady his pulse before knocking gently on the door. It moved inwards, unlocked. Pushing it harder now, the door opened slowly with the loud creak of a hinge in need of oil. After looking left and right down the corridor to ensure no one was watching, he tentatively stepped inside.

'Hello, Rochelle, are you there?'

There was no reply.

He moved forward into a room like that of any other chain hotel; the bathroom to his immediate right, a narrow, short hallway in front of him led to the main room, obscured from where he stood now.

Stepping into the belly of the room, he glanced towards the main sleeping space and his body recoiled at what he saw: Rochelle tied to an armchair; a small hand-towel stuffed into her mouth to gag her. Her eyes wide, she writhed and squealed as Marty stepped closer.

Opening his mouth to speak, Rochelle's squeals jumped in volume. He was suddenly aware of someone behind him and turned, instinctively raising his arms to defend himself, but it was too late. Something heavy smashed down on his head and his world turned black.

CHAPTER 43

Marty opened his eyes and took a moment to focus on the scene in front of him. His head was twisted awkwardly to the right; it felt heavy and waves of pain throbbed upwards from the back of his skull – like the world's worst hangover. His face was squashed against whatever he was lying on. As his eyes adjusted in the dim light of the room, he could see he was still in the hotel room, facing his own reflection in a mirrored wardrobe. He blinked furiously as the memory of his meet with Rochelle crashed over him; the open door, the look of abject terror on her face as he had walked into view and discovered her tied and gagged in a chair. Being struck from behind.

He sat upright and swung himself round to face the mirror, noticing his jeans, shoes and socks were missing. *Strange*, he thought as he instinctively reached for the back of his head checking for damage; he found a golf-ball-sized lump above the base of his skull. On further inspection, he found blood on his fingertips, before catching sight of something in the mirror behind him. He leapt up, spinning round to face the room.

Lying on the floor next to the bed was the lifeless, naked body of Rochelle; a black belt used as a ligature grabbed tightly at her neck. Although she was face down, her head was turned and he could see her right eye facing upwards, staring at death in the distance. Next to her right hand was a small hotel iron, marked with blood at the tip: the weapon used on him. For a long moment, he sat staring at the body and for the first time saw Ashraf, the young man trying to become a woman. The naked body was smooth and tanned but unable to hide the distinctive masculine features, large hands, broad back and muscular neck and throat. Marty's heart went out to Ashraf and Rochelle; the struggle with their collective demons was finally over.

Scanning the room, he realised the twenty thousand was gone, unfortunate but not his biggest concern. Right now, he needed to find whatever it was Rochelle had offered to bring with her tonight that could prove his innocence. He moved quickly round the room, tossing bed sheets, pillows and blankets out of the way, searching for anything that might help him. After five minutes of frenetic effort, he was none the wiser and sat back on the bed facing the mirrored wardrobes. His reflection was almost too much to bear; he hardly recognised the dishevelled vagrant in front of him and he felt sick to his stomach.

He placed his head between his hands, allowing it to sink forward towards the floor, closing his eyes. His brain raced and a flurry of images played out in his mind's eye. He felt certain now he was heading for a lifetime, or a quick death, in prison. He moved to get up, stepping painfully on something solid. Looking down at his bare feet, he spied a set of keys on a key ring. On closer inspection, he noticed the key ring was in fact a USB memory stick and his heart lifted. Maybe it was nothing – but maybe, just maybe, it was something, *anything* that could help. He grabbed the keys and held them tight in his hand saying a silent prayer, lost in a moment of hope.

Suddenly, there was a loud bang on the hotel room door and a man's voice announced himself from the other side. Hotel security. Shit.

Panic engulfed Marty as he tried to figure out what to do. The door banged again, harder; the voice louder and more agitated this time. Whoever was on the other side wanted to enter urgently. It was only a matter of time before they forced their way in and found him alongside *another* dead body.

He needed to focus on getting out of the room and to do that he needed to find his clothes. Marty dropped to his knees and searched under the bed – nothing. He dragged the mirrored wardrobe door back quickly – again, nothing. All the time the banging grew louder and now there was an additional voice. He ran towards the bathroom and stopped to peer out of the spyhole into the corridor. Outside he could make out the distorted figures of a suited man and a uniformed security guard. *Déjà vu*, he thought. As if sensing his presence, the suited man moved closer and attempted to peer back through the lens. Marty retreated and darted into the bathroom as the banging stopped and the low murmur of conspiratorial conversation permeated the lightweight door.

Turning on the light, Marty found his jeans and shoes strewn across the bathroom floor. Quickly slipping on his jeans he realised his belt was missing, now wrapped around Rochelle's neck. *Not again.* He moved silently across the bathroom towards the main room hoping to retrieve it just as the hotel door lock released from the other side. Instinctively he jumped back, thrusting the USB into the pocket of his jeans before grabbing his shoes in one hand and switching off the light with the other. Pushing the door half closed, he pressed his eye to the gap created by the open hinge, allowing him a partial view of the main bedroom area. His heart was pulsing in his ears, his breathing rapid and shallow as the adrenalin rushed around his body.

The hotel door opened slowly accompanied by the unavoidable loud creak of the dry hinge and a man's voice cut through the deathly silence.

'Hello, Miss Tan. Miss Tan?' said the suited man tentatively, as he entered the room and moved slowly along the walkway towards the main bedroom area, closely followed by the uniformed security guard.

Seeing his opportunity, Marty opened the bathroom door, and stepped softly out into the tiny hallway behind both men. He was sure they could hear his heart pounding and stood motionless for a moment, frozen with fear. His feet felt rooted to the floor as he watched them move further into the room.

The words 'Run, Marty, run!' played on loop in his head. He knew his window of escape was fading fast and his mind raced through the two scenarios; stay and tell them the truth, or run like hell and try to find out who was doing this to him. There was no contest. Finding his focus, he finally lifted his feet and stepped quietly towards the door, now slightly ajar.

He heard a loud shout from behind him.

'Oh my God, I think she's dead!'

Marty's feet moved rapidly now as he yanked the door open, the creaking hinge instantly giving him away. Instinctively, he shot a glance back into the room and saw the security guard turn and face him, his mouth open in an incredulous expression. Marty did not wait for his reaction, bolting out of the room before sprinting headlong down the corridor, a shoe in each hand.

A sudden surge of energy pulsed through his limbs. He could hear footsteps behind him and the loud jangle of keys on a chain, which he guessed belonged to the security guard chasing him down.

The elevator was a no-go, far too slow. Instead, he darted down the first emergency exit he came to, slamming into the door on his left, launching himself down a flight of steps in one movement. He landed heavily on the small concrete square and fell forward against the rough breeze-block wall and deep window sill above it, dropping his shoes as he did. Retrieving them quickly, he took a deep breath, turned and raced down the next set of stairs three at a time, clearing two floors in thirty seconds.

Above him, he heard someone slam through the doors and join him on the emergency stairs. He did not stop to look, preferring to keep his head down, his shoes locked in both hands and moving as quickly as his bare feet would allow down the hard cold stairs. Finally, he reached the ground floor and a set of glass double doors that opened out to the rear of the hotel. A large sign to the right of the doors made it clear they were alarmed. As footsteps echoed above him, he did not hesitate – kicking the doors open, an alarm sounded a split second later.

He considered stopping to put on the shoes but the chasing pack were getting ever closer, so cradling them against his chest now he raced over the small patch of grass that led to the car park. Darting between the cars over the rough and painful concrete, he headed for the fence running along the perimeter of the hotel grounds. Shouts behind him ordered him to stop but he kept on running, reaching the seven-foot wooden fence in less than a minute. Stopping for a moment, he attempted to throw his shoes over it without success as they bounced noisily off the wooden panels and back onto the grass. Glancing behind, the security guard was less than fifty feet away. He had to leave them where they now lay.

Without knowing what awaited him on the other side, he took a couple of steps back and threw himself up onto the fence, his hands and feet scrambling for grip as he hoisted his sixteen-stone frame up the wooden panels like a cartoon character running on the spot. Suddenly the security guard's thick hand grabbed at Marty's right ankle and pulled him backwards. He could feel his own grip slipping at the top of the fence and his life, as he knew it, going with it. In desperation, he kicked out at the security guard, catching him hard on the nose with his heel. The man cried out and let go, and Marty took his chance, hurling himself headfirst over the fence, his arms flaying maniacally as the concrete rushed towards him. He landed heavily and with the wind knocked out of him, he rolled in considerable pain on the hard surface, gasping for air.

Taking a moment to get his breath and bearings, he concluded he was in the grounds of a deserted industrial unit.

As he looked up, he could see a pair of hands grabbing at the fence above him and the sound of feet scrambling on wood from the other side.

Getting to his feet, he hobbled as fast as he could, almost doubled over in pain towards Ringway Road; all the time the voices of the security team echoed behind him.

As he reached Ringway Road, he jumped the small metal fence with some difficulty, glanced left and right, before sprinting across the busy road into the fields and welcome cover of trees opposite. He continued running until he was well out of sight and could no longer hear the shouts of the chasing pack. Finally, when he felt it was safe, he stopped and dropped to his hands and knees, his lungs burning and screaming for oxygen. He vomited as the adrenalin and lactic acid reached a crescendo in his exhausted body, before slumping down onto the ground and rolling onto his back.

He was safe, *for now.*

CHAPTER 44

Staring at the Exchange Hotel jutting out of the thick treeline ahead, Marty could see the blue lights of the assembled police cars bouncing off the building and surrounding vegetation. They had taken no time at all to reach the hotel. By now, they were likely inside the room examining Rochelle's lifeless body. His thoughts turned to Simon, hoping he had managed to get away before the police arrived.

Checking his pockets, he still had the key ring USB from Rochelle's room but no money, no phone and, without any way of contacting Simon, no mode of transport. He was on his own. His best bet of staying out of reach of the police was to keep moving. The only realistic option for shelter tonight was his mum's house. Nestled in the residential suburb of Gatley, it was less than three miles away and in normal circumstances an hour's walk; as a barefoot fugitive, it would clearly take longer. As the daylight began to fade, he checked his watch and the luminous face sprung to life; it was just before 10pm, which meant he would get to his mum's before midnight. Standing slowly, he offered one last look towards the hotel before setting off across the fields in the general direction of Gatley.

Marty's first challenge presented itself when he hit the large council estate on the edge of Wythenshawe. Moving gingerly with his head down he hobbled as quickly as his bare feet would allow over the weather-damaged asphalt. He passed the Horse and Jockey pub on his right, where what he assumed were a group of regulars had congregated smoking. He could hear music playing inside through the open doors and the men outside were laughing hard in the direction of a large, balding, almost spherical man in a red Manchester United football top. He was wildly gesticulating and telling either a joke or story in a loud, thick Mancunian accent. Marty turned his head away from the group and continued walking but they paid him no special attention. Evidently, it wasn't unusual to see a shoeless man hobbling through the streets after dark in this neighbourhood. He continued at pace glancing left and right as cars passed him in both directions. He moved alongside houses with a mixture of music, conversation and television filtering through the open windows on this hot summer's night, before taking a left turn down the side of Ringways primary school. He quickly found himself on the cool grass of the playing fields, which felt like a plush carpet under his feet.

Behind, he heard the sound of sirens filling the estate: common enough in Manchester, but just in case they were for his benefit, he began to run through the darkness of the school grounds, soon reaching the adjacent St. Anthony's Catholic primary school. Here, he stopped for a moment to catch his breath, listening for any signs of movement from the shadows. He checked his watch once more: 10.20pm.

The clear midsummer night was stubbornly refusing to let the sun set; the sky was still bright, and as the next phase of his journey would mean more time on the streets of Wythenshawe, he made the decision to take shelter for an hour until the majority of the neighbourhood would be asleep. Circling the main block of St. Anthony's school, he found a doorway covered by a thick shadow and took the weight off his throbbing bare feet. Leaning against the wall he closed his eyes and allowed his breathing to slow, suddenly realising he was utterly exhausted. A moment later, sleep enveloped him.

Sometime later, distant sirens jolted Marty awake and he shot upright, his chest heaving, sweat dripping from his nose. Disorientated, it took a moment for him to get his bearings and remember where he was – and his heart sank. He checked his watch, 11.11pm; he had been asleep for three quarters of an hour. The night sky was pitch-black now. It was time to get moving so he lifted himself to his feet, now painfully swollen.

Moving as quickly as he could through the quiet streets, he covered ground relatively easily and his energy levels increased as he planned his next move. He would get to his mum's house and let himself in. She was currently lying in the stroke unit of Wythenshawe Hospital, and since his father's death, she had lived alone so the place would be empty. She had always insisted on leaving a key inside the old dog kennel in the backyard, just in case of an emergency, and Marty said a silent prayer that she had not changed her habits.

After fifteen minutes, he ducked right, down the long sweeping road of Meliden Crescent and into the woods behind, allowing him total cover for the next quarter of an hour at least. He moved deep into the thick undergrowth taking care as he did to avoid anything sharp sticking out of the uneven ground and low-hanging branches. He stopped to give his feet some respite and checked his watch again: 11.40pm.

Around midnight he reached the main road of Cross Acres and stood in darkness at the edge of the wood weighing up his next move. Tired and bruised, he was tempted to spend the night within the safety of the trees, but he knew by morning he would be a sitting duck as he tried to move through the busy streets of Wythenshawe. He made his mind up to head for Cross Acres primary school and use their ample playing fields as a route towards the fields beyond, which would take him pretty much all the way to Gatley and his mother's house. By 12.20am, he had made it as far as Styal Road where he stopped to check for traffic, before crossing over into Hollyhedge Park running along the rear of his mum's house. A few minutes later he took shelter in the trees, staring at the house, suddenly filled with an overwhelming sense of love for his mum and deep longing for the safety of his childhood life.

He stepped out of the shadows to the edge of the garden and peered over the fence checking for any obvious signs of police presence, but saw nothing of note. Throwing himself up and over the fence in one noisy movement, he landed heavily in his mum's back garden. A dog started barking two doors down and a moment later the house lights next door came on, illuminating the back garden through the trestle fencing that ran the length of it.

He hit the deck and lay flat against the cool grass for at least a minute, holding his breath as he heard his mum's ageing neighbour Jack open his squeaking back door and step out into his garden. Marty tilted his head just enough to see the old man, who appeared a lot older than he remembered; something approaching eighty. In his right hand, he held a heavy-duty torch like a spear, whipping it erratically back and forth across his own lawn, before reaching the fence and casting the torchlight towards Marty's prostrate body. With the beam now just millimetres from his stricken face, Jack's wife Silvia barked something from behind him causing him to turn. Marty could not make anything out, but Jack obediently switched off the torch and headed back inside. 'Shit, that was close!' Marty whispered to himself.

He waited for the lights next door to go out before moving to the dog kennel and reaching inside. His relief was palpable as his hand touched the house key, hanging in its usual position on the small hook just inside the entrance. He slumped back onto the concrete patio slabs staring at the key cradled in his right hand, smiling as he thought of his mum; even in hospital, she was able to get him out of trouble.

It was then that he heard a car pull up at the front of the house, followed by doors slamming and men's voices talking loudly as the flashes of torches moved down the side of the house. There was no time to run and he would never make it inside the house on time, so as quickly as his large frame would allow, he squeezed himself inside the tiny dog kennel head first.

His mum had kept the relatively small breed of Cocker Spaniels all his life, and the kennel that housed each of them in turn, matched their size. Marty had hidden in the small wooden box many times as a child and still remembered how to squeeze inside, but seven-stone heavier it was not as easy as he recalled. He pushed his head forward, his chin pressed against his chest and the back of his neck almost parallel with the back wall, the weight of his body pressing heavily on the base of his skull. With great difficulty, he managed to cross his legs under him as a child would sitting on the floor and curled his feet together as best he could. Finally, in position, he held himself very still, taking quick, quiet breaths.

Outside he could hear two men talking as they surveyed the house, but could not tell if they were police or something even more dangerous. Either way, if they found him, he was dead.

As one of the men moved to a spot beside the kennel, Marty squeezed his feet closer to his body; he did not know how long he could hold his position and feared his bulky frame would cause the weathered timber to split. Cramp began gripping at his right thigh and he resisted the urge to cry out, gritting his teeth as the pain became unbearable. He soaked it up as the men continued their discussion. With each passing second, his limbs shook more vigorously and his feet began to lower against his will. *Don't give up Marty! Don't give up!* Conjuring the strength to hold himself inside the kennel a fraction longer, he listened to the movement outside; *they were leaving!*

A moment later, he heard the sound of car doors slamming and their vehicle moving away down the street. In an instant, Marty's buckled frame exploded open, crying out in relief as he did, before squeezing himself out of the kennel and finally hobbling to the safety of his mum's kitchen.

CHAPTER 45

After a fitful night's sleep on his old bed, Marty rolled off the bare mattress fully clothed and moved slowly to the window, gently poking his fingers through the venetian blinds and scanning the street outside. He checked his watch: 5.38am. The suburban world around him was yet to wake and the slowly emerging sunlight and early morning silence reminded him of days gone by as a fledgling radio presenter working his way up the ladder; up and out of his parent's house long before dawn, heading into the city to cover the early breakfast shift from 4am. Simple days he longed for once more.

Confident there was no one, police or otherwise, watching the house outside, he headed to the bathroom.

He pulled the light cord down noisily and his mum's weathered eighties decor appeared in front of him, the olive-green corner bath covered in an array of his mother's Avon products scattered around its edge. To the right, a mirrored bathroom cabinet reflected back a man he hardly recognised, eyes bloodshot, hair wild, falling just below his ears, the dressing on his neck a dirty grey now. Into day three of growth, his beard appeared almost white and with the dust of last night's trek embedded in the lines of his face, he looked like a vagrant. He could smell his own body odour, like strong onions, rising up from his sweat-stained shirt. His teeth were covered in a sticky film, the taste in his mouth sharp and stale. He wanted nothing more than a long hot bath and a shave, but hot water steaming into his mother's drains could easily alert someone to his presence. Instead, he ran cold water over his face and scrubbed his armpits clean before washing his hair in ice-cold water. He cleaned his teeth with his finger and toothpaste from the cabinet before towelling off and heading back to his bedroom in search of any of his old clothes still in situ.

After a quick rummage, he found a storage box under the bed containing a blue Manchester City sweatshirt that would have been baggy on a younger Marty but now fitted snuggly around his gut. It smelled a little stale and dusty but at least it was clean and dry. In the same box, he found a pair of battered Converse high-top trainers he had loved as a 'twenty-something', some matching Man City football socks and a blue Chicago Cubs baseball cap. He also found an old piggy bank full of change in his mother's bedroom and quickly carried his stash downstairs to the lounge room, cloaked in darkness from thick blackout curtains.

To avoid any unwanted attention from the neighbours, he left the lights switched off.

He was desperate to find out what was on the USB from Rochelle's room but his mother didn't own a computer and he decided the next best thing would be to check the news for the fallout from the airport hotel.

Negotiating his way through the darkened room, it wasn't long before he fell foul of his mum's abject love of clutter, banging his shins painfully against a new and unexpected metal-edged coffee table directly in front of the thickset 1990s-era TV. He tried his best not to scream out, swallowing the pain and rubbing his shin furiously as he switched on the ancient TV at a low volume.

His mother had never agreed with subscription TV and without access to twenty-four-hour rolling news he turned to the BBC and waited for the morning show to start at 6am.

Still rubbing his painful shin, he settled back into his mum's battered old sofa. Sitting there, he could almost smell his mum and dad, his mind instantly flooded with images of his childhood; the three of them watching TV together without a care in the world. The memories quickly gave way to guilt, guilt that he may have caused his father's death, and the fact his mother was now lying alone in a hospital bed.

To distract himself he emptied the piggy bank onto the soft leather couch and counted out just over twenty pounds in change.

A few minutes later, the BBC's swimming hippos graphic appeared on screen and the continuity announcer introduced their flagship *Breakfast* programme. Marty sat forward and waited for what he guessed would be the inevitable 'trial-by-media'; he would not be disappointed.

Delivered over a dramatic news theme, CCTV footage of Marty running from Rochelle's room, opened the show with the caption – RADIO STAR CONNECTED TO SERIAL KILLINGS. The show's anchors, Sam Davenport and Neil Bainbridge, wasted no time in setting the scene.

'... Manchester and the UK wake to a further twist in the story of the fugitive radio host Marty Michaels...'

Bainbridge handed straight back to news reporter Suzanne Callaghan live from outside the Airport Exchange Hotel, as she proceeded to walk the audience through the events of the previous twenty-four hours, scene by scene. The CCTV footage of Marty running from the room played as she explained security had discovered the body of a woman in her room at the hotel. They had not named the victim and Callaghan went on to explain that moments after discovering the woman's body, *'prominent radio shock-jock'* Marty Michaels, already wanted on an outstanding murder charge, had been seen fleeing the scene. They played the footage of Marty running from Rochelle's room, followed by additional video of him chased by security as he jumped over the fence at the back of the hotel. Unconfirmed reports suggested the police had not ruled out foul-play and that the two victims may have known each other. Those same 'unconfirmed reports' – which Marty knew from his own experience, had come from within the Force – suggested the victim may also have been sexually assaulted.

Marty sat wide-eyed, mouth open but unable to speak. He couldn't have looked more guilty if he had tried: two dead bodies, both supposedly sexually assaulted and killed by the same means, and this time, CCTV footage of Marty running from the murder scene. For a moment, he even questioned himself; had he *really* been drugged or knocked out? He knew there was darkness within him; he had battled it for most of his adult life, burying it in alcohol and more latterly cocaine. Had the demons finally taken hold of him? Had he raped White and Rochelle before killing them? Was he really a monster, schizophrenic even? His mind raced, searching for answers, until a familiar face appeared on screen and drew him back to the TV. APC Blake was making a statement outside Ashton House, presumably from the previous evening. Cameras flashed all around him and microphones emblazoned with radio and TV station logos battled for screen time under Blake's chin.

'I can confirm a body was found this evening in a guest room at the Manchester Airport Exchange Hotel. We urgently need to locate Marty Michaels who we believe was in the room with the victim around the time of death, and who witnesses saw running from the scene some time later. Two days ago, Mr. Michaels, who was under house arrest charged with the murder of Paul White, broke the terms of his bail and left his Prestbury home travelling into Manchester. Shortly afterwards we know he booked an appointment at the victim's place of work before going

on the run as officers closed in on his location. He evaded capture, resurfacing this evening at the Manchester Airport Exchange Hotel. Regrettably, he left the hotel before security or police could question him. We are appealing to the public to come forward with any information they may have on his whereabouts, and we urge anyone who may be helping Mr. Michaels to hand him over to the authorities or risk arrest. I have my best team working on locating Mr. Michaels and we've drafted in additional officers from across the county to help us in this manhunt. In light of recent events, I would remind the public not to approach Mr. Michaels who is regarded as dangerous, and instead, ask them to call the emergency helpline which is being displayed on the screen now.'

A barrage of questions followed but Marty had heard enough and switched the TV to mute. It struck him that Blake was choosing his language very carefully for maximum effect, as if trying to convict Marty live on TV; *'... evading capture... manhunt... not to approach Mr. Michaels... regarded as dangerous...'*

With the increased number of police looking for him, Marty knew the clock was ticking and whoever checked his mum's place last night could be back again this morning; police or not, he didn't want to be here when they arrived. Switching off the TV, he laced up his Converse sneakers and pulled on his cap before scooping the coins into the pockets of his jeans and heading towards the back door. Before he could reach it, he heard screeching tyres and the sound of cars coming to a sudden stop on his mother's driveway; blue and red light flooded through the smoked-glass front door, bouncing off the white walls of the hallway around him.

They were already here.

CHAPTER 46

There was no time to stop and think. He fumbled with the lock on the back door, rushing into the garden at the rear of the house. Shouts from police officers echoed from the field behind; they were boxing him in. He considered the dog kennel again, but with the sun coming up, he knew he would be easily visible in daylight.

Multiple footsteps began to echo down each side of the house accompanied by the audible click and buzz of police radios. Out of the corner of his eye, he spotted the opening to the old coal chute running into the coal bunker and cellar under the house. He raced towards it, pulling up the heavy metal grate and forcing his thick frame into the hole, sliding quickly and heavily into the darkness, before reaching up and pulling the grate back over his head, just as a team of officers swarmed into the garden. He crouched perfectly still trying to regulate his breathing, which in the confined space sounded like it was amplified through a Marshall stack.

Peering up towards the daylight, he counted four uniformed officers pacing around the garden. A moment later, he heard a loud muffled bang above his head coming from the direction of his mum's front door followed by an intense rumble of feet, rushing through the house across the floorboards, along the hallway and into the kitchen. It was hard to make out how many people were above him, but Blake was true to his word, they were looking for him en masse.

Above him, the footsteps continued to move around the house, interspersed with the murmur of voices, and he could hear a mixture of heavy and light objects being dropped around the ground floor.

Two of the officers in the garden stood close to Marty's position now, chatting idly to each other about last night's match at Old Trafford, an unexpected European defeat for Manchester United from what he could make out. One of the officers glanced towards Marty's location and he instinctively ducked, making an unnecessary amount of noise. The conversation tailed off as one of the men moved closer to the coal chute, kicking the grate with his booted foot.

'Mick, have you seen this?' he shouted to his fellow football fan who duly wandered towards his partner who had squatted down peering into the darkness below, 'Any idea what this is?' he asked.

The second officer crouched down next to him and grabbed at the thick metal.

'Looks like a coal bunker to me. Me nan used to 'ave one when I were a kid…'

'Do you reckon you could fit a bloke in one of those?' asked the first officer.

Staring up at the two men from the darkness, Marty's body tensed, his mouth bone-dry. He was sure every officer within a square mile could hear the loud clicking of his tongue against his palate.

As both officers began to pull at the grate, Marty edged himself towards the back wall of the bunker in a vain attempt to avoid capture. Grandiose images flooded his mind of Saddam Hussein dragged from a hole in the ground.

'Pass us your torch,' said the first officer and his mate duly obliged, shining the thick beam directly into the bunker.

'It looks pretty big.'

'Yeah, me nan's was massive. You'll have to get into the hole to see it properly,' said the second man.

'Bollocks to that! I'll get stuck!' the first one said, patting his ample belly for effect.

Both men laughed and the second officer suggested going in through the connecting door in the cellar. They both agreed it made sense and one of them headed into the house, whilst the other stayed guarding the grate. Trapped, he racked his brain for a solution, but drew a blank.

Suddenly there was a commotion in the house above. He could hear someone rushing to the back door, which opened a split second later, allowing Marty to hear a voice he had come to know well in the last week: Detective Chief Inspector Phillips. He could not make out what she was saying, but it was important enough for the officer above the grate to jump to his feet and follow her, and the rest of the team back into the house without protest. A moment later, the entire team appeared to leave by the front door.

Marty waited, cowering in the darkness for at least five minutes in case any of the team came back, but nobody did.

Finally convinced it was safe to come out, he climbed back up the chute with some difficulty, coughing loudly as he eventually collapsed on the concrete patio outside, stifling an involuntary, maniacal giggle as he did.

He could not believe his luck: another minute and one of the officers would have come face to face with their fugitive.

DCI Phillips would never know just how close she had come to finding the most wanted man in the UK.

CHAPTER 47

Peering through the tiny gaps in the wooden gate at the side of his mum's house, Marty spotted two uniformed police officers leaning on a panda car on the street at the front. They appeared to be alone and were idly chatting about something, but nothing he could hear. Retracing his steps, he tiptoed across the garden and lifted himself back over the fence and into the woods beyond. Crouching, he moved slowly through the rough terrain along the fence line that led to the various neighbours' gardens. He passed a number of houses until someone opening a gate ahead of him stopped him dead in his tracks and he darted for cover behind a tree.

He took a quick look at the man and could see he was pushing a mountain bike, wearing full cycling regalia: black Lycra shorts and a tight-fitting yellow jersey, black gloves and a bright red helmet. He turned to face the house where a woman was shouting something Marty couldn't quite make out. Whatever it was, the man reacted with agitation, muttering under his breath as he laid his bike gently on the ground and stomped off back in the direction of the house.

Marty's mother had always told him 'never to look a gift-horse in the mouth', and now he knew the value of her wise words. Jumping from behind the tree, he ran through the gate, grabbed the mountain bike and ran as fast as he could back into the woods, pushing it over broken branches and twigs before a moment later straddling it and attempting to pedal. Behind him he could hear the man shouting as he began to give chase. It was an expensive model and the cleated pedals required special shoes that fixed the rider's feet in place. Marty's flat and now wet Converse trainer slipped from the pedal as he tried to get the bike moving; the heavy metal block spun full circle and slammed painfully into his shin. He cried out in pain but angrily tried again, this time getting enough weight on the pedal to get the bike moving forward, slowly at first, over the bumpy terrain. He could hear the man was gaining ground behind him and considered ditching the bike and making a run for it, before finally gaining momentum; a second later he was up and running, putting distance between himself and his pursuer. With a surge of power, he was finally clear and pedalling with all his might as he headed into the freshly cut grass and safety of Hollyhedge Park.

Five hundred metres later, he stopped as he hit Altrincham Road. Glancing behind, he saw the man was still giving chase, waving his arms and shouting, which would soon draw unwelcome attention from passers-by. He had to keep moving and headed towards Longley Lane. After about half a mile, he pulled on to the side of the road by the recycling centre, attempting to catch his breath.

In spite of his new-found transport, he knew he could not make it alone and needed help to stay off the grid. He desperately wanted to contact Simon but could not remember his mobile or home number. He figured the best thing to do was call Rob, his number ingrained on Marty's brain after fifteen years without change.

Surprised and relieved to find a working payphone close by, he eagerly pushed in some of the loose change from his mum's house and pressed the sequence of numbers. Frustratingly, it rang out after about ten seconds.

'Bloody typical!' Marty said angrily.

He tried again with the same result.

'The man's an idiot. He's never bloody there when I need him!'

He tried one more time and just as he was about to give up, he heard the familiar voice of Rob.

'Hello?'

'Rob! Thank God!'

'Marty? Where have you been?' Rob sounded surprised to hear from his client.

Marty wasted no time.

'I didn't do it, Rob! I didn't kill Rochelle. I'm being set up!'

'OK, OK, I believe you Marty, I do, but this is really messed up now. Where are you? Can I come get you?'

'No, I have to keep moving. I've stolen a bike and the police will be looking for it pretty soon. If I hang around, they'll find me in no time.'

'OK then, can you come here to my place?'

'No chance, they'll be looking for me there too. We need neutral territory, somewhere they wouldn't think of.'

There was a moment of silence between the two men as both considered the options. Rob spoke first.

'How about the city?'

'Have you gone mad? It's wall-to-wall CCTV in there!'

'I know that but it's the Manchester Marathon today, there'll be tens of thousands of faces milling about, the roads are shut and the police will be focused on the runners and the crowds, and potential terror threats. If you can wear a cap or something to cover your face, it'll be a great place to blend in.'

Marty considered the idea and he had to agree it had merit. Although it was a big risk to put his now-infamous face into a crowd that size, after four days on the run his beard was thick and almost white, and his Cubs cap had a large peak that could help him hide his face. He nodded into the mouthpiece.

'OK, let's do it. Where do you suggest?'

'Well, it starts at Portland Street at 11am so it'll be really busy up there first thing. How about somewhere nearby, behind the library maybe?'

'That could work; there are some trees by Mosley Street we could use for cover. What time shall we meet?'

'It's just gone eight now; ten?' offered Rob.

Marty looked around him to ensure he was still alone.

'OK, see you under the trees at the back of the library at ten,' he said and hung up without waiting for a response.

He figured he was about eight miles from the city now and with two hours until the meet, felt confident he could make it on time – as long as he could stay out of sight.

*

Marty left the bike in the car park of an office block just off St. Peter's Square and hoped it would still be there if he needed it later – but in today's world he knew it was unlikely. As he walked away, he hoped his mum's neighbour was insured.

It was 9.30am. He had half an hour to kill before meeting up with Rob and intended to use the time to his advantage. A nagging doubt had been building inside him on his journey into the city, paranoid that someone had been listening to his call with Rob. If that were true, he planned to spot *them* before they spotted *him*.

Last Christmas, Marty had championed a campaign to raise awareness of the homelessness crisis in Manchester. It was commonplace now to see people living in tents across the city and more and more people were dying from the effects of harsh winters. Highlighting the issue, Marty had gone undercover and posed as a homeless person, trying to understand the challenges faced every single day. The results were gut-wrenching. Never had he felt more invisible sitting on the pavement of Manchester's busiest street, Deansgate. The best way to *disappear* is to *appear* homeless – because people will look anywhere but directly at you. Grabbing an empty Starbucks cup from a trash can and with his cap covering his face, he sat down where he could see the location for the meet as well as all routes in.

As Rob had suggested, the streets were teeming with people, dressed in numbered vests and running gear, all excitedly chatting about their plans for the race. It was a warm summer's morning and the sun was shining brightly. As expected, sitting on the ground holding a cup, nobody wanted to make eye contact. For a moment he smiled to himself; the UK's most wanted man, hiding in broad daylight and in full view of the city!

At around 9.45am, Marty spotted Rob entering Albert Square on the corner of Lloyd Street and his spirits lifted; seeing his oldest friend gave him hope he could still find a way out of this mess. Dressed in his usual crisp grey suit and white shirt, he was on the phone. *Typical*, thought Marty smiling. Despite the urge to do so, he resisted the temptation to run to the relative safety of Rob; he had to remain vigilant in case he was being followed.

Rob appeared tense and engrossed in the call. *Nothing unusual there*, thought Marty; he was after all one of the UK's most prolific agents. However, there was something else that did not quite fit. His eyes were darting around Albert Square, and as he finished the call, he took what looked like a large intake of breath and closed his eyes for a moment. A man Marty had never seen before joined him, dark-skinned with jet-black oiled hair wearing a black tailored suit and white shirt open at the neck. He was muscular, taller than Rob at about six foot three and wearing sunglasses. The two men did not greet each other but spoke quickly as Rob pointed towards the library before they separated and the dark-haired man walked in the opposite direction, immediately pulling out his phone to make a call. Marty followed the man as far as he could before turning to locate Rob, who had started to walk towards the library and the location of the meet.

He instinctively knew something was very wrong as he moved quietly and slowly behind Rob, scanning the area around him for signs of anything unusual. Rob reached the trees as agreed at the back of the library and stood in the shade with his hands in his pockets. Wearing his suit, he looked incongruous with his surroundings as waves of Lycra-clad runners walked past him towards the starting line without offering him so much as a cursory look. Marty had stopped by a payphone, all the time keeping his eyes on Rob and the surrounding area. Loading in some small change, he dialled Rob's mobile and watched as he fumbled inside his suit jacket pocket, checked the unknown number on the phone and then answered.

'Hello?'

'It's me,' said Marty flatly.

'Marty? Where are you, mate?' Rob asked looking around, his voice brimming with tension.

'I'm close by.'

'Let me know and I'll come and get you.'

'Were you followed, Rob?' Marty asked coldly.

The question clearly caught Rob off guard as he stuttered his response, spinning on his heels trying to locate Marty's position.

'*Followed*, me? No, why would you say that?'

'Did you meet anyone on the way here, Rob?'

'Marty, what's this about?'

'Answer the fucking question, Rob. Did you meet anyone on the way to meet me – yes or no?'

'Of course I didn't meet anyone. I came straight here to pick you up, mate.'

Marty's heart sank. His best friend and agent, the one man he thought he could trust, was lying.

'Goodbye, Rob,' he said quietly and replaced the receiver with a heavy heart, glancing one more time at his erstwhile friend who was still calling Marty's name into his mobile. A moment later, he turned into the crowd and made his escape.

CHAPTER 48

Marty drifted along with the crowd of runners, keeping his head down and face hidden under the peak of his cap as he tried to come to terms with the fact Rob had lied to him. Worse still, he had potentially been trying to help someone catch him. It didn't make sense; he and Rob had worked together for over fifteen years, they had become very close and since David's death, Marty had considered him his best mate. Always there when he needed him, sorting out the mess Marty left behind and picking up the pieces when he went off the deep end, a more and more regular occurrence since the split with Rebecca. He would have bet his life on Rob's unwavering support in any situation, no matter how grave – and yet he had lied to Marty at a time when he needed him more than ever. *Why?*

After allowing himself to follow the slipstream of runners making their way to the starting line through the back streets of Manchester, Marty had unconsciously found his way to the top of Portland Street close to the Northern Quarter. Taking a moment, he realised he was less than a quarter of a mile from Williams's apartment. There was a chance the police had picked Williams up or followed him home, but the risk was negligible compared to staying out in the open. Ten minutes later Marty stood on the corner of High Street and New George Street staring at the front entrance to the reporter's apartment block. The area was a no-car zone and on a Sunday was pretty much deserted. Still, he took his time scanning the streets and surrounding buildings for signs of anything that might resemble a surveillance team – *whatever that might look like.*

Satisfied there was nothing obviously out of place, Marty crossed the street towards the front door. Checking the buzzer system he found one marked 'Williams', pressed the call button and prayed it was Williams's. The bell was the kind that continued to ring loudly until answered at the other end, and in the quietness of the deserted street, it sounded like an alarm going off, signalling to the world that Marty Michaels, murder suspect and fugitive, had arrived. Thankfully, it eventually stopped as a distant voice spoke quietly through the tiny speaker.

'Who is it?' the voice asked sharply.

'I'm looking for Simon,' Marty said quietly.

'What?'

'Simon, I'm looking for Simon.'

'Who are you?'

Marty began to feel vulnerable.

'Is this Simon Williams's apartment?'

'Tell me who you are or piss off,' came the reply.

This was all he needed, twenty bloody questions.

Looking around, Marty could see a young couple walking up High Street carrying bags of groceries and heading straight towards him. *Shit or bust, Marty.*

'It's Marty,' he shouted into the buzzer.

'Who?'

Marty turned his back to the couple still heading towards him and cupped his hands around his mouth attempting to channel his voice directly into the intercom.

'I said, it's Marty *Michaels*! Marty bloody *Michaels*! Now let me in, you deaf bastard!'

'Marty? Oh thank God!' The door buzzed open. 'Flat 37, top floor.'

Marty took the stairs and quickly found the top floor corridor and number 37. The door was open. Williams appeared sporting a black eye and swollen lip, beckoning Marty to follow him into the lounge.

'What happened?' Marty asked.

'I could ask you the same thing, mate,' Williams said as he offered Marty the couch, taking up his usual position in the armchair.

Having lost his twenty grand, Marty deflected the question.

'All in good time, Simon. For now, tell me who did that to your face.'

'Not one hundred per cent sure, if I'm honest. I was waiting for you in the car park of the Exchange, when I heard all hell breaking loose as you legged it out of the fire doors into the car park, followed by that security guard. As soon as you went over the fence, I got away sharpish and went looking for you, but because of the one-way system around the terminals, by the time I got to where you landed there was no sign of you. I hung about for a while but as soon as the coppers turned up and blue lights started flashing, I figured it was best I disappeared.'

'You did the right thing. Look, I appreciate you coming after me, fella, but the last thing I need is you banged up.'

'Yeah, well anyway, I drove home slowly, all the time keeping an eye out for anyone following me. Nothing looked out of the ordinary so after a couple of loops round the Mancunian Way I pulled in here and came upstairs to the flat. I dropped my laptop bag on the couch, cos I never go anywhere without my laptop, grabbed a Scotch and tried to figure out what to do next.'

Marty was desperate for Williams to get to the point.

'*And?*'

'And then I hear a knock on the door. Not the buzzer from downstairs, that actual door there,' he said pointing behind Marty. 'So naturally, after what's been happening to you, I shit my pants thinking who the bloody hell is this? The banging continues, steady but not loud, kind of gentle. After a few minutes, I eventually pluck up the courage to creep up to the peephole and I can see a man stood outside.'

Marty leaned forward. 'What did he look like?'

'That's just it. He's wearing a high-vis waistcoat and a hard hat with the brim covering most of his face, "National Grid" written on the front. I ask him what he wants through the door and he tells me there's been a gas leak and he needs to get into my apartment.'

'Tell me you didn't open the bloody door, Simon?'

'What was I supposed to do? Gas is gas, if it leaks, it can explode. So I asked for ID and he flashes it up to the peephole but I can't see it. I tell him that, so he tries again, but still I can't make it out. I tell him it's no use and he says I need to open the door. I agree but push the chain into place so he can't get in. Well, that didn't bloody work, did it? As soon as I released the door, he throws himself at it and smashes it into my face. I roll backwards and before I even hit the floor he hits me with something hard and knocks me out cold.'

Marty began pacing the room nervously.

'Jesus Christ! Who are these people?'

'I dunno, mate, but this guy was after something specific. When I came round my laptop was gone along with my car keys, but nothing else.'

'He nicked your car?

'That's just it, no. The laptop's gone but the car's downstairs in the garage. He's clearly given it the once-over but whatever it was he was looking for, he didn't find. He even left the keys on the front seat.'

'What would they want with your laptop? More to the point, how would they even know you were helping me?'

'I can only think someone was watching at the hotel and followed me. As for the laptop, I'm really not sure.'

'Anything on it that might be of value?' Marty said as he sat back down on the sofa.

'Just my notes on your story so far and the potential connection to the COMCO buy-out and China, but to be fair, it is just notes at this stage; nothing concrete or printable and I backed everything up onto this before we went out last night,' Williams said as he held up a USB drive. 'So it's annoying but not the end of the world,' he added and shrugged.

Marty suddenly remembered the keys and key ring left behind at the hotel by Rochelle. He rummaged in his pocket and held it up so Williams could see.

'What's that? Williams asked.

'I found these keys on the floor of the hotel just under the bed. There's a USB attached. If our friend Paul White was a computer-whiz, I'm hoping this was what Rochelle was going to sell me for the twenty grand.'

Williams looked puzzled. 'What do you mean *was* going to sell you?' he asked.

Marty sighed and sat back. 'You'd better get us a drink,' he said. 'It's a long bloody story.'

*

Williams listened intently as Marty explained how his night had unfolded from seeing Rochelle tied up, to finding her dead body and his subsequent escape as he went on the run from the police. He finished at the point where Rob had lied to him, then drained his glass and stared into the empty tumbler, as if looking for answers.

'So as you can see, I'm totally screwed. I'm wanted for two murders and my best mate is helping the police find me.'

Williams scratched his stubbly chin.

'Are you sure he was a copper?'

'Well, I guess so. Who else could it be?'

'There's a chance he could be working for the people setting you up.'

'No way, not Rob. He's a bit of wide-boy but he's not a total bastard. He'll be helping the police in some misguided way because he thinks I'd be better off giving myself up. It has to be that...' Marty's words tailed off; he was already starting to doubt them.

Williams took another gulp of Scotch and cradled the glass in the fingers of both hands.

'Look Marty, I don't know Rob, but I do know that whoever these guys are, they have killed at least two people that we know of, maybe more. They're powerful and dangerous so who's to say they haven't got to him as well?'

Marty shook his head but knew Williams could well be right as he glanced down at the key ring and USB cradled in his palm.

'Whoever is after me and whoever it is that's pulling Rob's strings, I'm pretty sure we should have a look at this and see if it holds any clues.'

Williams nodded as he grabbed the USB.

'I have a USB point on the TV; let's look at it on the big screen.'

The wall-mounted fifty-inch screen sparked into life as Williams worked the remote looking for the right input and Marty was quickly faced with a list of at least one hundred unnamed but numbered folders staring down at him.

'Jesus, look at this,' he said exhaling loudly. 'This could take a while.'

Williams nodded, a sudden cheerfulness coming over him.

'Journalistic nirvana…' he said smiling. 'Un-mined gold, fella, un-mined gold!'

Clicking on the first folder at the top of the stack revealed a greyed-out Word document of some kind that would not open on the TV and a QuickTime movie file which Williams quickly opened and fired into life. The video software built into the TV took a moment to convert the file before the progress bar and the counter at the bottom of the screen rolled forward in tandem. At first, the screen remained black, with voices in the distance neither man could make out, before a picture suddenly appeared. It took a moment to focus but it soon became apparent they were watching two people having violent sex in the doggy-style position, the camera shooting them at a slight angle from the front. The man was clearly middle-aged with a large potbelly and greying hair, naked apart from a pair of socks hanging loosely from his feet. The woman, or more accurately girl, was petite, her face obscured by her hair which hung over her face. She groaned every time the man thrust himself into her at a frenzied pace, his face red and bloated, his eyes wild as saliva fell freely from his open mouth onto her back. Marty did not recognise him and when the girl's face finally appeared, neither Marty nor Williams knew her either. The only thing that did look in any way familiar was the room around them, but Marty could not place it. They decided to move on, closing the video and trying the next folder in the stack containing similar footage of a different middle-aged man and another young girl. So the process continued, as they trawled the files looking for anything connected to Marty that could help prove his innocence.

After almost an hour, he was beginning to lose hope. So far all they had uncovered was a raft of home-made porn videos of older men and younger women having sex like teenagers expecting their parents home any minute; nothing of use at all. Standing, he cursed as he wandered over to the balcony doors and gazed out onto the city streets below.

'It's no use, Simon; I'm well and truly fucked,' he said without turning around.

Ever the investigative journalist, Williams was diligently working his way through the files searching for the slightest thing that might help them.

'Mate, until we've checked every file, you can't give up hope. Even then, in my experience, you look at them again from a different angle. That's how you find stuff that others miss,' he said.

Still staring out of the window, Marty exhaled loudly, placing his hands behind his head as he stretched his upper body out.

'I'm done fighting, Simon. There's too many of them and I've got nothing. I might as well face it – it's over.'

Blessed with a flair for the dramatic, Marty waited for the enormity of his words to land, but the silent response from the room behind him wasn't what he was expecting. After a moment, he turned to face Williams who was now totally engrossed in the latest file he was watching. Marty followed his gaze and what he saw stopped him in his tracks.

'Is that who I think it is?' he asked.

Williams nodded furiously, his eyes never leaving the screen, 'I think it is, mate. I think it bloody well is.'

Marty stumbled to the sofa and sat beside Williams, 'Oh my God! That's Assistant Police Commissioner Blake!' he shouted.

'Yep, and that young woman with her face in his groin is *not* Mrs. Blake!'

'No it certainly is not!' scoffed Marty as they watched a young woman performing oral sex on the police boss.

'Jesus Christ! This is gold,' proclaimed Williams, excitedly.

Marty's mind raced with possibilities.

'When is this video dated?' he asked.

'Er… I think it was about twelve months ago.'

Marty thought for a moment.

'Fast-forward and see if there's anything else on this.'

Williams obliged, and over the course of the video, they discovered APC Blake enjoyed a host of sexual positions and varying degrees of sexual violence with three young women, all of different ethnic origin. The full video ran for over two hours and it was clear he possessed unexpected stamina.

Satisfied they had exhausted the Blake video, they moved onto the next folder, disappointedly void of anyone they knew, as was the next and the one after that. The initial euphoria of Blake's video began to wane as Marty realised that whilst he had eyes on a juicy piece of gossip, he had precious little to help him stay out of prison.

As if sensing Marty's disappointment, Williams reassured him they had plenty of folders still to review and that he was sure one of them would hold the key to proving his innocence. Marty was not convinced and headed for the kitchen to make himself a hot drink. Fumbling his way around the small space looking for coffee and a clean mug, his mind wandered back to the rooms where the videos were shot; all identical in colour and layout, all very familiar to Marty. Suddenly, it hit him.

'That's it!' he shouted loudly and ran back into the lounge room to share his discovery with Williams. 'I've got it! I recognise where the videos were shot!' he stated proudly.

Williams turned; his face grave as Marty continued to beam at him.

'Didn't you hear me, Simon? I know where they were filmed! The Metropolitan – the Sky Tower,' he said excitedly, but something in the way Williams was looking at him made his blood run cold.

'What? What is it?' he asked as Williams's gaze returned to the screen and the paused video file that filled the TV. Marty followed his line of sight and a moment later flopped down onto the sofa.

'What the *fuck*?'

Staring back at him was a face he knew only too well, his agent and best mate, Rob.

'I don't believe it,' Marty said in a whisper.

'I know, mate,' said Williams sympathetically as they stared at the frozen image of a naked Rob being penetrated from behind by the man Marty had found dead in his hotel room – Paul White.

There was a moment of silence before Marty spoke, 'Play the rest of the tape, Simon,' he said flatly.

'Are you sure? You don't have to watch this shit, you know; I can do it.'

Marty's gaze never left the screen. 'Play the damn tape,' he growled.

Marty and Williams watched in uncomfortable silence as the movie file unfolded, revealing Rob's clear enjoyment of hardcore sex with men.

'But he's not gay!' Marty protested 'I've known him for almost twenty years and I've never seen anything that would indicate he's gay.'

'Doesn't mean he isn't. Some people can go a whole lifetime in the closet publicly, and have a long-term lover in private to match the wife and kids at home.'

Marty nodded his agreement but he still could not comprehend what he had just discovered.

'Seriously, though, in the early days, he and I had a threesome with a girl and he could, you know, *perform*.'

'Well maybe he's bi? If that's the case, he could easily get an erection in those instances.'

Marty tried to process this new information.

'Or alternatively, *you* gave him a stiffy!' Williams said, attempting to stifle his childish grin unsuccessfully.

'Piss off!' Marty replied throwing a cushion at him.

After a long moment, Marty took the initiative.

'Let's see who else is on here.'

Williams obliged and they began trawling the remaining folders, none of which gave anything away, until finally they reached the last remaining unopened folder.

'Right, mate, this is it. Here goes nothing,' Williams said and pressed play.

The image on the screen was of a darkened room, a bed in the centre of the shot with the body of a naked man lying prostrate across it, his face turned away from the camera. Like those before him, it appeared to be in the Metropolitan and from behind the lens, voices could clearly be heard, one a British male, the other an Asian female.

'Turn the bedside light on…' said the man, '… and pull his legs round towards the camera so we can see his dick.'

A woman appeared in shot with her back to camera and quickly dragged the motionless body toward the lens before turning to face the camera. Marty recognised Rochelle instantly. The man spoke again.

'How long ago did we slip him the Viagra?'

'Almost two hours now,' replied the woman as she turned on the bedside light, revealing the naked man sporting a full erection.

'Right, looks good. We just need to see his face,' he said as Rochelle stepped back into shot and carefully – and surprisingly gently – turned the man's face to camera. As Marty finally laid eyes on the unconscious man, he felt the urge to vomit. Even Williams appeared lost for words, eventually finding the strength to mutter, 'Oh shit.'

'It can't be… it just cannot be!' Marty said.

Williams pressed pause on the video and stared at Marty, his face a mixture of sadness and pity.

'Sorry, mate, but it is. That's *you* on the bed.'

Marty was struggling to comprehend what he was seeing, his own naked body, prostrate, unconscious and sporting an erection, being manhandled by Rochelle.

'Why don't I watch this on my own?' Williams said.

Marty shook his head. 'No, play the tape.'

Williams did as instructed and they watched together, Marty's body placed in various sexual positions with the man behind the camera revealing himself as Paul White. White, in turn, acted as Marty's lover, at one point performing oral sex on him. The process seemed oddly efficient as White and Rochelle discussed angles, shots and positions requested by a third party

259

who had now joined them off camera. The final act made Marty feel sick and violated as he watched White yanking his penis vigorously until he ejaculated into a plastic container.

'That explains your semen in his mouth,' Williams said.

'It explains how they got it but not much else,' Marty replied.

Williams and Marty watched on as the couple placed the gimp mask on Marty's head and positioned him on the bed, pulling the covers over him like parents covering their child at bedtime; probably the most surreal image Marty had ever seen. As the couple began to tidy up, White appeared to accidentally knock the camera, forcing it to spin and catch the reflection of the full-length mirror on the wall, opposite the bed. For a split second a man's face appeared before the camera was switched off, ending the movie.

'Go back,' Marty barked.

'Hey?'

'Go back to the point where the camera gets knocked to the side.'

Williams obliged, running the tape back to the final moments.

'Pause it,' said Marty, 'and run it back shot by shot.'

Again, Williams did as asked and, frame by frame, the picture unfolded until they came face to face with the third person in the room.

'Jesus Christ, Rob, what did you do?' Marty said.

'What it is, Marty?'

'Rob Woodcock,' Marty muttered. '*You bastard.*'

Williams looked like he would burst. 'Are you going to tell me what we're looking at, Marty?' he said loudly.

Marty pointed to the screen and spoke in a measured voice. 'The man in the mirror, that's the guy I saw talking to Rob this morning in Albert Square.'

'No way!'

'I think it's fair to say that he's not a bloody copper.'

Williams nodded his agreement.

'In fact, based on this evidence, you were right – Rob is working for the same people that set me up.'

'This is so messed up,' Williams said pouring himself and Marty another large Scotch each before draining his glass noisily. 'What do you wanna do?'

'Well firstly, I wanna kill that son of a bitch Rob Woodcock; if I'm going down for murder, I may as well make the most of it!'

CHAPTER 49

The journey south to Rob's Wilmslow home through Sunday evening traffic had taken just under thirty minutes from the Northern Quarter. Both men had agreed that using Williams's car presented too much of a risk, and borrowing a VW Golf pool car from the Guardian's Manchester offices, Williams had driven with Marty hidden from view laid out across the back seat.

As they approached Rob's impressive detached Victorian villa, partially hidden behind thick oak gates and a high red-brick wall, Williams spotted a Ford Mondeo parked at the end of the street, two men sat in the front.

'I think we have a couple of coppers watching the house,' Williams said without turning his head towards Marty.

'How do you know they're coppers?' Marty asked.

'Because they look very bored!' Williams joked as they continued at a steady pace towards the two men. 'Right, keep your head down,' he said before locking eyes with the driver who stared back intently as they passed. Marty held his breath and pushed himself down onto the fabric of the back seat.

'What if they run a check on this car?' he asked

'If they do, they'll find it registered to the Guardian Media Group; and why would they worry about one more reporter, scoping out Marty Michaels's agent's house?' Williams said as he brought the car to a stop, a safe distance from the two men, all the time keeping his eyes on them in the rear-view mirror.

'I dunno, Simon. Seems like we're taking a big risk,' Marty said.

'Look, we'll pull up here a good distance away from the coppers and *I'll* watch the house. If they leave, we'll go in, if they don't then we'll think of something else, won't we?' Williams said cheerily and slowly began performing a three-point turn, moving the car to a position where he could clearly see the men as well as the entrance gate to Rob's house.

Lost in thought, Marty stared at the back of the seat ahead of him and both men remained silent. He began to feel his eyes become heavy and a moment later he drifted into sleep as his mind and body gave way to exhaustion.

His dream was frenzied and vivid, seeing David and his father trapped in a burning car, slamming their hands on the windows as they screamed for help but made no sound whatsoever, Rob and the mystery man watching on. Marty tried to scream for help but his jaw was locked shut. He wanted to run to them, but his legs would not move and, from a distance, a voice began calling his name over, and over.

'Marty!' Williams said prodding him from the front seat as he woke up with a start, his heart jumping as if it would stop for good.

'Sorry to wake you, but looks like we have movement,' Williams added.

Marty resisted the urge to sit up, instead taking some time to gather himself as Williams continued to narrate the scene in front of him.

'Rob's gates are opening and it looks like a car's leaving…'

'What kind of car is it?'

'Range Rover.'

'Colour?'

'Metallic-grey, I'd say.'

'That's Rob's. Can you see who's driving?'

'Hang on a minute...' Williams said craning his neck, '... he's looking away from me but he's dark skinned with a shaven head.'

'Sounds like him,' Marty said as Williams urged the driver to look towards him and Marty.

'Come on, fella, check both ways for traffic...' he said before exclaiming excitedly, '... we have a winner! It's Rob all right.'

Marty was desperate to lift himself up for a proper look but stayed low. 'What now?'

'Well, if the coppers don't follow him, that's exactly what we'll do,' Simon said, his voice brimming with excitement. It was clear to Marty that Simon loved the thrill of chasing a story as much as he used to.

Simon fired the ignition on the Golf and depressed the automatic handbrake switch.

'Looks like the coppers aren't moving, mate – so we are!' he said cheerfully and set off after Rob's Range Rover, which had reached the end of the street and was signalling left towards Alderley Edge.

Simon stayed a safe distance behind Rob's car and when he was confident the two men weren't following, Marty sat up in the back seat to help stave off his growing sense of nausea.

They drove for around fifteen minutes into the affluent village of Alderley Edge, once home to David and Victoria Beckham during his playing days at Manchester United. As a resident in the next village of Prestbury, Marty knew it well but had no idea where Rob was heading; he never mentioned having friends near the 'Edge'.

As they pulled into *f* Road, one of Manchester's most exclusive addresses, Rob began to slow and indicated that he was turning left into one of the houses. Williams pulled into the side of the street behind a row of parked cars with Rob still in clear sight, and killed the engine as the two men sat in silence, their eyes fixed on Rob's car.

A minute passed before the large wooden gates in front of the Range Rover began to open slowly. Rob moved the big car through, and the gates closed behind him.

'Who could he possibly know that lives there?' Marty said loudly.

Williams was in a more thoughtful mood. 'Not sure but there's one way to find out,' he replied, picking up his mobile phone.

'It's seven o'clock on a Sunday night; who on earth are you ringing now?'

'A source,' came the sharp reply, as the iPhone connected and rang four times before it was answered. Williams got straight to the point.

'It's me. I need an address check.'

Marty could hear someone speaking back to Williams but could not make out what they were saying as Williams nodded.

'Blackfarm Road, number twelve… yep… thanks,' he said and ended the call.

Marty's interest was piqued. 'Who was that?'

'Like I said, a source,' Williams said smiling, 'and you know I can't reveal a source.'

'Seriously, who I am going to tell?' Marty protested.

'Let's just say he's very well connected and leave it at that,' Williams chuckled.

For the next thirty minutes, the two men sat in silence, all eyes on the gates to the house, their focus punctuated only by the occasional car, which would cause Marty to duck down, out of sight.

Eventually Williams's phone began to vibrate and as he pulled it from his pocket, Marty spied the contact name on the big screen simply said 'T'.

Williams wasted no time. 'What you got?' he barked.

The voice on the other end sounded efficient and continued unabated despite Williams's seemingly constant commentary, 'Right… yeah… OK… I guess that makes sense… no shit!'

Marty stared at Williams with wide eyes and his mouth open urging him to share his new-found information but Williams just smiled and held up his index finger indicating Marty needed to be patient, before pulling a notepad from the inside pocket of his jacket and scribbling notes furiously. Marty attempted to read them but Williams had horrific handwriting and he eventually gave up. After five minutes, Williams thanked his mystery caller and rang off.

'What? Who lives there?' Marty begged.

Williams smiled and nodded. 'This is all starting to make sense now,' he murmured.

'What is? For God's sake, this isn't a game show – give me the bloody low-down, will you?'

'All right, keep your wig on,' laughed Williams. 'Turns out the house is leased from a company in the village called Edge Estates to a business based in Jersey going by the name of Delta Holdings. Now Delta Holdings have diverse interests all over the world in newspapers and magazines. They're a big outfit and in Europe their CEO is a guy called Frank Fairchild.'

'Should I have heard of him?'

'No, I don't suppose you should, but he's an American with a very interesting past. Turns out, Fairchild worked for the US government some years ago in one of their intelligence-gathering agencies, mostly in Asia. His records are sealed, which is quite normal for CIA, NSA types etc., but my contact rang his counterpart in New York who gave him an off-the-record brief.'

'What did he say?' Marty asked eagerly.

'Fairchild joined the agency after five years in the Navy SEALs, the US equivalent of the Special Boat Service...'

'I know what the SEALs are!' Marty said impatiently.

Williams looked hurt before snapping back at Marty, 'Do you want this information or not?'

Marty raised his hands in apology. 'Sorry, please go on.'

'As I was saying, Fairchild joined the agency in 2005 after five years with the SEALs. He spent the majority of his time in South East Asia, mainly Laos, feeding 'intel' to the authorities on heroin manufacturing and distribution. He was there until 2009 when he was involved in a bungled raid to catch South East Asia's biggest drug smuggler. The guy, who they had been after for years, escaped from certain capture and he's been on the run ever since. Fingers pointed at Fairchild and many suspected he was actively involved in the escape but there was no proof. The one man who did make a bona fide claim against Fairchild died in a car wreck a couple of weeks later. The top brass suspected it was more than just a coincidence but Fairchild's alibi worked out. One week after the accident, Fairchild resigned.'

'Wow... he sounds like a proper nasty bastard.'

'Doesn't he?'

'So how does he go from spook to CEO? And how is he connected to Rob?'

'That I don't know but it's about time we found out,' Williams said, starting the engine before pulling the car away from the curb and heading back to the city.

CHAPTER 50

Back at Simon's apartment, the two men got busy digging into the mysterious Frank Fairchild's past and present. Using a borrowed laptop from the Guardian offices, they trawled through the web looking for anything that might explain how Fairchild had risen from special-ops operative to CEO of Delta Holdings' European operations. Delta themselves were a conglomerate with a wide variety of worldwide interests including oil and gas, mining and media. Their European division had been built in the seventies on a host of newspaper and magazine titles across France, Germany, Spain and the Nordics. In the last two years, they had been rapidly expanding into Central and Eastern Europe – the Czech Republic, Poland and even Russia – but they had yet to buy in the UK. This was hardly surprising though, as falling circulations had led to a number of big-name heritage magazines and broadsheets closing their operations in the last twelve months. The digital revolution was squeezing traditional media out of the UK.

Williams was a skilled investigator but it soon became apparent that Marty had become too reliant on researchers over the years to be of any real use in uncovering anything meaningful on Fairchild, so he left Williams to it and switched on the big TV. He flicked to the BBC News channel and felt a mixture of relief and loss when his ex-wife, Rebecca, appeared in front of him presenting the bulletin. She seemed to be growing more beautiful as each year passed and looking at his own bloated and disheveled reflection in the mirror opposite, he felt ashamed of what he had become. Having once been so athletic, fierce and determined, he hardly recognised the overweight, unkempt and defeated man before him. How had it come to this, and how had he let go of the one true love of his life?

Marty turned up the volume and sat heavily on the couch as Rebecca revealed the latest on his situation. Despite the obvious discomfort he suspected it was causing her, she remained staunchly professional, displaying no emotional connection to the fact her ex-husband was now a fugitive, wanted in connection with two murders; or was it simply that she really *didn't* care – that she had long since given up any feelings for him? He dare not contemplate that reality, focusing instead on what she was saying.

'Talk105 star Marty Michaels remains at large tonight with the last confirmed sighting at the Manchester Airport Exchange Hotel yesterday evening. Michaels is wanted for questioning after a body was discovered in a room he was seen leaving some time later, before fleeing the hotel grounds on foot. It is believed he stole a mountain bike in the Gatley area at around eight o'clock this morning and made his escape. There have been no sightings since. Manchester Police Assistant Police Commissioner Blake today urged the radio host to give himself up.'

The programme cut to Blake standing in the front of Ashton House, a host of logoed microphones including Talk105 in front of his mouth as cameras flashed in his eyes. He looked as sanctimonious as ever, thought Marty.

'Marty Michaels, who is currently awaiting trial for the murder of Paul White, last week broke the terms of his bail and went on the run. Last night officers were called to the Manchester Airport Exchange Hotel when a man fitting

Michaels's description was seen running from a room where detectives found the body of a woman. At this stage, we have not been able to identify the victim but we are treating this death as a homicide. We would very much like to speak to Mr. Michaels and would urge him to give himself up. I would also ask that any members of the public who may have information that would help us locate Mr. Michaels do so as a matter of urgency. In light of the seriousness of these crimes, I would urge the public not to approach Mr. Michaels and instead call the situation room number on your screen now. I will not be taking questions at this time. Thank you,' he said and turned on his heels as he marched back inside the building.

As Rebecca reappeared on screen, Marty noticed her guard drop; a fleeting sadness flashed across her face, reminiscent of the day she had finally walked away from him. He felt a guttural shame gnawing at his core. She had never done anything but love him and he had let her down, pushing her into the arms of another man. His world had turned upside down in the last couple of weeks but one thing had not changed: his ability to hurt the people he loved the most.

Marty muted the TV and dropped his head into his hands as he stared at the floor trying to calm the anxiety building inside him. His attention was suddenly drawn to Williams, who began speaking on the phone.

'Hi, it's me. I need some information…'

Marty lifted his head before stepping up from the couch and wandering over to where Williams was sitting in front of the laptop, continuing to give orders to the person on the other end.

'Don't worry about where I've been; just write this down, will you? I need everything you have on the financials of Delta Holdings. They're a publishing company based in Jersey but I suspect they're backed by business elsewhere in the world. I want everything you can find, no matter how trivial, OK?'

Williams spotted Marty staring at him and gave him a reassuring nod and a thumbs up.

'It doesn't matter where I am right now, just send me the information when you get it, but call me first, OK? Great,' he said and ended the call.

Marty was perplexed.

'Who the hell was that?'

Williams raised his arms in mock defeat, leaning back in his chair, his voice suddenly soft.

'Take it easy, it's just my assistant.'

'Who for all we know could be working for the people who set me up!'

Williams stood to face Marty.

'Don't be stupid. Laura is one hundred per cent trustworthy,' he said flatly.

'Really, and did this Laura know you were taking me to see Rochelle on Saturday night?'

Williams looked away but said nothing.

'She did, didn't she?' Marty was shouting now.

Williams turned back to face Marty and nodded, 'OK, yes she did, but she's not working for anyone but me. I promise.'

Marty turned his body away like a petulant teenager and let out a frustrated growl. 'With everything that's gone on, how can you know that for sure?'

'Look Marty, I know she's not working for anyone else… because, well, because I'm sleeping with her; have been for almost a year now.'

Marty turned to face him.

'You're sleeping with her?'

Williams nodded, 'You could say she's kind of like my girlfriend,' he added.

Marty eyed him suspiciously, 'You're sleeping with your assistant?'

'Yes.'

'So how old is she?'

Williams blushed. 'She's twenty-nine,' he said, unable to stop a self-congratulatory smile creeping across his face.

Marty found himself giggling now too, 'And how old are you?'

'Forty-three,' Williams said sheepishly.

'Bloody hell!'

'Marty, she's smart and I trust her with my life. She's also a bloody fantastic researcher. If there's anything to find, she'll get it and she'll get it super-fast.'

Marty shook his head before exhaling loudly, 'I really hope you know what you're doing Simon, because I'm not sure I like the fact *my life* is essentially in the hands of *your dick*, so to speak!'

Simon smiled. 'I do, Marty. Just give her an hour and let's see what she can find.'

Marty nodded and scratched his stubbly chin.

'And it is a very nice dick... so she tells me. Now, I don't know about you, but I could do with a drink,' Williams said before clapping his hands together and heading off to the kitchen in search of whisky.

*

Right on cue, almost an hour later, Williams's mobile rang and he jumped from the armchair, racing over to the desk to answer it, 'Hi Laura,' he said softly.

As Laura spoke he took spurious notes in shorthand, nodding and saying 'yeah' and 'OK' for about ten minutes until he finally rang off and turned to Marty.

'Told you she was good!' he declared with a smile on his face.

Marty lifted himself from the couch and covered the floor quickly, keen to see what he had.

'What did she say?'

Williams unlocked the laptop and opened the internet browser.

'Firstly, Delta, although based in Jersey, are actually financed out of Switzerland, which is always a red flag for me. I mean, if your goal is to be tax efficient then Jersey's 'non-dom' status is more than enough. But if you want to hide your finances – then it's either Switzerland or the Cayman Islands.'

'So how does that help me?' Marty asked.

'You know, for a man in the entertainment business, you have no appreciation of a dramatic build-up, do you?' Williams said, half-smiling.

'Right now, more drama is the last thing I need.'

'Fair play. I'll get to the point.'

Marty's face betrayed his frustration. 'If you could…'

'Well, the Swiss holding bank for Delta is Ganner and Luchsinger International, the same bank that financed the failed takeover of the Fontaine Group back in 2011. Not only that, Ganner and Luchsinger International procured the investment when COMCO created EXPO C and the takeover of Fontaine.'

'That's some coincidence…' Marty said.

'Indeed it is!' replied Williams excitedly. 'Laura is convinced that if we can get access to their records, we'll find out more than just how much money they've got, but also who from Delta was involved in each deal.'

'So how would we do that? I can barely turn my computer on in the morning without help!' snorted Marty.

'And therein lies the problem of being a famous celebrity, my friend – too many people doing too much stuff for your lazy ass!' Williams said patting Marty on the shoulder, who nodded his sage agreement.

Williams said nothing as he tapped the pen in his hand against his teeth and drifted into thought. A moment later, he stood up from his chair and paced across the room toward the TV set.

'What is it?' Marty asked.

'The USB from Rochelle, it had a document on it that wouldn't open on the TV, right?'

'Yeah, so?'

'Well, according to Rochelle, White was a whizz with computer systems.'

'And?'

'Jesus, Marty. Has your brain gone soft with all those yes men around you? Is the hard-nosed investigative journalist ever gonna show his face and help *me* help *you*?' Williams said, his voice brimming with exasperation.

Marty looked defeated. 'That's right, kick a man when he's down, why don't you?'

Williams continued unfazed and yanked the USB from the TV. He returned a moment later, plugging it into the laptop and opened the file.

'White was super-tech-smart. He cleverly managed to make copies of videos that implicated some of the most powerful people in the UK. I'm guessing a man like that may also know how to access bank accounts and transaction details too.'

Marty was nodding now as the Excel icon finished loading on the laptop screen and the document opened in front of them both.

There was a moment of silence as they cast their eyes over the document, before Williams finally spoke.

'And I'd be bloody right in my assumption!' he said excitedly as he began scrolling down a list of names, dates and transactions from Ganner and Luchsinger International to various accounts in the UK.

'Jackpot,' Marty whispered. 'Bloody jackpot!'

CHAPTER 51

The list of names on the Excel file was extensive and at a rough estimate accounted for just short of a million pounds' worth of transactions made over a five-year period from Ganner and Luchsinger International to a host of personal accounts in the UK. Sitting side by side, Williams and Marty had scanned the file looking for anyone that stood out. It had not taken long to find three members of the current prime minister's government and various high-profile officers within the Greater Manchester Police. The list also contained a myriad of journalists and paps, the now-deceased Paul White, and COMCO CEO, Colin Burns. Suddenly his stance made sense; if Marty was at the centre of a conspiracy to discredit him, who better to have on the payroll than his boss? Marty felt sick to his stomach.

Williams continued to scroll through the names, occasionally shouting out well-known faces in UK media, government and the police.

Then Marty spotted something. 'Go back,' he said.

Williams began to scroll back through the document. 'What did you see?'

'Something that I really hope is just my eyes playing tricks on me,' Marty said flatly, before shouting, 'Stop!'

Williams looked at Marty, then back to the screen, 'What are we looking at?'

'Definitive proof of the ultimate betrayal!' Marty said.

'What?'

Marty tapped his pen on the laptop screen. 'Wooten Limited,' his voice ice-cold.

'Wooten Limited, should I know it?'

Marty sat back in his chair, his hands framing his face, and said nothing for a moment as he stared at the name on the screen in front of him. Williams continued to look between him and the laptop, clearly desperate for an answer.

'Marty? What the bloody hell is Wooten Limited?'

Marty shook his head slowly and exhaled loudly. 'Wooten Limited is the original trading name for Rob Woodcock.'

'Rob?'

Marty nodded. 'It was his first attempt at business after he retired from football. The name is a mixture of Woodcock and his squad number, ten – Wooten.'

'Jesus, Rob's actually on the payroll,' Williams whispered.

'He changed the name about five years ago to Global Sports and Media, said it sounded more impressive and credible; but he's clearly kept the accounts alive.'

'And you're sure it's Rob's old company – not a coincidence?'

Marty let out an ironic chuckle. 'I think that's highly unlikely, don't you?' Marty replied. 'He lies to me about meeting me alone, and instead turns up with a guy who's connected to stealth porn movies featuring the great and the good of Manchester. We then follow him to a house leased by Delta Holdings, and his old business accounts have been receiving money from the same Swiss account that has been paying my CEO – who, by the way, publicly hangs me at the first opportunity. Sound like a coincidence? It's him all right!'

Williams said nothing, turning back to the Excel spreadsheet as Marty stood and walked over to the big windows that overlooked the city. He didn't want to believe that his closest friend and agent could be part of this nightmare, but he knew deep down he was, and in a strange way he felt a sense of relief. Knowledge was power and, hour by hour, he and Williams were putting more and more of the pieces together. He remembered his father's words to him as an awkward, bullied teenager: *'Marty, if you can see your enemy, you can beat him, no matter how big or powerful.'* These words, over a twenty-year career, had inspired him to challenge some of the world's biggest names in entertainment, sport and politics. Thinking of his dad made him smile and his mind turned to David. If they were both still alive today, they would be telling Marty to fight; that it's not over until it's over; that *they* would never give up on him, so *he* certainly wasn't allowed to!

Marty turned back to the room, bristling with renewed energy now. 'Right, let's find out who else is going down for this!' he said as he rushed to sit down. 'And you can start with that slippery lawyer of mine, Andrew Johnson. If they got to Rob, Andrew would be the obvious next one on the list!'

After another hour of searching they had found nothing to link Andrew to Ganner and Luchsinger International, but both men reasoned the smooth-talking lawyer was not one to leave himself exposed. Further investigation was required. Williams put a call into Laura who had promised to come back within the next couple of hours and once again, she was true to her word. This time, Williams put her on speaker and after a brief introduction she shared what she had discovered.

'I've looked at every alias I can think of for Andrew Johnson, but there's nothing to link him or his associates to

Ganner and Luchsinger International – so as far as I can see, he's clean,' she said efficiently.

Williams was nodding as Marty stared intently at the iPhone. Laura continued.

'I took a look at the other names you asked for and again found nothing on DCI Phillips or her associates Jones and Bovalino; they look clean financially and from a brief look at their professional records, they appear to be good coppers.'

Marty twisted his face towards the phone on Williams's hand. 'Depends on your definition, I guess,' he said sarcastically.

Williams ignored him. 'Anything else? How about APC Blake?'

'Interesting, this one,' Laura replied. 'Blake's as clean as a whistle as you'd expect, so I had a look for his wife and daughter.'

'And?' Marty asked impatiently.

'Well, nothing on the daughter, and the wife appears nowhere under her married name, so I ran her maiden name – and bingo! I found a significant payment from Ganner and Luchsinger International which dates back to 2014.'

Williams smiled broadly. 'Laura, you're a diamond!'

Marty could almost hear the girl blush on the phone as she thanked him for the compliment.

'And how about the other guy, Fairchild?' Williams continued. 'Any idea how he made it from Navy SEAL to CEO?'

At the other end, Laura took a moment to find the documents she had printed and returned to the phone.

'OK, so there's a mixed bag of info on this guy. As you know from your contact, he was involved in the first Iraq war with the SEALs, before moving into special ops and one of the dark groups within the US government. Suspected of leaking information to the other side in Asia, he left not long after the only witness against him died in a car accident. I picked up his trail a year later when he began working in private security, assigned with protecting assets for Delta Holdings in volatile, war-hit cities like Erbil and Mosul in Iraq. He was soon running their security operation around the globe and, after a couple of years, he took over as Acquisitions and Development Director of their overseas oil, gas and mining division.'

'Sounds like a bit of a leap!' Williams cut in.

'Yeah, I thought that,' Laura said, 'but apparently his connections in Asia gave him a distinct advantage. Delta secured lucrative contracts in mining. He's been on the payroll for over ten years and continues to climb. As we know, he's now CEO of their European operations, spearheading their media investment strategy.'

'Did you get anything else?' Marty chipped in.

'Well I'm not sure if it's any use but his right-hand man is a guy he met during his early days in private security – Saleem Bulzar, an Algerian national. This guy's a real piece of work. He was born in Paris in 1974 to Algerian parents in the notorious Clichy-Sous-Bois district of the city – where the Paris riots started in 2005. He spent some time as a teenager in detention centres before joining the French Army where he excelled and ended up in the 13th Parachute Dragoon Regiment – one of their special-forces units – completing multiple tours of Iraq and Afghanistan until a severe head injury sustained in a firefight saw him medically discharged. When he recovered, he turned his hand to private security where he met Fairchild; the pair have worked together ever since.'

'Do you have a picture of this guy?' Marty asked.

'Sure, I'm emailing it to you now,' replied Laura. 'Oh, and his nickname is Buzzard – quite appropriate I'd say.'

A second later, Williams's email pinged and he greedily clicked open the attached image from Laura.

'That's the guy!' shouted Marty as he stared at the screen. 'He's the same guy!'

'What guy?' Williams said looking closer.

'The man who met with Rob and was in the mirror in the video!'

Williams put his hand to his mouth and whispered through his fingers, 'You're right. Jesus, Marty, what have you got yourself into?'

CHAPTER 52

After finishing the call with Laura, Marty and Williams debated what to do next. It was clear the size and scale of the war against Marty was far greater than either could have ever imagined. Based on events so far, it was evident that the longer Marty stayed at large, the greater the risk to both their lives. Marty had suggested Williams cut his losses and let him sort out his own mess, but the big journalist would hear nothing of it; when he committed to a story, he stuck to it, *no matter what*. Instead, he had suggested something entirely different, which Marty had instantly rejected out of hand, calling him crazy and 'off his head'. Somehow though, Williams had persuaded Marty that it was his best chance of proving his innocence, and after a somewhat heated exchange, he had reluctantly agreed.

Finding himself once again laid out across the back seat of the VW Golf, he was beginning to wish he had not.

DCI Phillips lived in a modest Victorian terraced house on a quiet cul-de-sac in the bohemian suburb of Chorlton-cum-Hardy. She had bought the place as a newly appointed DC as a 'doer-upper' and over the last ten years had lovingly restored it to its former glory, adding a large extension to the kitchen and creating a small but private decked area to the back.

Positioned opposite the house, Williams prepared himself to go in as Marty shared his nervousness from the rear of the car.

'Simon, I'm *really* not sure this is a good idea – *at all!*'

Williams turned to face Marty and smiled reassuringly. 'Trust me, I'll be in and out in a flash.'

Before Marty could protest further, he opened the driver's door and got out. 'Back in a bit,' he added before slamming the door, leaving Marty in total silence.

*

Marty checked his watch again and realised Williams had been gone for almost twenty minutes, not part of the plan. Had something gone wrong? Were the police on their way? Had Phillips arrested him for aiding a fugitive? Was she part of the corruption? As the questions raced, he began to panic and lifted his head to check for anything suspicious. Just as he did, there was a flurry of movement towards the car and the rear door thrust open. Instinctively he covered his face with his hands, closing his eyes as he waited.

'You all right, Marty?' he heard Williams say, before unravelling his arms and lifting his head up.

'Jesus! You took your bloody time!' he barked as he sat upright.

Williams smiled. 'You can't rush these things; it needed a delicate touch, plus I had to show her some of the videos to prove there's a lot more at play here than just you. Anyway, she wants to talk to you and has agreed it's off the record and she won't nick you... for now at least!' he said half-laughing.

'And you're sure we can trust her?'

'I'd be lying if I said I was, but we're running out of options and she's one of the few people who we know *isn't* on the

Ganner and Luchsinger payroll,' Williams said very matter-of-factly.

Marty nodded; he just wanted it all to be over.

Climbing out of the car, he pulled his cap down over his forehead and followed Williams towards the open door leading into Phillips's house.

Stepping into the hallway, the height of the ceilings and the absolute warmth of the place surprised him, emanating from the soft-coloured tones, restored staircase and parquet floor in front of him with a myriad of pictures and photographs running along the wall. He continued to follow Williams through to the back of the house into an open-plan kitchen-diner. Detective Chief Inspector Phillips sat on a tall stool behind a large cooking island cradling a glass of red wine. Next to her was an open laptop. Her hair fell loosely across her shoulders and she was barefoot and wearing a white T-shirt and jeans. Behind her, he could see the sun setting through the large glass doors that ran along the back of the house.

'Mr. Michaels, I have to admit, this is something of a surprise,' she said breaking into a wry smile.

Marty shifted uncomfortably and nodded. 'You're telling me.'

'DCI Phillips has agreed to hear you out, Marty, so it's time to do what you do best, mate – *talk*,' Williams said.

Over the next hour, Marty explained everything that had happened from the moment he woke in the Metropolitan, to his ill-fated rendezvous with Rochelle, plus Rob's attempts to lure him into the hands of the man known as Buzzard. Williams then filled in the blanks around COMCO and EXPO C's China Project, Delta Holdings and the long list of people being paid by Ganner and Luchsinger International.

When both men had finished, Phillips sat quietly for a moment as if considering exactly what to say. Eventually she pushed her glass away and slid off the stool as she spoke.

'If I hadn't seen the videos and the documents for myself, I'd have to say that's a pretty wild story you've both concocted. As it is, though, with the evidence you've gathered, I'm inclined to believe you could well be one of the victims here, Marty.'

Marty visibly softened and suddenly felt exhausted. The sense of relief was palpable.

Williams clapped his hand in triumph and slapped Marty on the back.

'Told you she'd go for it. You're innocent and together we're going to prove it!'

Phillips moved across the kitchen and returned with her briefcase, pulling out a USB stick and pushing it into her laptop.

'I'm making a copy of these files, always better to be safe than sorry.'

Both men nodded.

As Phillips busied herself on the laptop, she spoke without looking at them. 'I have to say, I've always had my doubts about Blake, but I never had him down for something like this. It all seems a bit too risky for a man waiting to collect a substantial pension.'

Marty nodded. 'The bastard was supposed to be my friend; we were golfing buddies,' he said.

Phillips looked up from what she was doing. 'I'm sorry to break it to you, Marty, but befriending you was a directive from above. It was the only way to shut you up and, at the time, that was a top priority,' she said smiling sympathetically for a moment, before returning her gaze to the laptop screen.

'Well he's gonna wish he'd never heard of Marty Michaels by the time I've finished with him,' Marty grunted loudly.

Phillips finished up and handed the USB back to Williams.

'OK. By rights I should be taking you into custody and sharing my concerns about Blake with the Commissioner – but he's no use at all, a bloody show pony fit for nothing but PR sound bites. If we're going to do this, we're going to have to do it ourselves.'

'Suits me,' Marty said.

'And me,' Williams agreed.

'Are you sure you don't want to bring that hot-shot lawyer of yours into the loop?' Phillips asked.

Marty shook his head vigorously. 'Nope. I don't trust him. If Rob's turned on me, Andrew won't be far behind.'

'You don't *know* Andrew helped set you up,' said Williams. 'He wasn't on the list of Ganner and Luchsinger International, was he?'

'Doesn't mean he's not on the payroll; he's a smart bugger and if anyone can hide a paper trail, it's Andrew Johnson. I should have trusted my guts on this one, I had a feeling he was up to something all along,' Marty said.

Phillips eyed Marty for a moment before responding. 'As you wish, but if I'm going to get involved I need my team on this, and that means enlisting the help of Jones and Bovalino.'

Marty could not hide his disgust. 'Forget it – no way. They're part of this too. There's no way they can be trusted!' he said dramatically.

Williams cut him off. 'Hear her out, will you?' he pleaded.

'I won't. They're a couple of arseholes who treated me like a common criminal, embarrassed me and have a major axe to grind because of some copper called Freddie Tate! There's no way on God's earth I'll let them near me again!' he said, folding his arms in protest.

Williams ignored him and turned his attention to Phillips. 'Who is this Freddie Tate they're talking about?' he asked.

Phillips ran her right hand through her hair before closing the laptop. She looked at both men and took a breath.

'Freddie Tate was a good copper. Came up through Henley with Jones; best buddies in fact. Sadly, he got himself into a bit of bother with the horses and casinos and racked up a crippling amount of debt. Anyway, remember the time you were wrongfully arrested for soliciting and a couple of detention officers wanted you to pay for their silence with the press?'

'I do,' Marty said louder than necessary.

'Tate was part of the detention team that night, and he knew what the two coppers were up to. When you kicked up a stink, the guys in question were lucky not to go down and agreed to resign quietly, but Tate was suspended whilst the PSD looked into whether he was involved. Two weeks into his month-long suspension, his wife found him dead in the garage, hosepipe inside the car. Apparently, he'd been suffering from anxiety and depression most of his adult life and the suspension and potential discharge was just too much to bear. He left two kids behind and the absolute tragedy was, he was posthumously exonerated.'

Marty raised his hands in defence. 'But that wasn't my fault! I didn't accuse him. I didn't even know who he was, for God's sake!'

'Your empathy does you credit,' Phillips said, her tone sarcastic.

'Look, I'm sorry the guy killed himself, but I only went after the two coppers who tried to blackmail me. Jones and Bovalino can't lay the blame for Tate's suicide at my door!' Marty insisted.

Phillips nodded. 'I agree with you, Marty, I really do. Look, let me talk to Jones and explain what's going on. He's a first-rate copper and I'm sure I can make him see reason. Plus, if there's one person Jones hates even more than you right now, it's Assistant Police Commissioner Blake!' she said laughing.

CHAPTER 53

Marty and Williams said their goodbyes and got back in the car; it was dark so Marty sat in the front this time.

He had reluctantly given Phillips permission to bring Jones and Bovalino into the loop because she had insisted on it, but the reality was he didn't trust either of them and felt very uneasy about their involvement, particularly given their views on Tate's death. However, Phillips had assured him that once both men had seen the videos and banking documents, they would be powerful allies he could count on.

Williams started the engine and stared at Marty in silence for a moment. 'Are you sure you're OK with all this?' he asked.

Marty looked out onto the dimly lit street and shook his head.

'It doesn't feel right, Simon, but what choice do I have? I need someone from the police to believe me, but I just don't trust Jones and Bovalino. I'm not even sure I fully trust Phillips, to be honest. I mean what if it's a set up and we get back to yours and find a bloody SWAT team waiting for us?'

Williams chuckled. 'It's not LA!'

'You know what I mean, armed police, guns, dogs; I'd be a sitting duck,' Marty said.

'It's easy for me to say, I know, but my gut tells me she's on our side and my gut is rarely wrong, mate.'

'Exactly; *rarely* wrong! What if this is the one time *it is?*'

Neither man said anything for a long moment. Marty eventually broke the silence, sighing heavily.

'The reality is, if I don't trust her, then I'm on my own and well and truly fucked...'

'You've got me, mate; I'll tell your story!' Williams said.

'Really, Simon? Do you think for a second that you wouldn't be locked up *immediately* for harbouring a fugitive? Besides, without a fair and proper investigation, anything you did write would be fish and chip wrapping in a week and I'd be back in Hawk Green at the mercy of McCloud and Keats. No, I have to trust her; she really is the only hope I have of getting my life back.'

Williams nodded. 'Shall we head back to mine then?'

'Yeah. I don't know about you, but I could do with a drink!' Marty said.

'Now you're talking,' Williams laughed.

*

The two men travelled in silence from Chorlton back towards the city through the suburbs of Whalley Range and then Hulme before Williams turned onto the Chester Road roundabout. A moment later, they reached the Mancunian Way and headed towards the Northern Quarter. The Hulme Arch appeared on the right as they passed over Princess Parkway before the highway cut through the university buildings on either side. Marty felt a sudden sense of appreciation for the city he had called home all his life.

Williams made Marty aware of a car travelling unnecessarily fast behind them and moved into the left-hand lane to let the driver pass but instead the car pulled in behind theirs, almost bumper to bumper. Marty dropped his head to check the off-side mirror.

'What's this guy's game?' he said angrily.

'I dunno, but if he gets any closer he'll be in my boot!' Williams said, before pressing the accelerator, attempting to distance himself from the other driver, who matched his speed and remained dangerously close to the back of the VW Golf.

Marty turned and attempted to get a look at the driver, but the headlights switched to full beam at this range were almost blinding.

'Shit, I can't see a bloody thing!' Marty said.

'He's having a laugh, this bloke!' Simon shouted as he moved into the outside lane, the ghosting driver mirroring his actions a split second later.

'Get the fuck away from him!' Marty screamed.

'I'm trying but he's stuck to me like glue!'

The two cars were now hurtling along the dual carriageway at ninety miles per hour, almost double the speed limit for this winding stretch of road. They passed over the A6 and rounded the long bend that followed as Williams pulled the car back into the inside lane. This time the chasing car stayed on the outside, creeping forward so its bonnet was just parallel with the rear wheel of the VW.

'What's he doing?' Marty shouted, his body turned, his eyes fixed on the car. 'Why doesn't he pass?'

'I don't bloody know!'

As they approached the railway bridge at the junction with Temperance Street, Williams was struggling to keep the car steady as their speed touched ninety-five. A split second later, both men heard and felt the deafening crunch of metal on metal as the mysterious car rammed the rear wheel of their VW from right to left. Williams grappled with the steering wheel as he attempted to stop them spinning out of control. It was useless; they were travelling too fast. He had lost all control. As the car began to fishtail, both men screamed, silenced a moment later as the VW slammed sideways into the stone base of the bridge.

CHAPTER 54

Marty opened his eyes, blinking slowly as he tried to focus. The dashboard airbag had deployed covering him in a fine white powder and a smell like gunpowder filled his nostrils. Turning his neck painfully to the right he saw Simon slumped forward onto the spent driver's airbag that covered the steering wheel. His face was a mixture of blood and powder, turned towards Marty, eyes closed. Attempting to reach out his right hand and touch him, Marty cried out, pain shooting across his chest and ribs.

'S-S-Simon…' he managed to whisper without response.

He knew he needed to get out of the wrecked car but moving was the last thing he wanted to do in that moment. He closed his eyes and attempted to breathe through the pain that flooded his torso and for a moment sat in total silence, allowing his rapid pulse to settle. As the pain began to dull a little, he became aware of something that sounded like running water coming from outside of the mangled car. *Shit, petrol!* He opened his eyes to see smoke slowly rising from the crumpled bonnet in front of them – they had to get out now. Unclipping his seatbelt, Marty attempted to open the passenger door but it creaked noisily and resisted his efforts. The sound of running liquid continued to seep into the car and Marty's panic began to rise.

'Simon!' Marty shouted this time in an effort to wake him, but his companion remained motionless, 'For fuck's sake, Simon, wake up!' he bellowed, with no response.

Yanking at the passenger door handle wildly he rammed the heel of his left foot into the base of the door as he attempted to get it open. It moved a little but defiantly stayed shut; the impact of the crash must have squashed the car frame over the door. He took a short breath, gritted his teeth and stretched his body to the right, pressing his fingers into Simon's neck, feeling a very faint pulse. He was alive, just.

Marty yelled as loud as he could into his ear once more, 'Simon! Simon! Come on, mate, wake up!'

With no response, he changed tack, dragging himself over the handbrake before slumping heavily onto the back seat and his battered ribs, crying out in pain.

Petrol fumes hung thick in the air. He knew it was only a matter of time before the hot car ignited the running liquid. Crawling on his hands and knees, he leant his full body weight against the rear door. Mercifully, it opened at the first time of asking, catching him off balance, and he fell forward onto the hard ground below.

Winded by the impact he screwed his face up as he rolled onto his back, waiting for the pain to subside. A moment later, he heard footsteps to his left and opened his eyes.

'Are you OK, mate?'

Marty looked up to see a middle-aged, portly man standing over him with a similar-aged woman by his side, a grave expression on her face. As he attempted to lift himself onto his hands and knees, the man offered him an outstretched hand, helping him to his feet.

'We've got to get Simon out,' he said as the woman stepped forward, eyeing him suspiciously, as he avoided her gaze.

'Here, aren't you that Marty Michaels?' she asked, craning her neck to see his face.

'You're mistaken,' he shot back, without making eye contact.

'No I'm not! George, he's that Marty Michaels...' she said looking at the man, her accent thick Mancunian, '... that fella off the radio, you know, the one who's been killing all those prostitutes!'

Marty stared directly at the woman now, shaking his head, 'That's not true! And it really doesn't matter who *I* am, we need to get *Simon* out of that car right now!' he shouted as the man and woman began backing away.

'Best you wait for the emergency services, mate,' the man said nervously, 'he could have a spinal injury or something,' he added, glancing left towards the woman.

Marty stepped towards them, his hands open 'OK, OK, *I am* Marty Michaels, but I didn't do what they're accusing me of, I'm innocent. Please, you have to believe me. *He* really needs your help,' he pleaded, pointing towards the car.

The man wrapped his arm across the woman's chest protectively, pushing her firmly behind him and shook his head, 'Look, mate, we don't want any trouble, we're good people. I think it's best you wait for the police,' he said as he turned and ushered the woman quickly away towards a car parked on the side of the road, its hazard lights flashing.

'Fuck!' Marty shouted before turning back towards Simon.

He was soon frantically pulling at the driver's door but like the passenger side, the impact had crushed it shut. Leaning through the broken driver's window, he checked Simon's pulse; faint but still there. Growling through the immense pain from his chest and ribs, he stretched as far as he could to unclip Simon's seatbelt and gently pulled his heavy torso back against the driver's seat.

'I'll get you out of this, buddy,' he said tenderly, cradling Simon's face with his hands.

In that moment, the smoke from the engine intensified, catching Marty's attention, and he stared wide-eyed as it turned from a steam-like grey to a thick black plume. A second later, a small flame appeared from the side of the crumpled bonnet. He didn't hesitate. Grabbing Simon under both arms with every ounce of strength he could summon, he began dragging him through the shattered driver's window. A minute later, and the big man's head and shoulders hung outside the car. Jamming his foot against the driver's door, he grabbed Simon's arms and heaved backwards but lost his grip, falling painfully onto the asphalt.

'Damn it!' he shouted in frustration.

As quickly as his broken body would allow, he got back to his feet and repeated the process, this time lifting Simon further out of the car, his face now pointing towards the ground. All the time Marty kept his eye on the growing number of flames flickering from under the bonnet.

Sirens filled the distant air. *Ambulance? Police?* It didn't matter. All that mattered was saving Simon; he wasn't about to let another mate die. Focused on the task in hand, he jammed both feet against the car door once more, pulling over and over, edging Simon further out until his torso hung lifelessly over the bottom of the door's window frame. Gasping for breath, with one final effort he managed to pull the big man free, falling backwards as his did, closely followed by Simon's seventeen-stone frame, which landed heavily on top of him.

The sirens moved ever closer.

Winded for a second time and struggling for breath he rolled Simon carefully onto his back, before lifting himself onto his hands and knees. Surveying the car, he could see the flames had spread the length of the car bonnet now and acrid black smoke filled the air. Time was running out.

With renewed strength, Marty jumped to his feet, grabbed Simon's arms and began dragging him backwards, but his own injuries and Simon's dead weight made it desperately difficult. Inch by inch, Marty pulled as the flames raced closer and closer to the fuel tank. *Come on, Marty.*

The sirens were upon him now and as he dragged Simon backwards, he glanced over his shoulder to see two police cars stop simultaneously about thirty feet away, closely followed by a fire engine, the sound of its hydraulic brakes slicing through the air. The chase was over but that wasn't important now. Saving Simon was all that mattered.

'Help me!' he shouted in the direction of the watching police and fire crew, before turning back to Simon, tightening his grip and heaving backwards in a flurry of short steps, 'It's gonna be OK, mate!' he shouted at Simon's lifeless body. 'It's gonna be OK.'

A split second later, the flames reached the fuel tank and with an enormous roar, the car exploded and a blast of flame blew Marty backwards off his feet.

CHAPTER 55

A loud beep repeated and echoed from the distance, quickly drawing closer until the noise seemed to have a will of its own, powerful enough to force Marty's eyes open into the semi-darkness. It took him a moment to orientate himself with his surroundings; he was in a private room in some kind of hospital, windows with closed blinds surrounding him on three sides, and a myriad of machines running parallel to both sides of his head. A heart monitor, the source of the beeping, pinged out a steady rhythm next to his left ear. One third of the bed was raised at a forty-five-degree angle under his back, and he was facing the door wearing a light blue gown that fitted loosely around his torso. His body from the waist down was covered by a crisp white sheet, in turn wrapped in a soft woollen blanket.

His mouth was bone-dry and his face and right arm felt hot, like a terrible sunburn. Attempting to touch his skin, he felt a sharp pain in his left wrist and heard the clatter of metal on metal; he was handcuffed to the bed. Wildly, he yanked at the cuff, and his ribs and left shoulder felt like they would explode, causing him to cry out in agony.

The door opened noisily as the blinds rumbled against the glass and a uniformed nurse appeared – a short Asian woman with a soft round face and thick dark hair pulled back tightly from her face. She offered a polite, thickly accented 'Hello' with the briefest of smiles, then moved steadily through the room, checking charts, pushing buttons on the various machines and eventually stopping next to Marty's handcuffed hand.

'What happened to me?' Marty asked.

'You don't remember?' the nurse replied.

Marty shook his head. 'I was in the car with Simon driving through Whalley Range and that's all I remember.'

The nurse smiled sympathetically. 'You were in a car accident two days ago,' she said. 'You've been deeply sedated since then.'

Marty flashed back to the car chase around the Mancunian Way.

'The driver…' Marty managed to stutter. 'Is he OK?'

'Mr. Michaels, try not to upset yourself. You have sustained some serious injuries.'

'Never mind me. Simon – what happened to him?' Marty barked.

The nurse looked at him and a sadness flashed across her face. 'Your car hit a bridge at high speed, the driver took the brunt of the impact. They say you dragged him from the wreckage.'

Marty's mind flashed back to the aftermath, Simon's body slumped over the steering wheel.

'You saved his life, Mr. Michaels. The car exploded and you were within reach of the blast. You came here to the burns unit; he went straight into theatre on the night of the crash. He's in intensive care now,' she said, squeezing his hand.

'Will he make it?'

The nurse smiled softly. 'He's stable and in good hands; the doctors are doing everything they can.'

'I want to see him.'

The nurse shook her head. 'Mr. Michaels, you're in no fit state to go anywhere. You suffered second-degree burns to the left side of your face and arm, three broken ribs, and severe ligament damage in your left shoulder from the seatbelt; and besides...' she said pointing at his left wrist, '...your "bracelet" means you're not going anywhere.'

Marty gently touched his bandaged right hand to his face and could feel the coarse texture of gauze against his fingertips. He pulled at his cuffed hand once more and let out a frustrated growl as it dawned on him he was going back to prison. In a weird way, he felt some sense of relief; no more running. Soon, though, the fear of what lay in store for him in Hawk Green overwhelmed him and he closed his eyes hoping to shut out the images flashing through his head.

A moment later, the nurse moved towards the door and as she opened it, Marty heard the distinctive tones of Andrew Johnson. Opening his eyes, he saw his lawyer standing at the end of the bed, his tan briefcase resting in front of him on the mattress by Marty's feet.

'Jesus, Marty, you look terrible. Are you in much pain?'

After Rob's betrayal, he no longer trusted Andrew and it showed on his face.

'What do you want?' he said curtly.

Andrew stepped around the bed and sat down in the armchair to Marty's right.

'I'm detecting a certain amount of hostility from you. Is everything OK?'

Marty rattled his left wrist against the metal frame. 'I'm cuffed to a hospital bed with second-degree burns and broken ribs after some lunatic tried to kill me by ramming me and Simon off the road. So no, everything is not OK!' he said.

'Yes, an unfortunate incident,' Andrew said.

'Unfortunate? It was attempted murder!'

Andrew nodded sagely. 'I've spoken to the doctors and they say your friend is stable,' he said.

'Do they think he'll make it?'

'At this stage, they really don't know, but thanks to you he's got a fighting chance. Another minute in the car and he'd have gone up with it. As it is he suffered severe internal injuries as well as multiple fractures, so the next forty-eight hours are critical.'

Marty closed his eyes again. He had warned Simon to step away from all this before he got hurt, but now it was too late. God, he had made a mess of things.

'Marty,' Andrew said his tone softer now. 'I need to talk to you about Rob.'

'I know all about that bastard!'

'You do? How? Who told you?'

'Nobody. I saw it with my own eyes, Andrew.'

Andrew looked puzzled. 'I don't understand. You've been unconscious for two days, how could you have seen *anything*?'

Marty looked at Andrew, his own expression now one of confusion. 'I found out a couple of days before the crash. Caught him lying to me and working with the guy who was more than likely driving the car that rammed us,' he said.

Andrew looked at the floor for a long moment before speaking. 'So you *don't* know.'

'You're not making any sense, Andrew. What are you talking about; what don't I know?' Marty protested.

Andrew lifted his head and stared straight at him. 'I'm sorry, Marty, Rob's *dead*.'

Marty let out an involuntary laugh, catching himself as he did. 'Is this a joke?'

Andrew's body visibly softened. 'I wish it was, Marty; I really do. They found his body in his car in Hulme a couple of days ago. The police said he'd been shot at close range in the chest with a small-calibre firearm – essentially a handgun.'

Marty blinked furiously trying to process what he was hearing. 'There must be some mistake, I only saw him the other night.'

'No mistake, Marty. The police released his identity yesterday.'

Marty closed his eyes for a moment as a single tear ran down his cheek.

'When did it happen?'

'They found his body the morning after your accident so I'm guessing the night before.'

A world of emotions flooded Marty now – fear, anger, guilt. Rob's betrayal had hurt him deeply, but to think his closest friend for so many years was now dead, filled him with sadness. He also felt very frightened; the people he was up against were steadily removing all loose ends.

'I want to speak to Phillips,' he said suddenly.

'That's not possible, Marty.'

'Why not?'

'She's been suspended,' Andrew said flatly.

'She's what?'

Andrew exhaled loudly before sharing the details. 'Footage of you entering and leaving her house has been all over social media for the last two days. She's been suspended pending an investigation, and the reality is she could be looking at serious prison time for harbouring a fugitive,' Andrew said.

'She didn't harbour anybody – I was with her for an hour at the most.'

'Well that's not how APC Blake saw it, and he's gone on record saying that if found guilty, she'll get no special treatment; that corruption has no place in the Greater Manchester Police.'

'That snake! He's the one who should be arrested – he's as bent as they come!' Marty raged.

'I'm sorry, Marty, but people are now suggesting it was Phillips who helped you remain at large for so long.'

Marty let out an ironic chuckle. 'What a load of shit – I stayed off the radar because I have half a brain and managed to stay one step ahead of them.'

Andrew nodded. 'Look, I know it doesn't look good for you right now but I promise you can trust me.'

'Really? Because about four hours after I told you I was going to meet Rochelle, she ended up dead and I was running for my life!' Marty snorted.

Andrew raised his hands in self-defence. 'I swear on my mother's life, Marty, the only person I told was Rob – and that was against my better judgement. He was worried about you and insisted I tell him. I really didn't think it could hurt. Why would it, he was your best mate?'

Marty shook his head in disbelief. 'So Rob set me up.'

'I'm afraid it certainly appears that way. Look, I'll do whatever it takes to get you out of this, I promise,' Andrew said.

Marty lay back into the pillow, suddenly aware of his injuries and the sheer weight of his own body. 'It's pointless, Andrew, whoever's behind this wants me in prison or dead, and now there's no one to stop them. DCI Phillips was my last hope and knowing how deep this corruption goes, she's as screwed as I am – *well and truly.*'

CHAPTER 56

It took Marty fifteen minutes flat to bring Andrew up to speed on everything he and Simon had been up to in the last few days, and by the time he had finished he was exhausted. Andrew had sat quietly taking notes on a yellow legal pad nestled in an expensive-looking leather case, nodding and scribbling furiously as he did. When he was finished, Andrew had assured him he would investigate everything Marty had shared and would be in touch soon. He would also be in constant contact with the hospital in case they tried to move him back to prison without telling anyone. Marty required protective custody and only his expensive legal team could ensure that, apparently.

After Andrew had left the room to head back to his offices in the uber-trendy Spinningfields district, Marty closed his eyes and allowed himself to listen to the sounds of the room around him, the rhythmic beats and tones of the machines monitoring his vital signs. Eventually he drifted into a dreamless sleep. Finally, some peace.

It was some time later that he woke with a start, convinced he was falling, his heart jumping so powerfully in his chest it caused him to cough. He must have been asleep for some time; the room was now cloaked in darkness. A feverish sweat covered his body and his blue gown was saturated at the neck. Rubbing his right hand along the back of his head, he felt a thick wetness on his palm, a stark contrast to the dryness of his throat.

'She's awake!' a spiteful voice said from behind his head, in a South London accent. Marty recognised it immediately and instinctively tried to pull himself up off the mattress to face Detective Sergeant Jones, but his cuffed hand ensured he was unable to see him standing directly behind him. Frightened, he waited for whatever was coming next.

'I knew Phillips was wrong to trust your bullshit story,' Jones hissed from the darkness, the soundtrack of the machines adding an eerie edge to his words. 'Always been a soft a touch that one, but not me, I had you pegged right from the start. From the moment I pulled that damned gimp mask off your head at the Metropolitan, I knew you were a predator that needed to be caged.'

Marty breathed deeply as he attempted to steady his racing pulse. When he spoke he was calm, but the reality inside was very different. 'Don't you think a man deserves to see his killer?' he said.

Jones laughed. 'Kill you? Me? I'm not here to kill you, Marty. I'm a copper, I don't kill people; I *protect* people,' he said as he moved to Marty's right and into his line of sight for the first time. 'But thanks to you, everybody thinks I'm corrupt,' he added unfolding a copy of the *Manchester Evening News* in front of Marty's face. The front-page headline: 'TOP COP HARBOURS DOUBLE MURDER SUSPECT' above a picture of Marty and Simon talking to Phillips in her kitchen, clearly taken from the rear of the house; probably with a telephoto lens based on the grainy quality of the picture.

Jones pulled the paper away, folded it into the shape of a baton and continued talking as he moved around the room, smacking the paper into the palm of his hand rhythmically as he did. 'Thanks to you, another good copper's life and career are in tatters, and me and Bov are guilty by association. Technically, both banned from this hospital – they think we might help you escape! I had to ask an old mate to look the other way, just so I could get past your security detail outside the ward.'

Marty kept his eyes locked on Jones, expecting an attack at any moment. 'So if you're not here to kill me, why *are* you here?' he asked, afraid of what the answer might be.

'I'm here to ensure that *you* know, without any room for doubt, that I'll do whatever it takes to protect Phillips; she's one of *us*. She tried to help you because she believed you. If you do anything to prejudice her case, hurt her, or drop her further in it, there is nowhere they could put you or lock you up where you'd be safe from me and Bov. Do you understand, Marty?'

Marty nodded his agreement. 'Look, I don't expect you to believe me, but I'm telling you the truth. I didn't kill White or Rochelle. I was set up! I have video proof that shows I was unconscious in the same room as White when they claim I killed him. And I'm certain it shows a glimpse of the real killer.'

Jones turned to face Marty now, his interest piqued. 'You still have a copy of the videos you showed to Phillips?' he asked quietly.

Marty nodded. 'Yes. Well at least I did when I left her house that night. The memory stick should be in the small front pocket of my jeans.'

Jones flashed an awkward smile and shook his head. 'I wouldn't hold out too much hope of ever seeing that again, Marty. Everything you touched will be in the hands of the forensic team by now,' he said as he headed towards the door.

Marty's heart sank; his final thread of hope was gone.

Jones opened the door and waited a moment for the blinds on the inside to stop rattling before delivering his parting shot. 'Do you know the irony of all this, Marty? You've spent your whole adult life chasing the news: hunting people, exposing secrets and ruining countless lives – and to what end? You now find yourself handcuffed to a hospital bed surrounded by coppers, with every detail of your sordid existence filling pretty much every column inch of the local rag. What a total waste of life,' he said as he threw the folded-up paper at Marty's chest. 'I'd check out page seven if I was you, you may find it interesting,' he added and left the room.

Marty stared at the closed door for a long moment as the blinds once again rattled against the glass, before carefully picking up the paper with his bandaged right hand, clumsily thumbing through to page seven. What greeted him caused him to double-take. Underneath a headline reading, 'MICHAELS OUTSMARTED THE COPS TIME AND TIME AGAIN', was a small handcuff key Sellotaped to the page along with a yellow Post-it note that read: *'When the alarm sounds take the fire door to the left of your room, head for the basement and get in the laundry bin. Destroy this note.'*

Marty laughed loudly and kicked the end of the bed in celebration. 'You bloody beauty!' he said as right on cue the fire alarm began to ring out.

He greedily grabbed the key to unlock his left hand and began pulling the IVs from his arm; he had no time to waste.

CHAPTER 57

As the alarm wailed loudly, Marty, barefoot and wearing only his blue gown, peered cautiously out into the corridor, which appeared empty. His police guard had walked right towards the nurses' station at the other end of the ward and was gesticulating wildly at the round-faced nurse who had been in Marty's room earlier. Glancing quickly to his left, Marty spotted the emergency exit door a couple of metres away. Checking left and right one more time, he made a run for it as best he could and bundled through the door in one noisy movement, drowned out by the screech of the fire alarm. He waited for a moment but aside from the ear-splitting noise, everything appeared quiet.

In front of him, a large sign informed him he was on the fourth floor. Without looking up, he moved as quickly as his broken body would allow down the concrete stairs. They felt cold underfoot and within less than a minute, he had reached the bottom of the stairwell and a sign marked 'Basement'. He opened the door partially and peered through the small gap onto a large concrete slab elevated above the ground, a loading bay. Opening the door further, the area appeared deserted aside from a collection of laundry bins that covered the ground from the edge of the concrete, back to where Marty was standing now. '*Get in the laundry bin*' Jones's note had said, but which one had he meant? Marty stepped out through the door and surveyed the area trying to decide which they meant for him. It was then he noticed the same *Manchester Evening News* newspaper Jones had given him moments earlier, hanging over the top of one of the bins in front of him. Moving closer he saw the now-familiar headline, 'MICHAELS OUTSMARTED THE COPS TIME AND TIME AGAIN'. He smiled, confident this was no coincidence; he climbed painfully inside, pulled the used sheets over his head and waited.

Finally, the ear-splitting tones of the fire alarm relented and Marty was suddenly aware of his own breathing, heavy and laboured under the sheets. His poor heart couldn't take any more of this fugitive lifestyle; he was too old for this shit.

The noise of heavy metal shutters opening startled him and he took a deep breath, holding it whilst a truck backed into the bay from outside, the reversing alarm echoing loudly around the big space. The engine died. A door slammed. A moment later, he heard the sound of the truck's hydraulic gate dropping onto the concrete, followed by the rattle of laundry bins rolling across the concrete floor and into the back of the vehicle. The process repeated five or six times around Marty until finally he felt his bin wobble as someone grabbed either side firmly.

'If you can hear me, tap the side of the bin,' said a man's voice, in an elevated whisper laced with a thick Liverpool accent.

Marty did as requested before the man spoke again. 'Do as you're told and you'll be OK. Stay quiet and keep your head down, and if we're caught, you're on your own, mate. Tap again if you understand.'

Marty repeated the process and the bin was suddenly on the move rolling inside the back of the truck. A second later, the hydraulic gate closed and a moment after that, Marty heard the man climb into the cab and close the door up front. The engine roared into life and they were on the move.

The truck moved slowly for a few minutes before coming to a stop, the hiss of the brakes echoing through to Marty, who instinctively tightened his body, wondering what was happening outside. He held his breath and not for the first time in the last week, prayed silently to a god long forgotten.

The Liverpool man's voice seeped through from the opening behind the driver's head up front.

'You watching the derby this weekend, Decka?' he said cheerfully, no hint of nerves in his delivery.

Marty's heart was pounding and he closed his eyes as he tried to regulate his breathing, *quietly.*

'No, mate, it's our Candy's wedding so I'm on strict instructions – no football,' a second man said, his voice a lazy Mancunian drawl, as if every word was a prisoner.

'Sod that, you can't miss the derby. You need to get that app on your phone, you know the one Jimmy was talking about the other night – the dodgy streaming,' the Liverpool man replied. It was evident these two men knew each other well.

'I need to get one of them smartphones first, though,' the second man added, before his radio crackled into life, an inaudible burst of conversation Marty couldn't hear.

'Echo three to base – no sign here, all clear,' said the second man.

The Liverpool man's voice seemed to crack slightly as he spoke. 'What's up, Decka?' he sounded nervous now.

'Apparently that pervert off the radio has got out of his room and they're locking the building down trying to find him,' he said.

'Bloody hell!'

'I know, that's all we need. The coppers'll be all over this place in a few minutes.' said the second man, 'Throwing their weight around, telling me security's not good enough. The arrogant pricks!' he added venomously.

'The last thing I need is the filth searching my van. I'm out of here!' said the Liverpool man.

The second man sounded distracted and agitated now. 'Yeah, yeah, whatever.' he said as he moved away.

A moment later, the truck roared into life and they were on the move again. *Maybe God was listening after all*, he thought.

CHAPTER 58

Five minutes after leaving the hospital, the lorry came to a sudden stop; a moment later, the tailgate deployed once again. With no clue as to what was going on, Marty kept his head low and waited for whatever was coming next.

'It's OK, you can come out now,' said the now-familiar voice of the man from Liverpool.

Marty followed the instruction lifting his head tentatively from under the sheets above the rim of the laundry bin. He finally saw the driver who had navigated his passage out of the Central Manchester hospital; a short, chubby, pale-skinned man with a stubbly chin, buzz cut and black T-shirt stretching over his protruding belly. His forearms were thick, covered in the green-and-blue hues of fading tattoos.

'Is this me done now?' he asked someone to the left side of the lorry, and Marty was more than surprised by his own reaction when he saw the striking features of DCI Phillips hidden under a navy blue baseball cap as she walked into view. *Thank God.*

Nodding her head, she threw a plastic bag towards Marty. 'Put these on quickly and come with me,' she said before turning to face the Liverpool man.

'So I'm off the hook, right?' he asked.

'Yes, Tommo, you're off the hook but if I ever catch you with anything even *remotely* hot again, you'll be back in Hawk Green in a heartbeat! Understand?'

Tommo nodded furiously, before making himself scarce.

Phillips moved to the rear of the truck, watching Marty as he stepped out of the laundry bin, emptying the plastic bag of its contents, 'Some jogging bottoms, trainers and a sweatshirt Jones organised for you. Not sure they'll fit,' she said.

Anything that wasn't a blue hospital gown was good by Marty, and he grabbed at them greedily. 'What you doing here?' he asked.

'I'll tell you in the car. Just get your clothes on and let's get moving.'

'I bet you say that to all the boys,' Marty said smiling.

Phillips turned and walked away in silence.

Two minutes later, Marty approached Phillips who was leaning against her rental car, the logoed number plate giving away its identity.

'You'd better get in the back. There's a blanket to cover yourself,' she said flatly.

He did as requested and they were soon on the road.

'Why do the switch in Burnage of all places?' he asked from the back seat.

'Why not?' countered Phillips, adjusting the rear-view mirror so she could see him lying down, 'It's as good as any; close to the hospital and frankly, people round here are good at turning a blind eye; I've seen it often enough as a copper!'

They drove for a couple of minutes without speaking before Marty broke the silence.

'I need to know something – what was with the newspaper hanging over the laundry bin? Why did you want me to get into that particular bin?' Marty asked.

Phillips glanced in the mirror and then back to the road. 'Because it was the only one that wasn't on CCTV,' she replied. 'It was specifically positioned in the blind spot of the loading bay. You can thank Jones for that, it was his idea.'

Marty nodded his approval. 'I will! By the way, Jones was very convincing in my hospital room. I really thought he wanted me banged up forever!'

'Yeah, I'm sorry if he freaked you out but we had no idea who might be listening in or watching your room. As much as Jones wants to help, he has a wife and two kids and can't afford to end up on the outside like me,' Phillips said.

Marty nodded and took a moment to reflect on his latest escape, as if watching an elaborate movie plot unfold. Totally surreal.

'So where *are* we going?' he asked.

'The Captains Lodge Hotel on the way to the airport.'

'The Captains? The place will be heaving with holidaymakers!'

'Exactly! Most of whom will be in the bar. The only thing they'll be focused on is starting their holiday as they mean to go on. Plus, I stayed there last night so we can go straight to the room.'

Marty considered it for a moment. The idea had merit.

'OK, so what happens when we get there?' he asked.

Phillips smiled as she glanced backwards, 'We put into action my brilliant plan to prove you're innocent, and I wasn't harbouring a fugitive,' she said enthusiastically into the mirror.

'Why do I get the feeling I'm not going to like it?' Marty said, half smiling.

'Trust me, Marty you will *love it!*'

He shook his head, pulling the blanket over his face, 'Of course I will. I mean, based on the last few weeks, what could possibly go wrong?'

CHAPTER 59

The Captains Lodge Hotel stands twenty stories high just five miles from the airport on Manchester's city limits, a classic example of sixties concrete architecture. Thousands of excited holidaymakers pass through its small functional rooms every week. The perfect place to blend in.

With Marty sporting a baseball cap and sunglasses, he and Phillips had made it through the recently renovated reception without issue and hid themselves away in a twin room on the seventh floor, overlooking the busy car park at the rear of the hotel.

Feeling the full effect of his injuries, Marty had lain on the bed, his torso propped upright by a couple of pillows and fallen into a deep sleep. He woke with a start some time later; 4am according to the clock radio next to the bed. Phillips was asleep in the armchair opposite, opening her eyes as Marty coughed.

Moving across the room, she sat sideways next to his waist and leaned in close to assess the damage to his face.

'That looks sore.'

'You think?' Marty replied sarcastically, immediately apologizing when he saw Phillips's reaction.

'I'm told you're a hero now,' Phillips said impassively.

'Hardly. I pulled Simon out of the car wreck, but who wouldn't in that situation?'

'You'd be surprised, Marty. Most would have left him there, hoping the fire brigade would do the dirty work. If you'd taken that option, he'd be dead.'

Marty considered her argument and nodded lightly, 'I guess so.'

'I know so, Marty. Those burns are living proof,' she said pointing at the gauze covering the right side of his face. 'You were above him when you were dragging him backwards and shielded him from the blast.'

'There *was* a couple that stopped to help, but they backed off when they realised who I was. As if I was some kind of *monster.*'

Phillips nodded, 'That's how you've been painted by the media, Marty. Another high-profile celebrity abusing his power!'

'But that's not fair! I never abused my power,' he said dramatically.

Phillips raised her eyebrows and stared at Marty for a moment, 'Really?'

'No!'

'So in almost two decades at the top you've never intentionally used your influence to damage someone else's reputation or career?'

Silently staring back at Phillips, Marty knew he was kidding himself. Since his dad and David died and Becks walked out, his anger had become a living thing. Some days he felt his only release came from lashing out and hurting others. He knew it was wrong, even when he was doing it, but he couldn't control it. Exhaling loudly he slowly nodded his agreement.

'I guess I have been a pretty horrible human being,' he said sadly.

'Maybe, but even if you have, you don't deserve what's happened to you.'

Marty appeared deep in thought.

'Have you checked social media since the accident, maybe my "heroics" have helped my cause?' he asked hopefully.

Phillips took out her phone, opened her web history and presented it to him, 'The crash was well documented but the story they're telling is that *you* were driving dangerously, swerving in and out of cars and hit the bridge. Nothing about pulling Simon out.'

'How can they get away with that? Simon was driving and we were rammed off the road!'

'If nobody witnessed it then whoever's behind all this can write whatever story they want!'

'But the couple, they turned up after just a few minutes. They must have seen something.'

'If they did they aren't talking, Marty.'

'And the nurse and Andrew, they both said I'd pulled Simon from the car. How did they know that if there were no witnesses?'

'I can only imagine the police or firemen would have mentioned it to the paramedics when briefing how you were injured, but after the crash the story was worldwide in a matter of minutes. A handful of people telling the truth cannot compete with the soap opera people *want* to be true; that you, Marty Michaels, a wealthy, powerful, celebrity-turned-fugitive on a killing spree, ran out of luck and brought about his own downfall. Swiftly brought to justice by the boys in blue.'

Marty sat open-mouthed unable to speak as he tried to process what Phillips was saying.

'I know it's shitty, Marty.'

'Bollocks is what it is! I mean, I know I've been a bit of a bastard but who the hell would want to do this to me?'

'The same person that's making me out to be a bent copper.'

'*And who the fuck is that?*'

Phillips smiled now, 'I thought you'd never ask!'

CHAPTER 60

Phillips handed Marty a thick file and returned to her position facing him on the edge of the bed.

'I've been digging through the files you gave me. Take a look at this lot,' she said with gusto.

Marty obliged and over the next few minutes flicked through the loose pages in silence.

'So what am I looking at, more financial records from Ganner and Luchsinger?'

'On the face of it, yes, but with a little imagination, we could be looking at proof Delta Holdings and Frank Fairchild are behind what's happening to you.'

Marty looked puzzled, 'I don't get it. How does any of this tie Fairchild or Delta to me?'

Phillips took back the file and carefully selected a single sheet before passing it back.

'Check the name and date on the highlighted account third from bottom.'

'Mrs. S. McAndrew?'

'And the date?'

'March 2012,' he said shrugging his shoulders, 'Should that mean something to me?'

Phillips chuckled, 'It's a good job *I'm* the detective. Do you remember the Manchester pathologist who killed himself a few years back?'

Marty took a moment to respond. 'The little fella, the guy who worked on my dad and David's post-mortems? Hung himself, didn't he?'

'That's the one. Remember his name?'

'Can't say I do, to be honest. It was all a bit of a blur at the time.'

Phillips stared silently at Marty for a moment before tapping the paper in front of him, 'Dr. George McAndrew.'

'Jesus! S. McAndrew was his wife?'

'Yes. As that account shows, she received a single payment in March 2012 of two hundred thousand pounds, around the time David and your dad died. McAndrew was the lead pathologist at Wythenshawe Hospital and theirs were the last two post-mortems he performed. A day after he published the results, he killed himself.'

'Bloody hell! So what, are you saying Fairchild killed him?'

'I don't think so, no. I'm pretty sure he killed *himself*. But as you said before, David had been sober for a long, long time. Why would he suddenly start drinking again?'

'I honestly can't imagine he would. He detested his old life.'

'So, knowing that, it's not too much of a leap to think someone could have doctored David's blood results.'

'McAndrew, but why?'

'Well, going through the post mortem report it appears he had the early onset of Alzheimer's. I can only assume, he was dying and wanted to look after his wife.' said Phillips.

'I don't get it. Why would anyone go to the effort of making it look like David was drunk if he wasn't?'

'*To cover their tracks.* Drink-driving offers a neat and tidy result; no need to look too closely at the car, and the killer walks away.'

'But McAndrew, why make two hundred grand and then kill yourself?'

'Maybe it was guilt at what he'd done, or fear of what lay ahead, we'll never know.'

'So how do we prove it?'

Phillips stood now and walked over to the window, 'That's just it. I'm not sure we can.'

Marty's frustration boiled over, 'Well, what bloody use is this?' he shouted, slamming the list of accounts with the back of his hand.

Phillips ignored his tantrum, 'To a judge and jury, not much. To us, it goes some way to proving Fairchild and Delta are bad people with a web of connections that keeps on growing. With so many police and government officials on the payroll they *have* to be the ones pulling the strings now.'

'And what if they aren't? What if it's a massive coincidence and *someone else* is behind all this?'

Phillips turned back to face him, her expression one of resignation, 'Well then, we're fucked, well and truly, mate.'

The room fell silent for a long moment.

Eventually, Marty spoke, 'So, we have *one* theory based on some pretty thin evidence?'

'Pretty much, yeah. Still, it's more than we had yesterday,' Phillips said brightly.

Marty moved off the bed and tentatively stretched his aching body in front of the window, shielded from the outside world by a white net curtain. Phillips rummaged through a rucksack on the office chair opposite the bed.

'Here it is!' she said triumphantly.

Marty turned away from the window, 'Here *what* is?'

Grabbing his right hand, Phillips placed a small bundle onto his palm. Looking down he could see a hair-thin wire, slightly bulbous at one end with what looked like a cigarette lighter attached.

'What's this?' he asked, clueless.

'*That* is the latest piece of undercover recording kit as used by Her Majesty's finest in the Greater Manchester Police, liberated by Jones not long after I was suspended.'

'And we need this for what exactly?'

'Recording a confession, of course!'

Marty laughed, 'And who exactly is supposed to be giving us this confession?'

'Fairchild.'

'Fairchild? Are you serious?'

'Deadly,' said Phillips.

Marty shook his head, 'How? How?' he repeated.

'Simple, using your considerable skills as an interviewer, you get him to tell you what he's been up to.'

'Well, why didn't you say that? I'll get him on the show tomorrow,' Marty said facetiously.

Phillips dropped into the small armchair next to the window, folding her arms and staring at Marty intently.

'OK, smart-arse. How many celebs and politicians have you managed to get under the skin of in the last fifteen years? Hmmn?'

Marty thought for a moment, 'Well, it's hard to say. I've kind of lost count.'

'Exactly! So why is it so ridiculous to think that you could get Fairchild to confess?'

Marty took his time to answer, 'Well, when you put it like that, I guess it's not. But you're forgetting one thing – to get him to open up I need to be in front of him.'

'Agreed and you will be. The plan is I'll drive you to his house tonight!' Phillips said confidently.

'What? Are you mad?'

'You said it yourself, Marty. The only way to get him to talk, is to speak with him face to face.'

'So what? We just drive up to his house, ring the bell and start talking when he answers the door?' Marty shot back sarcastically.

'Pretty much. You tell him you want to meet to make a deal. Money for White's documents. He takes the bait and you go to work wearing that,' she said, pointing at the wires in his hand. 'That bit on the end is a super-powerful directional microphone, capable of picking up any noise directly in front of it, as long as it's within a ten-metre range.'

'*Any noise?*' he said twisting his face, 'How are we supposed to get clarity on Fairchild's voice if it's picking up everything else? It'll be a mishmash of every sound in the room.'

Phillips's smile returned. 'I'll calibrate it from the receiver, which also acts as a recorder,' she said.

Marty was confused. 'So how do *you* calibrate it? Isn't it going to look a little bit suspicious if he's talking to me and a copper is sat recording him?' Marty shot back.

'Funny, aren't you?' Phillips said, half-laughing now. 'No. The mic and the receiver have a range of one hundred metres. As long as I'm in the grounds of the house, then I can pick up the signal. When he starts talking, you just need to make sure you're in front of him, and I can pick out his voice. Once it's locked in, he'll be the focus of everything we hear.'

Marty listened intently as he inspected the tiny kit in his hands more thoroughly. He had to admit the idea had *some* merit, but was essentially crazy: virtually impossible. Still, he had nothing to lose at this stage.

'Well, it looks like we have a plan that couldn't possibly go wrong,' he said, his voice brimming with sarcasm. 'As my dad would say, in for a penny, in for a pound.'

CHAPTER 61

'So you're clear what you have to do?' Phillips asked Marty as she tested the range of the receiver and the direction of the microphone taped to his chest, just below the neckline of his black Adidas sweatshirt.

They had stopped a few streets away from Fairchild's Alderly Edge home and were now standing on the pavement at the side of the hire car.

'I'm going to call Fairchild on the number programmed into your iPhone here,' Marty said raising the handset so the screen and number were visible to Phillips. 'How did you get his house phone, by the way?'

'Found it in a document on the USB,' Phillips replied.

'Seriously? That's lucky!'

'No luck involved – I'm a bloody good detective,' she added proudly.

'And you're sure it works? That it's current?'

Phillips nodded. 'Yep, I called the other night pretending to be one of those marketing companies asking for Mr. Fairchild. Whoever answered was not at all interested in whatever I was selling. It works all right.' Phillips pressed on. 'So when you get through, then what?'

'I'll tell him I want to meet face to face to make a deal – enough money to get me out of the country. In exchange, he gets the remaining copies of the sex tapes plus the bank details that connect Delta Holdings to government and police corruption. I'll tell him if he doesn't give me what I want, the data goes to the police in exchange for a deal.'

Phillips nodded. 'You tell him you'll be waiting by the front gate. When he lets you in, I'll sneak through the gates as they're closing.'

Marty was beginning to feel anxious, 'What if they've got cameras on the gate?'

'I'm sure they will, which is why you're going in after the sun goes down. I'll follow the car through in the shadows. I was a candidate for SCO19 – I'm a natural at covert operations!' Phillips said smiling.

Marty nodded. 'OK, OK,' he repeated as he tried to psych himself up for the deadly game of cat and mouse that lay ahead.

Phillips checked her watch. 'Right, it's almost nine-fifteen, time for me to get into position opposite Fairchild's. You ready?'

Marty took a sharp intake of breath to calm his rapid pulse. He had butterflies in his stomach reminiscent of his first ever radio show, coupled with a growing sense of nausea. He nodded silently and turned away for a moment trying to compose himself, before turning back and reciting the running order of events they had planned. 'OK, so I call him at nine-thirty to set up the meet. When I pull up to his gates, I activate my full-beam headlights in case anyone is looking down the drive, to help shield you. When you see the full beam go on, you run to the rear of the car and follow me through. I drive to the front of the house while you move to a point in the garden where you can hear me through the mic. I go inside the house, get Fairchild to confess, and as soon as he does, Jones and Bovalino arrive to arrest him and Buzzard, before they kill me. That sound about right?' he said, his tone facetious.

'You're going to be OK, Marty, I promise,' Phillips said patting him on his shoulder causing him to cry out in pain, 'Sorry,' she said extending her arm, 'and good luck.'

Marty shook her hand, careful not to aggravate his injuries, 'Thanks, Phillips. I have a horrible feeling I'm going to need it in there.'

CHAPTER 62

As the sunlight began to fade on the horizon, Marty sat in the driver's seat of the rented Ford Mondeo staring at the iPhone in his hand. He and Phillips had agreed he would make the call at 9.30pm sharp. The illuminated screen told him he had just under ten minutes to wait before reaching out and stepping into the unknown, and potentially deadly, world of Frank Fairchild. Glancing up he checked the street ahead, and then behind in the rear-view mirror. He saw nothing. Sounds of a summer's evening floated gently on the breeze. It reminded him of Rebecca; she loved this time of night, the chatter of the birds and hum of distant traffic of journeys unknown. God, he missed her and his heart ached for his old life and his beautiful ex-wife. He checked the time on the iPhone once more: 9.22pm. 'Bugger it,' he muttered under his breath, 'I've got enough time.' He opened the phone icon on the handset.

Luckily, Rebecca had kept the same number since buying her very first mobile back in 1998, the eleven-digit code forever burned into Marty's memory. Punching in the sequence, he hesitated for a split second but soon pressed on. A moment later the phone began to ring, eventually ringing out and activating the voicemail. 'Damn it,' Marty said and tried again, the outcome the same. He tried a third time, with still no answer. Deflated and feeling desperately lonely, he tried one last time.

'Hello?' a man said on the other end.

Marty didn't recognise him. After many nights of drunken calls to his ex, he had grown familiar with her husband's voice. This man was definitely not Sean.

'Do you want Rebecca?' the man asked, his voice flamboyant and colourful.

Marty, caught off guard, replied, 'Er, yes, I do.'

'Hang on, I'll get her,' he said cheerfully. A moment later Marty heard the voice of the only woman he had ever loved.

'Hello?' Rebecca said softly.

Marty was stuck for words for a moment.

'Hello?' she asked again. 'I don't think there's anyone there,' she added to someone at her end.

'Hi, Rebecca,' Marty managed to mumble as he attempted to stop her from hanging up.

'Marty?' Rebecca said sounding surprised.

'Hi, Becks,' he said softly.

'Jesus, Marty, where the hell are you? Are you OK?'

'I thought you'd be on air?'

'What? No, not till ten.'

'I didn't do it, Becks; I didn't kill anyone.'

There was a long pause on the end of the line before Rebecca spoke again. 'Your escape is all over the news, Marty – please give yourself up. You can't keep running.'

'I know that, Becks, but I'm innocent and tonight I'm going to prove it to the world!' he said firmly.

Rebecca's voice was soft but brimming with concern. 'Marty, what are you going to do?'

'I'm going to get the killer of White, Rochelle and Rob to confess!' he said firmly.

'Marty. Let me come and get you. I can help tell your story.' Rebecca's voice betrayed her fear as it jumped up an octave. In a perverse way, it gave Marty a sense of comfort; she still cared enough to worry about him.

A wave of calm rolled over him. His voice was even when he spoke. 'Becks, please don't worry about me. When I'm done, you'll know the truth.'

'Please, you don't have to prove anything to me.'

'I don't have a lot of time so please just listen. I need to tell you how sorry I am for driving you away…'

'Please, Marty, don't…' Rebecca cut across him.

'For once in your life listen to me!' Marty shouted and Rebecca was suddenly silent. He pushed on. 'I'm sorry for the way things ended and I know I lost the best thing that ever happened to me when you left. When Dave and Dad died, a piece of me did too. The good piece. The caring, human, real me burned in that car with them. What was left behind was the shell I am today; a drunk, coke-addicted arsehole who's been eaten up by anger. That anger has made me bitter and twisted and I've gone out of my way to ruin other people's lives. I actually started to take pleasure in seeing other people's misery. Well, karma has finally paid me back; the hunter has become the hunted.'

'Oh Marty, I am so sorry…' Rebecca interjected.

'Don't be, Becks! The last three weeks have been hell. But in a strange way, I've found the old me – the Marty who just wants to live; the Marty who appreciates life and doesn't care about money, or fame or power; the Marty who believes in justice and doing the right thing. Whatever happens tonight, Becks, please remember me that way.'

'What are you saying?'

'Please look after my mum; she'll be lonely. I want her to remember the real me, not the bullshit they created.'

'Marty, you're scaring me.'

'I gotta go, babe…' he said without thinking; it was the name he had always called her when they were together. 'I love you, Becks,' he added.

'I know you do,' Rebecca said softly as Marty moved to end the call. Inadvertently, he turned it into a FaceTime connection, revealing the sad but beautiful face of his ex-wife on the screen in front of him.

'I never was very good with technology,' he said smiling and gave her a wink before ending the call.

CHAPTER 63

Marty pulled the car up to the big wooden gates and flicked his headlights to full beam, looking around intently trying to spot Phillips, but he couldn't see her. He took a deep breath and watched the iphone screen for a moment as it slowly processed the sequence of numbers and eventually connected. Marty lifted the handset to his ear and waited as four rings went by before it was answered. The male voice on the end was heavily accented, a mixture of Middle Eastern and French. 'Hello?'

Marty hesitated.

'Hello?' the man said again.

Marty managed to control his nerves and finally spoke, just as the man was about to hang up.

'Hello, I'd like to speak to Frank Fairchild,' he managed to say.

'Mr. Fairchild is not available, goodnight,' the man said.

Marty spoke louder now as the man attempted to end the call, 'Tell him it's Marty Michaels and if he still wants to buy COMCO, he needs to hear what I have to say. I'm outside the gate and ready to talk.'

There was a pause at the other end before the man replied. 'Wait,' he said and pressed the mute button. Thirty seconds passed before the man returned. 'Follow the drive and park outside the front door,' he said gruffly and a moment later, the gates began to part in front of Marty.

He moved the car forward and continued glancing in his rear-view mirror for signs of Phillips as the long, curved drive opened up onto Fairchild's palatial home, which looked more New York Hamptons than Alderly Edge. He prayed she had made it through, otherwise this was all for nothing.

As he brought the car to a stop, the double-height front door opened and Buzzard – the man Marty had seen with Rob in Manchester and in the background of the sex tape – moved out onto the illuminated stone steps. He was wearing a dark suit and white shirt open at the collar and his jet-black hair was gelled back against his head. Marty opened the car door and the man signalled for him to follow as he stepped back inside the house, where he waited with both hands in his pockets.

Marty tentatively and somewhat painfully moved through the front door, struck by the opulence and scale of the building: it was enormous. The reception hall felt cavernous with a sweeping staircase on either side of the opposite wall leading to a mezzanine balcony.

Buzzard kept his eyes fixed on Marty at all times. Up close now, he was surprisingly tall, probably six-five and clearly still very athletic. His face was fearsome, the right side heavily scarred, with most of his right ear missing. Thick wrinkles forged in the heat of desert warfare surrounded his black, soulless eyes. He wore a well-maintained beard and a single diamond stud earring in his remaining left lobe.

'Put your arms up and spread your legs,' he said, his accent more French than Middle Eastern up close. 'I need to check you for weapons.'

Adrenalin rushed through Marty's body as he imagined what Buzzard would do if he found the tiny microphone fixed to his chest, and the transmitter positioned carefully in the crack of his backside. Slowly, he followed the order. Buzzard stepped forward and expertly, and surprisingly gently, frisked him, starting with his arms, then his shoulders, his broken ribs causing him to grimace, before running his hands down his legs. Marty waited as Buzzard stood up and slowly patted his chest from behind. He held his breath and closed his eyes waiting for the inevitable. Nothing happened. Buzzard stood behind him for at least ten seconds without saying a word. Finally the big man spoke, 'OK, you're clean.'

Marty exhaled just a bit too loudly as Buzzard stepped in front and turned to face him causing his suit jacket to billow, revealing a gun big enough to take out an elephant. Marty wondered if it had been a deliberate move to remind him what was at stake; funnily enough, nothing had ever been clearer.

Evidently satisfied, Buzzard ushered Marty to follow him into an enormous lounge room. Wall-to-ceiling glass ran the length of the space overlooking the rear garden, and an outdoor pool, its lights giving off a soft blue hue. With a retracted glass wall and polished oak floorboards, the lounge appeared to morph into the outdoor decking that covered the patio, and a cool evening breeze flowed easily through the house. Out on the decking, a man Marty recognised from Laura's files as Fairchild, sat on a plush outdoor sofa, looking relaxed as he read a book and sipped what appeared to be Scotch. Finally – Frank Fairchild.

As Buzzard and Marty approached, the man looked up. 'Mr. Michaels, good evening,' he said with a broad smile and stood to greet his guest. 'Will you join me in a whisky?' he asked, his American accent rich and melodic. *Texas*, thought Marty.

He knew from Laura's research that Frank Fairchild was forty-eight years old; around six foot two, built for action as opposed to the corporate life he now lived. He had movie-star looks, his clean-shaven face chiselled and lightly tanned, accentuated by his salt-and-pepper hair, cut short and deliberately messy. He wore a cream linen shirt opened loosely at the neck over crisp navy blue cotton shorts and his long muscular legs ran into a pair of tan-coloured espadrilles. His heavy metal watch glistened against the light from the pool.

'No, I'm good, thank you,' Marty said flatly.

'Quite right too,' Fairchild said with a wink as he held up his own glass. 'This stuff'll kill you!' he added before draining the remaining whisky.

Marty said nothing, fearing his voice would betray his raw nerves.

'Another one please, Buzz, and then you can finish up for the day,' Fairchild said as he handed Buzzard the empty glass, before ushering Marty to join him on the sofas. Marty attempted to sit without exacerbating his injuries; easier said than done, and not unnoticed by Fairchild.

'Your injuries look pretty painful, I must say. Mind you, that was a nasty accident you had, wasn't it?' he said. Marty, who finally found a comfortable position, chose not to respond. Fairchild continued. 'God, I love this time of night in the summer. Britain is like nowhere else on the planet on nights like this,' he said passionately as Buzzard returned with his drink, before disappearing into the house without a word.

Fairchild took a swig of the whisky and savoured it a while, his eyes closed, before opening them and locking his gaze on Marty, saying nothing for a moment. Finally, he spoke. 'So, Mr. Michaels, is there a reason I'm now harbouring the UK's most wanted man?'

Marty nodded. 'I have something you want and you have something I need,' he replied.

Fairchild flashed a smile. 'And what might those two things be, Marty? Can I call you Marty?' he asked, but it was clear he wasn't asking for permission.

Marty sat back in the chair in an attempt to appear at ease but the exact opposite was true. In all his years, he had never felt so nervous and he was struggling to keep his racing pulse at bay. Still, he knew to have any chance of opening him up, he had to get Fairchild talking. 'I have evidence of widespread corruption that implicates Delta Holdings and key members of the British government, the Greater Manchester Police, members of the board of COMCO and even the prime minister. If I go public, you can forget your purchase of COMCO, which considering the lengths you've gone to, to keep me out of your way, is not something I think you want to happen.'

Fairchild smiled but his eyes remained cold. 'And why do you think anyone will believe you, Marty, considering your recent activity?' he asked flatly.

'Maybe they will, maybe they won't; but even if none of it sticks, it'll shine a light on what is a very dodgy deal. Your close ally, the prime minister, will have to go, meaning you lose your cosy trading deals, and the stink around it will mean the deal between Delta and COMCO could never go ahead. Why would a man like you take the risk?'

Fairchild nodded and took another swig of the whisky. 'So, what do you want, Marty?'

Marty took a long breath before replying, his words almost stuck in his throat. 'Cash, plain and simple.'

Fairchild smiled broadly now. 'Cash? I have to say that's a surprise coming from an upstanding man like yourself, but hey, cash is king after all,' he said taking another drink. 'How much does it cost these days to buy the formerly incorruptible Marty Michaels?'

'Two million sterling transferred to an offshore bank of my choosing,' Marty said without hesitation. 'Two million and I disappear forever. I hand over all the evidence I've gathered and you get COMCO without any interference.'

Fairchild cocked his head at a slight angle and stared at Marty before reaching into the pocket of his shorts and pulling out a USB drive Marty instantly recognised. 'And what if I already have this evidence you're talking about in my possession? What if, after your very unfortunate car accident, my associate Buzzard was on hand at the hospital to retrieve the USB he so carelessly missed at the airport hotel?' he said laying the memory stick on the table between them, a broad smile appearing on his face.

Marty's eyes darted to the drive and back to Fairchild. 'What makes you think I didn't make a copy?' he said, trying to appear unfazed.

Fairchild sat back and cradled the thick tumbler in both hands now, his eyes still locked on Marty's. 'Oh, I have no doubt you made a copy and I have no doubt that Detective Chief Inspector Phillips fully intended to use it, but you see, that's the thing with evidence, it's only any good if someone actually sees it, and I'm not sure she'll be showing it to many people when she's dead,' he said coldly.

Marty flinched despite his best efforts to appear calm and together.

'You don't really think I'm stupid enough to let DCI Phillips roam around the grounds of my house whilst you do your best to distract me, do you?' he said swigging from the tumbler and pointing with his index finger for Marty to look behind him.

Attempting to appear in control, Marty swivelled his body, slowly turning to the sight of Buzzard holding a gun to Phillips's head, her eyes wide, her mouth gagged with tape, her wrists bound in front of her with cable ties.

'It looks like you are running out of options, Marty Michaels,' Fairchild said smugly, toasting him with his glass. 'And I'm pretty sure I just saved myself two million pounds!'

CHAPTER 64

Not for the first time in the last three weeks, Marty felt like he was living his life inside a movie script, sitting here on a chair in Fairchild's enormous lounge room facing DCI Phillips, herself on a matching chair. Her hands were still tied in front of her and the tapc remained in place over her mouth. A large smoked-glass coffee table separated them both, Phillips's phone, used to call Rebecca and Fairchild, sat on the table in front of Marty. To his left stood Buzzard, motionless, his oversized gun trained on Marty's head. Directly behind Phillips, Fairchild was standing with his back to the room, staring out onto the pool and the garden beyond, his right hand in his pocket, the left cradling the small listening device Buzzard had just removed from Marty's underpants and chest. Ironically, the room was silent apart from the soundtrack of the summer's evening floating in from outside.

Fairchild turned to face Marty but remained silent, repeatedly tossing the small transmitter in his left hand, as if working something through in his mind. He walked towards Phillips, pulling his free right hand from his pocket and placing it on the detective's shoulder, causing her to flinch as he did.

'It's amazing how small technology is these days, don't you think?' Fairchild said looking directly at Marty, his southern drawl more prominent now.

Marty said nothing and with Phillips gagged, Fairchild turned his attention to Buzzard, 'Imagine if we'd had shit like this when we were in the field, Buzz – we'd have been unstoppable!' he said enthusiastically, his right hand still gripping Phillips's shoulder.

Buzzard nodded in silence, his eyes and gun still fixed on Marty.

Fairchild's tone was playful now. 'What was the plan, Marty? Were you hoping to record a confession?'

Marty nodded. 'Something like that,' he said flatly, already tiring of the big Texan.

Fairchild moved away from Phillips, walking casually across the room towards Marty.

'And what were you expecting that I'd confess to, White's murder, the lady-boy's, Rob's? Impossible. You see, *I* didn't kill them,' he said smiling. 'No… it wasn't me… it was Buzz here! This crazy French-Algerian motherfucker, he killed them *all*.'

Marty flinched hearing the truth about Rob's death.

Fairchild wandered over to a cabinet positioned behind Buzzard, opened a large drawer and took out a pair of latex gloves, pulling the left one on slowly as he spoke with his back to Marty. 'You must be wondering why your closest friend and agent of nearly twenty years would betray you?' he said turning to face his audience, noisily, and purposely, Marty suspected, cracking the latex against his wrists.

Marty felt the hate building inside him, like a small fire spreading through his insides. It took every ounce of control he could muster to stop himself leaping from the chair and taking his chances with Fairchild, but the man was an expert in unarmed combat, not to mention Buzzard's unflinching aim. Coupled with his own injuries, Marty didn't stand a chance.

'I'm sure you're about to tell me,' he said sardonically.

Fairchild finished putting on the right-hand glove and reached into the drawer again, this time fishing out a small black handgun, before walking back across the room and taking a seat on the large sofa adjacent to Marty and Phillips. 'He was gay, Marty,' he said with a broad smile.

Marty's mind flashed to the video he and Simon uncovered, but did everything he could to keep his face deadpan.

'But then if you saw the videos you already knew that,' Fairchild added. 'You see, Marty, he was a closet fag with Afro-Irish parents. He would have done anything to stop them seeing that video of White hammering his ass like a randy dog, not to mention his macho footballer clients. They don't take kindly to homos in that world – I mean, when was the last time anyone came out in soccer? Literally, decades ago, Marty. Decades! If that video went viral – well, his life was pretty much over. Shamed by his parents, shunned by his friends and clients. The choice was very simple, we destroy *his* life, or he helps us destroy *yours!*'

'You bastard!' snorted Marty, losing his cool.

'Me? I'm not the one you should be shouting at, Marty! How do you think you ended up in a hotel room you never booked, with no clue how you got there? How did we get CCTV showing you drinking with a male pro? It was Rob – *all of it!* He was the one who cloned your credit card and booked the room. *He* told Rochelle how to order the drugs from your dealer. *He* invited you to the Sky Lounge and spiked your drink so we could get you in the room with White and his lady-boy lover. Of course, the beauty of using 'ludes is they can wipe out any memories from the previous eighteen to twenty-four hours, which is why I'm guessing the whole thing was a mystery to you,' Fairchild said effusively, waving the gun as he spoke.

'Rob would never do that to me; not knowingly,' Marty said.

'Oh, he *would* and he *did*, Marty. Rob gave the police and the press the heads-up on the morning of your arrest. It was thanks to him you were slashed in segregation, he told us when your lawyer would be visiting. And when you arranged to meet White's lover at the airport hotel, Rob again provided the information, gleaned from Johnson. You see Marty, Rob's been pulling your strings all along.'

Marty did not want to believe what he was hearing about his oldest friend, but in his heart, he knew it was the truth.

'The fact is Rob Woodcock destroyed your life, everything you held dear; everything *you ever cared about*, rather than let it happen to *him!*'

Marty was trying to process what Fairchild was saying but he had so many questions. 'But the money? The Swiss bank payments, why pay someone you were blackmailing?'

Fairchild stood up from the sofa now and leaned towards Marty, the gun just in front of him, 'Oh, I wasn't always blackmailing him. No, when I first met Rob it was all very civilised, actually. You see, I've been hatching this plan for revenge ever since you got in my way with the Fontaine takeover. Your fucking preaching and posturing all but killed the deal and cost my associates a lot of money. You made me look powerless and I can't have that, Marty – not in my world. I have a well-earned reputation as someone who can fix *any* situation, problem or person; but not you, it seemed. If I was going to remain the top man in my business, I needed to find a way to get to you – and on a grand scale to really make my point.'

'You're crazy!' Marty said.

'Maybe,' Fairchild said smiling. 'So I pulled in a few favours from some old friends at the agency, who hacked into your phone and those of your closest associates. Various bosses, that lawyer of yours and your agent. It really is amazing what people talk about when they think no one is listening. It became evident Rob was having a little trouble with his finances – not to mention his *big* secret. Turns out he was being blackmailed by a young man he had been seeing. The boy had lied about his age, saying he was twenty-one when actually he was just sixteen. When Rob found out the truth he ended it, but the kid would not leave quietly, threatening to go to the Sunday papers with sex tapes – unless of course Rob paid him for his silence. Seeing the opportunity, I used my influence to make that issue go away and he was naturally very relieved. He believed all I wanted in return was to get close to you to help me get the inside track on buying COMCO – which, in a way, was true. He was happy to let me do that so I put him on the payroll with a monthly retainer and I became his client. However, the real reason for getting close was to work out the best way to *destroy you*,' Fairchild said staring deep into Marty's eyes.

Marty held his gaze.

Fairchild straightened and moved next to Buzzard, 'Anyway, when your father and producer died driving your car, I couldn't hide my disappointment it wasn't you. He didn't react too well to that. Told me he wanted out and dropped me as a client. Stopped taking calls, blanked emails etc. I needed more leverage; and all it took was a hot boy and a video camera—'

Marty cut across the big Texan, 'Did you kill them?'

Fairchild smiled and glanced at Buzzard, 'Now why would you think that?'

'Because David was seven years sober and there's no way he would have driven my dad home drunk.'

'You read the coroner's verdict, Marty. It was death by drink-driving,' Fairchild said nonchalantly.

'The blood results were faked!'

'Now who would do a thing like that?'

It was clear Fairchild was enjoying the exchange.

Marty could feel the hate growing inside him, 'George McAndrew, that's who – his wife was on your fucking payroll!'

Fairchild was clearly impressed, 'My, you have been busy haven't you?' he said glancing at Marty and Phillips in return, 'Did you come up with that theory all on your own or did the good detective here help you?' He said before pulling the tape noisily from her mouth.

'We know it was down to you. You killed them both and we'll prove it!' Phillips said breathlessly.

Shaking his head, Fairchild laughed dramatically, walking across the room and leaning in close to Phillips's face, his voice almost a whisper, 'You'll prove nothing when you're dead, sweetheart,' he said, holding his face next to her left ear as he sniffed her hair deeply. 'Women always smell so wonderful, wonderful!' he said loudly.

Marty's eyes followed Fairchild as he straightened and walked back towards the edge of the room and stared out over the pool, glowing in the garden. Buzzard had not moved an inch.

'So because I stopped you buying Fontaine you wanted to kill me?'

'Pretty much,' Fairchild said without turning around.

'But you killed David and dad by mistake?'

'Unfortunate, that one.'

'So why not kill me back then? You clearly had the muscle to make me disappear.'

Fairchild turned to face Marty now, 'You took their deaths badly. The word was, you were smashing so many drugs in the aftermath, your pretty little wife was on the verge of leaving you. You being a highly strung 'performer', I thought you might save me the trouble and kill yourself. Sadly, as evidenced by your presence here today, that wasn't the case.'

'You're a piece of work,' Phillips said turning her head towards Fairchild.

'Thank you,' he said enthusiastically.

'So where does COMCO fit into all of this?' Marty asked.

'Drugs,' Fairchild shot back. 'Or more accurately, lots of drug money. You see, I'm very well connected in South East Asia, have been ever since my days in the agency. In fact, it turns out I'm one of the world's biggest distributors of heroin, and I need lots of different accounts and transactions to clean the money which that kind of trading generates. The only reason I got into Delta in the first place was the need to look legit. Buying COMCO fills a hole in my distribution and banking network, and as an added bonus, the British government fully supports non-doms paying as little tax as possible. I like that.'

'Jesus, Simon was right,' Marty said, barely audible.

Phillips cut in, 'So why set up Marty for the murder of White and Rochelle? Why go to all that trouble?'

'A couple of reasons really. Marty was the prize asset of COMCO. With him as the poster boy, the share price was ridiculously high. Killing him would've made him a martyr with little impact on the stock. Ruining him destroyed the share price in a matter of days, meaning the terrified shareholders are now ready to accept a much lower price than the business is actually worth.'

'Which you are more than willing to offer…' Marty added.

Fairchild smiled and flashed his perfect white teeth. 'Naturally,' he replied. 'Secondly, after that stunt you pulled in his first interview, the prime minister and a lot of powerful people in government were panicking that you had a hit-list of paedophiles in Parliament. He was convinced you were about to expose another scandal on a par with Yewtree.'

'But that's absurd, I was speaking hypothetically – there's no list! I made it up for the interview. I just wanted to see him squirm a little,' Marty interjected.

'Personally, I never thought there was a list, my friend, but Fay got real spooked by it, rambling about skeletons in closets. Made me think he was worried that *he* was on your list; not a great way for a fledgling leader to begin his new government, is it? And he came to me for help. You see, we go way back, me and Nick.'

'Asia...' Marty said as he started to make the connection, 'Let me guess, you guys met when he was out there drumming up future business as Minister for Trade?'

'Now you're getting it, Marty!' Fairchild said emphatically. 'We met at a state dinner in Laos and I was able to share my desire to expand Delta into the UK. He offered to use his influence to help me. I offered my *special* services in return – namely doing any dirty work needed to help him become prime minister. He was dangerously ambitious and it made for the perfect alliance.'

'So Fay's corrupt?' Phillips said.

'Jane, that's a very strong word. I prefer, *entrepreneurial*.'

Marty could not hide his disgust, 'He's fucking bent! The bloody prime minister's part of this!'

'Tomayto–tomahto,' Fairchild said casually waving the gun. 'Anyway, when you started shouting about that *list*, I was the first person he called to make it go away. *He* needed you quiet, and *I* needed a low share price. Win–win. Seeing how quickly Yewtree turned so-called heroes into monsters, it seemed the obvious choice to bring you down. One of the first things they teach you in the agency: use your enemy's greatest strength against him. You were a self-righteous, arrogant bigot and bully who used his dominant media presence as a weapon. What better way to destroy you than turning you into a sex-fiend serial killer and feeding you to the media wolves?'

'Jesus Christ,' said Marty, his words barely audible as Fairchild chuckled to himself.

'And lastly, Marty, if you want the whole truth, framing you was actually a lot of fun; all part of the game,' Fairchild said as he reached down to pick up Phillips's phone, 'I love winning, Marty; *love it!*'

Marty was lost for words. A *game?*

'What's the access code on this thing, sweetheart?' Fairchild said without looking at Phillips.

'Go to hell,' she replied defiantly.

Fairchild glanced at Buzzard who remained vigilant and completely focused, his gun trained on Marty's head, before turning slowly to face Phillips. 'Now, now, Jane. Considering your position, you should be doing everything you can to get on the right side of me,' he said casually as he moved next to Marty, staring straight at her. 'Tell me the four-digit access code,' he demanded more forcefully as he placed his gun against Marty's kneecap, 'or I'll put a bullet through his knee right now.'

Marty tried to look unfazed but failed as his eyes widened and his leg instinctively flinched.

'I'll count to three, Jane,' Fairchild continued. 'One… two…'

'OK! OK! Jesus! OK! It's just a phone, what do I care? Zero, one, one, seven,' Phillips said quickly.

Fairchild tapped in the code and flashed a smile. 'Thank you. Now where is Twitter on here?' he asked himself as he wandered back across to Phillips, pressing the gun heavily into her kneecap. 'Got it! OK, Marty, username and password please?'

'For what?'

'Your Twitter account, Marty, Twitter!'

'Why do you want to access my Twitter account?'

Fairchild let out an exasperated breath. His right hand still pressing the gun into Phillips's knee, in one lightning quick movement he lifted his left elbow and smashed it down onto the bridge of Phillips's nose, causing her to scream out in pain as blood quickly poured down her face.

'Just give it to me. Or your pretty little friend here won't stay *pretty,* for long,' he said coldly yanking Phillips's head back with his left hand so Marty could see the damage inflicted with just one strike, as she coughed up blood.

Marty gave him what he wanted. 'At Marty Michaels five,' he said quickly before adding the password, 'Becks81, capital B.'

Fairchild smiled. 'Can't let go can you, Marty?' he said as he accessed the account and began typing, narrating aloud. *'It's time for my final performance, tonight I finish this and my legacy will be complete.* That should do it,' he said laughing and placed the phone back on the table in front of Phillips. He then pulled a combat knife from his back pocket and in a flurry of movement sliced through the detective's restraints. 'See, Jane, it pays to be nice to me,' he said returning the knife to his back pocket.

Phillips rubbed her wrists and flexed her fingers as the blood returned and Fairchild strolled casually across the room, stopping behind Marty, pressing the gun painfully against the back of his head.

'Do you know what the world will think when they read that tweet, Marty?' he asked, not waiting for an answer. 'They'll wonder what you mean by *legacy,*' he added as he cocked the gun then pressed it harder into the back of Marty's head. 'Then they'll see what you did here – in my house – and everything will become crystal clear.'

Marty tried to appear calm, unsuccessfully, as the heavy gun dug into the base of his skull. 'What are you talking about?'

Fairchild continued. 'The world will finally see you for what you are, a deranged man caught up in a seedy world of revenge and betrayal. You will reach new levels of fame! Marty Michaels – the man who strangled his lover during sex and killed his lover's partner in a jealous rage. Sadly, his agent discovered what he had done, so Marty killed him too, murdering him with the same gun I have in my hand right now,' he said pushing the cold metal further into the base of Marty's skull to make his point. 'Before coming after me, Frank Fairchild, the businessman trying to buy his beloved COMCO, breaking into my home and shooting my head of security as he tried to protect me...'

'What?' Marty managed to say before Fairchild pulled the gun away in one rapid movement. A deafening explosion erupted next to his left ear.

The smell of gunpowder filled the air. Marty watched as Buzzard recoiled violently backwards and slumped to the floor, dark red blood oozing from his stomach across his white shirt.

Phillips screamed and Marty's eardrum felt like it would burst with the ringing white noise that consumed it, as Fairchild continued without missing a beat.

'... after which he tried to kill me,' he said and crouched down directly behind Marty, speaking into his right ear. 'Luckily though, DCI Phillips, despite her suspension – *good cops never give up etc.* – had followed him. Thank God, she had, because she saved my life. *But* in doing so, our heroine tragically lost hers...'

A split second later, Fairchild stood and fired another shot, this time at Phillips. Her chest exploded and the force of the bullet pushed her backwards onto the floor, her body suddenly shapeless like a rag doll.

Fairchild's tone was playful now, almost childlike as he walked over to the prostrate figure of Phillips on the floor. 'Oh dear, it looks like you've killed a police officer,' he said, turning to face Marty. 'All that's left for me to do is to wrestle the gun from your hand – and kill you in self-defence.'

Buzzard groaned from his position as a dark red pool of blood began to creep across the floor.

Marty was in shock. The piercing pitch rang through his left ear as his gaze fell on the dying man. 'You shot your own man! You killed an innocent woman in cold blood! *A fucking police officer!*'

'Casualties are a necessary consequence of warfare,' Fairchild replied, his voice void of any emotion.

Marty turned his gaze back to Fairchild now. 'You're an animal, pure evil!' he spat.

Still holding the gun in his gloved hand, Fairchild walked back towards Marty and leaned forward so his eyes were level with his. 'I'm neither of those things, Marty; I am in fact a certified sociopath,' he said calmly. 'The CIA's full of them,' he added. 'You see, an animal acts on instinct and the act of being evil requires *emotion*; a calculated and complicit decision to go against any empathy you may *feel* for another living thing. Whereas for me, every move is calculated to deliver me the optimum outcome. I have no empathy and *I feel nothing* when I take a life; it is a mere necessity to keep me in front of the next man. I am not evil, Marty, I am a highly trained assassin who realised that killing someone in the boardroom is just as primal as killing someone in the jungle.'

Marty glared at Fairchild, hate seeping through every pore in his body. 'So how will you explain the fact I've never fired a gun in my life, let alone in your house? I've seen enough on forensics to know without gunshot residue, there's reasonable doubt.'

Fairchild chuckled, his tone mocking, higher in pitch as he imitated Marty. *'I've seen enough on forensics...* Do me a favour! You're a fucking DJ and I am an ex-CIA operative with ten years of black ops experience. I've *forgotten more* than you could ever hope to learn about forensics, and more importantly, I know how to make a crime scene look exactly as I want it to. This isn't my first rodeo, sweetheart. Trust me, when I'm finished, there'll be *no* reasonable doubt whatsoever. Zero, Marty. *You* are going to die and *I'm* going to carry on living my fabulous life. I will be the new owner of your beloved COMCO, laundering millions and millions of my filthy drug money in the process,' he said as if describing his plans for the weekend. 'Imagine that, COMCO a front for drug-running,' he added as he stared at Marty for a long moment, saying nothing, his face void of any emotion.

Eventually he straightened, turning away from Marty as he did. In that split second, Marty's instincts took over. With one Herculean effort, he hurled his broken body at Fairchild, knocking him sideways as he did. Both men crashed heavily onto the large glass coffee table. It shattered into tiny pieces under their combined weight of over five hundred pounds.

Marty landed on top of Fairchild giving him the upper hand and he began raining punches down on his opponent's head, a rookie mistake. The big Texan smashed his fist up into Marty's solar plexus, disabling him instantly. Marty slumped forward as Fairchild pushed him off and slammed him head first into the shattered glass on the hardwood floor, three times in rapid succession. Dazed, Marty tried to catch his breath and blood flowed from his head into his eyes and down the back of his throat. Fairchild thrust his knee into the base of Marty's back, raining punches into Marty's broken ribs. Explosions of agonising pain surged through his body as each blow landed. He began coughing up blood and gasped desperately for air as

Fairchild stood and kicked him hard in the same broken ribs, causing him to scream out in pain.

Fairchild reached for his combat knife in his back pocket, but realised it had come loose in the fight. Spotting it poking out from under the sofa a few feet away, he stood and walked casually across the room to retrieve it. He returned to stand over Marty who was lying motionless, face down in a pool of his own blood and broken glass. Dropping to his knees, Fairchild held the knife in his right hand and leaned in close, pressing the blade to Marty's bloody right ear. His voice was cold and measured as he spoke, no hint of emotion. 'Do you know, of all the people I've killed in my life, Marty, this will give me the greatest satisfaction,' he said, running the blade lightly from Marty's ear to his mouth. 'I cannot tell you how much I've enjoyed setting you up and destroying your career in the glare of the media. It really has been enormous fun. *But.* Even though you've been a worthy opponent – probably one of the best I've ever faced, in truth – you're simply no match for me. I own everyone in this city; the Assistant Police Commissioner, your CEO Colin Burns is my bitch. Goddammit, even your prime minister is in my pocket! How else do you think that asshole got himself elected in just three months? It was me, Marty, me. I used hackers to rig the election. I got Nicholas Fay into Number Ten, and helped protect his paedo pals in government! Me. Frank-fucking-Fairchild. *I own each and every one of them.* I decide who lives and who dies, and I'm afraid in this game, you die!' he said as he rolled Marty onto his back.

Marty coughed up blood and opened his eyes, staring up at Fairchild who casually straightened his hair with his left hand, his right hand still holding the knife, before smiling down at him.

Through bubbles of blood, Marty managed to speak, his voice a determined low growl. 'Not if… I can help it!'

Fairchild laughed loudly and placed the sharp blade under Marty's chin, his tone mocking, his voice measured. 'What you gonna do, Marty, tell on me? Haven't you noticed? No one is listening to you anymore. You're a murderer. Your beloved audience think you're a sadistic sex-killer. An when I'm done telling them about my nightmare ordeal here, how you shot Phillips and Buzz in cold blood, even your own mother will see you that way.'

Marty coughed up more blood as he attempted to speak. 'But it's not true,' he managed to say.

'The truth?' Fairchild chuckled. 'No one cares about the truth anymore, Marty. They care about the story, *the drama*. Anything to brighten the sad, pathetic lives they live out on Facebook, Twitter and Instagram. The truth is what *I* say it is. I own UK media, and tomorrow morning that same media will tell the world that Marty Michaels was a rapist, a murderer, a cop killer – and they'll *believe it!*'

Marty managed a bloody smile now. 'Why wait until tomorrow?' he said as he lifted Phillips's iPhone in his left hand. 'Did you get all that, Rebecca?' he said, blood gurgling in his throat.

Fairchild's smile vanished as Marty turned the phone around to reveal the bright, active screen. A FaceTime call connected to a number he didn't recognise.

Marty filled in the blanks, 'Smile, Frank Fairchild; you're live on the ten o'clock news!' he said, a broad smile breaking across his face.

Fairchild pulled the knife away from Marty's neck and leant back across his thighs. He stared at the phone stony-faced for a long moment, his face the picture of calm before finally losing control. 'No! No! No! That's not how this ends!' he screamed, rage descending on him. 'That's not how this is supposed to go,' he added and raised the knife high in the air. 'I still win, Marty, because you're still going to die!' he said maniacally as he thrust the heavy blade down towards Marty's chest.

In that moment, a deafening bang filled the room, and Fairchild's face seemed to freeze in time, as a dark patch of blood began to spread from the charred hole that had appeared in his cream linen shirt. A split second later, Marty felt the full weight of the big Texan as he slumped forwards on top of him, his broken ribs causing him to cry out and drop the iPhone to the floor.

Attempting to get out from under the big man, he kicked his feet and grabbed at the leg of the sofa. He managed to wriggle free and lifted himself painfully up onto his hands and knees.

Across the room to the right of the chair she had been sitting on when Fairchild shot her, Phillips lay face down on the floor, the black handgun in her bloody right fist.

'Phillips!' Marty shouted as he crawled slowly over the glass towards her.

Gently he rolled her onto her back, revealing a gunshot wound to her chest just above her left breast. He checked her pulse; she was alive – just. Fairchild had missed her heart. 'Wait here, Jane! I'm gonna get help!' he said and crawled back to pick up the phone where he was relieved to see Rebecca's face, still connected, her expression grave.

'Oh my God, Marty. Are you OK?' she asked.

'I need an ambulance at Fairchild's house on Blackfarm Road. DCI Phillips has been shot.'

Rebecca nodded furiously. 'The police are on their way, Marty. Emergency services too.'

'Thanks. I was hoping you got all that, by the way?'

'We heard *every word* Marty, as did most of the UK live on the ten o'clock news,' Rebecca said proudly.

Marty smiled as the echo of sirens filled the room. 'Sounds like the cavalry. I'd better go,' he said, ending the call.

A moment later, he heard the front door being broken down. 'Armed police!' came a shout from behind him, followed by the now familiar London tones of Detective Sergeant Jones who ran over and crouched next to Phillips. 'Medic!' he screamed loudly as his eyes locked on Marty. 'All went according to plan, then?' he said sarcastically.

Marty chuckled now. 'Not quite, Jonesy... not quite!' he said as he coughed up blood and slumped sideways to the floor.

EPILOGUE

The heavy November rain pounded the soil covering the grave, forming small puddles that fed tiny rivers of water down the mound of mud towards thick sodden grass. It was hard to believe it had been almost six months since those few short weeks had brought murder and 'media-madness' to Manchester.

It had taken the public no time at all to move on from the events that had left five people dead, a prime minister disgraced and countless members of the police charged with corruption. The scrolling TV news, Twitter and Facebook feeds had dissipated, and now the carnage of that night at Frank Fairchild's house in Alderly Edge was a distant memory for most; old news. Some people, though, could never forget.

Staring down at the grave, Marty closed his eyes and tried his best to bury the pain that burned inside him.

Cleared of the murders of White and Rochelle, time had passed in a blur. Despite the offer of a new mega-money contract from COMCO, TV and book deals, he had decided to take an open-ended hiatus to try and make sense of everything that had happened to him. After countless therapy sessions, he was fully aware he had to move on from the terrible events that had cost him so dearly, but it took every ounce of strength he possessed just to get out of bed each morning. Flashbacks and nightmares of the rape haunted him in the night and the realisation that his father, his producer and his agent were murdered weighed heavily on his shoulders. Although he tried hard not to blame himself, he could not escape the feeling that clawed at his mind a thousand times a day: *their deaths were on him.* His dad's and David's, at least.

Staring down at the grave, he allowed his shoulders to rise and fall gently as he began to weep silently, visualising the lifeless, lonely body buried below his feet.

A soft, warm hand reaching out to touch him halted his tears. Marty turned and his heart lifted as he gazed down at Rebecca, drinking in her luxurious scent which cut through the rain as the fingers of her right hand tightened around his.

'I miss him too, you know,' she said softly.

Marty nodded, 'It's hard not to. He was such a lovely man. I wish I was more like him; calm, sweet and kind.'

Rebecca smiled, 'You are, Marty, you're *just* like him.'

Marty offered a sad smile in return, shaking his head. 'Not me, Becks, I'm like my mum; loud, neurotic, impatient.' He said softly, 'They were the perfect match in many ways. Yin and yang. I still can't believe it's six years since we lost him. It kills me to think I'll never see him again. Or David.'

'I know. I know,' Rebecca said, leaning her petite frame against his, attempting to shelter from the rain, which seemed to worsen in a matter of seconds. 'Are you up to seeing Rob's grave?'

Marty's body tightened at the mention of his name and he said nothing for a moment as he fought the wave of emotions that flooded his body, 'No, Becks. I can't, I just can't.'

Squinting against the rain, Rebecca lifted her head to face him, and smiled softly, 'OK Marty. There's no rush.'

'That's just it, Becks; I'm not sure I'll ever be ready. He took so much from me, how do I ever forgive him?'

Rebecca stared back at him for a moment and squeezed his hand tighter still, nodding. 'Give it time. I know it's no consolation, but he suffered too in all this. He wasn't a bad man. He was lost and scared. Just like you were.'

'Yeah, but I didn't kill anyone!' Marty snapped back.

'No, that's true but then neither did he.'

'*As good as!*'

Rebecca opened her mouth to speak but seemed to stop herself and turned her face away from the rain. They both stared in silence at the headstone in front of them: GOD BLESS PETER CHRISTOPHER MICHAELS – LOVING HUSBAND TO MARGARET AND FATHER TO MARTY.

'God bless, Dad,' Marty whispered into the rain.

'It's time to go. You said we'd be at your mum's house for one,' Rebecca said softly, her mouth forming a warm smile.

Marty stared down at the woman he still loved with all his heart, 'I really do appreciate you coming to see Mum on Dad's anniversary. She's really looking forward to seeing you.'

'I love your mum, you know that.'

'I know, but are you sure Sean is OK with it?'

Rebecca nodded, 'He's fine. Probably on the phone to Hong Kong or Shanghai anyway,' she said patting him absentmindedly on the chest. 'Banking never sleeps,' she mumbled into the wind.

'Would you mind dropping me at Simon's after Mum's? He's still not fully mobile and I want to make sure he's got everything he needs.'

'Of course babe; whatever you want.'

Marty's heart jumped hearing her call him *babe*. He wished to God he could rewind time and never let her go. 'Thanks, Becks,' he whispered as he closed his eyes and held her close for a moment, relishing every second, before reminding himself she was married to someone else. 'Come on, you, Mum will be wondering where we are and she's talked about nothing else but cooking you her world famous Yorkshire puddings. *Remember those?*'

Rebecca craned her neck in an exaggerated arc as she looked up at Marty. 'Oh God, no!'

Marty laughed, pulling her close again. 'Take one for the team, Becks!'

They held hands as they walked down the path, letting go as they reached Rebecca's car.

As Marty opened the passenger door, he took one last look at his dad's grave up on the hill in front of him.

'Sleep well, Pops,' he said softly, 'sleep well.'

ABOUT THE AUTHOR

For twenty years OMJ Ryan worked in radio and entertainment across the UK and Australia, collaborating with household names, celebrities and music icons, accumulating a host of international writing and radio awards.

In 2018 he followed his passion to become a full-time novelist, writing stories for people who devour exciting, fast-paced thrillers by the pool, on their commute - or those rare moments of downtime before bed. Owen's mission is to entertain from the first page to the last.

Hailing from Yorkshire, Owen has lived and worked in Leeds, Manchester, Sheffield, Glasgow, Sydney and Melbourne, before settling in the north east of England with his wife Kim and son Vaughan.

If you would like to be kept up to date with new releases from OMJ Ryan, visit his Facebook page, or www.omjryan.com if you have any feedback you would like to share.

ACKNOWLEDGMENTS

This book would not have been possible without the expertise, guidance, help and support of so many people, who willingly took calls, replied to emails and answered SMS messages at all hours of the day and night, as I wrestled with the story and, eventually got ready for launch.

My wife Kim has been with me throughout this incredible journey and her belief in me never wavered, even when mine did. She's also an amazing sounding-board and always my final proof reader. Thanks Babe.

My wee man Vaughan, when you're old enough to read it I hope it'll make you proud of daddy.

To mum, dad, Simon, Suze, Doreen, Kay, Jill, Deb, Cath, Emma K and Kim G who read the many first drafts, and gave me invaluable feedback to help hone the final story.

I owe a huge debt of gratitude to DC James Eve, Simon 'Harry' Harrison QC and 'Andy' who helped guide me through the complexities of the British legal system.

Thanks to Rebecca for the introduction, and Lloyd for the advice on switching the story from Sydney to Manchester.

Sinead and Sophie, my proof readers.

Roland, Kathleen and Andrew at the Writers Studio in Sydney, NSW.

And finally thank you to Dan and Aaron who helped bring my vision for the cover to life, as well as Chris W, DP, Stuart, Arlene, Jon, Katie, Ali, Lisa, and Steve who supported my launch strategy.

Oh and thank you, to you – for buying 'Media Monster'. I hope you enjoyed it.

29812200R00218

Printed in Poland
by Amazon Fulfillment
Poland Sp. z o.o., Wrocław